Praise for *Over Hexed*

"A snappy, funny, romantic novel."
—*New York Times* bestselling author Carly Phillips

"Filled with laughs, this is a charmer of a book."
—The Eternal Night

"The same trademark blend of comedy and heart that won Thompson's Nerd series a loyal following."
—*Publishers Weekly*

"Thompson mixes magic, small-town quirkiness, and passionate sex for a winsome effect."   —*Booklist*

"A warm and funny novel . . . you find yourself cheering. I would definitely recommend it."
—The Road to Romance

"This novel was brilliant. I laughed until I cried, and it was a very fast read for me. This genre is the beginning of a new series for Thompson, and if this novel is any indication of the following books, then Thompson has hit the jackpot."

—Romance Readers at Heart

"Vicki Lewis Thompson has a true flair for humor. Pick up *Over Hexed* and be prepared to be amused, delighted, and satisfied as Vicki Lewis Thompson takes you on an unforgettable ride."   —Single Titles

"Vicki Lewis Thompson sure delivers with *Over Hexed*. . . . A lighthearted tale that won't soon be forgotten."   —Fallen Angel Reviews

"With her wonderful talent of lighthearted humor, Vicki Lewis Thompson pens an enchanting tale for her amorous characters, steeping it in magic and enough passion to scorch the pages."   —Darque Reviews

"Vicki Lewis Thompson has created another romance blended with humor to make you beg for more."
—Once Upon a Romance Reviews

continued . . .

And for the other novels of Vicki Lewis Thompson

"Count on Vicki Lewis Thompson for a sharp, sassy, sexy read. Stranded on a desert island? I hope you've got this book in your beach bag."
—Jayne Ann Krentz

"Wildly sexy . . . a full complement of oddball characters . . . sparkles with sassy humor."
—*Library Journal*

"A riotous cast of colorful characters. . . . Fills the pages with hilarious situations and hot, creative sex."
—*Booklist*

"Smart, spunky, and delightfully over-the-top."
—*Publishers Weekly*

"[A] lighthearted and frisky tale of discovery between two engaging people." —*The Oakland Press* (MI)

"Delightfully eccentric . . . humor, mystical ingredients, and plenty of fun . . . a winning tale."
—The Best Reviews

"A funny and thrilling ride!"
—Romance Reviews Today

"A hilarious romp." —Romance Junkies

"Extremely sexy . . . over-the-top . . . sparkling."
—*Rendezvous*

"A whole new dimension in laughter. A big . . . *Bravo!*" —A Romance Review

WILD & HEXY

Vicki Lewis Thompson

AN ONYX BOOK

ONYX
Published by New American Library, a division of
Penguin Group (USA) Inc., 375 Hudson Street,
New York, New York 10014, USA
Penguin Group (Canada), 90 Eglinton Avenue East, Suite 700, Toronto,
Ontario M4P 2Y3, Canada (a division of Pearson Penguin Canada Inc.)
Penguin Books Ltd., 80 Strand, London WC2R 0RL, England
Penguin Ireland, 25 St. Stephen's Green, Dublin 2,
Ireland (a division of Penguin Books Ltd.)
Penguin Group (Australia), 250 Camberwell Road, Camberwell, Victoria 3124,
Australia (a division of Pearson Australia Group Pty. Ltd.)
Penguin Books India Pvt. Ltd., 11 Community Centre, Panchsheel Park,
New Delhi - 110 017, India
Penguin Group (NZ), 67 Apollo Drive, Rosedale, North Shore 0632,
New Zealand (a division of Pearson New Zealand Ltd.)
Penguin Books (South Africa) (Pty.) Ltd., 24 Sturdee Avenue,
Rosebank, Johannesburg 2196, South Africa

Penguin Books Ltd., Registered Offices:
80 Strand, London WC2R 0RL, England

First published by Onyx, an imprint of New American Library,
a division of Penguin Group (USA) Inc.

First Printing, June 2008
10 9 8 7 6 5 4 3 2 1

PUBLISHER'S NOTE
This is a work of fiction. Names, characters, places, and incidents either are
the product of the author's imagination or are used fictitiously, and any resemblance to actual persons, living or dead, business establishments, events, or
locales is entirely coincidental.

The publisher does not have any control over and does not assume any
responsibility for author or third-party Web sites or their content.

If you purchased this book without a cover, you should be aware that this
book is stolen property. It was reported as "unsold and destroyed" to the
publisher, and neither the author nor the publisher has received any payment
for this "stripped book."

The scanning, uploading, and distribution of this book via the Internet or via
any other means without the permission of the publisher is illegal and punish-
able by law. Please purchase only authorized electronic editions, and do not
participate in or encourage electronic piracy of copyrighted materials. Your
support of the author's rights is appreciated.

For Debbie Macomber, who understands this crazy business better than almost anyone. Thank you for your friendship and for so generously sharing your hard-earned knowledge. May I someday be as savvy and well organized as you!

ACKNOWLEDGMENTS

No author is an island, or even a small continent. I wouldn't be able to function without my valuable people connections. That's especially true of my daughter and assistant, Audrey Sharpe. I've also enjoyed wonderful support from everyone at New American Library, especially Claire Zion, Hilary Dowling, and Elizabeth Tabor. My professional life would truly suffer without agents Robert Gottlieb and Jenny Bent. Thank you all for making me look good!

Prologue

"**I** had a chat with our lake monster this morning." Dorcas Lowell gazed at her companions from behind her black marble desk. How she enjoyed dropping bombshells during Monday staff meetings.

Her husband, Ambrose, and her assistant, Maggie Madigan, looked gratifyingly shocked. Sabrina, the black cat curled in Ambrose's lap, sat upright and blinked, which was as shocked as Sabrina ever allowed herself to be.

Ambrose recovered first, and he was furious. "Look, we agreed you wouldn't—"

"The lake monster speaks English?" Maggie leaned forward in her chair.

"Who cares?" As Ambrose stood, Sabrina leaped onto the polished desk. "You should never have gone there alone. Anything could have—"

"But nothing did." Dorcas stroked Sabrina and smiled at her husband. He was so cute when he was mad. He would never have approved of her going to see the lake monster alone, but she'd known instinctively that was the way to approach the problem.

Ambrose glowered at her. "You might have been killed."

"Nonsense." Dorcas gently extricated her notes from underneath Sabrina's paws. "Would you like to hear my report?"

Ambrose sat down with a martyred sigh. "Might as well, considering you risked your life to get it."

"I did nothing of the kind." Dorcas put on her jeweled reading glasses and consulted what she'd written. "In a nutshell, Dee-Dee is lonely."

"Hold on, Dorcas." Ambrose obviously still had his snit going. "Matchmaking for humans is one thing, but we're *not* matchmaking for a lake monster. End of story."

"Why not?" Maggie's voice quivered with anticipation. "Couldn't you bring a mate to the lake?"

"Ye gods." Ambrose glared at his wife. "Please don't tell me you're considering that."

"No, sweetie, I'm not."

Maggie made a sound of protest. "But—"

"Sorry, Maggie. It's out of the question." Dorcas turned to her with a tolerant smile. From the moment Maggie had discovered that Dorcas and Ambrose had magical powers, she'd acted like a kid with a new Xbox. When she'd moved here from Houston to get married, she'd immediately asked to work for them in their matchmaking business. A nonmagical person such as Maggie usually thought that witches and wizards could do anything.

"I don't understand the problem, Dorcas," Maggie said.

"Transporting a grown male lake monster here would take more powerful magic than Ambrose and I could manufacture by ourselves."

Ambrose snorted. "You think?"

"But you guys have connections. The Grand High Wizard was just here this weekend. I'll bet he—"

"He wouldn't do it," Dorcas said. "For one thing, it violates the original contract made with Dee-Dee when she arrived here, which says she's not to have any contact with people, magical or non. Cecil would never approve."

"But you've already had contact," Maggie pointed out.

"Which I hope Cecil never discovers, but I happen to think this needs solving. Unfortunately, bringing in a mate couldn't be done without somebody noticing. Imagine a creature the size of the Goodyear blimp cruising over our unsuspecting neighbors. You don't see that so much here in Big Knob, Indiana. The residents would get hysterical."

"And then we'd have a monster hunt on our hands," Ambrose added. "Once they're alerted to strange creatures in the area, they could easily find George. The only reason they haven't discovered that a dragon lives in the forest at the edge of town is because it never occurred to them there was one there."

Maggie nodded. "I see your point. I don't want to endanger George."

"Neither do I," Dorcas said, although most of the time she longed to give that silly dragon a kick in the patoot. If he'd paid more attention to his duties as the Guardian of Whispering Forest, she and Ambrose would be off the job and headed home to Sedona by now. Instead, by order of the Grand High Wizard, they were stuck in this one-dragon town until George earned his golden scales. They'd already waited months for that, and there was no end in sight.

"So if we're not going to find Dee-Dee a mate," Ambrose said, "what are we going to do about her?"

"I'm not sure yet." Dorcas tapped her glowing pen against her lips. "She needs more study."

Ambrose's scowl had returned. "Next time, I'm going with you, and I'm bringing my staff. Did you even take your wand along?"

"I went unarmed, to gain her trust. And you may *not* come with me next time. This is delicate. Something only a woman would understand."

"Then can I go?" Maggie looked as if she could barely contain herself. She obviously loved being an insider, the only Big Knob resident who knew that Dorcas was a witch and Ambrose a wizard. Even Maggie's husband, Sean, didn't know, although he'd been their first nonmagical client. Sean thought they were relationship counselors.

"Maybe you can go," Dorcas said. "But let's wait a bit. I wouldn't want Dee-Dee to think I'm gossiping about her secrets. She's vulnerable right now."

Ambrose rolled his eyes. "Nothing that weighs two tons is vulnerable, Dorcas."

"That's what you think. Okay, what else do we have this morning, gang?"

"I have something." Maggie reached into her briefcase, pulled out a folder and shoved it across the desk toward Dorcas. "You both know Jeremy Dunstan. He's a good friend of Sean's." Maggie's eyes sparkled whenever she spoke of her husband.

As Dorcas thought of the match she and Ambrose had orchestrated between Maggie and Sean, she reminded herself that being sentenced to dragon duty hadn't been all bad. The Grand High Wizard's decree had lost some of its sting now that she and Ambrose were using their matchmaking skills on the good citizens of Big Knob.

"Of course I know Jeremy," Ambrose said. "I was just in his Internet café yesterday, surfing the Web."

Dorcas wasn't surprised. The Internet was Ambrose's new fixation. He'd recently created a MySpace page for himself. "Does Jeremy want our help?" she asked Maggie.

"Of course he wouldn't want it," Maggie said. "But he needs it. I'm sure we can figure out a way to help him without his knowledge."

Intrigue. Dorcas relished it. Smiling at Maggie, she opened the folder and found a neatly typed prospectus for a new matchmaking scheme between Jeremy and

Annie Winston, sister of Melody. Melody was getting married next weekend with Annie as maid of honor and Jeremy as best man. Nice setup.

Dorcas flipped through the contents of the folder. It was a common story. Back in school, shy Jeremy had lost out to the football hero, but now Annie and the football hero were divorced. "Jeremy still loves her?" Dorcas asked.

"That's what Sean says." Maggie ran a hand through her short red curls. "I wormed the story out of him this weekend."

Dorcas continued to read. "Annie was voted Miss Dairy Queen the summer before her senior year. What's that all about?"

"It's Big Knob's annual Dairy Festival that takes place next month," Maggie said. "It's the highlight of June around here, and according to Sean, being elected queen is a huge deal. I'm sure Jeremy was intimidated by that, too."

Dorcas looked at Ambrose. His anger over the Dee-Dee incident seemed to have subsided. Although Dorcas ran the Monday morning staff meetings, Ambrose kept track of appointments, so he would know if they had time for this project.

She closed the folder. "What do you think, Ambrose? Can we fit Jeremy into the schedule?"

Her husband reached for the appointment book sitting beside his chair and thumbed through it. Because matchmaking wasn't a full-time job in a town with only 948 residents, and because it usually involved unsuspecting clients, they'd decided never to charge for it. To stay busy and bring in a little extra cash, they'd taken on some marriage counseling, as well.

He glanced up. "We can make the time providing you lay off this Dee-Dee situation for now."

Dorcas recognized blackmail when she heard it. But *for now* was a vague term, and she could work around it. She scratched behind Sabrina's ears. "Okay."

"Then I guess we're in business," Ambrose said. "Jeremy and Annie will be our next matchmaking clients. When does Annie arrive in town?"

"Today."

Ambrose closed the appointment book and stood. "Then we'll have to work fast."

Chapter 1

"**S**uck it in." Melody tugged on the back zipper of Annie's peach-colored matron-of-honor dress.

"I used the measurements from when I made your wedding dress," their mother said, sounding anxious. "But I must have transposed some numbers."

"It's not your mistake, Mom." Annie was too mortified to admit that she was twenty pounds past those old measurements. She'd planned to lose the weight before the wedding. Then Melody had moved up the date by six months.

But, fat or skinny, Annie looked hellacious in peach, which might be why Melody had chosen it, the little snot. The bridesmaids would be in pale blue, but Melody had saddled Annie with a contrasting color, a color that made her skin look sallow and her blond hair brassy.

Annie held her breath, closed her eyes and prayed the damned zipper would close.

"Got it!"

When Annie opened her eyes, Melody and her mother stood looking at her. They were in identical poses, hands on hips, gazes scanning the dress. Neither of them seemed pleased.

That made three of them. Annie could imagine the

picture she presented stuffed into this tight dress—like a shrimp ready for the barbie.

"Too much cleavage," her mother said.

"My thoughts, exactly. Maybe a brooch." Melody walked over and tried to drag the edges of the neckline closer together.

Annie stepped back. "I wouldn't do that if I were—" The sound of popping seams said it all.

"Oh, dear." Her mother hurried over and touched the splitting side seams, as if she could work some healing magic by a laying on of hands. "Faulty thread. I must have used faulty thread and I just didn't notice."

"The problem's me." Annie couldn't bear to have her mother take the rap for this. "I've gained a little weight." Thumbscrews wouldn't get her to admit how much, though.

"And it looks good on you," her mother said with characteristic loyalty. "You were always too thin. Don't worry. I'll take care of the dress."

"Yeah, Mom can fix it," Melody said. "She's a genius when it comes to letting things out. She fixed Sharon Fugate's prom dress so nobody could tell Sharon had gained thirty pounds."

"I haven't gained thirty pounds." Actually, she had, but she'd shaved off ten in the past three months. She'd counted on having more time to unload the rest.

"My mistake." Melody was clearly loving this.

Annie longed to grab her sister around the neck and give her a knuckle rub like the ones they used to inflict on each other in the old days. But she couldn't blame Melody for enjoying this moment.

Everything had come so easily for Annie. She'd been an honor student and an athlete, the school softball team's best pitcher in Big Knob's history and a whiz at her SATs. No one had been surprised when Annie had collected the coveted title of Miss Dairy Queen, a scholarship to Northwestern, a wedding ring from Zach Anderson, and an on-camera job at WGN News in Chicago.

A little sister who'd struggled in Annie's shadow for years could be forgiven for gloating now that Annie's lucky star had lost its glitter. The divorce from Zach had been humiliating, followed by the loss of her glamour job at WGN. Unfortunately she'd discovered that in a pinch, food could take the place of love and fame.

Now she looked less like the Dairy Queen and more like the Dairy Cow. It wasn't Melody's fault. The peach dress, however, *was* Melody's fault. Melody just hadn't realized it would be overkill.

"Let's get that dress off and let me work on it." Annie's mother unzipped the dress with much less effort, now that the seams had given way.

"I'm thinking a lace shawl, to cover your cleavage," Melody said.

"I'm thinking duct tape, to cover your mouth." Annie couldn't help it. She was trying to be charitable, but she had only so much patience, especially because she'd been starving herself ever since Melody's phone call four days ago announcing the new and exceedingly imminent wedding date.

Melody's chin lifted like it used to do when she was five. "It's *my* wedding!"

"It's *my* cleavage!"

"Girls, girls." Annie's mother bundled the dress up and took it over to her sewing table. "You're too old for this kind of nonsense."

"And too busy." Annie reached for her clothes. "I have to get going."

"Where to?" Her mother spoke around a mouthful of pins.

"That new Internet café of Jeremy's." Pulling on her black slacks (slimming) and buttoning her cream-colored blouse (flattering), she slipped on her shoes and grabbed her trench coat.

The trench coat had been a silly purchase, now that she thought back on it. But after she'd left WGN, the reporting job at the *Chicago Tribune* had been a welcome lifeline, a way to salvage her pride. In celebration, she'd bought what she considered the ultimate journalistic badge, a black trench coat. Besides, it helped cover the added weight.

Fortunately, Big Knob's May weather was still cool enough to justify wearing the coat. Annie wondered how Melody would feel about having her matron of honor walk down the aisle with it on. The trench coat would look a hell of a lot better than that peach number.

"Do you have to go right now?" Melody said. "Georgia and Carol are coming over to help me with the favors. We could use an extra pair of hands."

"I'll help when I get back." Annie grabbed her purse and started for the door. "The first installment of my Life in a Small Town series is due in an hour. Thank God Jeremy has high-speed access in that café he opened a couple of months ago."

"Just don't miss dinner," her mother said. "I made apple pie."

Annie knew that. She'd smelled it baking the minute she'd arrived this afternoon and figured the pie was in her honor. Joy Winston was famous for two things: her seamstress skills and her apple pies. Her talent with a needle had kept the family afloat after Ralph Winston had died from an undiagnosed heart condition when the girls were six and four.

Ralph had been an insurance agent who'd sold plenty of car and home policies but had never believed in life insurance, not even for himself. His financially strapped widow had sold the agency and opened the Knob Bobbin Sewing and Fabric Shop. After sewing had become a job instead of a hobby, she'd used her baking to relax after work.

That apple pie cooling on the kitchen counter would

taste like ambrosia, and Annie didn't dare eat a single mouthful. "I'll be home for dinner," she said. "But I'm not really all that hungry these days, so don't expect me to eat much."

Melody rounded her eyes at Annie. She wasn't fooled, not for a minute. She knew Annie was dieting like crazy.

Annie's mother glanced up and took the pins from her mouth, always a signal that she had something important to say. "You're beautiful just as you are. I never liked how you had to worry about your weight because you were on camera all the time. Plus Zach was too obsessed with your weight. You look better this way. Healthier."

"Thanks, Mom." Annie smiled at her and wished, just a little bit, that she could come back home to live in her mother's nonjudgmental circle of love. Six months ago, when she was going through the divorce, phone conversations with her mom had been her lifeline. But she was a big girl—a little too big at the moment—and she couldn't come running to Mommy, who would feed her apple pie and insist she wasn't fat, just healthy. "See you guys later."

Word traveled fast in Big Knob, so Jeremy knew that Annie had arrived at her mother's house at approximately one forty-five this afternoon. Although outwardly he seemed calm as he dealt with customers at the Click-or-Treat Café, internally he was wrecked, wondering how soon he and Annie would run into each other. In a town this size, it wouldn't take long.

As he moved through the café late in the afternoon, the crowd was mostly teenagers doing homework. Normally he got a kick out of their wacky brand of humor, but today he was too distracted to appreciate it.

"Hey, dude, you keep crashing into poor Megabyte." Seventeen-year-old Tony Gambino looked up from his keyboard. "Good thing that dog has a forgiving nature or you'd be missing a leg by now."

"Yeah. Sorry, Meg." Jeremy leaned down to scratch behind the Irish wolfhound's ears. Stumbling over Megabyte was easy to do considering the space she took up as she sprawled on the floor, but normally Jeremy was more careful.

Not today. Annie was in town. Originally the wedding had been scheduled for October, months away. Jeremy had counted on having time to get himself mentally prepared. But plans had changed.

Until last week, the groom had worked in Evansville, which was only a short commute. Then his company had abruptly transferred him to Waikiki, which made for a slightly longer commute. Melody and Bruce had decided to bump up the wedding to this weekend so they could begin their life together in Hawaii.

Jeremy couldn't be happier for both of them, except that now his reunion with Annie, a woman he still had hot dreams about ten years after they'd graduated, was suddenly upon him. No official wedding festivities including him and Annie would take place until the rehearsal and rehearsal dinner on Friday night, but he'd see her before then, guaranteed.

The possibilities were endless. They could accidentally meet in the Hob Knob Diner during lunch, or at the Big Knobian Bar at happy hour, or while strolling around the town square window-shopping. No, wait. He never window-shopped. But they could bump into each other buying Bradley's famous chicken salad at the deli. Then again, Jeremy might take his kayak out on Deep Lake at the very moment she went there to watch the sunset.

Or she could walk into his café right this minute and take all the guesswork out of it. Jeremy almost dropped the carafe of Jumpin' Java Blend he'd been about to pour into Tony's mug. Everyone got free refills on the flavor of the day, but as an employee, Tony got free refills all the time, anyway. Tony probably had way too much caffeine in his system.

At the moment, Jeremy didn't have the brain cells available to cope with Tony's caffeine problem. He was too busy trying not to stroke out at the sight of Annie standing just inside the café's front door. She was ten times more beautiful than he remembered. The black trench coat gave her an *X-Files* look that he found wildly exciting. Then again, Annie would look wildly exciting in a faded flannel shirt and baggy overalls.

"Hi, Jeremy." She smiled and walked toward him.

"Hi." *Brilliant, Dunstan. Surely you can do better than that.* "Long time no see." No, apparently he couldn't do better than that, not when he was looking into those incredible blue eyes.

"It has been a long time." She glanced around the café. "Nice place."

"Thanks." He liked her hair like that, chin length and sleek.

"Didn't this used to be Billie's Bobble-Head Shoppe?"

"Right. Billie decided right after Christmas to downsize and move to a house two blocks from the square. The timing was perfect for me, so here I am." *And here you are, standing in my café.* He still couldn't believe he was face-to-face with the woman of his dreams.

"Is that your dog?"

"Yeah. That's Megabyte. She's sort of a mascot for the café."

"She's huge."

"And harmless." Jeremy couldn't stop looking at Annie. Her skin glowed, just as soft and touchable as he remembered. Even softer, maybe. The new job with the *Tribune* must agree with her. She seemed more cuddly than before. Not that he'd ever had the chance to—

"Hey, can I get my refill?" Tony asked.

"Sure." Still staring at Annie, Jeremy tilted the carafe in the general direction of Tony's coffee mug.

"Hey, dude, watch out!"

Jeremy glanced down in time to see a stream of hot coffee headed for the computer keyboard, a keyboard missing its plastic cover because Tony had taken it off after complaining about a sticking key. It was one of those slow-motion moments in which all the ramifications flashed instantly through his mind—the coffee splatters on Tony, the ruined keyboard and, most of all, the humiliation of having Annie there to see it.

But the coffee never reached the keyboard. Instead it defied gravity, reversed direction, and ran backward into the carafe. Jeremy gazed at the carafe in stunned silence.

Tony's mouth dropped open. Then he laughed and began clapping. "Excellent trick, dude! Hey, people, you won't believe what I just saw our man Jeremy do. He's a freaking magician!"

Kids left their computers and clustered around, asking questions and wanting a repeat. Even Megabyte lumbered to her feet and cocked her head at Jeremy.

"I have no idea what happened." Jeremy looked at the carafe. Had somebody tampered with it? Switched it with some trick model?

"Sure you do. Don't be modest." Ambrose Lowell appeared at his elbow looking more trim and sophisticated than most fiftysomething guys. "That was amazing. One of the best tricks I've seen in ages."

Jeremy hadn't heard him come in, but then it had been really noisy right after the incident with the coffee. "Seriously, you guys. I swear I don't know what—"

"That was very cool, Jeremy." Annie gazed at him with interest. "I don't know how you did it, but what a realistic performance."

Jeremy glanced at her. He didn't know what the hell had just happened, but Annie had never looked at him that way before, like he was someone to be reckoned with. Only a fool would keep insisting he was clueless.

"Thanks." Then he finally remembered his manners and introduced Annie to Ambrose. She was such a big celebrity in town that everyone else already knew her.

She shook hands with Ambrose, and Jeremy was a little jealous that Ambrose got to do that. Sure, Ambrose was old enough to be her father and happily married to Dorcas, but some women were turned on by that graying-at-the-temples look.

Too bad Jeremy and Annie had the kind of in-between relationship where they knew each other too well to shake hands but not well enough to hug. That meant he didn't get to touch her at all. Bummer.

The other kids begged Jeremy to do the trick again, but when he refused, they eventually headed back to their respective computers. Megabyte resumed her spot on the floor. Only Ambrose and Annie continued to hang around.

"Your carafe stunt was great," Annie said. "I desperately needed something like that."

"You did?" Fulfilling her desperate needs was a longtime fantasy of his. He'd just never expected to do it with a coffee carafe.

"My editor wants me to write a series of pieces on the joys of small-town life. I told him there wasn't a whole lot to write about in Big Knob, but he insisted. You've just given me the lead for my first story—'Tired of big-city bustle? Try some small-town magic.'"

Letting her believe what she wanted was one thing. Having her write a story for the *Tribune* claiming he was a magician made Jeremy uncomfortable. "Just so you know, that was a complete—"

"Tour de force," Ambrose said. "I consider myself a minor talent in the field of illusion. If you're willing to divulge some of your secrets, I'll divulge some of mine."

Jeremy had no secrets, and he definitely had to put a stop to this. "The thing is, I don't—"

"I think magic is fascinating." Annie gave Jeremy another admiring glance. "I'm sure you don't want to give away any tricks of the trade, but can you tell me where you learned how to do stuff?"

"If he's anything like me, he's self-taught," Ambrose said. "Right, Jeremy?"

"Right." Frantically Jeremy tried to remember if he knew *any* magic tricks. There was one having to do with cards that Sean used to try on people, but Jeremy couldn't remember it.

"So do you put on performances here in town?" Annie asked.

"No. In fact, I—"

"I get it," Ambrose said. "You're still in training, aren't you?"

Jeremy met Ambrose's gaze. It was as if the guy sensed Jeremy's dilemma and was trying to help him out of a jam. What if he took lessons from Ambrose? Jeremy could trade him computer time for it.

Oh, who was he kidding? With only a few days to work with, he'd never become polished enough to convince Annie he was a true magician. He'd be exposed as a fraud, and that light in her eyes would disappear.

"Okay, I have my angle," Annie said. "Internet café owner by day, aspiring magician by night. Even your café name, Click-or-Treat, fits right in." She dug a flash drive out of her purse. "I need a computer. I have thirty minutes before deadline. Where do you want me?"

Right here, next to me, forever. "Over in the corner there is fine." He gestured with the magic carafe. She was on a tight deadline, and what kind of guy would sabotage that by convincing her she had no story?

Of course, he was allowing her to write something that wasn't true, and that wasn't good, either. What a mess. But his moral angst didn't stop him from wanting to watch her take off her trench coat before she sat down in front of the computer.

As she slipped the coat off her shoulders and hung it over the back of the chair, he gulped. Her body was as voluptuous as ever. More so, if you asked him.

"What a babe," Tony murmured. "I like older women. I could sure see myself—"

"Watch it," Jeremy said.

Tony put up both hands. "Sorry! Didn't know you had dibs. Say, could you do that trick again?"

"No."

"Then how about my coffee?"

Jeremy looked at the carafe, not sure what to expect from the damned thing. "Let me get a fresh pot. Ambrose? Coffee?"

"You bet." Ambrose followed him over to the counter.

Jeremy walked around it and took a full carafe from under the coffee machine spout. Placing a mug on the counter, he poured it full. "I'm not a magician, Ambrose," he said in a low voice.

"I know."

"So what do I do about that? I can't turn into one overnight."

"Not overnight, no." Ambrose picked up his mug. "But come by the house tonight after you close up. Maybe I can teach you how to fake it."

"I don't know. That sounds risky. I could screw it up royally."

"True. But do you want the girl or don't you?"

Jeremy blinked. "Look, Ambrose, I'm not about to become one of your matchmaking clients. That was fine for my buddy Sean, but I prefer to blunder through on my own."

"Suit yourself. But if you ask me, you could use a little magic."

"I'll just tell her the truth. I'll take her some coffee,

and then I'll let her know that there's been a misunderstanding, and I'm not a magician."

Ambrose pulled a handkerchief out of his pocket. "And to ease your confession, which will ruin the story she's writing for her paper and possibly get her in trouble with her editor if she ends up with no story at all, you can give her this rose."

"What rose?"

"This one." Ambrose flicked the handkerchief and produced a red rose glistening with dew.

Jeremy stared at it. Then he glanced at Ambrose. "Okay," he said. "Your house. Nine o'clock."

Chapter 2

So Jeremy Dunstan was in training to become a magician. Annie was fascinated, and as a result, her first installment of the small-town series seemed to be writing itself. She craved surprises, which was one of the reasons she'd left predictable and boring Big Knob for the excitement of Chicago. Working as a journalist there meant no two days were ever the same.

Yeah, surprises are great, except when the surprise is that your husband is leaving you for someone else. Getting that shocking news right after Annie had broken her ankle during a skiing vacation designed to rejuvenate their marriage was not fun at all. But to be honest, she couldn't claim total surprise. She and Zach had been on the skids for a long time before the ski trip.

The mechanics of the divorce hadn't taken long. She'd had the cast taken off the day before she became officially single. By then she was also officially overweight. The combination of restricted mobility and depression had added the hated thirty pounds in no time.

Shoving those crummy thoughts aside, she focused on her story. As she worked, the aroma of coffee and chocolate tickled her senses. She glanced sideways at a steaming mug and a chocolate chip cookie on a napkin. Both had appeared as if by magic, and she smiled. Jeremy had always been the considerate type.

She welcomed the coffee, both for the comfort and for the caffeine boost. But the cookie was off-limits. The mug had the Click-or-Treat logo on it—a computer terminal wearing a Zorro-type mask. Cute. She'd bet Jeremy had designed it.

Blowing across the hot liquid before taking a rejuvenating sip, she returned her attention to the computer screen. Fortunately the Internet café owner–budding magician story took shape quickly. Keeping track of the time display in the corner of the screen, Annie pulled in some of her previous knowledge of Jeremy to round out the profile, contrasting his quiet teenage persona with his emerging showmanship.

Opening this café and becoming a successful entrepreneur seemed to be bringing out new elements of Jeremy's personality. She wondered whether any other secrets lurked under that introverted exterior. In any case, she had her first story ready to go, and a lead on a second one. Tomorrow she'd visit Billie Smoot's relocated bobble-head shop for another slice of small-town life.

Right before she hit the SEND button on Jeremy's story, she realized that her editor might want a shot of him. He'd told her to take a digital camera along, just in case. He wasn't expecting great photography from her, thank God.

The shot needed to be posed, not candid, because she wanted to make sure she had a full frontal view of Jeremy's T-shirt with the Click-or-Treat logo on it. And he should be holding a carafe. She wouldn't bother asking him to do the magic trick again because her digital camera wasn't fast enough to pick it up.

She pulled the camera out of her tote. This would have to be fast. She had about five minutes before deadline. Jeremy moved around the café refilling coffee mugs and answering questions about various Web site searches.

Camera in hand, she approached him. "Can I get a quick picture?"

He looked up, and a flush crept up from the collar of his T-shirt. "Uh, I'm not very photogenic."

"Dude, don't be stupid," the teenager named Tony said. "This is promo we're talking about here. Can I be in it?"

"Me, too!" A pretty blonde who reminded Annie of herself at that age hopped up from her chair.

That started the stampede, and Annie decided to go with it—Jeremy surrounded by teenagers. "Hold up the coffeepot, Jeremy," she said.

"He should totally do the magic trick," Tony said.

"No." Jeremy looked extremely uncomfortable.

"I couldn't capture it with this camera, anyway," she said and was glad to see him relax a little bit.

But he still seemed stiff and self-conscious. "I'm not sure this is a good—"

"Yes, it is," Annie said. "Hold up the carafe and smile."

"But—"

"Just do it." Tony nudged him. "You'll be famous."

"Not my goal." Jeremy held up the carafe, but he wasn't smiling.

"Okay, everybody. Say cheese." Annie hoped that would prompt Jeremy to smile. She had new respect for the staff photographers. How did they handle a reluctant subject?

"Forget that cheese thing," Tony said. "Everybody say *hot sex*."

They all laughed, including Jeremy, and Annie snapped the picture. She took a quick look at it and was surprised. Jeremy was cuter than she'd thought.

"Perfect! Thanks, guys." She hurried back to her computer so she could upload both her story and the digital shot, along with a caption for the photo.

Done. Sitting back with a sigh of satisfaction, she picked up the coffee mug and realized she'd drained it. She'd also eaten the cookie. All of it. Shit. With no gym in sight, she'd have to run a couple of miles tonight to work off that cookie.

"More coffee?"

Glancing up, she found Jeremy standing beside her with a coffee carafe in one hand. "Is that the magic pot?"

"Nope. No tricks this time. Just a refill."

She consulted her watch. "Thanks for the offer, but I'd better get going. I promised Melody I'd help her make favors tonight."

"Right. Wedding stuff. I need to call Evansville about the tux order."

Annie made a face. "Please don't remind me about wedding clothes. It's a painful subject."

"It is?" He looked surprised. "I thought women liked dressing up."

"We do if the outfits are flattering. But Melody picked out this hideous peach color for my matron-of-honor dress." She shuddered. "I look truly disgusting in it."

"I seriously doubt that." He gazed at her, his gray eyes warm and friendly behind the lenses of his wire-rimmed glasses.

"Trust me, it's true." As she met his gaze, she noticed something she hadn't seen in a guy's expression for some time—sexual interest. It felt damned good.

So it was only Jeremy, the class geek, who was giving her The Look. Sometimes a girl had to take what was available. Besides, Jeremy was far from ugly, as she'd recently discovered after taking his picture. He had a strong jaw and good cheekbones, and he'd filled out quite a bit since they'd been in school together.

He also had really nice eyes, something she'd never noticed before. His plastic-framed glasses had been replaced by trendy metal-rimmed ones, and his thick brown hair looked more stylish than she remembered.

To be honest, she hadn't paid much attention to Jeremy, period. He'd been so shy in school, always in the background of any activity. Although she'd made good grades, too, she'd never let homework interfere with her social life.

How times changed. The whole mess with Zach had screwed up her confidence to the point that she no longer had a social life. Maybe that explained why she was soaking up the warmth coming from Jeremy.

"So you sent the story in?" he asked.

"Yep. Thanks for being such a good sport about the picture."

He shrugged. "I just—"

"I know. The whole thing was sort of abrupt. But the picture turned out great." She picked up her camera. "Want to see it?"

"Uh, that's okay." He backed up a step.

Not wanting to force the picture on him, she put down the camera. What a contrast to Zach, who would have wanted to see the image immediately and would have insisted on retakes until he was satisfied that he looked sufficiently hot in the photo. "Anyway, I hope they run the picture with the story," she said. "Does anyone in town subscribe to the *Trib*?"

"I do here at the café."

"I would think you'd get it online, instead."

"Well, I can," Jeremy said, "but people around here seem to like reading the print edition. They might claim to get all the news they need from the *Big Knob Gazette,* but everyone who comes in here sneaks a glance at the *Trib*."

"Great." She pushed back her chair and stood. "Then they can check out the story." She pulled her coat off the back of the chair.

"Guess so. Here, let me help you with that." Setting

down the carafe beside the computer, he held the coat while she shoved her arms into the sleeves.

"Thank you." The brush of his hands across her shoulders felt nice. Casual touch didn't happen so much these days now that sexual harassment had become an issue. Which was a good thing, of course. People shouldn't be subjected to unwanted caresses. She just hadn't realized that living alone in the city would throw her into a virtual touch-free zone, and she missed human contact.

Oh, who was she kidding? She missed male contact. She missed sex. Right after Zach left, she'd thought men were all creeps and she could easily live without them. Six months later, she was ready to acknowledge that they had a few redeeming qualities.

Buttoning her coat, she turned to Jeremy. "I need to settle up. What do I owe you for the computer time and the goodies?" Maybe it was her use of the word *goodies,* or the direction her thoughts had taken when he'd helped her on with her coat. Whatever the reason, she suddenly found herself wondering how Jeremy would be in bed. How totally inappropriate.

"It's on the house." He picked up the carafe again.

"No, seriously. Let me pay you."

"That makes no sense. You just did a story on my café. Like Tony said, that's free publicity."

"Which you didn't ask for. Which you even tried to avoid, as I recall." She really liked looking into those gray eyes. His obvious sexual interest soothed her battered ego.

"I'm just not comfortable in the limelight."

"Yet you're training to be a magician. There must be an extrovert in there trying to get out." She enjoyed the thought of that. She wouldn't mind being around for the transformation.

"It's only a hobby."

"But a fun hobby. Listen, I need to pay you. I'll be

coming in every day to file a new story, so I can't have you comping me all week. That's not fair."

"We could say it's for old time's sake."

"Or I could buy you a drink over at the Big Knobian after you close up shop here."

The invitation obviously surprised him, but it surprised her, too. She must be in serious need of male companionship if she'd hit on the first guy she came across in Big Knob. She'd said it, though, and she couldn't very well take it back now.

He looked conflicted. "Actually, I'm supposed to be meeting someone."

Whoops. "Of course. I shouldn't have assumed that—I mean, a terrific guy like you would be seeing someone. My bad."

"That's not—"

"No, really, don't worry about it. I've been gone a long time, and I've lost track of who's dating who around here." Clutching her tote, she backed toward the door. "I'll get my little sis to give me a cheat sheet so I don't make those kinds of mistakes again." In fact, she wouldn't be making any mistakes at all, because she would eliminate all thoughts of men and sex from her mind.

"I'm not meeting a woman!" Jeremy said it loud enough that all activity in the café stopped and everyone's attention turned to them.

"Oh. *Oh.*" Annie blushed. She'd always had lousy gaydar, and here was proof. She'd hit on someone who batted for the other team. She'd been so caught up in her own deprivation that she'd imagined sexual interest where there was none. He'd probably been admiring the cut of her cream-colored blouse and trying to guess the designer.

Tony was the first to comment. "Hey, I'm cool with that, Jeremy, my man. To each his own, is my motto."

Jeremy groaned. "That's not what I meant at all.

It's a . . . a business meeting. I'm not . . . I don't want you to think that I'm . . ."

"I wasn't thinking anything," Annie lied.

"So what do we have going on here, gayness or straightness?" Tony asked. "Inquiring minds want to know. We're not here to judge. We're just curious."

Annie turned toward the kid, who was too precocious for his own good. "It's none of our business. Let's just drop it." And then she hurried out of the café before the situation grew any worse.

"So now Annie thinks I'm gay." Jeremy sat on a purple sofa in the Lowells' parlor, with Megabyte sprawled at his feet in her normal floor-rug pose. Jeremy wished he could be naturally relaxed like his dog. Instead he had to rely on the mug of Irish coffee Ambrose had just handed him. He'd had a rough day.

"Don't worry about a little miscommunication," Dorcas said. "That can be fixed." She and her black cat, Sabrina, occupied a red wing chair set at a right angle to the love seat, while Ambrose leaned against the mantel, sipping his Irish coffee. Sabrina kept eyeing Megabyte and arching her back, but Meg took no notice.

"I don't know how to fix it." Then Jeremy realized he was asking for the very thing he didn't want—matchmaking services. "Wait. Forget I said that. I'm really not here for that kind of advice."

"Even if it's free?" Over the top of her mug, Dorcas focused her amber gaze on him.

He was sorely tempted because he couldn't figure out his next move where Annie was concerned. But he was twenty-eight years old, for God's sake. He shouldn't have to consult Dear Abby on this issue. "I'll work it out," he said.

Dorcas nodded. "No doubt over a nice meal."

"You think I should ask her out?" He envisioned a quick and embarrassing rejection. Before he risked asking for a date, he had to clear up her misconceptions about him.

"I think it would be a good move." Dorcas looked as if she understood good moves. A sleek brunette in her fifties who dressed with big-city flair, she didn't seem to belong in a backwoods place like Big Knob.

"But she won't go out with me."

"I'll bet she would," Ambrose said. "Most women aren't prejudiced about gay guys."

Jeremy clenched his jaw. "I don't want her to go out with me under false pretenses. Damn, if only I'd known what to say. But I'm not quick on my feet in a situation like that, and she left so fast. I couldn't very well run after her insisting I'm heterosexual." He took a large gulp of the Irish coffee. The drink was strong and had an unusual taste . . . maybe amaretto.

Ambrose's lips twitched. "No, running down the street proclaiming your virility would have been worse. But Dorcas is right. Get the date, which will allow you plenty of time to clear up the misunderstanding."

Ambrose sounded so urbane, so . . . un–Big Knobian. Jeremy had never been able to figure out what Ambrose and Dorcas were doing in this small town handing out relationship advice. But here they were, and here he was, listening to that advice. He couldn't argue that they had a good point.

"I have Tony closing up tomorrow night," he said, "so I could leave the café by five. I could take her to the Hob Knob for an early dinner. That's even assuming she'd go, which I still say she won't."

Ambrose set his mug on the mantel. "Well, you can be sure of it if you throw in a little magic."

"That's the other thing. I appreciate your offer, but there's no way you can teach me enough to make her believe I'm a magician. I'll be the goofy guy getting tangled in colored scarves and dropping coins on the floor."

"Not on my watch." Ambrose crossed to the love seat. "Drink up. I'll mix you another one."

"Is that a good idea?" Jeremy appreciated how the drink had softened the painful memory of Annie leaping to the wrong conclusion about his sexuality. But he was here to learn something, not get wasted.

"It's an excellent idea," Dorcas said.

"But shouldn't I be looking for ways to sharpen my reflexes?"

Dorcas shook her head. "You need to sharpen your instincts, not your reflexes." As she stroked Sabrina, the cat turned her back on Megabyte and curled up in Dorcas's lap.

"She's right," Ambrose said. "At the moment, logic is getting in your way. Another Irish coffee, and you'll let go of your preconceived ideas of what you can and can't do."

"You mean I'll lower my inhibitions."

Ambrose nodded. "That's another way of putting it."

"Bottoms up, then." Jeremy drained his mug and handed it to Ambrose.

Once Ambrose had left the room, Jeremy turned to Dorcas. "I'm serious about what I said before. This is about magic tricks, not matchmaking. Asking Annie out is a good idea, but I'll take it from here."

"I'm sure you will."

"Or I won't." Jeremy thought the statistical chances that he would become romantically involved with Annie were roughly a million to one. "Magic or no magic, I'm not counting on anything. I mean, Annie's a city girl now. Our lives are going in completely different directions."

"What will be, will be." Dorcas fell silent as she continued to stroke the cat.

Sabrina, however, lifted her head and fixed Jeremy with a green-eyed stare. Then she made a little noise low in her throat that seemed to be a definite comment on the situation. If Jeremy didn't know better, he'd swear that Sabrina had just told him he was full of it.

Chapter 3

Annie's fitting for her dress went slightly better early the next morning, but nothing could be done about the overriding problem of the god-awful color. Annie felt overwhelmed by peachyness, drowned in peachnicity, ambushed by peachability.

"That'll do nicely," her mother said.

"Perfect," Melody agreed with a yawn. They'd stayed up late making favors while their mother finished the alterations.

Annie hadn't been able to face trying on the dress at midnight, so she'd put it off until this morning. The three women had been up since five because everyone had a tight schedule today. Joy had left the Knob Bobbin in the care of her lovable but scattered assistant the day before, and she wanted to go in early and straighten out any cash-register issues.

Melody, traveling at warp speed these days, had scheduled an early-morning consultation at the local flower shop, Beaucoup Bouquets. When a wedding was bumped up by six months, everyone involved had to scramble. Annie was determined to be a supportive sister and help where she could, but she also had another story to file by this afternoon.

The dress wasn't worth struggling over. She gazed into the full-length mirror, the one that used to give her much better news than this, and resigned herself to the inevitability of the peach dress wrapped around her extra twenty pounds. By moving the wedding date and choosing this color for her matron of honor, Melody had guaranteed that she'd be the most beautiful Winston daughter in the room come Saturday's wedding. And that was as it should be on a woman's wedding day.

Feeling noble and virtuous, Annie unzipped the dress and stepped out of it. "Great job, Mom," she said. "Thanks for letting it out."

"No problem." Joy took the dress and hung it on a padded hanger. "And now I have to run. No telling what sort of mess Cecily made of the receipts yesterday while I was gone."

"We need to take off, too," Melody said. "Since Gwen offered to open early for us, I promised we'd stop by the Hob Knob to pick up cinnamon rolls and coffee before going over."

"Gwen?" Annie pulled on stretch jeans that were too tight. No cinnamon rolls for her this morning. "You mean Gwen Dubois?" Gwen had been one of Annie's closest friends in school, but over the years they'd lost touch.

"Yep, that's her," Melody said.

"I take it she's helping her folks run the flower shop."

"Actually, she's running it by herself," Melody said. "A couple of years ago Elaine and Andre moved to a double-wide in Yuma because of Elaine's arthritis. They left Gwen the business. She's done well, too. Seems to have a green thumb."

"Huh. I somehow thought she'd be traveling the world by now." Annie remembered how Gwen used to say she was going to France someday to trace her ancestors. But maybe worries about her mother's health and the pressure of taking over the business had kept that from happening. "Is she married?"

Melody shook her head. "I don't even think she's dating anyone."

Their mother switched off the light over her sewing table. "What happened with Jeremy? Weren't they going out?"

"Oh, God, that was a disaster." Melody rolled her eyes. "Jeremy's parents and her parents were into this *Fiddler on the Roof* thing, hoping to match them up because the 'rents were friends and they thought Jeremy and Gwen were so much alike. Well, they are, which resulted in zero chemistry."

Annie thought of yesterday's awkward conversation with Jeremy and wondered whether gender issues had been the real problem. But she had no intention of broaching the subject.

"That's too bad," Joy said. "And in a town this small, I wonder if either of them will be lucky enough to find someone."

Annie thought Gwen had a fighting chance, but if she was right about Jeremy, he didn't have a prayer of finding a significant other in the conservative confines of Big Knob, Indiana.

From the minute Jeremy climbed out of bed in the morning, he had the nagging feeling that something significant had changed. For one thing, he was naked, and he usually slept in pajama bottoms. For another thing, he was awake before Megabyte, who was snoring away on the braided rug next to his bed.

As he pulled on the clothes he'd left on a chair in the bedroom, she lifted her head and gazed at him as if he'd gone crazy. Maybe he had. The birds weren't even chirping yet, for chrissake.

"Come on, Meg. If I'm up, you might as well get up, too." His utilitarian apartment was located above the café, so in order to let Meg out to do her business he had to walk downstairs. Making doggy protest noises, she lumbered after him.

"I don't get it, either," he said. "I haven't been up this early since I was a kid."

He halfway expected to see something out of place when he walked through the café, but everything there looked perfectly normal. Meg headed reluctantly out the back door into the chilly morning air, peed quickly and headed back up the stairs to the apartment. Jeremy followed, all the while looking for clues as to why he'd bounced out of bed like the Energizer Bunny.

Standing in his tiny kitchen, he fed Meg and remembered he'd forgotten to start the coffee downstairs. He never forgot to start the coffee. He always required caffeine, and plenty of it, to feel human in the morning.

Something was going on, but he couldn't figure out what. He prowled the apartment and gazed out the windows, expecting to find some evidence of change. His building was located on the east side of Second where it intersected with Fifth, and he had windows in the front and side of his apartment. From the side window he could see the old house that had become the headquarters of the Big Knob Historical Society, his mother's pet project.

The front windows looked across the intersection toward the town square. At this hour, when the sun huddled below the hills east of town, the square was empty except for the life-sized statue of Isadora Mather standing in front of the gazebo. His mother, Lucy, had spearheaded the fund-raiser to erect the statue honoring the wife of the town's founder, Ebenezer Mather.

Lucy Dunstan loved nothing better than digging into old attics looking for local history, and the residents had given her carte blanche to do that. On one of her excavations she'd unearthed an old journal describing how Isadora's herbal remedies had saved many Big Knobians during a smallpox epidemic in the early 1800s.

According to the journal, Isadora had also inspired

the layout of the town's five main streets. Her husband, Ebenezer, had created a five-pointed star and proclaimed it a tribute to Isadora, his shining star. Consequently the town square was actually a pentagon, but everyone called it a square because that's what people expected to find in the middle of a small midwestern town.

As Jeremy gazed at the statue, it slowly took on an eerie glow, as if lit from within. He blinked and rubbed his eyes. Still glowing. The hills continued to block the rising sun, and besides, sunlight wouldn't create that effect.

When the sun finally did come up, the glow gradually faded. Had the town installed a type of dusk-to-dawn device inside the statue? He could easily have missed that innovation because he was never awake this early unless he set an alarm.

But a light inside the statue wouldn't explain what he'd seen. Nothing would show through bronze. He'd just have to ask his mother about it. She was the authority on that statue.

Suddenly he was eager to start the day, and yet he hadn't put a single drop of coffee into his system. Peeling off his clothes, he headed for the bathroom to shave and shower. He was into his second chorus of "Eye of the Tiger" before he realized he was singing. *Singing.* Jesus. No wonder Meg was standing in the doorway staring. What was wrong with him?

By rights he should be hungover after spending the evening with Dorcas and Ambrose. Those two sure could put away the booze. After the second Irish coffee he'd lost track of how many he'd had, and most likely they'd kept up with him.

He'd also lost track of the magic lesson. Maybe they'd all decided to party, instead, because he had no memory of learning hat tricks or how to manipulate a deck of cards. But he did have a vague recollection of

Ambrose dancing a dorky cha-cha to Frankie Avalon's "Venus." And there had been something strange going on with the black cat, too. . . .

He turned to his dog. "I'm swearing off Irish coffee, Meg. It makes me see weird things, like that black cat dancing the cha-cha with Ambrose. I'll bet you didn't see anything like that."

Meg whined and wagged her tail.

"Don't say you did just to make me feel better. I'd rather not have a dancing cat in town, thank you very much. Or a glowing statue, for that matter. I like Big Knob the way it is. Quiet. Predictable. That suits me fine."

But it doesn't suit Annie, does it? The thought sent out sparks as it blazed through his hyperactive brain. Annie had left town for the same reason he'd stuck around, which meant that lusting after her was an exercise in futility. Just as well that he recognized that, because apparently he hadn't learned any magic last night.

Even so, he didn't want to leave her with the impression that he was gay. The part he did remember from his time with the Lowells was their suggestion that he ask Annie out.

Come to think of it, hadn't they sent him home with a bottle of wine from their private collection, in case the wine would come in handy? Still holding his razor, he walked into the small kitchen and glanced around. Sure enough, a bottle sat on the counter.

He leaned down and read the label. Mystic Hills Winery, bottled in Sedona, Arizona. Although he was no wine expert, he'd never heard of winemaking in Sedona. But Dorcas and Ambrose seemed far more educated in those things than he was, so he'd take a chance the wine was decent.

In order to share it with Annie, though, he had to make a date with her. No time like the present. Setting down the razor, he went to his land-line phone in the living room and thumbed through Big Knob's slender phone book.

Belatedly he realized how early it was. He was all set to apologize, but nobody answered at the Winston house. The old Jeremy would have left a message and let it go at that, but the old Jeremy seemed to have left the building. The new Jeremy intended to track Annie down, talk to her directly and get a commitment for tonight.

He called the Knob Bobbin.

"My, you're up early this morning, Jeremy," Joy said.

"Tell me about it. By the way, you don't happen to know anything about a new lighting effect on the statue, do you?" With only one statue in town, he didn't have to be more specific.

"Lighting effect?"

"It glows."

"I haven't heard anything about that, but I can't imagine how you could make a bronze statue glow."

"I guess you're right." Jeremy felt ridiculous for bringing it up. He really would save the question for his mother. "Anyway, I was wondering if you could help me find Annie. I tried your house, but no one answered."

"We've been up since before dawn and we're all running around like chickens. Is it something about the wedding?"

"Yes." The answer came to him instantly. No hemming or hawing. No searching for the right thing to say, which would have been his normal behavior. Just a clear and confident *yes*. He couldn't go through all the festivities as best man with the matron of honor thinking he was gay. Simple as that.

Life had never been that simple for him before, but this morning his thoughts were clear on the subject of Annie. She might never be interested in him because he lived in a place she found boring. Now that he hadn't learned any magic last night, he didn't have that to intrigue her, either. But he had other attributes, damn it, and he wanted her to know exactly what she was missing by rejecting him.

"You could try Beaucoup Bouquets," Joy said. "Annie and Melody went over there to finalize the flower order. They're probably still there."

"Thanks." As Jeremy said his good-byes and disconnected, he wondered whether his name would come up over at Beaucoup Bouquets. What if Annie mentioned her suspicion that he was gay? What would Gwen say to that? She couldn't disprove it, that was for sure.

He'd tried to work up some passion when he'd kissed her, but he'd felt almost nothing. He liked Gwen and he was completely heterosexual, contrary to what Annie thought. He probably could have taken Gwen to bed purely for the release, but that wouldn't have been fair to either of them.

Back in his college days he hadn't been so principled. He'd had a couple of relationships that had very little emotional commitment. To admit that he'd never been able to care about anyone the way he cared about Annie sounded juvenile, so he didn't admit it. But he was secretly afraid that was the truth of the matter.

Gwen answered the phone. He hadn't talked to her on the phone since they'd agreed to stop dating. They'd left some things unsaid, and now that didn't seem right.

"Hi, Gwen. It's Jeremy."

She laughed. "I know who it is. We dated for months."

"Yeah, and I'm sorry it didn't work out. I'm also sorry that I never told you how great you are. We're not right for each other, but I hope some guy comes along who is right for you, because you deserve someone special and he'd be a lucky son of a bitch to have you."

"Wow. That's quite a speech, especially for a quiet guy like you at this hour of the morning. Either you stayed up all night and are wired, or you've had way too much coffee since you climbed out of bed."

"Neither."

She hesitated. "You're not taking something, are you?"

"Taking something?"

"You know—one of those antianxiety drugs. I would hate to think that you—"

"Good God, no." But what she'd said gave him an uneasy feeling. What if Dorcas and Ambrose had slipped something into his Irish coffee? That would explain why he felt like king of the hill this morning.

"Well, okay, then. So is that all you called about? To wish me a nice life?"

"No, although I do. Is Annie there?"

"As a matter of fact, she is. Let me get her."

"Thanks." At the prospect of speaking with Annie, his adrenaline level spiked, but he didn't feel nervous. Damn, he hoped this confidence wasn't the result of Irish coffee spiked with Prozac. That would suck.

"Hi, Jeremy."

He would recognize her voice anywhere. Nobody else had that husky undertone that had been so distinctive on WGN that he'd have known it was her with his eyes closed. Her voice made him—and most likely the male population in general—think of sex.

For one wild moment he considered growling playfully into the phone. That would be waaay out of character. "Hi, Annie. Your mom said I might find you there."

"We're finalizing the flower arrangements. If you want to weigh in on the boutonnieres, now's your big chance. Melody's leaning toward a rose instead of a carnation, and Bruce is in a meeting, so I guess that leaves you as the decision maker."

He didn't give a flip if the guys had to wear dandelions, and Bruce wouldn't, either, but he knew women usually cared about stuff like that. "I'm sure a rose will be fine."

"I'll tell Melody. In fact, would you like to come over and take a look at the plan for the flower arrangements? You might have some ideas."

"Ideas about flower arrangements?" Then it hit him. She thought he had a knack for such things. He wanted to set her straight—ha, ha—right then and there, but a phone conversation, especially with other people able to hear her end of it, wasn't the place. "I know nothing about flower arrangements," he said.

"Oh. Okay."

"I was calling to see if you'd have dinner with me tonight. I have something I wanted to talk to you about."

In the silence, he could imagine what she was thinking—that he wanted to explain about yesterday. Which he did, but not in the way she might guess.

"You mean at the Hob Knob?" she asked finally.

It was the only place in town that served complete meals, and he'd thought about going there, but it didn't fit his image of this date. "They still close at six and they don't serve wine." He, however, could serve it. But where?

"I remember the Hob Knob closes early," she said. "People hardly ever have dinner out around here."

That had to be a far cry from her life in Chicago. So that was settled. He couldn't take a big-city girl like Annie to the Hob Knob at five o'clock.

He thought quickly. Dinner in his apartment wouldn't work because the café would still be open. The noise filtering upstairs would ruin the ambiance. "Ever been kayaking?"

"No. Are you into that?"

"Yep. Bought myself one last year. I could borrow a second one so we could both go."

"But I've never—"

"You're athletic. I could teach you in no time." He couldn't believe he was overriding her objections. He would never have had the confidence to do that yesterday.

"I have been sort of curious about kayaking."

"Great. Then let's have a picnic supper on the far side of the lake tonight." He couldn't believe these words were coming out of his mouth. He sounded so damned sure of himself it was scary.

"Won't it be dark by the time we paddle back?"

"Yeah." And he liked that idea. "But the moon's almost full and I have a couple of high-intensity flash-lights we can hang around our necks. We should be fine." They would be more than fine. Having Annie alone in the woods sounded like heaven to him. It was even early enough in the year to beat the mosquito season.

"Well . . . then I guess I could do that," she said. "But let me check to see if Melody needs me for anything tonight."

As he waited for her to come back on the line, he glanced down at Megabyte, who stood watching him as her tail swept slowly back and forth. She always seemed to sense when he was making plans that didn't include her.

"I promise to take you for a run before I leave," he said. The dog flopped down on the floor and sighed as if knowing she'd been relegated to second place.

"Jeremy?" Annie returned to the phone and she was laughing. "You still there?"

Always. "I'm here." There was more laughing in the background. Once upon a time he would have been convinced the laughter had something to do with him, but today he didn't let himself think that.

"Melody says it's no problem as long as you don't let me drown in Deep Lake. She'd have trouble find-ing a new matron of honor so close to the wedding."

Chapter 4

After being reassured that life jackets would be involved in her virgin kayaking experience, Annie hung up the phone.

"So what was that all about?" Still grinning, Melody picked up her cinnamon bun. She apparently found the idea of Jeremy pursuing Annie hilarious. "He must have an agenda if he tracked you down at the crack of dawn in order to ask you out. That's major enthusiasm."

"I'm not sure what it's about." Annie looked away as Melody bit into her cinnamon bun. Her sister had tried to talk her into buying one, but Annie had stayed strong. It hadn't been easy. The Hob Knob had the best cinnamon rolls Annie had ever tasted.

Instead of watching Melody eat, Annie glanced over at Gwen, not sure how this invitation of Jeremy's might be affecting her. Gwen had joked with Melody about Jeremy's eagerness, but that might have been a cover-up. No telling if he'd broken her heart, but if he had, she was hiding it beautifully.

Gwen had always been a class act, and Annie had been happy to discover she still was. She was also the kind of woman a makeover team would love.

Her brown hair could use a more flattering cut, but apparently she'd never cared to experiment with haircuts, or makeup, either, for that matter. Her clothes

did nothing to show off her figure, and her glasses
didn't compliment her face at all. A few simple
changes and one of her flowers tucked behind her ear,
and Gwen would be dynamite.

"I'm glad Jeremy's dating again," Gwen said. "He's
a great guy."

Annie searched for envy in her friend's brown eyes
and found none. Still, she would play it safe. "I don't
consider this a date."

Melody finished off the cinnamon roll. "If it walks
like a date and talks like a date, then it must be a
date."

"Then it's a date with no future." Deciding to meet
the Gwen-and-Jeremy dilemma head-on, Annie focused on her friend. "Mom said you and Jeremy used
to go out."

Gwen sighed. "God, we did. We surely did. I can't
believe we gave in to parental pressure at our age, but
they kept throwing us together and making it obvious
how thrilled they'd be if we became a couple."

"I'm sure they made it sound cozy," Annie said.

"Oh, definitely. Before my folks moved to Arizona,
they used to play pinochle with the Dunstans every
Thursday night, and I'm convinced they spent a good
part of the evening picking out names for the children
Jeremy and I were supposed to have."

Melody licked her fingers and picked up a book of
flower arrangements. "Manipulation to the max."

"It was, but I can see their rationale. We got along
fine, and Jeremy's even cuter now than he was as a
teenager. I should have wanted to jump his bones,
but . . . I didn't."

Annie wondered if Gwen's built-in gaydar had
warned her off, but she said nothing.

"After a while," Gwen continued, "I figured out he
wasn't sexually interested in me, either. One night we
finished off a bottle of wine, got slightly smashed and
admitted that we had no interest in becoming lovers.

Both sets of parents were crushed, but that's the breaks."

"Good thing you could be honest with each other," Annie said.

"Amen to that." Gwen gazed at her. "Now that we're talking about this, I seem to remember Jeremy had a crush on you back in school."

"He did?" Annie had never noticed anything of the kind.

Gwen laughed. "Don't look so shocked. Half the boys in school had a crush on you. You were the—"

"I've decided to add daisies to the bridal bouquet," Melody said. "I've found an arrangement I really like here on page twenty-three. But I want to keep the white roses. They're the focal point, the serious wedding flowers. The daisies are a dash of whimsy, just like it says here in the catalog."

Gwen exchanged a glance with Annie and smiled. "Sure thing." She walked over to where Melody sat on a stool with the book open on the counter in front of her. "Adding daisies is a brilliant idea."

In that moment, Annie decided she'd missed having a friend like Gwen. In all the years they'd spent together, Gwen had never acted jealous of Annie's accomplishments and popularity. Annie couldn't say that about too many people, including her sister. She definitely couldn't say it about her ex-husband. She wouldn't be so foolish as to lose touch with Gwen a second time.

Dorcas stood on the front porch and gazed with distaste at the red scooter parked there. Ambrose had bought the stupid thing last winter, and he loved it. Dorcas did not. But their only other mode of transportation was her hand-carved broom, and they didn't dare ride that in the middle of the day.

They'd scheduled a noon appointment with George in the Whispering Forest as an experiment to find out if the dragon was capable of getting up that early. A Guardian of the Forest had to switch from night to day shifts occasionally to properly patrol the area. George had the habits of a teenager—awake until all hours of the night and asleep most of the day.

Because of that he was useless at daytime patrols, and that had to change or he'd never earn his golden scales. George earning his golden scales was the key to allowing the Lowells to leave Big Knob and return home to Sedona. Dorcas still thought the punishment that had sent them here had been too harsh, but there had been no appeal.

Intent should have counted for something, and she'd meant to help Thaddeus Hedgehump with erectile dysfunction, not cause him more problems. The solution had seemed obvious—bespell Thaddeus so he became aroused at the sight of his wife wearing support hose. Unfortunately, Dorcas had neglected to make the spell specific to his wife's support hose, and Thaddeus had become a bit of a problem at the Witch and Wizard's Senior Center.

Dorcas and Ambrose still might have escaped with a slap on the wrist, except that Thaddeus happened to be the Grand High Wizard's brother-in-law. Banishment to Big Knob had been the sentence, with no reprieve given until they'd rehabilitated George.

George was better, but far from ready to assume his duties. Desperate for a way to keep him awake during the day, Dorcas had promised him a special treat if he'd show up at the clearing by noon. He adored presents, so he might arrive on time.

"Let's ride!" Ambrose strutted out the door wearing his leather motorcycle jacket, leather chaps and a red bandana tied around his head.

Dorcas couldn't decide which was more embarrassing, the silly little red scooter or Ambrose tricked out like a Hells Angel. "I think it's time we bought a car."

"Now, *that* would be ridiculous. We've made out fine borrowing Maggie's when the weather's bad. We don't need a car."

"If you want to talk about ridiculous—"

"I don't. I want to ride over to see George and sell him on the joys of sunshine." He tucked a journal inside his leather jacket and zipped it up.

"What do you have there?"

"My ammunition. I've been collecting quotes from famous people about the value of rising early. I plan to read them to George."

Dorcas rolled her eyes. "Oh, that'll work."

"You have a better idea?"

"I do." Dorcas patted her pocket. "Chocolate-covered espresso beans."

"You're kidding."

"Nope."

"You're seriously planning to give high-octane caffeine to a two-thousand-pound dragon who's ADD?"

"Ambrose, he's not ADD. He uses that as an excuse, and you know it. George is just lazy and a little immature."

"In that case, my quotes are exactly what he needs." Ambrose unzipped his jacket, took out the journal and opened it to the first page. "The early bird gets the—"

"The early bird gets the chocolate-covered espresso beans. You won't win points with George by pushing worms, my love. Now, wheel that red monstrosity down the steps and let's do this. Otherwise we'll be late, and that's a poor example to set."

"Right." Ambrose grabbed the handlebars. Then he paused. "Do you think Sabrina wants to come?"

"Probably not. She's sleeping." Sabrina was tired from her big adventure this morning, but Dorcas didn't want to mention that just now.

"Then let's go." Ambrose started the engine.

With a grimace of resignation, Dorcas climbed on behind him.

"I stopped at Click-or-Treat this morning," Ambrose said as they putt-putted down the bumpy sidewalk and onto the street.

Dorcas leaned closer so she could hear him. "And how's Jeremy?"

"Walking and talking like an alpha male. Annie's article with his picture that showed up in the *Tribune* this morning didn't faze him a bit. He accepted all the fanfare coming his way as if he was used to it."

"Excellent." Dorcas was glad the spell had worked. She'd been a little concerned about allowing Jeremy down in the basement during the circle ceremony, but that's what the spell book had called for, so they'd risked it. "Does he remember anything about last night?"

"Not much. He asked me if I liked Frankie Avalon, so he might have registered that we were playing 'Venus' on the stereo."

Dorcas groaned. Ambrose had a thing for that song and insisted on playing it whenever they worked a matchmaking spell. Sabrina aided and abetted by dancing the cha-cha with him as they circled the cauldron.

"I don't think it's a problem," Ambrose said. "He was pretty fuzzy headed by the time we took him to the basement."

"True. You do make great Irish coffee." Dorcas waved as Sean Madigan drove past in his truck. No doubt he was heading to their house to take Maggie out to lunch.

"Jeremy didn't think he'd learned any magic, though," Ambrose continued, "so I demonstrated that he could do a coin trick and manifest a red rose if he said *abracadabra.*"

"I still say we shouldn't have used that old cliché. Nobody says *abracadabra* anymore."

"Not in our crowd, but it sounds right to a guy like Jeremy. He tried to analyze the tricks, but I managed to convince him it was an intuitive thing and analyzing would screw him up."

"Good thinking." Dorcas hung on to Ambrose as he braked to a stop and allowed Clara Loudermilk to cross the street in front of them.

It was obviously Clara's day at the Bob and Weave Hair Salon, because a purple cape covered her ample bosom, her hair was wrapped in foil and she carried her Chihuahua, named Bud, in her arms. Clara was too impatient to wait at the salon while her hair color processed, so she ran errands while the dye worked its magic.

"Good morning, Clara," Ambrose said. "Good morning, Bud."

Bud, of course, started frantically barking. Bud barked at everything.

Clara eyed them with suspicion. "I think that scooter upsets Bud. I've noticed he's very sensitive to the color red." Tucking the squirming dog under her arm, Clara marched across the street.

"Nice to see you both," Ambrose called after them.

Dorcas laughed. "You'll never charm Clara. She doesn't trust anyone unless they were born and raised here."

"Forget Clara. I'm working on the dog. I think he likes me better already." Ambrose piloted the scooter past the square and continued on Fifth in the direction of the Whispering Forest.

Outside of town, trees covered in new green leaves arched over the two-lane road. Dorcas took a deep breath and savored the loamy scent of plants coming to life. Up ahead, the granite splendor of Big Knob thrust 192 feet into the air.

Dorcas gazed at the town's namesake. "How long since we've had outdoor sex?"

"Too long. I'm not used to these cold winters."

"Me, either." Back in Sedona they'd been able to

have outdoor sex almost year-round, but sex in the snow wasn't her idea of fun.

"I don't think we should try it in the Whispering Forest, though," Ambrose said. "Just our luck George would decide to patrol at that very moment and he'd be traumatized for life."

"He would, now that we've become parental figures to him."

"The lake's not such a good spot for outdoor sex right now, either," Ambrose said.

"Because of Dee-Dee?"

"Dear Zeus, I forgot about her!" Ambrose swerved onto the side road leading into the forest and stopped the scooter in a spray of loose dirt.

"Ambrose, for Hera's sake! What's wrong with you?"

Turning in his seat, he looked back at Dorcas. "Jeremy and Annie will be kayaking across the lake this evening. We have to stop them!"

"We'll do no such thing."

"But what about Dee-Dee? We don't know what she might do. We can't endanger—"

"I talked with her again this morning. In fact, I took Sabrina with me."

Ambrose's face turned the color of merlot and he could barely speak. "You—you *promised* you wouldn't pursue that if we took on Jeremy and Annie's case!"

"I said I'd put it on the back burner. Which I have. I got up very early, before we had anything scheduled, so that's back burner to the tenth power. You didn't even know I was gone, did you?"

"That's beside the point, and you took *Sabrina*. She would have been a one-bite snack for that creature, a cheese puff, a snickerdoodle, a—"

"Nonsense. Dee-Dee's a vegetarian. Anyway, now Sabrina and Dee-Dee are friends. Dee-Dee took Sabrina on a ride around the lake this morning."

"She *what*?"

"It's really adorable, Ambrose. Sabrina perches on Dee-Dee's head, and off they go. Sabrina sits up there with her ears back and her fur blowing in the wind. She *loves* it. I wish I'd had a camera."

Openmouthed, Ambrose stared at her.

She patted his cheek. "Don't worry about Dee-Dee, sweetheart. I'm on the case."

Jeremy expected to see Annie sometime during the day because she'd have to send another story to the *Tribune*. He thought she might come in after lunch, but he was pleasantly surprised when she showed up before noon.

Click-or-Treat was busy. A whole crowd of teenagers often stopped by during their lunch hour to check e-mail, and today they'd also shown up to check out his story in the *Trib*. Consequently the place was jammed when Annie walked in the front door.

She was carrying her black trench coat instead of wearing it, and when he got a look at her tight jeans and form-fitting red T-shirt, he felt like a cartoon character with spring-loaded eyes. *Boing.*

He waved to her and she waved back, but a quick glance around the café told him that every terminal was in use. He evaluated who he could bump to give her access and settled on Tony, who was supposed to start working in twenty minutes, anyway. "I need you to take a break," he said as he approached the teenager. "Annie's here to file her story for the *Tribune*."

"You've got it, Boss." Tony signed off and stood. "Look, I've been thinking about her, and if you're not inclined that way, then how about if I—"

Jeremy grabbed Tony by the back of the neck. "Listen up. I am not gay," he said in a low voice that sounded so macho he almost ruined the effect by laughing. He couldn't explain this sudden personality change of his, but he was beginning to realize it was fun.

Tony held up both hands. "Easy, dude. I believe you. Never thought you were. Seriously."

"Yeah, you did, but it's okay." Jeremy gave him a friendly push toward the counter. "Have a macchiato on the house."

"I'm all over that." Tony gave Annie a smile as he walked by her on his way to the counter. "Welcome back."

"Thanks." Her answering smile seemed to light up the entire café.

"I cleared a terminal for you." Jeremy watched her approach as X-rated fantasies danced in his head. Tonight, they'd be alone on the far side of the lake. He might never have another chance like that, and he was determined not to blow it.

"Looks like you booted Tony off."

"Tony doesn't have a newspaper editor breathing down his neck." Jeremy would love to breathe down Annie's neck, and nibble her earlobe, and take that gold hoop earring in his teeth, tugging gently while he—

"Annie!" Bobble-head shop owner Billie Smoot, her impossibly blond hair sticking out in all directions and something red staining her orange sweatshirt, charged through the front door. The bobble-head dolls she clutched in each hand gyrated madly as she rushed over to Annie's terminal. "I found Dolly Parton and Cleopatra!"

Annie leaped up, seemingly as excited as Billie. "Terrific! Did you find Jesus?"

Billie sighed. "I couldn't find Jesus. I searched high and low, but either I've lost him or I sold him and forgot to write it down in my ledger."

"I'm glad you didn't lose Dolly." Tony ambled over sipping his macchiato. "She was my favorite bobble-head."

"She's very different, all right." Billie jiggled her hand. "Only one with a bobble head and bobble boobs."

"Yeah," Tony said, gazing at the doll with an expression of worship.

"I've lost the stand, though. Without that stand, if you set her down she falls flat on her face."

"No duh." Tony reached for the bobble-head. "I'll buy her for half-price."

Billie jerked Dolly out of reach. "She's not for sale. This is a priceless, one-of-a-kind bobble-head, and I could still find the stand. I probably lost it in the move." She surveyed the café. "What a nightmare that was."

"It was a trying time for all of us," Jeremy said. Selling the building to Jeremy and moving had been Billie's idea, but getting 527 bobble-heads out of here and into her new digs had been more than she'd bargained for. She'd insisted on bubble-wrapping each one. Twice.

In the end, because Jeremy was so desperate to get his business up and running, he'd helped wrap. The process had dragged on for days, and the pop of a bubble-wrap chamber still made him quiver.

"Too bad about Dolly's stand," Annie said. "But we can make do without it for the picture." She dug in her tote and pulled out her camera. "Stand right there and I'll get a shot of you holding both of them."

"Egads, I look like a fright. Bad hair day. And the ketchup exploded when I was doctoring my scrambled eggs this morning." Billie shoved the bobble-heads into Jeremy's arms. "You hold 'em."

"I'll be glad to hold Dolly," Tony said, his gaze hopeful.

"That would be cute," Annie said. "Two guys, each with a sex-symbol bobble-head." She glanced at Billie. "Okay with you?"

"If he's careful."

"Yes!" Tony punched a fist in the air. "I'll be in the *Trib* holding a Dolly Parton bobble-boob doll!"

"And holding it very carefully," Jeremy said as he turned over the doll.

"No problemo, dude." Tony took the doll and only made it jiggle once before squaring up next to Jeremy for the picture.

Annie clicked the shutter. "That's good. Now all we need is a little magic to make this complete."

Jeremy prayed the trick would work the way it had this morning with Ambrose. He made a fist with his free hand. "Abracadabra!" When he opened his hand, a red rose lay across his palm, its petals glistening with dew. He had no clue how he'd manifested that rose.

Ambrose had said it was an instinctive thing, but Jeremy was beginning to think there was something very peculiar about Ambrose. For now, though, Jeremy had decided to muzzle his curiosity and reap the rewards. Like, for instance, Annie's admiration.

"Bravo!" She put down her camera and clapped enthusiastically. "That was terrific, Jeremy. I don't know how you did it."

"Professional secret," he said.

"I'm sure." Annie picked up her camera again. "That stunt is going in the story." She snapped another picture of Tony clutching Dolly and Jeremy holding Cleopatra and a perfect red rose.

Billie peered at Jeremy. "You were always such a quiet boy, Jeremy Dunstan. Since when did you get so jazzy?"

Jeremy looked over at Annie and winked. He'd never winked at a girl in his life, but this time it came easily. Then he turned to Billie. "People change," he said.

Chapter 5

The clearing was empty when Dorcas and Ambrose climbed off the scooter.

"He's not here," Ambrose said. "Typical."

"We'll wait a while." Dorcas paced the clearing and studied the surrounding forest of pine and oak with a few sycamores sprinkled in. Was that a pair of disembodied eyes floating in the shadows? George loved to use his gift of invisibility, where the only thing anyone could see were his red eyes . . .

Ambrose crossed his arms over his chest. "I'll bet he's still snoring away in his cave."

"We'll give him a few minutes." Dorcas sat down on a stump in the middle of the clearing.

"Do you think we should tell him about Dee-Dee?"

"I'm not sure. I—wait a minute." Dorcas held up her hand. "I smell smoke."

"And where there's smoke, there's me!" George materialized in a dramatic flash of light. He towered twelve feet in the air and might have looked fearsome except for his loopy grin and the white iPod dangling around his neck.

Dorcas had given him the iPod months ago. She had called it a peace offering and Ambrose had called it a bribe. Whatever it was called, George was never without it. Dorcas kept him supplied with downloads and believed the iPod helped keep the relationship cordial.

"Great Zeus!" Ambrose leaped aside to avoid being smacked with the dragon's swishing tail. "Did you have to startle us like that?"

"Absolutely, dude. That's how I get my groove on. So what's the four-one-one on this Dee-Dee chick?"

Dorcas decided he might as well know. He'd find out eventually, and better that he hear it from them than from one of the forest creatures. George regularly played Texas hold 'em with the raccoons, and raccoons were known for spreading gossip.

"Dee-Dee's a lake monster," Dorcas said.

"Okay. I'm cool with that. But what does a lake monster have to do with yours truly?"

"Well, nothing, really. But I thought you might hear stories that she's living in Deep Lake and wonder about her."

George blinked. "She's living right behind your house?"

"Yes."

"You're gonna send her packing, right? Big Knob is a one-monster town, and I'm it."

Just like that, Dorcas came face-to-face with sibling rivalry. No wonder she'd never had children. "For one thing, she's been here longer than you have."

"So what? Once I showed up, she was overkill, excess baggage. She might as well suck it up and leave."

Dorcas sighed. "It's not quite that simple. She's huge, and we can't just spirit her away."

"That's your story."

"And it's not only her size." Dorcas wished she'd never started this conversation. She glanced over at Ambrose, hoping for some backup, but he merely shrugged, the turncoat. "Dee-Dee's lonely."

"And you know this how?"

"I've talked with her."

"Isn't that special." George's lower lip stuck out in what could only be called a pout. His wicked teeth and the horn on his snout made the expression look a little strange, but there was no denying his reaction. "Can't she make her own friends? I made *my* own friends. I'm sure there's a fish or two she could hang out with."

"I doubt she'd have much in common with them."

"So you're all about Dee-Dee now. That's cool." George attached his earbuds and began undulating to the music only he could hear. "Uh-huh, oh yeah, uh-huh, uh-huh, uh-huh."

"George," Dorcas said, loud enough that she figured he could hear through the earbuds. "You are our primary responsibility. We'll never shirk our duty to you because of Dee-Dee."

"Shirk away." George kept dancing. "See if I care. I suppose you forgot my present. Or maybe you gave it to Miss Lonely-in-the-Lake."

Dorcas clenched her jaw as she despaired of George ever maturing into his Guardian position.

Ambrose finally stepped into the fray. "You aren't acting like a dragon who deserves a present," he said. "In fact, I was planning to read something to you, but now I've changed my mind."

George stopped dancing and took out his earbuds. "You were going to read to me?"

"Yes, but I—"

"Nobody's ever read to me before."

Dorcas sensed a disaster coming. If George expected to be entertained and got a lecture instead, the meeting would deteriorate even more. "Ambrose isn't going to read you a story, George. He just copied out a bunch of quotes that he thought you should hear."

George looked at Ambrose. "At least somebody still cares about me." He glared at Dorcas before sitting down with a thud that shook the ground. "I'm ready, dude. Lay it on me."

Ambrose settled himself beside George and pulled his journal out from inside his jacket. Dorcas watched in amazement as he read about the joys of early rising and George hung on every word. There the two of them sat, the wannabe biker and the rebellious dragon whose scales were mostly still greenish brown. But as the reading session continued, Dorcas swore the tips of George's scales began to change color.

Annie treated the kayaking date with Jeremy the same as she would an outing with a girlfriend. That made her preparations supereasy. She wore an old pair of walking shorts, a T-shirt, and a Northwestern University sweatshirt to keep her warm.

A little lipstick and a quick brush through her hair, and she was ready. When he pulled up in front of the Winston house at five thirty, two kayaks tied on top of his Suzuki Samurai, she grabbed her purse and went out to meet him.

Jeremy turned to her with a smile as she hopped in the car before he had a chance to shut off the engine. "Either you're eager to go or you don't want me talking to your mother and sister."

"Trust me, you don't want to go in there. They're wrestling with the seating arrangements for the reception. As it stands, the entire town will be gathered around table one, because that way, nobody will be offended."

"You're right. I'm staying out of that."

"But I do really want to go kayaking. It's always looked fun to me, but I never knew anybody who could teach me how to do it."

"Then I'm your guy." He pulled away from the house. "You look great, by the way."

"Thanks, but these are really old clothes." Ever since seeing Jeremy at Click-or-Treat today, she'd been trying to figure out what was different about him.

The easy compliment was a typical example. Yesterday he would have stuttered over it. Today he was as smooth as glass.

"You looked great earlier today, too," he said with the same calm assurance. "I just didn't have a chance to say so."

"Billie and her bobble-heads do tend to take over." She glanced at him and discovered that his profile was quite nice to look at. The leash he'd attached to his glasses made him look like the athletic type, but it was more than his accessories turning her on.

Until this moment, she'd never taken the time to notice all of his attributes—his thick, dark hair, strong nose, sensuous lips, and square jaw. She could tell he'd shaved before picking her up, which gave him points in her book.

"We need to get something straight." Then he laughed. "Absolutely straight. That's me, Annie." He flashed her a grin. "I'm not even slightly gay."

The words registered, but the grin was the part that supercharged her libido. She couldn't remember the last time she'd been that attracted to a man's smile. Well, yes, she could—Zach when they were sophomores. He'd been able to make her panties wet with a smile before she even understood what wet panties were all about.

Now she knew all about the wet-panty syndrome, and Jeremy, of all people, was creating the same effect. "I guess I jumped to conclusions."

"Yeah, well, I didn't explain myself well. I'd told Ambrose I'd come over to his place so we could talk magic. He was the guy I was seeing."

The whole magic schtick was working on her, too. She'd never known a magician, but she'd seen *The Illusionist,* and the whole concept of a magician oozed mystery and sex appeal. Any man who could say a magic word and produce a perfect red rose sprinkled with dew would certainly get her phone number. If he played his magic cards right, he'd probably get a whole lot more than that.

But she was jumping the gun. Right now they were having a friendly conversation, and she needed to hold up her end. "Ambrose seems like a fascinating person." She thought Jeremy was ten times more fascinating, but she wasn't ready to tip her hand quite so soon. "I wonder if he'd let me interview him for my next story."

"You could always ask. He and Dorcas came to town last summer, and nobody can figure out the attraction to Big Knob. You haven't met Dorcas yet, but she's pretty polished, too. They both seem to belong in some upscale boomer community with gourmet restaurants and art galleries lining the street."

"Maybe it's the beginning of a trend—sophisticated urban dwellers head for the classic simplicity of small-town America. How's that for a story angle?"

"Very good." He turned down the dirt lane that led to Deep Lake. "I can see why you've done so well in Chicago."

"I'm hanging on by my fingernails in Chicago."

Jeremy pulled into a parking space close to a small beach and turned to her. "That's not the word in Big Knob. In this town you're a superstar."

She couldn't pretend that she didn't like hearing that. "Then I shouldn't spoil the image."

He reached across the console and took her hand. "Couldn't happen. Not with me. I've had a crush on you since I was fourteen."

She drew in a quick breath. So Gwen had said, but Annie hadn't expected Jeremy, always the shy type, to say it out loud. "That's very flattering."

"I'm not here to flatter you. And I'm not here to be your pal." He looked into her eyes. "You might as well know this up front, Annie. I want you."

To Annie's complete surprise, the feeling was mutual.

*   *   *

Dorcas watched from her kitchen window as Jeremy loaded a picnic supper and a couple of rolled blankets into the cargo area of his red kayak. He also tucked in the bottle of wine she and Ambrose had given him.

Dorcas stroked Sabrina, who sat on the windowsill and was also observing the activity down by the lake. "Everything's progressing nicely, Sabrina." The cat purred in loud approval.

As Jeremy instructed Annie in the proper use of her paddle, things became quite cozy down on the beach. Dorcas could feel the sexual vibrations from where she stood in the kitchen.

By the time Jeremy had helped Annie put on that silly skirt thing that kayakers had to wear and settled her in his kayak, the heat between those two was so obvious it made Dorcas smile. Jeremy was making all the right moves, even to the point of giving Annie his kayak, a beauty that Sean had built for him, and taking the substandard blue one for himself.

Judging from Annie's body language, she was responding with enthusiasm to all that gallantry. They were off to a great start, but Dorcas had studied the file Maggie had supplied the day before. She'd also made a few discreet inquiries this afternoon about Annie Winston.

This was a woman who wouldn't easily give up the excitement of big-city life without a good reason. Dorcas decided it might be wise to provide one.

"Come on, Sabrina." Dorcas grabbed her leather jacket from a peg near the back door. "Since Ambrose is still at Click-or-Treat playing with his MySpace page, this is the perfect time for us to meander down to the lake."

Normally Jeremy hated the part where he had to wade into the cold water of Deep Lake. Fed by an underground stream rumored to originate in northern

Canada, the lake never seemed to warm up, even in
summer. This time of year it felt glacial.

At the moment, glacial was exactly what he needed
to cool his heated body parts. Helping Annie learn the
basic paddling stroke had created some self-control
problems. He prided himself on his ability to keep his
urges at bay, but he'd never been this close to Annie
before. To complicate matters even more, she'd begun
sending *I'm available* signals.

During the brief lesson, she'd relaxed against him
as if daring him to take her in his arms. He damn
near had, probably would have for sure if he hadn't
remembered that Dorcas and Ambrose's kitchen window looked out on this tiny beach area. He wasn't in
the mood to put on a show.

But he was definitely in the mood. Annie's voice
had dropped into the ultrasexy range, and when her
gaze met his, it was warm and welcoming. As a result,
he was hard and hyperventilating.

The torture continued. He had to make sure her
life jacket was cinched up, and then show her how to
put on the protective skirt. By the time he'd helped
her into the kayak, he was shaking from the effort to
restrain himself. He tightened the noose holding the
skirt around the cockpit opening, making it water-
proof.

During a normal kayaking lesson, Annie would have
to roll the kayak and demonstrate she could loosen
the skirt and get out safely. But neither of them were
in wet suits, and the lake was so calm that Jeremy
couldn't see putting her through that exercise.

He'd save that part for another time, if there ever
was another time. This was only supposed to be a
brief introduction to the sport. He stepped deeper into
the icy water and shoved the red kayak out onto the
lake.

He'd given her his boat because he wanted her first
kayaking experience to be a good one. Sean, whose

carpentry skills were amazing, had built this one for him and had insisted on painting it red, supposedly to give Jeremy some pizzazz in his new sport. The kayak sure was visible.

The blue one he now pushed into the water belonged to Bruce, who was responsible for Jeremy getting into kayaking in the first place. It wasn't a particularly good one—the rudders didn't react well—and Bruce was leaving it in Big Knob when he and Melody moved to Hawaii.

He'd offered it to Jeremy, who was glad to have it for this date but didn't really want it permanently. He had high standards in most things, which probably explained why nobody but Annie had ever interested him.

Annie floated in her kayak, her paddle held in both hands, and waited for him to pull alongside. The lake was as still as Jeremy had ever seen it, which was good for Annie's first try at this. Wind and choppy water made the learning curve steeper, and he'd have felt more obliged to explain the rollover technique. Most beginners weren't crazy about that maneuver, and it might have put Annie off.

"It's incredibly beautiful out here," she said. "We're just catching the beginning of the sunset."

"Uh-huh." He had a tough time appreciating the sunset when there was Annie to look at. Her cheeks were flushed and her eyes sparkled with excitement. He'd thought she could never look more beautiful than she had riding on the float as Miss Dairy Queen the summer of her junior year, but he'd been wrong. Tonight he saw more than a pretty girl. Annie had turned into an incredibly voluptuous woman.

"Thank you for suggesting this," she said. "What a fantastic idea."

"Wait and thank me after you've paddled across the lake," he said. "You'll be using muscles you didn't know existed, and you might be a little sore."

"I don't care. I had sore arm muscles plenty of times when I was a softball pitcher." She lifted her paddle and dipped it into the water. "Am I doing it right?"

"Not bad. Remember to twist at the waist and make that figure-eight pattern I showed you."

"Right." She started off. "If you follow behind me, you'll be able to check my technique."

"Okay." He'd planned to follow, anyway, so that she could set the pace. "Looking good, Annie. You'll probably take to this the way you did to pitching."

"You know, I miss softball. I thought about joining an adult league in Chicago, but there was never time."

Once again he was reminded of the difference between big-city and small-town living. In Big Knob they always seemed to have time for the extras. For one thing, nobody ever got stuck in traffic.

This evening on the lake was a perfect example of the pace of life around here. Except for the occasional twitter of a bird settling down for the night, there was no sound except the liquid slide of their paddles through the water. No honking horns, no jackhammers, no blaring music, no sirens.

"Look, there go Mr. and Mrs. Mallard." Annie stopped paddling long enough to point out the ducks crossing their path. They left a V-shaped wake that fanned out over the otherwise smooth surface as they swam toward the shore.

"In another few weeks we'll have ducklings around here."

"I remember. They're just too cute, like a miniature flotilla."

"Yeah." Jeremy loved the ducks, the lake, the trees. He craved this kind of peaceful setting, especially after a day spent in the café, which might well be the noisiest place in town if you didn't count the school gym during a basketball game.

Annie's voice drifted back to him. "Are the Knob Lobbers still competing?"

"Yep. If you were going to be here next week you could see our first home game." But she wouldn't be here next week. Because that depressed him, he decided not to think about it. "Have you figured out a story for tomorrow?"

"Maybe. I saw Clara Loudermilk heading into the Bob and Weave today, which reminded me about her husband Clem and the bra patent that made him so rich."

"You'd never know he was rich to look at him. Still dresses in denim overalls. Clara's the one who's spending the money. Sean built her a high-end sun-porch this past winter."

"But Clem's the one I want to interview. I know he's shy, but if I can get him to talk about his inven-tion, that would make a great story. I'll bet lots of women in Chicago wear that brand and have no idea the inventor lives in a little town in southern Indiana."

"I'm sure you're right." But Jeremy wished she hadn't brought up the subject of women's underwear. The bulky life jacket she wore and the kayak skirt disguised her figure so that he'd been able to tempo-rarily subdue his animal instincts. But thinking about bras brought those instincts roaring back.

He wondered if she wore a black bra under that red T-shirt. In his fantasies, she dressed in black lace underwear, the perfect complement to her blond hair. But he wouldn't really care if she happened to be wearing plain white cotton tonight, so long as he had a chance to find out.

Yes, he might be rushing the relationship to be con-sidering that kind of move already, but he didn't have much time to work with. By Sunday she'd be gone. He'd already announced his intentions and she hadn't run screaming, so only a fool would hesitate. He was no fool, and for some reason he'd overcome his usual hesitation, too.

Although he enjoyed kayaking, tonight he was much

more excited about the land part of this adventure. Fortunately that would start soon. They'd made good time, and the beach on the opposite side of the lake was only a couple of minutes away.

Twilight had created intriguing shadows on the sandy beach ahead. The shadows would give them privacy. He planned to build a small fire once they got there, more for atmosphere than anything else. The food was already cooked, and he didn't want a bonfire that would light up the place. Darkness and seclusion would work better for what he had in mind.

"Almost there," he said. "You're probably getting tired."

"Not particularly. I can't get over how quiet it is out here. You could hear a pin drop."

"I know. I've never seen the water this still."

As if on cue, little ripples slapped the sides of his kayak. Then the ripples turned into small waves that rocked both boats. Strange. There was no wind.

Annie looked back at him. "What do you suppose is causing—" Then her eyes got huge and she screamed.

Jeremy twisted around to look and found nothing there. Something *had* been there, though, something that caused substantial waves to rock both kayaks.

"Jeremy!"

He turned back and saw that she'd drifted parallel to a particularly large wave approaching her boat. "Turn into it!" he yelled.

But whatever she did with the paddle only made things worse. The kayak flipped, taking her with it.

Dear God. Jeremy stroked quickly and came up beside the upside-down hull. Loosening the skirt and ripping off his life jacket, he dived into the water. She was trapped under there, and he was the imbecile who hadn't taught her how to get out.

Chapter 6

Her lungs burning, Annie struggled to pry the skirt loose from the kayak. Her fingers were trembling too much and she couldn't budge it. *That thing I saw . . . it was in the water . . . with me.* She'd never been so sure she'd die.

When she felt movement next to her, her heartbeat hammered in her ears. The creature would eat her. It would pull her out of the kayak like a clam from its shell and gobble her up.

She hoped it wouldn't hurt much. Too bad she couldn't write the obituary. It would be one hell of a story. Probably make the national evening news.

But she wasn't ready to die, damn it! She struck out, flailing with both arms. Maybe she could gouge out the creature's eyes so it couldn't see her. She hit something solid and bubbles tickled her face.

Then she was dragged out of the kayak, skirt and all. Any minute she expected to feel the chomp of huge teeth. Yet she was suddenly released, and her life jacket caused her to pop to the surface.

Gasping and coughing, she tried to scream again, but she didn't have the lung power. She prayed that Jeremy was close enough to hit the thing with his paddle. Maybe he could stun it, or . . . oh, who was she kidding?

She was doomed. The paddle would be like a

matchstick to something that size. She was grabbed from behind. No! She wouldn't give up. She would resist until she had no strength left.

"Hey! Stop fighting me!"

The voice was hoarse, and a moment passed before she registered it as one she knew. Jeremy! She tried to tell him they were in terrible danger, but instead she sounded like a woman gargling her morning mouthwash.

In the dim light, a dark, menacing shape drifted closer. In a panic, she kicked out, knocking it away.

"That's the boat! We need it!"

Poor Jeremy. He didn't know that a measly kayak would be no protection against a monster of the deep. But maybe it was better than nothing. She allowed him to tow her over to the boat by the shoulder of her life jacket. She kept her chin in the air so she wouldn't swallow any more water.

"I'll boost you in," he said.

That's when she figured out that this was the kayak he'd been using, not the one she'd overturned. He shoved her into the cockpit with more strength than she would have given a computer geek credit for. She was wedged in sideways, which was partly because of the protective skirt she still wore.

Jeremy hung on to the side until the kayak stopped rocking. "Can you get all the way in?" He sounded tired.

She wondered if she'd done any damage when she'd tried so hard to get away from him. "Maybe. Give me a second." She coughed up more water. "Jeremy, there's a monster in the lake."

"I doubt it."

"Don't you dare say that!" She coughed some more. "I saw it!"

"Yeah, you saw *something,* but it wasn't—"

"I saw a monster." She shuddered, both from the cold and from the memory of that prehistoric-looking long neck, small head and beady eyes. If the rest of the creature matched the length of the neck, it was at least the size of an eighteen-wheeler.

"Okay, whatever. Work yourself into the kayak. Then, if you can hold my glasses, I'll try to locate one of the paddles."

"No! You can't go swimming around out there. It will eat you."

"Annie, I'm freezing and I'm sure you're freezing."

"I'm pretty cold."

"To get to shore we need at least one of the paddles. Here." He handed her his glasses, still attached to the leash. "I'll be right back."

She peered after him, but soon all she could do was listen to him splash around searching for the paddle. Heart pounding, she held her breath. What if the next sound she heard was an agonized scream? She didn't know what she could do to help, with no weapon.

She heard no scream, but something made a flapping sound overhead. An owl? She glanced up at a dark shape hovering at least twenty feet above her. It looked too big to be a bird.

Her stomach clenched in fear. Was she going crazy, or was Big Knob becoming the scene of some horror flick?

"Got it!" Jeremy called out.

She looked in the direction of his voice and could vaguely see a paddle waving in the air. When she glanced up again, whatever she'd seen was gone. A kite. Some idiot was flying a kite out here. That would explain what she'd seen, if only there happened to be a breeze blowing.

"And here's the other one," Jeremy said. "Excellent!"

She heard him kicking his way back toward her and decided she'd better get situated before he got there. Moving cautiously, she eased her waterlogged self down into the opening. Her shorts and sweatshirt weighed a ton and the soggy material squished against the seat as she settled in.

The paddles bumped the side of the kayak. "All set?" Jeremy asked.

No, I just saw something weird in the sky, too. He already thought she was imagining monsters everywhere, so she decided not to mention it right now. "Just so you know, I'm not fastening the skirt."

"That's fine. Here, hold both paddles. I think I know where the other kayak is."

She took both paddles and shoved one down into the opening next to her legs. "Forget the other kayak. Hang on and I'll paddle us in before the monster attacks." *Or we get plucked up by some flying monkey.*

"There is no monster and I'm not forgetting it. That's the kayak with the food and the wine."

"How can you think about food at a time like this?"

"You'll thank me later." He swam away from the boat.

"That's assuming you come back," she muttered, keeping her voice low in case either of the creatures might be listening. Her teeth started chattering as she stared out into the darkness and scanned the sky.

Then over the tops of the trees rose the almost-full moon. In the faint silvery glow she could make out the upside-down kayak and Jeremy swimming toward it. She prayed nothing would break the surface of the lake or swoop down from above, either.

At least now she had a paddle and could go to his rescue. Exactly *how* she'd rescue him, she had no idea. With small bears, you were supposed to stand as tall as you could and look menacing. But this wasn't a bear and it wasn't small. She hadn't read the manual on how to intimidate a lake monster or a flying monkey.

Yet if these creatures were predatory, why hadn't they struck again? Could all this be the result of some elaborate hoax? Someone would have to go to a lot of trouble to make such a lifelike creature come out of the water, even if they'd created only the head and neck.

Something that large would require more than one person to manipulate. Maybe two or three people, all wearing scuba gear, could accomplish it. But she couldn't sell herself on the idea. The thing in the air could have been a radio-controlled model plane of some sort. But she wasn't buying that explanation, either.

She'd developed into a decent journalist because she had a sixth sense about fake news versus the real deal. She didn't think what she'd seen was fake. And if the two sightings were real, she might be sitting on the story of the century.

Now, there was a concept. Instead of shivering in the kayak worrying that she and Jeremy would become monster food, she should be figuring out how to confirm the sightings and make herself famous. Hardly anyone at the *Tribune* took her seriously because they thought of her as a talking head from WGN. If she found the equivalent of Nessie plus some prehistoric flying creature right here in Big Knob, her reputation as a reporter would be guaranteed.

On the debit side, if she broke the story before she was sure of what she'd seen and it turned out to be a few teenagers playing a practical joke, her reputation would be in the toilet. Although she didn't really *want* to see either creature again, she'd need to if she planned to stake her career on them.

Wild things usually had a routine to their behavior. She should come back here with a camera, probably about the same time in the evening. If she could be sneaky about it, then that would somewhat rule out the practical jokesters. Several people knew she and Jeremy had planned to come out here tonight, so pranksters could have gotten the word. There were few secrets in a small town.

Yet the idea that someone had gone to that kind of trouble boggled her mind. Why? To what purpose? Okay, teenagers didn't need a purpose other than to create havoc, but still. This would have involved intensive engineering.

Jeremy reached the kayak. He had to be physically drained by all he'd done so far, and the kayak was weighted down with food, wine and blankets. Yet he managed to flip it upright and scramble in. She was impressed.

Glancing over in her direction, he made a megaphone of his hands. "Can you paddle over?"

She could. It was the least she could do after the way she'd treated him like a punching bag when he'd tried to rescue her. Holding the leash of his glasses between her teeth, she began to paddle. The breeze she stirred up made her colder, but the exertion warmed her, so it was a trade-off.

"That's close enough." He reached out a hand. "Give me the other paddle."

She stretched it across the distance between them.

"Thanks. Keep holding on and I'll pull you closer so I can get my glasses." He maneuvered the kayaks until they bumped up against each other with a hollow thunk.

She handed over the glasses, and he put them on. "I can't believe these didn't end up at the bottom of the lake. Dumb luck, I guess. You okay?"

"Sure." Making it through all the drama was sort of exhilarating.

"I was thinking as I recovered this kayak that I owe you the chance to bail on this evening. We can paddle back if you want. I'll even hook a towline on your kayak so you don't need to do any work. This hasn't gone quite the way I'd hoped."

"No, but it certainly hasn't been boring."

He laughed. "No, it hasn't, but I never intended to almost drown you. You have a right to be nervous about how the rest of the night will go."

Truth be told, her nerves were giving way to excitement about the possibility of a scoop. And she was curious about how Jeremy planned to save this date. It would take quite a bit of ingenuity, but she had a feeling Jeremy was an ingenious guy.

She gazed at him across the dark water. "I can't see how it could get any worse."

"That's what I'm counting on. The picnic is viable because the food's zipped into plastic bags. The blankets are also protected, and I always keep my matches in a watertight container. I could build us a fire. We have wine. We can still do this thing."

"It appeals to me in a *Survivor* kind of way." Besides, she wanted to talk to him about the monster and the creature in the sky. She could come here tomorrow night by herself, but she wouldn't mind having backup. Jeremy was the sort of steady, dependable guy a girl could count on in a situation like this. He'd proved that tonight.

"So you're up for it?" He sounded hopeful.

"Sure, why not?"

"Great. Head for the beach. That kayak doesn't handle as well as mine, but you have some experience now."

"Oh, yeah. I'm a freaking expert."

"Annie, you've done a super job. It's not your fault that you dumped. I'll be covering you from behind."

In spite of her newfound courage, a shiver ran through her. "I thought you didn't believe we were in any danger."

"I don't, not really. But if kids are playing a prank, stuff can go wrong. They might not mean to cause harm, but they could miscalculate. That's what I'm watching out for."

He'd be a good person to have on her side, she
thought as she propelled the kayak toward the shoreline. Besides that, he was turning into one hot number,
with his heroics and his manly skills. She wondered
how he planned to get them both dry, and if it involved taking off any clothes.

Dorcas greeted Ambrose with a martini and a smile.
"How was your afternoon?"

Ambrose gave her a kiss and took a sip of his martini. Then he walked into the parlor and set the martini glass on the mantel. "I have to remember that
Jeremy's the guy when it comes to the Internet." He
leaned down to give Sabrina a scratch behind her ears
before peeling off his red bandana and unzipping his
motorcycle jacket.

"Problems?" Dorcas lounged on the purple sofa
and drank from her own martini. She had to admit
Ambrose looked good in the jacket and leather chaps.
The scooter was what sounded the wrong note in the
tune. Now, if Ambrose had a *Harley* . . .

"Tony was running things." Ambrose divested himself of the jacket and chaps and laid them on the red
wing chair. Sabrina wound herself between his legs,
purring loudly. When he picked up his martini and
went to join Dorcas on the sofa, Sabrina followed and
settled herself between them.

"Tony's a good kid," Dorcas said.

"He's a good kid, but he doesn't have Jeremy's ex-
pertise." Ambrose rubbed Sabrina under her chin. "I
screwed up the MySpace page and deleted some
things that Tony couldn't recover. Jeremy could have
done it, I'll bet."

"Yes, but Jeremy needed a break."

"True." Ambrose took another drink of his martini.
"That reminds me. I assume you kept your eye on the
beach this afternoon?" Relaxing into the cushions, he
draped his arm over the back of the sofa.

She had to tell him. She'd known that from the moment the red kayak had gone bottoms up. "Yes, I did. Would you like me to refresh your drink before I tell you all about it?"

Ambrose lowered his glass and looked at her.

"What?" She twirled the stem of her glass between her fingers.

"I have more than half my drink left. If I didn't know better, I'd think you wanted me good and mellow before you hit me with the bad news."

Dorcas waved a dismissive hand. "It was nothing, really. In fact, the whole incident played to our advantage in this matchmaking project, if you ask me."

"Dorcas . . . ?" Ambrose stared at her, eyebrows lifted.

She cleared her throat. "I don't know if you've thought this project through, but even if we help Annie and Jeremy get together, that's no guarantee it'll turn out well."

"We never guarantee that, anyway. We don't interfere with free will."

"I understand that, but Annie has a great job in Chicago and she considers Big Knob boring. Even if she falls in love with Jeremy, I can't picture her being happy here."

Ambrose groaned. "What have you done?"

"Let me get us each another drink." Dorcas grabbed his glass and headed down the hall. Ambrose was going to be furious with her, no matter how she explained things. She couldn't avoid telling him, but she could procrastinate.

Moments later he walked into the kitchen. "I just checked your broom and the bristles are damp."

She poured a generous amount of gin into both martini glasses. "I did some low flying over the lake."

"Because . . . ?"

"After what happened, I couldn't leave them out there to fend for themselves. I had to make sure they were both okay. I'm sure Dee-Dee didn't mean for that to happen, but—"

"*What?*"

She turned to find Ambrose advancing on her, his silver-gray eyes molten with fury.

"Hold on a minute, Ambrose. It's not what you think."

He paused only inches from her, waves of anger rolling off him. "Dee-Dee attacked them, didn't she?"

"No." Dorcas swallowed. "I . . . sort of asked her to . . . make an appearance."

"Dear Zeus! Are you out of your magical mind?"

"Listen to me for a minute. Annie's a reporter. I wanted to give her a reason to stick around beyond this weekend."

"Precisely. She's a reporter. What are you going for, bringing the entire team of *20/20* to Big Knob?"

Dorcas had acted on impulse, and only later had realized the potential risks, but she wouldn't admit that to her husband. "It won't happen that way. Annie's too smart to break the story until she's investigated it thoroughly for herself. I can manage Dee-Dee so that Annie never gets quite enough information to go public."

A muscle twitched in Ambrose's jaw. "Sounds as if you didn't manage her all that well tonight. And you still haven't told me what happened."

So she did, minimizing the danger of Annie becoming trapped under the kayak and maximizing Jeremy's heroic response. "I made sure the kayaks and paddles didn't drift too far away," she added. "And now I know more about Dee-Dee's wave-creating potential. Next time—"

"There will be no next time." Ambrose's expression remained jungle-cat fierce.

Although Dorcas wasn't about to take orders, she didn't relish going head-to-head with her beloved, either. She preferred persuasion. "Think about it. If

Dee-Dee can keep Annie here a little longer, it's worth the risk. Those two deserve to fall in love, and I want to do everything in my power to make it happen."

Some of the fierceness left Ambrose's eyes and he let out a long breath. "I admire your dedication and I understand how much you want soul mates to find each other."

"It's my life's purpose, Ambrose."

"I know, but you're forgetting why we're here. Our first responsibility is to George, not our matchmaking clients."

"Yes, but—"

"If you mess around with Dee-Dee and somehow jeopardize George's presence in the Whispering Forest, I hate to think what would happen, both to George and to us, for causing such a disaster."

Dorcas fell silent. "You have a point." She hated when that happened, but Ambrose was right about George. They couldn't allow anything to happen to him. He was their sworn duty at the moment.

"I'm glad you admit that. And I hope to hell you really can control that lake monster."

"Oh, I can. No worries." Dorcas said it with as much confidence as she could muster. She couldn't have Ambrose doubting her on that score after the way she'd disregarded his warnings about making contact with Dee-Dee.

Dorcas was glad she'd befriended the lake monster and thought ultimately that would be a good move on her part. But she couldn't deny that she'd disturbed the contract Dee-Dee had lived with for years. That kind of rigid contract was bound to unravel eventually, but Dorcas had helped the process along.

Now that Dee-Dee had broken her contract, would she follow Dorcas's directions to the letter? Probably not.

Chapter 7

Jeremy insisted on doing the he-man work of dragging the kayaks up on the sand, but Annie announced that she'd been a Girl Scout for as long as he'd been a Boy Scout. She wanted to help make the fire. Consequently, he left her to dig a pit in the sand while he went in search of wood.

He didn't roam far, though, and kept glancing back to make sure she was okay. Fortunately his glasses had held up through the whole ordeal so he could see just fine. He needed to stay alert, because somebody could be out here bent on mischief, and he didn't want Annie scared any more than she had been.

Come to think of it, he should have expected some sort of prank tonight. The teenagers who hung out at his café treated him like a big brother. He understood those dynamics. As a kid brother himself, he'd done some horrendous things to ruin his older sister's dates.

The seniors were bouncing off the walls, anyway, because of their upcoming graduation. There wasn't a whole lot to do in Big Knob, and that meant they had to manufacture their own fun. Jeremy and Annie had been handy.

Reasoning that out helped, but he was still ready to knock some heads together. Maybe tomorrow he'd talk to a few kids and see if any guilty remarks came tumbling out. They needed to know that what had seemed like a harmless joke could have hurt someone.

When he located a couple of dead branches and dragged them back down to the beach, he found Annie on her hands and knees lining the pit she'd dug with stones.

"Nice job," he said.

"Thanks." She took another stone from the pile she'd made and tucked it into place. "I know how to do this, and I have the badge to prove it."

"I believe you." He started snapping off twigs to use for kindling.

She glanced up. "How about the monster story? Do you believe me in that case, too?"

He spoke with care. "I believe someone wanted you to see a monster."

Putting the last rock in place, she sat back on her heels and ran her fingers through her wet hair. "If that was a trick, then it was the most professionally rigged stunt in the history of Big Knob. Whoever did it needs to work in Hollywood. Seriously."

"Another good reason to find out who did it. We can set him or her on a new career path." He cracked a small branch against his knee and hoped he looked manly doing it.

"Let me help." She stood and came over to pick up one of the dead branches. Then she cracked it over her knee as neatly as he'd just done. "Where are the matches?"

"In the kayak." He needed to remember that she'd been a top athlete in school and could probably best him at most things. If he'd imagined that he'd be in charge of the operation and thereby look like a hero, he'd been dreaming.

"Since you know where the matches are, why don't you let me finish this part?"

He couldn't argue with her reasoning, so he laid

down the branch he'd been working on and walked, shoes squishing in the sand, back to his kayak. Once there, he unloaded everything—matches, food, wine and blankets. Especially the blankets.

She had a fire laid in the pit by the time he came back with his load of stuff. He set it down and tossed her the matches. "I have a couple of blankets," he said.

"Damn, I wish you'd mentioned that before. I'm freezing." She struck a match and touched it to the wood. The kindling didn't catch. She tried another match, and another. "It's not catching. Maybe you should use some magic."

What the hell? If it didn't work, he'd look silly, but they could laugh about it. He pointed toward the fire. "Abracadabra."

To his astonishment, the fire leaped to life.

"All right, Jeremy!" She stood and gave him a high five. "We could have used you at Girl Scout camp. Every time we failed to start the fire with one match, we got a lecture from Mrs. Rhodes."

"We were supposed to start a fire by rubbing two sticks together. I couldn't do that, either."

"But look at you now." Her gaze traveled over him, warm and admiring. "I'm dying to know how you do that."

Me, too. "I'd tell you, but then I'd have to kill you." He was beginning to wonder how many things that *abracadabra* worked for.

"Okay. Secret order of magicians and all that. Well!" She clapped her hands together. "I'm ready for one of those blankets. I see we have a pink flowered one and a blue snowflake one. I assume I get the pink."

He'd thought so, too, when he'd packed them. But now that the blanket might be touching her bare skin, he changed his mind. "Take the blue." He picked it up and handed it to her. "It's softer."

"I'm impressed with a man secure enough to own a pink flowered blanket, let alone wrap himself in it."

Jeremy shrugged. "It's a hand-me-down from my family. My mom knew I needed a spare blanket to carry in the kayak and she wasn't worried about the color."

"Well, neither am I. Thanks for giving me the softest one."

As he considered what he was about to say, his heart beat faster. "Listen, about the blankets, I'm not sure what your plan is, but I think it's counterproductive to wrap them around our wet clothes. In five minutes we'll be just as clammy as we were before."

"I had the same thought, unless you have some magic drying charm."

"I'm afraid not." Even if he did, he wouldn't use it. The other possibility was too tempting.

"Then let's try this." She picked up one stick with a fork on the end and jammed it into the sand close to the fire. Then she found a second one of about the same length and planted it a few feet from the first. Finally she propped a straight stick across the forks. "Clothesline."

"Clever." He gulped. She was way ahead of him.

She turned and walked away from the fire. "Don't look."

"I won't if you won't." He grabbed the pink blanket, walked in the opposite direction and kept his back to her. As he shucked his wet clothes, he could hear her doing the same.

The sound of her undressing should have, by all rights, given him a boner. But he was so cold that everything was shrinking. He hoped she *wasn't* sneaking a peek. She might not understand how cold could affect a guy.

"I won't turn around until you say so," she called out.

"Okay." He moved fast as the cold night air hit his

testicles. Soon he was draped in the blanket. All he wore besides that were his glasses, still attached to their trusty leash.

In theory this concept had sounded sexy—both of them naked and loosely wrapped in soft blankets. That was before he'd decided to give her the blue one, leaving him looking like Chief Pretty-in-Pink.

But at least he was warmer, and maybe, once they were settled beside the fire and his privates had returned to their normal size, he wouldn't feel so ridiculous. "Ready," he said, and turned around.

She stood on the opposite side of the fire, her bare feet scrunched into the sand and the rest of her covered from neck to ankles in the blue blanket he used on his bed all winter. Her hair looked as if she'd been in swimming and hadn't bothered to comb it out. Seeing her like this, mussed and naked except for the blanket, *his* blanket, was more arousing than he ever could have imagined.

She was a present ready to be unwrapped, and he was more than ready to do that. He couldn't assume that she had similar thoughts, but she had come up with the clothesline idea, so they might be on the same page.

No question the plan was logical and practical. But there was serious subtext. He wondered if she realized that or if she thought they would simply dry their clothes by the fire and put them back on with no hanky-panky in between.

She leaned down to pick up two bits of fabric and almost lost her grip on the blanket. "Whoops. You'd better turn around again until I get my clothes draped over the clothesline."

"Sure." He turned, and imagined he looked even sillier from the back. A blanket-wrapped woman was one thing. You pictured her throwing it off with a seductive smile. A blanket-wrapped man . . . not so much.

"There," she said. "Now I'll turn around while you hang up your clothes. I tried to leave you plenty of room."

Picking up the wet, sandy clothes he'd left in a heap, he faced the fire and her makeshift clothesline. Sure enough, her bra and panties were black and lacy. She'd put them very close to the flames.

"I hope your underwear doesn't catch fire."

She laughed. "That would take some explaining back at the Winston house. But it would be a great story for my grandchildren, wouldn't it?"

It would, which generated thoughts he had no business having. Until now, he'd been living for the moment, hoping he could fulfill his fantasy, if only for one night. But Annie was more than a one-night stand to him.

And that was his deep, dark secret—he wanted her on a forever basis. He wanted to be the father of her children, the grandfather of her grandchildren, the great-grandfather of her great-grandchildren, and so on through the ages. Wasn't ever gonna happen, but he wanted it, anyway.

"Jeremy? Are you finished hanging your clothes? I'm ready to cozy up to that fire."

"Yeah, right. Almost done." He started flinging his clothes over the stick and managed to knock it, along with her underwear, into the sand.

That meant picking up everything, including the delicate bits of black lace that had touched the areas he most wanted to touch, too. The cold air no longer had an effect on the family jewels. As he brushed the sand off her bra and panties, his penis rose to the occasion. Maybe he should just hang his briefs on that and be done with it.

Eventually he managed to balance his clothes and hers across the stick without knocking everything over. Then he stood and wrapped himself in the pink blanket. Because one part kept protruding, he decided to sit down and hide that bad boy under the folds of the blanket.

"All set." The wine and plastic bags filled with food and utensils were within reach, so he pulled them over and located the wine opener. Then, in an act of brilliance, he took off his glasses and tucked them in one of the plastic bags.

If he and Annie got cozy, he didn't want to have to deal with taking off the glasses. Yesterday he wouldn't have been thinking that far ahead. Tucking a couple of condoms in the bottom of the open package of napkins wouldn't have occurred to him, either. Today it had.

She settled down beside him, her left knee close to his right, but not quite touching. She brought the scent of the lake and a faint floral fragrance with her. "Now, let's see who gets voted off the island."

Her nearness and her nakedness under the blanket worked on his imagination, but he was determined to play it cool. "I promise you, my kayaking trips are never this scary."

"Then it must be my fault."

"No way." He used the weight of the wine bottle to hold the blanket in place as he worked the cork loose. The naked-in-a-blanket routine was more awkward than he'd anticipated.

"Maybe somebody still holds a grudge about the Miss Dairy Queen contest."

"After ten years? Nah. More likely it's the Click-or-Treat crowd trying to wreck my evening for the hell of it." The cork came out with a loud pop.

"I just can't believe someone could arrange all that on such short notice. It would take days, if not weeks, to build that head and neck. Then there was the thing that flew overhead."

"What thing?" He set a plastic goblet in the sand

and managed to pour wine into it without knocking it over or flashing Annie. "You didn't say anything about a flyover."

"We were kinda busy. And I was afraid you'd think I was crazy. At first I thought it was an owl, but it was too big for that. And it hovered."

"I'd say it was probably a kite." He handed her the wine.

"Thanks." She held her blanket closed with one hand and took the goblet with her other. "No, it wasn't a kite. I thought of that. No wind."

"Then a radio-controlled plane of some sort." He poured himself some wine and placed it carefully beside him. This blanket was a pain.

"I suppose it could have been remote controlled. Again, I don't see how the whole deal was arranged so quickly. We didn't plan our trip until this morning."

"So maybe it wasn't aimed at us." Wedging the cork back in, he rotated the bottle, screwing it into the sand so it wouldn't tip over. "Maybe some kids dreamed up the prank weeks ago and were waiting for their first victims to come along."

"That's possible." She glanced at him. "I want to get to the bottom of this. If it's a trick, then I can write a story about small-town teenagers finding unusual ways to get their kicks. If it's not a trick . . ."

"Don't worry. It's a trick. But at least it didn't completely ruin the evening."

"No, it didn't." She smiled. "I'm having a great time, Jeremy, in spite of everything. Maybe even because of everything. It's not every day a girl gets rescued from sudden death."

He knew she was joking, but the comment made his stomach clench. "I wouldn't have let anything happen to you. And for the record, I always believed you saw something. I'm just not into the monster theory."

She glanced at him. "I wish you'd seen it. That might have changed that logical mind of yours."

"I wish I had, too." If only she knew what was going on in his mind right now. It wasn't logical at all. All he could think about was kissing her.

They were tantalizingly close. He could lean over right now and make contact, but that would be a predictable move. The new Jeremy didn't make predictable moves.

Still, here they were, sitting together in the sand in front of a cozy fire. They were drinking wine and had nothing more than blankets covering them. The time was right for him to do *something*.

Ambrose had promised he could pluck coins from behind people's ears, even if he had no coin on him, just as he'd been able to manufacture a rose from thin air. These things made no sense, yet when Jeremy contemplated doing a magic trick, he had the strangest feeling that he had special powers.

As a kid he'd believed in superheroes, and maybe a part of him still did. What if Ambrose and Dorcas were not what they seemed? What if they were *space aliens*?

Whoa. If he was willing to believe that, he should have no trouble believing in a lake monster. And he did *not* buy that. Still, the magic tricks were very cool, however he was able to do them.

He set down his wine. "Hold still a minute." Brushing back her damp hair, he reached behind her ear. "Abracadabra." Sure enough, a quarter slipped into his fingers. It was warm, as if someone had been holding it.

"Found something," he murmured, and held up the shiny coin.

Her eyes widened. "You're *amazing*."

"So are you." This time he did kiss her, just touching her lips in tribute. Her mouth felt as he'd always imagined it would—like warm velvet. If Ambrose's magic tricks had given Jeremy the chance to kiss Annie for the first time, then Ambrose could be from Krypton for all he cared.

Her lips moved in response, settling more securely against his. And she sighed, her soft breath tickling his mouth. That sigh alone was enough to kick his libido into overdrive. He imagined holding the back of her head and thrusting home with his tongue. God, he wanted to do that.

But instead he controlled the impulse. This was a first kiss, not an all-out assault. His fevered brain had trouble remembering that, but he held on to his sanity with steady determination. He wouldn't overstay his welcome. Better to quit while he was ahead. Gradually he backed away from a mouth so plump and inviting, it could star in every lipstick commercial ever made.

Her eyes fluttered open and her gaze was dreamy. "You're one of the nice guys, Jeremy."

"You know what they say about nice guys."

Her answering smile turned slightly wicked. "I can think of one case in which finishing last would be a bonus."

Okay, now things were getting intense. He was having a tougher time staying James Bond suave. "Interesting thought."

"Interesting activity." Still smiling, she ducked her head and took a drink of her wine.

If she was trying to rattle him, she was succeeding. He fought the urge to throw her down on the sand—not classy. Instead he picked up his wineglass without fumbling. He'd never been that smooth. "I propose a toast."

She glanced up, her blue eyes warm. "Great idea."

"To Melody and Bruce."

She looked surprised, but she touched her goblet to his. "Practicing for the rehearsal dinner?"

"Nope. Thanking them for getting married and bringing you back to town."

"That's a lovely thing to say." Her voice was low and sweet. "Now I'm glad I did, but I was dreading it."

He hadn't expected her to say that. He hadn't meant to change the mood, either, but he just had. "Dreading it? Really?"

"Silly, huh?" She took another swallow of her wine. "This is great wine. Did you get it here?"

She obviously wanted to change the subject, so he went along with her. "In a way. Dorcas and Ambrose gave it to me out of their private stash."

Now that she'd admitted not wanting to come back, he thought about how she'd acted since she'd arrived. Although he'd been dazzled by her, maybe she hadn't been sparkling with the same bright confidence as before, and he'd been too smitten to notice.

If she was less sure of herself these days, he wanted to know who or what had taken the starch out of her. And then he wanted to fix the situation. He had a pretty good idea how to do it, too.

Chapter 8

Whoops. Annie hadn't intended to be so honest. She'd meant to flirt with Jeremy and tease him with possibilities. He looked cute and amazingly sexy wrapped in that blanket, despite the pink flowers. She had arousing visions of what was under that blanket, and she bet he had similar thoughts about her.

Telling him she'd dreaded coming home hadn't been part of her plan. Talk about a buzz kill. Whew.

She'd just have to keep the conversation light from here on. Wine was a neutral subject, so she'd go with that. "What's the wine label say?" she asked.

Setting his goblet in the sand, he turned the bottle so she could see the label. "Mystic Hills Winery. It's bottled in Sedona, which is where they used to live. It's even possible they owned the winery."

"I definitely need to interview them before I leave. There are more stories here than I thought. I suppose you know about Abe Danbury and his petition to ban canned laughter from all sitcoms." Good. She'd made it back to safe territory.

Jeremy seemed willing to follow her lead. "Everybody in town knows. Abe's obsessed with the subject. People avoid him like the plague." He took a drink of his wine. "If Abe keeps pushing that petition, he's liable to lose his bid to get reelected in the fall."

She laughed. "Politics are fun in a small town. I'd forgotten that."

"Don't let Abe hear you say so. He takes his job as mayor very seriously."

"That's part of what makes it fun. People are earnest instead of cynical." She was surprised to discover she'd finished off her wine.

"More?" He set down his goblet and picked up the bottle.

"Why not?" She held out her goblet for a refill. The evening was getting back on track, and she was feeling more mellow by the minute.

"I'm glad you like it." Jeremy poured her wine and topped off his own.

"I noticed Abe's wife, Madeline, is still waitressing over at the Hob Knob," Annie said.

"Yeah. I think she'll be there forever."

"And she's still pushing sugar." Annie shook her head. "She was determined to supply Melody and me with enough cinnamon rolls to feed an army. I had to get out of there fast." She glanced at her wineglass. "I shouldn't be drinking this, either, but it's so good."

Jeremy looked worried. "You're not diabetic, are you?"

"Oh, no. Just watching my calories." She hadn't meant to say that, either. Damn. Jeremy seemed to bring out all her hidden issues.

"You're kidding, right?"

"No, but that look of disbelief makes my ego do the happy dance. Thanks."

"By what anorexic measuring system are you fat?"

She took another sip of wine. Oh, what the heck. He was making her feel better about something that had bothered her for months, so where was the harm in that? "I'm twenty pounds over what I weighed when I married Zach. Two months ago I was thirty pounds over."

"I don't know where you're putting it. You look great."

What a nice guy. "I shouldn't be telling you any of this. Body issues are not a fit topic for a first date."

"Annie, if that's what an extra twenty pounds does for you, then you should have gained it years ago."

Bless him. He was saying exactly what she needed to hear. "Ah, Jeremy, you can't imagine how soothing that sounds, especially compared to the way Zach—" She stopped abruptly. Someone needed to give her a muzzle. "So how about those Cubbies? Think they're gonna win the pennant this year?"

Jeremy's expression was stormy. "Ask me if I give a damn. Annie, what about Zach?"

"Ancient history."

"One of my favorite subjects."

Well, she'd done it now. She might as well tell him. "He had a thing about women gaining weight after they got married. I didn't dare order dessert in a restaurant or he'd make a big deal out of it. I'm sure that's one of the reasons I ate everything in sight after he left. Hence the weight gain. I'll get it all off eventually."

"*He* left *you*?"

"Uh-huh." She drained her wine. "Not too many people know that, so I'd appreciate it if you'd keep it to yourself."

"I can't believe a guy would be stupid enough to give you up."

"I can't believe I was stupid enough to try and hang on to such a loser. I booked a skiing trip in a misguided attempt to rekindle our love. Instead I managed to break my ankle. He told me in the emergency room that he was leaving me for another woman, someone cuter and blonder. More adoring, too, I'll bet."

"What a gold-plated asshole."

"Thanks." Her heart warmed. The rest of her was feeling pretty receptive to him, too. She'd needed someone to say that, and so far, no one had. To be fair, she hadn't given anyone the opportunity.

She and Zach had been the golden couple, the envy of all their friends in Chicago. But the pressures at work and worry about her marriage had kept Annie from forging any deep friendships. When the breakup had come, she hadn't trusted any of those casual acquaintances not to gossip about the humiliating details, so she hadn't revealed them.

She'd had no confidants in Big Knob, either. Even her mother, Joy, didn't know the whole story, although she might suspect some of it. But Joy was still on friendly terms with Zach's mom, who was a good customer at Joy's shop. Annie saw no reason to poison that relationship.

So Jeremy was the first person who'd heard the naked truth about the breakup. For six months she'd been too afraid of what people might think or what they might say. But Jeremy made her feel safe. Maybe that was because he'd saved her from drowning not long ago.

She thought it was more than that, though. Jeremy was trustworthy. After dealing with a man who hadn't been, she had become better at figuring out who a girl could count on and who she couldn't. Jeremy had *count on me* written all over him. That made him very appealing.

Besides that, he was a magician. And more than a little good-looking. And brave. And strong. Yep, Jeremy had it going on.

"Zach didn't deserve you, Annie."

She gazed at him silently for a long time. Then she put her wine goblet in the sand. "What about you, Jeremy?" she said softly. "Do you deserve me?"

"I . . ." He swallowed. "I'll take whatever you're willing to give."

She took hold of the edges of the blanket and slid it down over her creamy shoulders. "It just so happens . . . I'm in a giving mood." She let the blanket go.

Jeremy's goblet dropped from his suddenly slack fingers, spilling red wine all over the pink flowered blanket. She didn't think he even noticed. How gratifying.

Usually she thought things through before she acted. But tonight she didn't feel like thinking. Warmed by the fire and Jeremy's adoration, she wanted to reclaim her sexuality.

With any other man, she would have worried about her body. Zach had demanded perfection and had quickly pointed out any developing flaw. The mental assault had been gradual and insidious. Then his warnings that she'd get fat had become a self-fulfilling prophecy.

Intellectually she knew she wasn't horribly overweight. But for someone who had been the hometown beauty queen, these extra pounds were humiliating. Thankfully, Jeremy didn't see it. He only saw the woman he wanted desperately.

For a moment she sat very still, sinking into his hot stare. Beside them the fire crackled and the scent of wood smoke filled the air. From now on she'd always associate that scent with Jeremy, who surprised her more with every minute they were together.

There was something to be said for a man who thought she was a goddess. She'd made the mistake of loving a guy who thought he was a god. She wouldn't be doing that again.

She held out her hand. "So far, you've been the best part of coming home."

His blanket fell to his waist as he reached out and wove his fingers through hers. His grip was surprisingly strong. "That's all I need to hear."

She had a couple of seconds to admire his broad

chest and the jet-black hair sprinkled over it before he wrapped his free arm around her and pulled her closer. Meeting him in the middle, she steadied herself by putting a hand on his bare shoulder. Her fingers encountered hard muscle. Yum. This could turn out way better than she'd expected.

No tentative kiss this time. He laid claim to her mouth with the enthusiasm of a man who knew what he was after. She tasted wine and pent-up frustration. She had the flattering thought that he'd been waiting more than a decade for this moment. What a rush to finally give him what he wanted as she opened to the eager thrust of his tongue.

When he released her hand and cupped her breast, she moaned. She'd missed a lover's touch more than she'd allowed herself to know. And Jeremy, praise heaven, knew how to touch a woman. He stroked and kneaded until she squirmed closer, wanting more contact.

He responded by easing her onto her back. How he managed to get the blanket under her at the same time, she had no idea. But after all, he was a magician.

Then he began kissing his way down her body, making magic happen everywhere his lips touched. She'd never responded like this, but Zach had never treated her this way, either, as if she were the most sensual creature in the universe. She writhed against the blanket, relishing every tactile pleasure—the warmth of the fire, the rub of soft fabric underneath her, the slide of his tongue along her rib cage.

She could guess where this journey would end, and that was more than fine with her. Modesty was highly overrated, especially when a man had the tongue of a magician. He wouldn't need to say any magic words to bring about the result he had in mind. All he had to do was . . . oh, yeah. Just like that.

Her hips lifted of their own accord as he zeroed in. Annie didn't have a lot of experience to guide her, but she had a hunch this was a blue-ribbon effort on Jeremy's part. In any case, she was slowly, gloriously, losing her mind.

One by one her other senses faded. The snap of the fire, the tang of smoke, the rustle of the blanket, even the exotic, liquid sound of Jeremy loving her—everything disappeared except the sensation building between her thighs. She trembled as her climax stalked her like a jungle cat.

Just there, so close, crouching, ready to spring. She groaned, wanting . . . wanting . . . and at last it was upon her, contorting her body and forcing cries of release from her throat. She was helpless before an onslaught so strong she was left gasping for breath.

Jeremy held her thrusting hips and drew out the pleasure until she was so filled with it that she begged him to let her go. He didn't. Instead he kissed the inside of her quivering thighs and told her how beautiful she was.

She felt beautiful, too, for the first time in months, maybe years. To think she'd dreaded her return to Big Knob. Yet Jeremy had been here all along—Jeremy and his talented hands, his supple mouth, his wicked tongue . . . she'd been missing out on nirvana without even knowing it.

Speaking of Jeremy's talents, she'd be willing to bet he had others. As he slid up next to her and feathered a kiss over her mouth, she became aware of a body part she had yet to meet. Considering the bounty she could feel pressing against her thigh, she would be a lucky girl if she could make its acquaintance. Sad to say, she could barely lift her little finger, let alone her hips.

She did, however, have enough energy to offer her gratitude. She gazed up into his face. Although it was in shadow, she could make out the faint gleam of his eyes.

"What a gift," she murmured. "What a heavenly gift. I don't know how to thank you."

There was a smile in his voice. "I do."

She detected a certain amount of strain, too, which was perfectly logical. She might have just experienced the gold standard when it came to orgasms, but Jeremy still lived in frustration land.

"I would love to," she said, "but you've wrecked me. I'm a shell of a human being."

"Give yourself a few minutes." He nuzzled her neck and toyed with her nipples.

She might not need a few minutes, after all. She was already well on the road to recovery. In point of fact, she sailed right past recovery and into arousal. She moved her leg so that her thigh rubbed his erect penis. "I have an idea."

He nibbled on her lower lip. "I like the way you think."

"We can reverse positions and I can return the favor."

"Or you can stay right where you are and produce the same effect." He pushed up on his hands and knees. "Don't go away."

"Are you saying that you have—"

"Yes."

Knowing he'd brought a condom excited her. When he'd said he wanted her, he'd been serious about it. She appreciated a man with drive, a man who knew how to go after what he craved. Fortunately, he craved her.

She laughed softly as she listened to him rummaging around in the plastic bags. "Now I know for sure you were a Boy Scout."

"So you don't think I was being presumptuous?" There was a soft ripping sound as he opened the package.

"Judging from the way things turned out, I'd say

no." The deep ache she felt surprised her. She'd just had an outstanding climax, and yet the snap of latex and the promise of Jeremy moving inside her made her impatient. She shifted her weight on the blanket. "Hurry."

"I'm here." He moved between her thighs. Then he rested his forearms on either side of her head and cupped her face with both hands. "Before this happens, I want you to know something."

Her pulse quickened in anticipation. "That you're generously endowed? I already figured that out. I'm quick that way."

"I'm not talking about body parts." He brushed his thumbs over her cheeks. "Please understand . . . I expect nothing."

She knew what he meant, but she chose to misunderstand. "I hope you expect to come."

"Oh, I will come." The husky note in his words betrayed his excitement. "But other than that, I expect nothing from you."

"Jeremy, I—"

"Nothing but this." He probed gently. "Just this." And he thrust home.

"Mm." She wrapped both arms around him and closed her eyes in ecstasy. "That's a lot."

With a sound that was part gasp, part laughter, he rested his forehead against hers. "I never thought I'd be . . ."

"But you are." She lifted her hips, taking him deeper. Her body hummed as if connected to the ultimate power source. Maybe she was.

"You are . . . perfect." Raising his head to gaze down at her, he drew back and glided in again.

Heaven. "We are perfect," she murmured. She hadn't dreamed sex could feel so good. "I think I've found my G-spot."

He laughed softly and moved against her. "You lost it?"

"Didn't think I had one." She pushed her hips upward, putting more pressure on her newly discovered pleasure point.

He began to stroke her more deliberately. "Apparently you do."

The friction became so delicious she could barely speak. "Oh, Jeremy . . . *Jeremy*!" With a cry she came. The glorious, full-body rush dwarfed anything she'd experienced before as the spasms moved through her in relentless waves. She felt them in her toes, her fingers, the roots of her hair.

While she was still absorbing the aftershocks and gasping for breath, he surged forward with a heavy groan. Locking himself tight against her, he shuddered, and the steady pulse of his orgasm thrummed inside her.

Good, so good. She stroked his sweaty back with trembling hands. To think she'd thought sex was sort of boring, an exercise more filled with work than wonder. But then, she'd never been with Jeremy.

He rested his cheek against her shoulder and struggled for breath. "Annie . . . that was . . . incredible."

"For me, too." And she wanted to add, *Is this it? Was one time all you needed for your fantasy?* But she was afraid to say it out loud, for fear it might be true. She didn't want it to be.

He sighed and nestled closer. But although he lay on top of her, she could tell he wasn't giving her his full weight. He was obviously bracing himself, which couldn't be comfortable if he felt as much like a rag doll as she did. He was a reasonably slender guy, so she figured he wouldn't be too heavy.

She tugged on his back. "Come on. Relax against me. I can take it."

He dropped like a stone.

"Oof! Hey!"

Instantly he pushed himself up again. He grinned down at her. "Couldn't resist."

"Jeremy!" She smacked him lightly on the shoulder and he nipped at her nose. She tickled his ribs and he yelped and withdrew from the battle.

At least she thought he'd withdrawn as he walked off into the shadows.

"Jeremy? You okay?"

"Yep."

Then she figured out he was taking care of the condom, because in seconds he was back, ready for a serious tickle fest. Soon they were shrieking and rolling around like five-year-olds. When they accidentally flipped off the blanket onto the sand, they were forced to stop before they ground sand into places that would be most unpleasant. They were both laughing so hard they had the hiccups.

As she held her breath in an effort to stop her hiccups, she gazed at him in the light from the dying fire. The kayak rescue had been thrilling, the sex had been fabulous, but Jeremy's playful side might be the most irresistible of all.

Uh-oh. Once upon a time she'd found Zach irresistible, too. Everything had seemed rosy in the beginning, but it hadn't turned out that way in the end. Now that she was finally putting her life back together, falling for some guy wouldn't be very smart. She'd already proved her judgment could be easily clouded, her goals set aside.

She swallowed a hiccup and let out a breath. She seemed to be cured. "So," she said. "Where do we go from here?"

In the dim light, his expression was tough to read. "That's up to you."

"I'm only six months into being single again. Tonight's been wonderful, but I'm not in the market for—"

"I know. That's why I said what I did."

Right before you helped me find my G-spot. Remembering how that had felt made her skin flush. "Would you rather quit while we're ahead? Just so things don't get messy?"

"No." His smile was just barely visible in the darkness. "I'd rather have tons of hot monkey sex until you have to leave town."

Chapter 9

Sound carried across the lake, especially at night. Knowing this, Dorcas had left Ambrose practicing some maneuvers with his wizard's staff while she took a stroll down to the water. Sabrina had chosen to stay with Ambrose, which was just as well.

Ever since he'd converted his staff to a collapsible model, he'd had problems with it. Something about screwing and unscrewing the sections disturbed the internal vibrations. With Sabrina there, he'd have backup if one of his spells got out of hand.

The air was chilly and the nearly full moon cast a streak of silver over the calm, dark surface. But events were far from calm on the far side. If Dorcas understood the sounds of feminine sexual satisfaction, and she most certainly did, then Annie was having a *very* good time.

Dorcas was glad Jeremy had decided to take the wine along. The additive Dorcas had perfected worked only with couples who were soul mates. Anyone else drinking it and having sex would experience a normal, ho-hum encounter. But if two people who were meant for each other imbibed the wine, they'd have mind-blowing, world-changing sex, the kind that gave Dorcas shivers.

Judging from what Dorcas had heard, the wine had worked to perfection. Maybe it was time to open a bottle of it tonight and share it with Ambrose. Eventually Jeremy and Annie would leave the lake, and then Dorcas could lure her lover outside for some waxing-moon sex. She thought the waxing moon produced the best orgasms, and Ambrose seemed to agree. They deserved some fun after their labors with George.

As Dorcas listened to Annie and Jeremy, she slipped off her shoes and walked through the sand to the edge of the lake. The water was so still that it barely lapped at the sand. The dark lake sounded like a cat grooming herself.

Cold as the water was, Dorcas felt drawn to it. One thing Sedona lacked was water. She stepped slowly forward until it kissed her toes. Although she winced at the freezing temperature, she stood her ground until her feet gradually became used to it.

She thought about Dee-Dee, who was probably hiding in her cave and brooding about the events of the night. The lake monster could breathe underwater for short periods, but she also needed air. Dee-Dee had described her cave as beautiful but lonely, a place hidden far under the hills beyond the lake, accessible only through the lake itself. Dorcas had taken pity on her and given her some back issues of *Wizardry World* in a Ziploc bag so the lake monster would have something to read.

"Hey, Dorcas. What's happening?"

Dorcas jumped and turned around. A woman walked toward her with long, purposeful strides. She was tall, with red hair cut very short. Beaded earrings hung almost to her shoulders. She wore thigh-high boots, a short leather skirt that displayed her belly button, and a fringed top that barely covered her breasts.

Strangers didn't just suddenly appear in Big Knob. Dorcas and Ambrose had decided that in order to do their best with George, they needed to keep unauthorized people out of the Whispering Forest. They'd achieved that by bespelling the exit sign on Highway 64.

Dorcas had put Ambrose in charge of that. If anyone in town expected a visitor, the whole town knew it and Ambrose turned on the exit sign. The rest of the time it stayed off. He'd turned it on for Annie and must have forgotten to turn it off again, because this woman was not a Big Knobian.

Or she's a witch.

As she drew closer, Dorcas noticed the silver pentagram nestled in the woman's considerable cleavage. Her face looked familiar, too. Dorcas knew her from somewhere, maybe Sedona. What was her name? The face was so familiar . . .

The woman held out a hand generously decorated with rings. "Isadora Mather."

"Isadora?" So this was the woman captured in bronze on the town square, the widow of the town's founder.

No one in Big Knob had a clue that their beloved Isadora had been, and still was, a witch. But the magical community knew that Isadora had used her magical skills to stem a potentially catastrophic smallpox epidemic here. That was in the mid-1800s, and Dorcas didn't think Isadora had been back since. She wondered what Isadora was doing here now.

She shook Isadora's hand, but she couldn't help staring. "Did you drive or fly?"

"Flew."

All righty, then. Dorcas didn't have to blame Ambrose for goofing up his exit sign duties. A witch on a broom wouldn't care about highway markers. "Aren't you supposed to be wearing a calico skirt and a sunbonnet?"

Isadora smiled, her teeth perfect and white. "I got rid of that fashion disaster the second Ebenezer croaked. Burned it with the rest of the house. Everyone in Big Knob thought Ebenezer and I died in the blaze, but the poor old guy had already gone to his reward by the time I lit that fire. I made sure it was hot enough to leave nothing but ashes."

"Clever."

"Believe me, I had plenty of long, boring evenings to come up with my plan." Isadora tossed her head, and her earrings glittered in the moonlight. "I took off for the gold fields and never looked back. San Francisco rocked then and it still does."

"So why show up now?" Dorcas was still trying to superimpose the image of the bronze statue on the town square onto this floozy straight out of a singles bar.

"I heard there was a little problem with Dee-Dee. Have you seen her tonight?" Isadora peered out over the lake. "I have a soft spot in my heart for that girl."

"So you had a previous relationship with her?"

Isadora nodded. "I guess Cecil didn't tell you. She appeared on my watch. Like it or not, I feel a certain amount of responsibility for her. I thought we could have some face time tonight so I could find out what's up."

Dorcas thought it was interesting that Cecil hadn't mentioned that Isadora was tied in with Dee-Dee. Knowing Cecil's conservative mind-set, he probably hadn't wanted to take the chance that Dorcas would summon this obviously flamboyant witch to Big Knob.

"So is Dee-Dee around?" Isadora asked.

"I'm afraid she's hiding in her cave at the moment. Tonight she—um—accidentally flipped a kayak."

"Yikes. What was she doing out with kayakers on the lake?"

Dorcas wasn't ready to admit that she'd kind of invited Dee-Dee to do what she'd done. "Well, she's lonely."

"So I heard."

"So lonely she's ready to chew the stalactites off the roof of her cave. If you ask me, she's also sexually frustrated, although she's too shy to admit something so personal."

Isadora fiddled with one of her earrings. "I can see how she would be. She's been there—what? Almost two hundred years? That's a long time with no nakey-nooky."

"Did you have a contingency plan for that?"

"Well, no." Isadora gazed out over the lake. "To be honest, I had my hands full when she showed up, a runaway teen lake monster. Giving her sanctuary in Deep Lake was dicey, but I decided to risk it because there was no way she was going back to her controlling parents."

Dorcas tried to keep her temper in check. "But didn't you know that she'd grow too big to leave and be trapped there? Is that any better than having a curfew?"

"Look, don't start. I did what I thought was best. That was also about the time the Wizard Council was saying they would transfer George to the Whispering Forest in some wizard version of tough love, and then there was the smallpox epidemic, which was not a lot of yucks, either. I was never cut out to be Florence freaking Nightingale."

"They did send George to the Whispering Forest, and he's—"

"Don't tell me. A pain in the ass. His parents let him get away with murder. What're you gonna do with a kid like that?"

Dorcas sighed. "Goddess knows, but Ambrose and I are going to figure it out. In the meantime, though, we could sure use some help with Dee-Dee. And since you're the one who set her up in Deep Lake—"

"With a contract, I might add."

"So you drew up that contract?"

"Yes, and if she's violating it, that's not my fault. I came here to help, but I'm not taking the rap for this, so don't think I am."

"But you came." Dorcas held on to that fact. "And I'm glad you're willing to help."

"Well, yeah." Isadora blew out a breath. "Like I said, she's a sweetie. I also thought I'd take a peek at that bronze statue they erected in my honor. What a shock that was. Did you ever see anything so hideous in your life?"

"I guess it's not exactly Venus de Milo."

Isadora grimaced. "That outfit makes me look fat. Early this morning I tried a few flame spells to see if I could melt the blasted thing, but all I managed to do was make it glow. I'll have to work on that."

"Oh, Isadora, don't melt it. The town put a lot of money into that project. They love the statue. It gives them a sense of history."

"If only they knew the true history. The only fun I had was putting a bug in Ebenezer's ear to lay out the town in the shape of a pentagram. Old coot thought it was a star. He didn't even get it when I created the walking trail connecting the points of the star. And here he was, a descendant of Cotton Mather of Salem fame. Don't you love the irony?"

Dorcas was quickly concluding that Isadora was a troublemaker who might not be much help after all. But Isadora cared about Dee-Dee and might have some ideas and/or some special powers that would help them solve that problem. Dorcas shouldn't look a gift witch in the mouth.

She also needed to remember her manners. "Do you have a place to stay while you're here?" Dorcas wasn't crazy about the thought of having a guest again so soon after bidding good-bye to the Grand High Wizard, but with Dee-Dee's future on the line, she had to make the offer.

"Thanks, but I found a room. I met Abe Danbury on the street peddling his petition against canned laughter. I happen to hate that stuff myself, so I told him I'd pass it around. One thing led to another, and he offered me their spare room. He's the mayor, right?"

"Yes, and if you want to keep him happy, you won't melt your commemorative statue."

Isadora pursed her lips. "We'll see. No promises. Oh, and FYI, I'm traveling under an alias so nobody makes the connection. I'm Isabel Moore for the duration. Well, if Dee-Dee's not coming out again tonight, I might as well go. There's a mudslide at the Big Knobian Bar calling my name."

"You'll think about the Dee-Dee situation, though?"

"Absolutely. I do my best thinking with a mudslide in my hand. See you." Turning, she tromped back up the dirt path toward the main road.

Dorcas hoped Isadora hadn't parked her broom at the end of the road. She might think nothing of zooming around on it, hoping to give the locals a scare. She was definitely a loose cannon, but if she could help with Dee-Dee, then Dorcas would put up with her and do damage control as necessary.

Jeremy didn't expect to see Annie again until the next afternoon when she came in to write her story about Abe and his petition. Because he felt the need for some advice, he left Tony in charge of the café during Tony's school lunch break and met Sean at the Hob Knob.

Madeline Danbury came around the counter with a couple of menus. "Sean called and said he'd be a little late. He told me to find you two a table in the corner."

"Thanks." He followed her over to a small table against the back wall. Waitresses had come and gone at the Hob Knob, but Madeline had become a fixture there. She brought in plenty of business, possibly because her permed white hair and rosy cheeks made people think they were eating at Grandma's house.

"How've you been, Madeline?" Jeremy pulled out a wooden chair and took a menu. He didn't need a menu, but Madeline believed in doing things by the book, so everyone got a menu.

"I was doing just fine until last night, when I found out Abe had offered our spare room to a loose woman." Her lips were set in a straight line of disapproval.

Jeremy had a moment of panic. What if someone had started a rumor about Annie being naked with him on the beach? What if she'd had a fight with her mother and sister over it and had to take refuge at Madeline and Abe's house? Surely she would have called him first.

"What sort of loose woman?" he asked cautiously. He hoped it wasn't Annie. Madeline was known for her conservative views on sex before marriage. She didn't believe in it.

"Someone named Isabel Moore," Madeline said.

Jeremy relaxed. "Never heard of her."

"Neither has anybody else. She waltzed into town in a skirt that barely covers the subject, long, drippy earrings, and boots like they wear on MTV. Abe says she's from San Francisco, which should tell you something."

Jeremy was intrigued by both the thought of a newcomer and the image of Madeline watching MTV. "Why's she here?"

"I don't know, but I mean to find out, seeing as how she's staying under my roof. She weaseled her way in by pretending to support Abe's petition. That tipped me off that she's up to no good. Nobody supports Abe's petition except me, and I have to, being his wife and all."

"Well, keep an eye on her for us, Madeline."

"Don't worry, I will. You want some coffee while you're waiting?"

"That would be great." Jeremy was always happy to drink a cup of coffee he didn't have to brew. He wondered what would happen if he pointed his finger at the espresso machine at the café and said *abracadabra*. Maybe when no one was around he'd try it.

Sean arrived just as Madeline was leaving to get the coffee. "Coffee, Sean?" she asked.

"You bet." Sean pulled out a chair and sat down. His dark hair was mussed and he looked very happy. He waited until Madeline had left before leaning toward Jeremy. "Sorry I'm late. Maggie had a mid-morning break and . . ." He grinned sheepishly.

"Say no more." In the past, Jeremy had never quite understood how Sean was willing to drop everything for a chance to be alone with Maggie, but he understood it now. If Annie crooked her little finger, he'd close the café in a heartbeat.

"I'm crazy about that woman."

"You might have mentioned that a few thousand times. But crazy looks good on you." When Sean and Maggie were dating last fall, Sean hadn't looked like his usual studly self. Everyone had been confused as to why Sean, the town Romeo, had suddenly become so awkward. Jeremy had put it down to raging hormones.

Considering how Annie was affecting him, he wouldn't be surprised if people could see a difference. He certainly felt like a new man, although in his case, hormones were having the opposite effect they'd had on Sean, making him more confident instead of less.

Sean picked up a menu and put it back down. "They should do away with these things. Everyone has it memorized."

"Madeline likes them." Jeremy thought about how to broach the subject of Annie.

"I get such a kick out of Madeline. Menus have to be passed out at a proper restaurant, even though no-body opens them. She's a color-inside-the-lines kind of woman." Sean nudged the menu aside. "So how's business at the café?"

"Fine." Maybe first he'd talk about the wine. "Dorcas and Ambrose gave me a bottle of that red wine you raved about."

"Cool. You try it?"

"Um, yeah. Annie and I had some last night."

Sean gazed across the table, his green eyes filled with speculation. "What'd you think of it?"

Jeremy lowered his voice. "Listen, do you think that wine makes everything . . . better?"

Sean looked as if he wanted to laugh, but he didn't. "I'm guessing that your use of the word *everything* means you and Annie—"

"We did."

"Congratulations, buddy. I can imagine what that means to you."

"But how about the wine?" Jeremy lowered his voice another notch. "Do you think there's some kind of aphrodisiac in it?"

"I don't know." Sean leaned toward him and kept his own voice low. "Maybe. I tried to buy some from them and they wouldn't sell it. Can't find it on the Internet, either. They're giving us another bottle on our anniversary, so I have a hunch there's something in there that makes good sex even better."

"Now I'm scared that the next time won't be as good. We drank it all."

"You could ask them for another bottle."

Jeremy shook his head. "I'm not one of their clients. That's not what this is all about."

"Oh? Then what is it all about?"

Madeline arrived with their coffee. "I assume you're both having the usual."

"I am," Sean said.

"Yeah, I guess," Jeremy said.

Madeline nodded. "I don't know why I bother to ask. I should automatically bring you both turkey sandwiches. I'll be right back."

"Wait a minute." Jeremy caught her arm. "Changed my mind. I'll have the French dip."

Madeline stared at him as if he'd sprouted tentacles. "French dip? You never have French dip."

"Then, it's about time. And I'll have the coleslaw instead of the fries, too."

Madeline frowned. "Something strange is going on with you, Jeremy. First those magic tricks and now the French dip and slaw."

"What magic tricks?" Sean asked.

"I can't believe you didn't hear about it," Madeline said. "There was even a story in the *Tribune*."

"I've been doing some work at the house the past couple of days and didn't come to town." Sean glanced at Jeremy with raised eyebrows. "What've you been up to?"

Jeremy shrugged. "Just fooling around." He happened to know that Sean had stayed home because he was renovating the room that would become a nursery. Maggie wasn't pregnant yet, but they were having fun planning for when it did happen.

"I'll tell you what he's been up to." Madeline pointed to Jeremy. "Showing off with a trick coffeepot on Monday and plucking a rose out of thin air on Tuesday. No telling what he'll come up with today."

"Interesting." Sean folded his arms and looked across the table at Jeremy.

"And don't you be doing any of that magic in here," Madeline said. "We like the place calm and orderly."

"I'll keep that in mind." Jeremy glanced up at Madeline. "Could you lean down here a minute? I think there's something behind your ear."

"And I know exactly what it is. A pencil."

"No, your other ear." Jeremy pushed back his chair and stood. "Abracadabra." He reached behind Madeline's ear and pulled out another warm, shiny quarter. Damned if the trick hadn't worked a second time. "Look what I found."

Madeline backed away from the quarter as if it had

cooties. "I don't trust magicians. Never did. I'll get your order, but you behave yourself, Jeremy Dunstan. I mean it." She bustled off.

Sean had his head down and his shoulders were shaking. When he looked up, his eyes were bright with laughter. "Outstanding. Where did you learn how to do magic?"

Jeremy reclaimed his chair. "Well, I—"

"That quarter trick was smooth, man. Puts my silly little card trick to shame. I'm impressed."

Jeremy thought about admitting that he didn't know how the tricks worked. But Sean had always been the cool guy while Jeremy had been the geeky one. Just this once, Jeremy wanted to be cooler than Sean.

"Ambrose gave me some tips," he said.

Sean nodded. "Makes perfect sense that Ambrose is an amateur magician. What a great way to get girls. Which reminds me, we never finished talking about Annie."

Jeremy ran his finger around the rim of his mug while he thought about what he wanted to ask. "When I first found out she was coming home, I told myself not to get my hopes up."

"Good thing you didn't give that kind of message to other parts of you."

Jeremy rolled his eyes. "Yeah, well. The thing is, I'm feeling more confident now."

"I should hope so. You had a significant encounter with Miss Dairy Queen. There are guys in this town who would kill for that chance."

"I know. Believe me, I'm grateful." Jeremy leaned closer to Sean. "I've tried to tell myself to be satisfied with a few nights of great sex, but instead I'm already trying to figure out how to get her to stay."

Sean finished off his coffee. "Which is where I come in, right?"

"Right. For a while there last fall, it looked like Maggie was going to choose the big city instead of you." Jeremy took a deep breath. "How did you get her to change her mind?"

"I'm not sure I can take any credit for that." Sean stared into his empty cup, as if thinking back to the scary days when he thought he'd lost Maggie forever.

"Maggie seems happy here."

"She is." Sean glanced up. "She's having fun working for Dorcas and Ambrose, plus she's getting a kick out of helping me restore the house."

"Annie really loves her job at the *Trib*. I can't picture her being happy at the *Big Knob Gazette*. If someone jaywalks across Fifth, that's a big news day."

Sean gazed across the table at his friend. "You might have it tougher than I did. Maggie's job in Houston wasn't totally satisfying to her." He hesitated. "Have you given any thought to relocating?"

"Well, that's way premature, but yes. And I would hate living in Chicago. I like small-town living—no traffic, no crime, no crowds."

"I know. I like it, too." Sean stared at him in silence for a few more seconds. "So when are you getting together with her again?"

"I hope tonight."

"After the bachelor party?"

"Oh." Guilt washed over Jeremy. He'd been so obsessed with Annie that he'd forgotten Bruce's bachelor party, the one he'd set up at the Big Knobian, the one he was the host for.

"Besides," Sean said, "won't Annie be at the bachelorette party being hosted at our house tonight?"

"Yeah, she will. And chances are both parties will run late."

"I'm guessing. Maggie told me not to come home until at least one in the morning."

Jeremy couldn't very well be pissed about that. The wedding was Annie's reason for being here. "Maybe I can see her beforehand." Then he remembered that Tony and Kira were driving into Evansville to see a movie and had specifically requested he not assign them hours this afternoon. "Or not."

Jeremy was quickly realizing how little free time was left. Tomorrow night might be it, because Friday was the rehearsal and rehearsal dinner, and Saturday night was the reception. During the day Annie had her stories to research and write, and he had a café to run.

"Whenever you see her again," Sean said, "I have a suggestion."

Jeremy looked at him. "What's that?"

"Don't be proud, buddy. Ask Dorcas and Ambrose to give you another bottle of that wine."

Chapter 10

Click-or-Treat was deserted at one thirty when Annie walked in to write her story about Mayor Abe and his gonzo petition. The petition was weird enough, but now Abe had an assistant, some woman from San Francisco who didn't seem to belong in Big Knob at all, although people commented that she looked vaguely familiar. Annie thought so, too, but Isabel's outrageous personality was the reason for including her in the story.

Once inside the door of the café, she glanced around, expecting to see Jeremy. He wasn't anywhere to be seen. Megabyte sprawled in her usual spot on the floor near the counter, so Jeremy had to be somewhere nearby.

Thinking about Jeremy made Annie nervous. She was more than a little embarrassed to meet him in the light of day after the hot encounter they'd had the night before. She'd never been that uninhibited during sex, not to mention that she'd dropped all her inhibitions on their very first date. She would have preferred to avoid him completely, but the café's high-speed Internet connection made it the only place in town where she could accomplish her assignment.

So here she was, feeling awkward. She'd never had this kind of morning-after, or afternoon-after, confrontation with a man. She'd dated Zach for so long that when they'd finally had sex, it hadn't seemed like a big deal. Come to think of it, sex had been a very little deal with Zach, who had been her one and only sexual partner. She hadn't realized how bad a lover he'd been until last night, when she'd experienced Jeremy's top-notch effort.

But now she wasn't sure how to act around him, especially in public. Thanks to the wedding, she'd have to spend lots of time in public with Jeremy. Her tummy churned at the thought. Getting naked and having sex on the beach had seemed to make sense at the time, especially after the lake-monster incident and sharing that bottle of great wine.

But upon waking up this morning, she'd decided having sex with Jeremy, or at any rate *more* sex with Jeremy, wasn't very bright. Casual sex wasn't something she knew anything about, and Jeremy didn't deserve to be her practice round.

She still intended to find out what the hell she'd seen in the lake last night, but that didn't have to translate into a repeat of their extracurricular activities. Besides, she was in Big Knob to be the matron of honor at her sister's wedding, not have an affair. The week's activities were already frantic enough, and none of it was supposed to be about her.

Before Jeremy had dropped her off at home, he'd mentioned getting together again tonight, and she'd readily agreed as if she had no other responsibilities. This morning Melody had reminded her of the bachelorette party at Maggie Madigan's house outside of town.

Maggie had offered her house because it was such a perfect place for a party, and everyone was pitching in with food, games and decorations. Annie felt honor bound to do her share, which meant she had no extra time today or tonight. She wouldn't be able to follow up on the lake-monster story today, which was a shame. She wouldn't have time to get horizontal with Jeremy, either, which was a good thing.

Her nervousness aside, it probably wasn't right for Jeremy, either. He might say he was fine with a brief fling, but she didn't really believe him. Yes, he was training as a magician and seemed more confident than she remembered, but that didn't mean he could handle casual sex any better than she could.

She took off her trench coat and hung it over the back of a chair facing the terminal where she'd worked the past two days. Then she walked over to Megabyte, crouched down and scratched behind the dog's floppy ears.

Megabyte shifted her weight and leaned into the caress while her tail thumped lazily on the floor.

Annie laughed. "Good thing I'm not about to rob the place."

"She's a washout as a guard dog, but I love her, anyway."

Adrenaline rushed through Annie's system. She stood as Jeremy walked toward her, and all her thoughts about staying away from this man exploded in a blast of fiery lust. Yesterday she would have been hard-pressed to describe Jeremy as sexy. Today, she couldn't imagine why.

She tried telling herself he was only Jeremy, a lanky guy in glasses wearing a black polo with the Click-or-Treat logo, worn jeans and sneakers. She'd known him all her life. *But not as well as I know him now.*

Understanding his ability to bring her to a crashing orgasm gave him a certain je ne sais quoi. The expression in his gray eyes turned her insides to jelly, and his mouth . . . Oh, God, his mouth was so sensuous, more than she'd ever realized.

Or maybe that was due to the fact that she'd felt that mouth all over her, especially in one particularly sensitive spot. During that activity she'd thrust her fingers into his thick, dark hair. She could feel the texture of his hair sifting between her fingers, feel the motion of his tongue as he . . .

"Annie?"

"What?" She cleared her throat and glanced away.

"Are you okay?"

"I—I'm fine." She pretended great interest in her surroundings. "So where is everybody?"

"It's usually slow this time of day. The kids come in during their lunch hour and again after school. Since nobody was around, I went upstairs to throw in a load of laundry."

"Oh." She hadn't stopped to think about him living upstairs, but of course he would. Billie had done the same thing.

Annie wondered about that load of laundry and whether it included the blankets they'd used last night and the clothes he'd stripped off and dried by the fire. No doubt.

She'd never forget the softness of that blanket he'd loaned her and the sensation of wrapping it around her naked body. That blanket had been a type of foreplay.

He continued to gaze at her as if he might be remembering all that, too. "I guess you need to log on."

"Yes." She needed a hell of a lot more than that. She needed him to slip his hard drive into her software.

Until she'd seen him standing there, she'd been able to convince herself that a sexual relationship would only complicate an already dicey week and create future problems for both of them. Now that they were eyeball to eyeball, she didn't give a flip. Complicate away, baby.

Instead of helping her get set up, Jeremy remained where he was. "I forgot about the bachelor and bachelorette parties tonight."

"Me, too." She wished he'd touch her, wished he'd

kiss her until she couldn't see straight, but anyone walking by would be able to glance in the café's large windows and catch all the gossip-worthy action, so that was a bad idea.

Yet maybe he'd thought of it, too. He lifted his hand as if he might reach for her. Instead he massaged the back of his neck. "Do you have any spare time late this afternoon?"

She shook her head. "After I finish my story I have to help decorate Maggie's house." Jeremy would have a bed upstairs. More condoms, too. Then again, she'd have to strip down in broad daylight, something she hadn't done for any man since she'd gained weight.

"Decorating shouldn't take too long," he said.

"Well, there's something else I have to do first, actually. I promised to provide a couple of games. I'll have to make them up, because I doubt any store in town would sell them."

His eyebrows lifted. "What kind of games?"

"The usual." She needed to get her mind off sex and onto her duties as the matron of honor. That would solve a host of problems. "I have to dream up twenty items a bride needs on her wedding night. Teams compete to see who produces the most using the contents of their purse. Then I have to get some butcher paper and create a pin-the-penis-on-the-man game . . ." So much for keeping her mind off sex.

Jeremy cleared his throat. "How long will it take to write your story?" The heat in his eyes said he wasn't thinking about newspaper work.

"About an hour." As she met the fire in his eyes, her heart beat faster. Maybe his upstairs bedroom was dark. At the very least he'd have a shade or curtains he could pull over the window. "But then I have to work on the games and have them over at Maggie's by four."

"What if I helped you with the games?"

That made her smile as she imagined him cutting out paper penises. "That's a generous offer, but I—"

"There's nothing generous about it. I want you to come upstairs with me," he said softly.

The urgency in his voice caused her body to hum in anticipation. *Say no.* But she didn't want to say no. "Jeremy, that's crazy. It's the middle of the day . . . and the café is still open."

"No, it's not." Breaking eye contact, he walked over to the glass door, reversed the sign from OPEN to CLOSED, and clicked the lock.

His simple gesture was enough to soak her panties. She loved it when a man took charge. Until yesterday, she hadn't seen Jeremy as a take-charge kind of guy. What a difference a day made.

Megabyte lifted her head, whined and started to get up.

"No, Meg. Stay."

The dog flopped to the floor again.

"If you close during the day, won't you be questioned about it?" Annie felt an obligation to put up a little more resistance. Going upstairs with Jeremy was an irresponsible thing to do when she had places to go and people to see. And she still wondered if either of them would be fine with ending everything when she left for Chicago.

"I'll tell anyone who asks that I had wedding business to take care of." He took her hand and smiled. "Technically, that's true. I'm bonding with the matron of honor."

"I shouldn't do this." But she allowed him to lead her toward the stairs, anyway. His grip was insistent, his hand warm and his touch electric. Her whole body wanted to party down. "We should be concentrating on the wedding."

Jeremy took off his glasses and hung them on the end of the railing. Then he tugged her up to the landing, where they were hidden from view. "I'd rather concentrate on you." He backed her against the wall and kissed her with a fierceness that would make an alpha male proud.

A girl could do worse. Annie kissed him back with equal ferocity. In no time they were gasping for breath and tearing at each other's clothes, right there in the stairwell.

Jeremy pulled his mouth away from hers as he stripped her sweater over her head. "I've been going insane from wanting you. I think of you every minute." The sweater dropped to the stairs.

"I've been thinking of you, too." She fumbled with his jeans, popped the snap and pulled down the zipper. Specifically, she'd been thinking of what was hiding behind that zipper.

"I've been dreaming of your breasts." After unhooking her bra, he let it fall and claimed her with both hands. She leaned into his caress and he groaned. "Damn, you feel so good."

"You, too." She slid her hand inside his briefs and wrapped her fingers around his penis. So silky smooth, yet so filled with power—the power to make her go off like a bottle rocket.

He closed his eyes with a low moan.

"Do you like that?" She stroked him and felt him tremble.

His reply was husky with need. "Oh, yeah." He sucked in a breath and squeezed her breasts. "Stop."

She did. When a man sounded choked up and ready to come, a wise woman backed off if she wanted more fun and games. Annie definitely wanted more fun and games.

He stood very still for a moment, his breathing rapid, his jaw tight, and his fingers flexing as he cupped her breasts. Slowly his eyes opened, and his gaze smoldered. He looked like a man on the edge. "We'd better get upstairs."

"Okay."

Giving her a quick, hard kiss, he released her breasts and grabbed her hand. "Come on."

They ran up the rest of the stairs like a couple of kids. She barely registered the contents of his living room as they dashed through a doorway on the left. His double-sized sleigh bed looked like a very nice antique, but she wouldn't have minded an inflatable mattress on the floor, so long as they were naked on top of it.

The only negative was the sunshine filling the room. He must have read her mind, because immediately he crossed to the window and pulled a cord. Wooden blinds clattered to the sill, muting the light. Much better.

"I don't want to take a chance anyone can see in," he said. "But we need more light." He walked back to the doorway and hit the switch, which turned on both bedside lamps.

Annie reached over and turned it off again. "I like it better dark."

He turned to her. "But I can't see you as well." Stepping closer, he drew her into his arms. "My eyesight's bad enough in good light, but—"

"Forget the light." She insinuated her hand inside his briefs again. She loved playing with her favorite action toy, but she also wanted to distract him. "It doesn't matter. We don't have much time, anyway."

He grasped her wrist. "If you keep that up, time won't be an issue."

"Short fuse?" She wound both hands around his neck and teased him with kisses.

"Damned short. I should have more control than I had last night. Instead I have less."

"I'll take that as a compliment." She kissed him again, this time using her tongue in ways that made him groan and start working on her slacks.

But when she tried to return the favor by trying to

take off his jeans and briefs, he gasped and backed away. "I'd better do that."

"Good. It'll be faster." And faster was what she wanted. Backing toward the bed, she kicked off her shoes and finished taking off her slacks and panties.

He stood immobile, watching her. "You look . . . incredible."

"Thank you," she said softly. The compliment warmed her, although she had to remember he couldn't see very well. "But one of us isn't undressed yet."

Never taking his attention from her, he stripped down, and it was her turn to stare. Yes, she'd experienced his very fine equipment up close and personal, but his magnificence made an even greater impression as he stood in front of her today. When she'd first glimpsed his considerable endowments, she hadn't known whether he knew how to use them.

Now she knew exactly how well he could manage, and that prior knowledge made her bold. One step back and her legs grazed the wooden rail of the sleigh bed. Lowering herself to the mattress, she lay back and held out her arms.

In the stillness of the room, she could hear him swallow. Her heart thumped wildly in her chest as she anticipated the pleasure they could find with each other. "I want you," she murmured.

"I want you, too. And I want desperately to see you better." Reaching behind him, he turned on the bedside table lamps.

Without stopping to think, Annie grabbed the edge of the comforter and pulled it over herself.

"Hey." He crossed to the bed and sat down beside her. "Are you really that shy?"

She let out a little wail of frustration. "I'm *lumpy*."

"That's sure not what I remember from last night."

"It was dark. Very dark."

He framed her face with both hands and leaned

down to kiss her forehead, her eyes, ...
mouth. And as he kissed her, he began to ...
had so many dreams about you. So many wet ...
if you must know. I finally have you in my bed, b...
not for long. And I'm greedy. Touch, taste and smell
are wonderful, but I want the visual, too."

"That'll ruin your fantasy for sure." But her resistance was melting. Adulation could do that.

"You can't possibly ruin it. I was the class geek. You were Miss Dairy Queen. I never thought I'd have a moment like this, but I do. Let me have it all. Please."

She let him ease the comforter away. Maybe it would be all right.

Jeremy sighed in obvious pleasure, and within seconds she realized it would be more than all right. It would be outstanding. Jeremy began to worship her body in a way that Zach never had.

He stroked her and murmured words of praise, licked her skin and moaned in delight, kissed every inch of her and described how he would make her come, and come again. Then he followed through.

Jeremy loved her with a fervor she'd only read about in books. She'd never been given three orgasms within ten minutes, never felt so much like a goddess that she lost all her inhibitions. With a man like Jeremy at the helm, she'd be willing to have sex under the lights of an operating room. He made her feel perfect.

And when finally he rolled on a condom and pushed deep inside her, her joy was so complete she thought she might levitate. She came again—*again*—and he followed quickly afterward with a hoarse cry of ecstasy. He deserved that ecstasy, she thought as she held him tight. He also deserved a woman who wouldn't bolt once the weekend was over. Too bad that wasn't her.

Chapter 11

Dorcas and Ambrose finished up a late lunch at the Hob Knob and stepped out into the sunshine.

Ambrose put on his leather motorcycle jacket but left it unzipped. "I might have to invest in denim for the summer."

"How about investing in a real motorcycle for the summer?" Dorcas had given this some thought and had decided she would be fine on the back of a Harley. It was tootling around on the back of a red scooter with a top speed of forty-five that set her teeth on edge, especially when Ambrose insisted on dressing like a big bad biker dude.

"I like the scooter," Ambrose said. "It's all we need for getting around Big Knob. A motorcycle would be overkill."

Dorcas rolled her eyes. She'd always assumed that every man secretly lusted after a Harley. She, however, had to marry the one guy in America who thought scooters were perfectly adequate. It was so terribly European of him. In Europe his scooter might have been cool, but in the great U.S. of A., it was not. Riding on the back of it, Dorcas felt like a dweeb.

She'd continue her campaign for a Harley and hope Ambrose would finally give in. If not, she might have to figure out a spell that would make the scooter look like a Harley. It would still only go forty-five miles an hour, but at least it would look stylin' on the streets of Big Knob.

"As long as we're in town," Ambrose said, "I'd like to check for messages on MySpace. It's so nice out, let's leave the scooter where it is and walk over."

"We can do that." Dorcas didn't even bother putting on her jacket, deciding to carry it over her arm instead. She fell into step beside Ambrose. "Maybe we can get an update on how Jeremy and Annie are getting along."

"Whatever you do, don't let on that you heard them last night."

"I wouldn't dream of it." But if Annie happened to be around, Dorcas wasn't above dropping a couple of comments about seeing something unusual in the lake. Good sex might make Annie happy, but it wouldn't guarantee that she'd stick around in the same way a good scoop might.

"I also think we need to invite Isadora to dinner," Ambrose said.

"Isabel," Dorcas said in a low voice. "You can never tell who might be listening."

"Isabel, then. But we need to talk to her and find out if she's thought of a solution to the Dee-Dee problem. I wonder if Isador—uh, I mean, *Isabel* has any pull with the Wizard Council."

"I wouldn't count on it," Dorcas said. "I think she's a renegade."

Ambrose glanced over at the bronze statue on the square. "She doesn't look like it in that pose."

"I keep telling you, she doesn't look anything like that statue, except for her face. She's also a lot taller than that. Think Nicole Kidman with very short hair."

"That's why I want to have her over, so I can evaluate whether she's going to be a help or a hindrance," Ambrose said. "Did you mention anything about George?"

"His name came up, if that's what you mean."

"Did you ask her not to go out there?"

Dorcas had a moment of uneasiness. "No." And now she wished she had. A party girl like Isadora and a screwup like George would be a bad combination. Dorcas could easily see Isadora wanting to sit in on the poker games with the raccoons.

"If you invite her to dinner tonight, we can outline our program with George and ask her not to interfere."

"I can't invite her over tonight," Dorcas said. "There's Melody's bachelorette party. I didn't think they'd want me to come because we're so new in town, but they do and I said I would."

"I completely forgot about that. I'm supposed to drop in at Bruce's bachelor party, too. They've reserved the Big Knobian for it."

"You mean it'll be closed to everyone else?"

Ambrose nodded. "It's just for one night, though."

"Yes, but that leaves Isabel with nowhere to go tonight. I can't picture her staying home watching TV with Abe, and she just arrived, so she wouldn't be invited to the bachelorette party." The more Dorcas thought about that, the more she worried. "No telling what she could get into while everyone else is busy with the two parties."

"You mean she might decide to pay George a visit."

"Right. If I thought she'd spend the night talking to Dee-Dee, I wouldn't be concerned. But I can't see Dee-Dee holding her interest that long."

"George would," Ambrose said.

"Oh, yeah."

"I think you'd better find out if you can bring a guest to the bachelorette party."

Dorcas nodded. "I think so, too, although that does put her geographically closer to George. I'll just have to keep an eye on her." As they reached the intersection of Fifth and Second, she glanced across the street to the building that housed Click-or-Treat and saw a woman out front. She wore a spring suit of pale green and her gray hair was cut in a simple bob.

Dorcas looked over at Ambrose. "Isn't that Lucy Dunstan, Jeremy's mom, standing outside the café?"

"I think so. I don't know her all that well."

Dorcas automatically checked for traffic before crossing the street. It was a habit from when they'd lived in Sedona and there actually *was* traffic. As she and Ambrose drew closer, she could tell that the person with her hands cupped around her face as she peered into the café was Lucy.

Lucy was only about five-two, but she had the commanding presence of someone much taller. Physically Jeremy had taken after his father, principal of Big Knob's K–12 school. At six-three, Franklin P. Dunstan towered over his wife, but Dorcas had never doubted that Lucy held her own in that relationship.

Dorcas wasn't surprised to see Lucy at Click-or-Treat. She was president of the Big Knob Historical Society, which had recently bought the house next to the café and planned to use it as a museum. According to town legend, the house was built on the same site as the homestead owned by Isadora and Ebenezer. Isadora had, of course, burned the original house to the ground, although no one except Dorcas and now Ambrose knew that.

Having the historical society headquartered in that historical location obviously thrilled Lucy. Then there was the added benefit of being close to her son's apartment and place of business. She could pop over and see him whenever she wanted to. Except this afternoon, judging from the way she was banging on the door and peering inside, the program didn't seem to be working for her.

"Hi, Lucy," Dorcas called out. "Anything wrong?"

"I hope not." Lucy rattled the door a few times. "Jeremy never closes the café this time of day. His Suzuki's parked around back, so he hasn't gone far."

"Maybe he's on some kind of errand for the wedding." Dorcas had a hunch something more intimate was going on, especially after glancing up to the second floor and noticing the blinds down, but she wasn't going to suggest that to Lucy.

"That's just it," Lucy said. "Bruce called me because he was trying to reach Jeremy—something about the bachelor party tonight. He's not at the Big Knobian, and Sean has no idea where he might be, either. I've tried a few other places, but I can't find him."

Dorcas's theory gained momentum. If Jeremy was upstairs with Annie, then the last thing he needed was his mother interrupting. "Did you try his cell?"

"Yes, and he's turned it off. That is so not like him." Lucy faced them, her forehead creased with worry. "I just need to know he's okay. I realize he's young and healthy, but that doesn't mean he couldn't have fallen on the stairs and knocked himself out. I can't be sure, but I think I heard someone groaning."

Dorcas bit the inside of her cheek to keep from laughing. The groaning clinched it. Jeremy and Annie were upstairs having an afternoon delight. His mother, who couldn't imagine her son involved in such a thing, thought he might be dying.

Glancing at her husband, Dorcas could tell that he'd come to the same conclusion about the encounter going on upstairs. But of course they'd be able to figure it out. They had prior knowledge of the relationship developing between Jeremy and Annie. Apparently the gossip hadn't reached Lucy yet.

Time to remedy that. Dorcas turned to Ambrose. "Will you excuse us a minute? We have some girl talk to take care of."

"Sure thing." Ambrose wandered down the street and stood in front of the old clapboard house that now belonged to the historical society. He pretended great interest in the plaque next to the front door.

Dorcas gazed at Lucy. "I'm sure your son's fine," she said. Then she proceeded to give Lucy a G-rated version of Jeremy's recent activities.

Jeremy had vaguely heard someone banging on the door downstairs, but a guy in the middle of a much-needed climax could be forgiven for ignoring it. Bracing himself above Annie, he gazed into her flushed face and felt a rush of gratitude. There was another emotion coming in the wake of that gratitude, but he wasn't ready to acknowledge it yet. He might never acknowledge it, because once he did, his life would never be the same.

Annie's chest heaved as she struggled for breath. He was gasping, too, but so happy. So very, very happy. This woman made him feel like a stud, and he would always cherish that.

She sighed, and it was a wonderful sound. "That was fantastic. I can't even tell you how fantastic."

"I'm glad." He could look at her forever. "It was great for me, too."

"I could tell." She smiled. "You groaned really loud." She reached up and brushed the hair back from his forehead. "Someone's banging on the door downstairs."

"I know. I'm trying to ignore it."

She started to laugh, which gave him all sorts of interesting sensations where he was still buried deep within her. He leaned down and nuzzled her ear, nipping at the lobe and the pearl earring decorating it. "What's so funny?"

"You've lived in this town all your life, and you think you can ignore someone pounding at the door of your business. Even I, who have been away for several years, know you can't do that. Is your truck parked in back?"

"Yes." He hadn't thought about his truck. Then again, he hadn't thought about much of anything except shutting down the café and getting Annie upstairs and out of her clothes.

"You'd better check and see who's trying to get in." She wiggled against him and kneaded his butt.

"I like it right here."

"I understand that, but you have responsibilities to your customers." She pinched him gently. "I don't want to be responsible for you going belly-up."

"If I do, can we try it with you on top?"

She was still laughing, but she gave him a harder pinch. "Go. Find out who wants you. Besides me."

He loved hearing her talk like that. She might be stroking his ego. She would probably still leave on Sunday. But for now, at this very minute, she wanted him. That was something.

Reluctantly he eased off the bed, detoured to the bathroom to take care of the condom, and walked back to the window. By lifting one of the wooden slats, he could see down to the street below. There stood his mother. Even worse, she was talking to Dorcas Lowell. He didn't have to think very hard to know what they were discussing.

Just then his mother glanced up at the window and waved. He allowed himself one pithy swear word and let go of the slat.

"Must not be good news," Annie said. "Who's out there?"

"My worst nightmare."

"What do you mean?"

Jeremy searched for the clothes he'd tossed on the floor with such joyful abandon not long ago. "The person who was banging on the door is my mother."

"Oh." Annie swung her feet over the edge of the bed. "Then maybe I'd better stay up here until she leaves. You could make up some story about needing to take a nap, or—"

"Not gonna fly. Dorcas Lowell is down there, too, and they're having a cozy conversation."

"So what?"

Jeremy pulled his shirt over his head and tucked it into his jeans. "The thing I didn't tell you about Dorcas and Ambrose is that they run a sort of matchmaking business in town."

"Matchmaking? That sounds so old-fashioned."

"I know it's weird, and there aren't that many matches to make in a place this size, so they do marriage counseling, too."

"Have they actually made any matches here?"

"Just one that I know of. Sean and Maggie." He glanced at her and his heart nearly stopped at how beautiful she looked sitting there naked on his bed. But she wasn't smiling.

"I'm beginning to put this together. They give you wine and teach you magic, both of which have a positive effect on me. Are they trying to match us up?"

"No!" At least Jeremy didn't think so. He wasn't positive that they weren't working some undercover operation even though he'd told them he didn't want their services. After all, he had taken the wine and a little advice.

"Are you sure?"

Jeremy sighed. This could become such a disaster. "They know I'm interested in you, but I told them I didn't want any matchmaking."

"Just some magic and a bottle of wine."

He didn't like the wary look in her eyes, and didn't think he deserved it, either. "Look, I told you straight out I wanted you. I was willing to take any help I could get along those lines. But that's not the same as matchmaking. Matchmaking is where you try to get two people to the altar, and that's not my goal."

"That's good, because I have zero interest in marrying anyone." She climbed off the bed and located her panties and slacks. "Been there, done that."

He knew she felt that way, yet it still hurt to hear her say so. "I get that you aren't interested in anything serious. We just happen to click sexually."

"Yes, we do." Her voice softened. "And I appreciate that more than you know. I just wonder how we're supposed to play this with your mother."

"It won't be easy. She was very disappointed when Gwen and I broke up. I thought when my sister had a baby that would take some of the pressure off me, but it hasn't. Now that my mom knows what having a grandkid is like, she wants a bunch more."

Annie nodded as she pulled on her slacks. "My mom doesn't complain, but I'm sure it's killing her that Melody's moving all the way to Honolulu. Even if she and Bruce have kids, they won't be close by. So I'm her only hope."

"So once the word's out that we're involved, the campaign will begin." Jeremy didn't hate the idea, but he could tell Annie did. So he said what he had to. "We could say we had a big fight, and then stay away from each other for the rest of the week."

She fastened her slacks and stood there, topless and tempting. "It's a thought, but that could mean bad juju for the wedding. The matron of honor and best man are supposed to be friendly."

Jeremy allowed himself a few seconds to admire her, maybe for the last time. "We've certainly fulfilled that requirement."

"Mm." Her gaze warmed under his hot appraisal.

He groaned softly. "I'd better go get your bra and sweater. The longer we stay up here, the worse the implication." Turning away with reluctance, he hurried through the apartment and down the first flight of stairs.

Her black bra and dark blue sweater lay on the landing in mute testament to the frenzy with which he'd pulled them off. He could have finished the job and made love to her right there on the landing, no problem. Correction, that would have caused a huge problem. He'd always been careful about birth control, but in this case he had to be scrupulous.

Then again, he might not have to worry about the issue ever again with Annie. Now that his mother, and likely half the town, would try to pair him up with Annie, she wouldn't want to have anything more to do with him. Maybe they wouldn't concoct an actual fight, but the effect would be the same—no more sex.

Grabbing the bra and sweater, he jogged back up the stairs and walked into the bedroom to find her peeking through the blinds.

"They're gone," she said.

"You're kidding." He walked over beside her and looked down to the street. No one was standing there. "That's amazing. I would have thought Mom wouldn't be able to resist putting me on the spot."

Annie let the slats fall back into place and turned to him. "Maybe she has something more subtle in mind."

"It's possible." Jeremy picked up his cell phone from the bedside table where he'd laid it before taking off his jeans. Flipping it open, he turned it back on.

Sure enough, there were messages, one from Bruce and two from his mother. He watched Annie hook her bra as he listened. What he wouldn't give to be allowed to watch her dress every day. Boy, was he a dreamer.

The message from Bruce was about whether Jeremy had arranged for any sexy entertainment for the bachelor party. He had. The belly dancer driving over from Evansville was a surprise that only Jeremy knew about.

As Annie pulled the blue sweater over her head, he listened to the first message from his mother, an earlier call asking where he was. The second one had been made two minutes ago. And it contained a bribe.

Jeremy glanced at Annie, who was running her fingers through her tousled hair. "I guess you've mentioned to a few people that you'd like to interview Clem Loudermilk about his bra invention."

"I did. I left a couple of messages on the Loudermilks' answering machine, but they didn't call back, so I talked to some other people to see if anyone could intercede for me. It would be a great interview."

"Looks like you can have that interview. My mother's tentatively set it up for Friday morning, if that works."

"Oh, it works. That would make a great piece for my last story in the series." The wary look was back in Annie's eyes. "What's the catch?"

"She wants us to come to dinner Thursday night. I have the distinct impression if we don't cooperate, the interview might somehow go away."

Chapter 12

"Here you go. Forty penises." Jeremy kept his voice down as he set a ten-by-twelve manila envelope next to the terminal where Annie was working. There were teenagers all around them surfing the Internet.

Annie was typing frantically to make up for lost time, but she couldn't resist taking a minute to tease him. "Couldn't fit them in a five-by-seven?"

"I thought the ladies should get a thrill."

"Or a laugh."

"Don't mock the help."

She grinned and glanced up at him. "I really appreciate this, Jeremy."

"My pleasure." His gaze lingered, and the longer he looked at her, the hotter the fire in those gray eyes. He lowered his voice and braced a hand on the desk so he could lean closer. "Thanks for accepting my mom's dinner invitation. It was blatant manipulation on her part."

"It was, but that's okay. If I were a mom, I'd want to find out the intentions of a woman who tempted my son into closing his business in the middle of the day."

Jeremy looked rueful. "Sometimes small-town living sucks."

"So move." She tossed it out lightly, like a joke, but it wasn't really a joke. She wondered if he'd ever considered it. That could make a huge difference in how their relationship turned out.

He held her gaze, as if he understood exactly what she was asking. "This will probably sound dopey, but living here just feels right to me. When I was at Purdue getting my degree, I couldn't wait to get back to this crazy little town with all its faults. It's my home."

She nodded. "I respect that, Jeremy." She hesitated, then finally decided it needed to be said. "Your folks do understand that I'm going back to Chicago on Sunday, right?"

"I'll make sure they do. And as for that dinner, don't worry about it. I promise they won't get out the shotgun."

Annie laughed. Then she lowered her voice. "And you'll go back out to the lake with me afterward so we can try and catch another glimpse of the monster, right?"

"Sure. There's no monster, but I'll go with you."

"Good. And no wine. I don't want to take a chance on missing it, so no hanky-panky, either."

"If you say so."

"I do." She wasn't planning to make out with him this time. Never mind that at this very moment his body heat and the scent of his aftershave made her squirm in her chair.

Tomorrow night she'd be strong. She had a potential story that could make her career and she couldn't take a chance she'd be canoodling with Jeremy when the lake monster appeared.

Of course, the whole town would think she'd gone to the lake with Jeremy so they could make out. That wasn't a bad cover for her investigation, come to think of it.

"By the way," Jeremy said, "I've sent one of the kids over to the deli for six feet of butcher paper. And no, he doesn't know what the project is I'm working on. But even if he did, he wouldn't be shocked. Kids know a lot more than we did at that age."

"I'm sure."

He straightened. "I'll bring you coffee and a cookie."

"*Yes* on the coffee. *No* on the cookie."

Jeremy frowned. "Annie, you are not f—"

"I'm not skinny, either. I would love for my dress to hang on me by Saturday."

With a little growl of frustration, Jeremy left to get her coffee. She couldn't expect him to understand. For whatever reason, he found her sexy the way she was.

That was gratifying for the time being, but she wanted to get back to her fighting weight, needed to be able to look at herself in the mirror without wincing. Back in Chicago she had an entire wardrobe that taunted her with her former measurements. She would wear those clothes again or know the reason why.

Five hours later Annie was blindfolded, dizzy and holding a nine-inch penis.

"To the left!" Gwen shouted.

"More to the left!" called Heather Tufts, a well-endowed former classmate who clerked at the Big Knob Hardware store now.

"Go straight ahead," said Maggie. She'd taken charge of the pin-the-penis-on-the-man game.

Definitely feeling her two cups of vodka punch, Annie lunged forward and stuck the taped end of the penis somewhere on the butcher paper. As everyone whistled and clapped, she lifted the blindfold and discovered she'd been dead on.

"When you're getting it regular, you know exactly where it goes," said Isabel Moore, the newcomer from San Francisco. Dorcas Lowell had brought Isabel to the party and seemed to be keeping an eye on her.

From the moment Annie had met Isabel at Mayor Abe's house, she'd felt as if she should know her.

Something about Isabel tickled Annie's memory, but she couldn't come up with what it was.

Melody held up her paper penis. She'd had at least three cups of punch and Melody never could hold her liquor. "I want to know, since Annie made these, if it's a representation of just what she's been getting. If so, I'm trading Bruce for Jeremy."

"How can it be a representation?" Annie said. "It may be long, but boy, is it flat." She'd given up protesting that nothing was going on between her and Jeremy. Everyone at the party seemed to know they'd been together at the lake last night and alone in his apartment this afternoon.

"That's right," Isabel said with a flip of her long beaded earrings. "Length isn't everything. Girth is important, too. Still, I find it interesting that Annie's brought us a stack of nine-inchers. If you get tired of Jeremy, honey-bunch, let ol' Isabel know, 'kay?"

"Jeremy's not—" Annie caught herself before she blurted out that Jeremy's penis was not nine inches long. Eight, tops. Better not say that, either. Better lay off the punch, or no telling what might come tumbling out.

"Not your boyfriend?" Isabel flashed her perfect teeth. "Then the field's wide open, isn't it?"

"Oh, who cares?" Melody made a face. "This is my party, not Annie's. So who's next?"

For once Annie was grateful for Melody's jealousy. "How about Dorcas?" She handed the blindfold to the woman Jeremy had said was a matchmaker. Dorcas didn't fit Annie's concept of a matchmaker, someone plump and gray haired with a sweet smile. Instead, Dorcas looked as if she could be running a Fortune 500 company.

Annie vowed to interview her before the week was over, because she sensed a story was connected to Dorcas and Ambrose. In the meantime, she wanted to find out what was going on with Isabel Moore.

She wanted to place her, but that wasn't the only issue. The bottom line was that she didn't like thinking of Isabel, with her short skirts, big tits and flashy style, getting her manicured fingers on Jeremy. Once Annie left, he might be a guy on the rebound. He could be vulnerable to the wiles of a woman like Isabel.

Grabbing another cup of punch, Annie walked over to where Isabel leaned against the mahogany railing of the stairway leading to the second floor. Before the party Maggie had given Annie a tour of the place, and the old Victorian was turning into a beauty thanks to Sean's carpentry skills. The staircase had been refinished and recently polished with lemon oil, judging from the way it gleamed.

But Annie wasn't concerned about architectural details at the moment. She wanted to find out whether she had to worry about Isabel Moore moving in on Jeremy come Monday morning. She put on her reporter's hat. "So how do you like San Francisco?"

"Love it. Great city." Isabel had to be at least five-ten, and the stiletto heels on her boots brought her to well over six feet.

Annie was determined not to be intimidated, even if she had to look up. "I hope to see it someday. Have you ever been to Chicago?"

"Not recently. Why?"

"I have the feeling we've met somewhere before."

"Afraid not."

"Hm." Annie sipped her punch. "I assume you flew here."

"You assume right." Isabel looked amused, as if she found a discussion of transportation silly.

Annie managed a smile. The punch helped with that. "So what brought you from a bustling city like San Francisco to a quiet little town like Big Knob?"

Isabel glanced away, but not before her green eyes revealed that she was hiding something from Annie. "I have a thing about phallic symbols." She took a sip of her punch. "This is terrible stuff. Wish I had a mudslide instead. It would make this party a lot more exciting."

Annie could believe that Isabel loved phallic symbols, mudslides, and wild parties, but that wasn't the whole story. There was more to Isabel than she was revealing. Maybe if they went somewhere more private, Annie could find out what it was.

"Have you seen Big Knob in the moonlight?" she asked. "The moon will be full tomorrow night, but it's almost there now. You get a great view from the back porch."

"So let's go, girlfriend." Isabel gulped the rest of her punch and set the cup on a table as she headed for the hall leading to the kitchen.

Annie located Maggie in the midst of the game in progress. "Isabel and I are going out to look at the moon," she called out. "We'll be right back."

"Don't be long," Maggie said. "We're playing truth or dare next."

"Hold me back," Isabel muttered.

Annie's curiosity grew as she followed Isabel out the kitchen door to the back porch. If she was so bored, why hadn't she taken a picture of Big Knob and left town? And why did she look so familiar?

Isabel crossed the back porch and walked down the steps to stand in the yard. Maggie had dug out the weeds that used to choke it and planted a few rosebushes and irises. The loamy scent of fresh potting soil mingled with the aroma of buds beginning to open.

As Annie had promised, the view of Big Knob was spectacular from here. It seemed close enough to touch, thrusting into the dark sky like a giant fertility symbol. A mist rose from the woods surrounding the granite spire, and the mist combined with the moonlight to soften its jagged contours.

"I could have an orgasm just looking at that thing," Isabel said.

Annie had to admit the rock had that sort of effect, especially on women. She couldn't help thinking of Jeremy standing in front of her this afternoon, his penis so proud and erect.

"So is Jeremy really hung like a horse?"

"Yes," Annie said dreamily. Then she snapped out of her punch-induced daze. "Did I say that out loud?"

"You sure did, honey-bunch."

"Isabel, I need to talk to you about Jeremy. You see, he's had a crush on me for years, and I—"

"You finally decided to give the poor boy a shot. Good move, Annie. There's nothing like years of frustration to make a guy try harder." She laughed. "Or *be* harder, for that matter. I'm sure he really concentrated on providing the big O."

Guilt washed over her as she thought about the truth of that. Jeremy must have been knocking himself out, and yet she kept reminding him the relationship was temporary. What a self-absorbed maneuver. She couldn't have sex with him anymore. It would only make things worse when she left.

That brought her back to the subject of Isabel. "I'll be going back to Chicago on Sunday. My life is there, not here."

"And your point is?"

"It's possible that when I leave on Sunday, Jeremy will be a little . . . upset."

"So it's casual for you and not for him."

"That's one way of putting it." She wasn't crazy about that assessment, but she didn't have a better way of describing the dynamics.

"And you want me to console him! I can do that. It'll be a sacrifice, but what are friends for?"

Gag me. Annie wondered if she was wasting her breath on Isabel, but maybe the woman had a conscience hidden somewhere under her wild-child exterior. "I'm asking you not to take advantage of the situation. I doubt you'll be relocating to Big Knob, and I can't bear to think of him being abandoned twice in a matter of weeks."

"So it's okay for you to take advantage of him, but not me? Sounds like a double standard, chicky-babe."

The truth hurt, and Annie reacted by mounting a counterattack. "You haven't known him all your life. I have."

"Oh, I see the distinction now. You're allowed to break a guy's heart if you've known him a long time, but he's off-limits if you just met him. Are those the rules in Big Knob?"

A headache started building at the base of Annie's skull. It could be a side effect of the punch, but it was probably because she was clenching her teeth so hard she was about to give herself a sore jaw. Isabel was right, damn it.

She let out a breath and rolled her shoulders. "You've made your point. I shouldn't have slept with him. I won't anymore. I'm asking you not to compound my mistake."

Isabel gazed up at Big Knob. "I'll think about it."

Annie stared at her profile. Damn, where had she seen that profile before? "Do you have relatives here?"

"Why?" Isabel turned her head.

"There's something so familiar about you."

Isabel seemed startled, but she recovered quickly. "I have one of those faces, I guess."

Annie couldn't shake the feeling that Isabel was somehow connected to the town. She tried to remember if one of the girls she'd gone to school with had run away from home. She couldn't think of anyone, but she'd ask Gwen. Gwen had a better memory for things like that.

A cool breeze whipped up, making Annie shiver. "We should probably get back to the party."

"You go ahead." Isabel turned back to the view of Big Knob. "I'm getting my phallic symbol fix."

"All right. See you in there." Annie started to climb the back porch steps.

"Oh, and by the way."

Annie turned back. "What?"

"Jeremy's a big boy, and I'm not just referring to his package. I think he can handle a little disappointment regarding his love life."

"Of course he can. I just—"

"You just know that you're setting him up for a gigantic disappointment, don't you? I could provide him a soft place to land, with only a little disappointment when I left. Think about that. Maybe you should be thanking me for cushioning the blow instead of warning me off."

Because she had no printable answer for that, she went inside. No matter how much she wanted to paint Isabel as the villain of the piece, the label wouldn't stick. Everything Isabel had said was right.

Annie, not Isabel, was the heartless bitch out to have a good time at Jeremy's expense. If he required some consolation after she left town, she shouldn't begrudge Isabel or Jeremy the experience. If she saw red at the thought of Jeremy and Isabel naked together, that was her problem, not theirs. She'd been back in town less than three days, and she'd already created a hideous mess.

Dorcas had been blindfolded when Annie left with Isadora, but once her turn was over she kept glancing at the hallway and waiting for them to come back. She couldn't stop Isadora from interacting with the citizens of Big Knob, but she'd like to keep those interactions to a minimum if possible. Isadora's reckless streak could blow their cover, and Dorcas didn't fancy a twenty-first-century witch hunt.

When Annie walked into the room alone, Dorcas hoped that meant Isadora had stopped at the bathroom on the way back down the hall. Several minutes later, Isadora hadn't returned. The Whispering Forest bordered Sean and Maggie's property, which meant Isadora had easy access to George if she took it into her head to pay him a visit. Dorcas had no choice but to quietly question Annie.

She had to wait until after Annie received her prize for winning the pin-the-penis-on-the-man game. The prize was a package of Day-Glo green condoms, extra large. Annie laughed and excused herself to go tuck the box in her purse. As she started down the hall, Dorcas pretended great interest.

"Those are a riot." She followed Annie down the hallway. "Can I see them before you put them away?"

"Sure." Annie paused and gave the box to Dorcas. Then she glanced back down the hall as if checking to see if the coast was clear. "Listen, as long as no one's around, I need to ask you something."

Dorcas handed back the condom box. "What's that?"

"Jeremy told me you and Ambrose are match-makers."

"That's one of our job descriptions. Our company is called Hot Prospects for that reason, but we offer marriage counseling, too."

"Just so there's no misunderstanding—I'm not in the market for another husband."

Dorcas had been expecting that sort of disclaimer, especially after the incident this afternoon in front of Click-or-Treat. Annie was probably feeling pressured. That wasn't a good thing.

"I understand completely," Dorcas said. "And for the record, Jeremy specifically told us he didn't want our services."

Annie nodded. "So he said. But I know you talked to his mother today, and Jeremy mentioned that she's eager to see him married. So I just wanted to make sure that no one had any illusions about my ultimate plans. I'm savoring my freedom right now."

"Makes sense." Dorcas desperately needed to find out what had happened to Isadora, but she couldn't let this golden opportunity with Annie pass, either. "I have something I wanted to ask you, too."

"Oh?"

"When you were out on the lake last night, did you see anything . . . unusual?"

Annie's gaze intensified. "Why?"

"Well, Ambrose and I have a view of the lake from our house. I'm not sure if you knew that or not."

"No, I didn't." Annie's full attention was focused on Dorcas. "Have you . . . seen anything?"

Good. The plan is working. "Yes. I think there's something unusual living in that lake."

Annie grabbed Dorcas's arm. "So do I! But Jeremy doesn't believe me."

"What have you seen?"

"Well, I saw this little head and long neck come out of the water." Annie gestured with both arms. "I freaked out, let me tell you. The rest of it had to be big, because it caused waves that made my kayak tip over."

"That sounds scary."

"I was plenty scared, but after we paddled to the beach and I started thinking about it, I realized that if it was real and not a kid's prank, I could have the scoop of the century."

"Oh, Annie, you really could."

"Have . . . have you talked to anyone else about this?"

Dorcas shook her head. "Only Ambrose, and he won't say anything, either. I wouldn't want people in Big Knob to think I'm crazy."

"But we can't *both* be crazy." Annie's eyes shone with eagerness. "Dorcas, I know this is a lot to ask, but I would love to get an exclusive on this. If you see anything more, will you let me know?"

"Be glad to. I think it's exciting."

"Me, too! I was planning to stake out the area tomorrow night and bring my camera. I don't dare break the story until I'm sure it's not kids playing a prank, but with you living right there, you might have other sightings. Before we leave the party I'll give you my cell number."

"Perfect." And so it was. Dorcas worked hard not to gloat. This was going so well.

"And one other thing. I would love to interview you and Ambrose for my small-town series in the *Tribune*. I think it's so interesting that you decided to settle in Big Knob."

Dorcas's smile faded. The Wizard Council might not be too pleased by a feature story in a major newspaper. And yet, an interview would be a great way to cement the relationship with Annie.

"Unless you'd rather not." Annie's smile faltered, too. "I don't mean to invade your privacy, but I—"

"Not at all. Come by tomorrow morning about ten. We'd be glad to do an interview." Dorcas had to follow her instincts, and giving the interview seemed like the best course of action. She needed to get to know Annie better.

Annie still looked doubtful. "If you're sure."

"I'm totally sure." And now she simply had to handle the Isadora situation. "By the way, did Isabel come back in with you?"

"Uh, no, she didn't. She wanted to stay out and look at Big Knob a while longer. I keep trying to think why she looks so familiar, too. I've seen her somewhere before, but I can't figure out where."

Dorcas's uneasiness returned. "Maybe she just has one of those faces."

"That's what she said when I asked if she'd ever been to Chicago. But I don't think Chicago is where I know her from, anyway. She's related to someone around here, I'll bet. Maybe a long-lost niece or daughter who decided to come home at last."

Dorcas wondered how soon Annie would see the resemblance between Isabel Moore and the bronze statue on the square. Maybe Isadora's idea of melting the thing wasn't so bad after all.

"I think I'll go out back and see how she's doing," Dorcas said. "She might be feeling a little shy and out of place."

Annie laughed. "Isabel?"

"Okay, maybe not. But I brought her, so I should check up on her." Dorcas patted the box of condoms. "Enjoy these."

"Thanks, but I can't."

"You can't?" Dear Zeus, now nothing seemed to be going smoothly, not even the sex. "Why not?"

"I won't be having sex with Jeremy anymore. It's not fair to him."

Dorcas tried not to panic. "Maybe you should let him decide that."

"Oh, he can say he'll be fine until he's blue in the face, but I don't believe him. When I leave he'll be devastated. I—"

"Annie!" Melody called from the living room. "Quit playing with the condoms and get back here! Everybody's waiting for you so we can start truth or dare because you have the best secrets!"

Annie glanced at Dorcas. "I have to go. This is no time to make Melody upset. But thanks for keeping an eye on the lake for me."

"No problem." Dorcas muttered a little prayer to Venus that Annie wouldn't be able to keep her vow of celibacy. Then she hurried out to the back porch.

Isadora was gone.

Chapter 13

When the belly dancer didn't show up at the Big Knobian, Jeremy was stuck for entertainment. The bachelor party limped along on beer and munchies and not much else going on besides sports on TV, which the guys could watch anytime. Sean suggested magic tricks, but Jeremy figured that could backfire. Everyone would pester him for the secret behind the tricks, and because he didn't know how he was accomplishing any of it, things could get ugly.

After a couple of rounds of drinks, somebody came up with the idea of crashing the bachelorette party. Jeremy was out of options and decided it couldn't hurt. Besides, he'd get to see Annie.

A mere two days ago that prospect would have sent him into a panic of indecision. His confidence in that department had grown exponentially. Instead of being worried about his reception, he looked forward to being with her.

Luckily they'd invited Chief Bob Anglethorpe to the bachelor party, so he led the way in his squad car with the dome lights flashing. Because they'd all been drinking, they drove slower than a funeral procession so nobody would get hurt. Jeremy took Bruce and Ambrose in his Samurai.

"I can't understand what happened to the belly dancer," Jeremy said as they followed Bob's cruiser up First Street and turned right at Fourth, headed for Sean and Maggie's house.

"Well, it's the thought that counts." Bruce sat beside Jeremy in the passenger seat, his face alternating red and blue as the cruiser lights flashed through the windshield. Bruce was a big guy who made the Samurai seem crowded. "This could turn out better, anyway. I've always wondered what bachelorette parties are like."

"Thanks for not being pissed." Jeremy had always appreciated Bruce's even temper. He'd need it with Melody, who'd had a chip on her shoulder all her life. Jeremy understood that. It couldn't have been easy being less attractive, less brainy, less everything compared to Annie.

"Where was the belly dancer coming from?" Ambrose asked from the backseat.

"Evansville," Jeremy said. "I asked Bob to check and there weren't any accidents along that stretch tonight. It's not like she could get lost on Highway 64, either. You can't miss the exit sign for Big Knob."

Ambrose made a funny little sound.

"You okay back there?" Jeremy asked.

Ambrose cleared his throat. "I'm fine. Thought I saw a skunk on the road, but either I didn't or you missed it."

"I would hate to hit a skunk, for a lot of reasons," Jeremy said. "After Sean saved a family of them living under his rental house last fall, I've become a real fan of skunks. I went out with him once to see the spot he fixed for them in the Whispering Forest. Pretty cool."

"You wouldn't catch me in the Whispering Forest," Bruce said. "That place is haunted."

"I don't know if it is or not," Jeremy said. "What do you think, Ambrose? Don't you and Dorcas have picnics out there?"

"I don't think it's haunted," Ambrose said.

"Try going out there at night," Bruce said. "You'll

change your tune. Back in school a bunch of us went out there, thinking we were big brave football dudes. First we smelled smoke, and then we saw these red eyes, and this spooky voice said, 'Go away.' If we could've run that fast on the field, we would've been state champs."

Jeremy laughed. "I remember you telling me about that. I still think it was Stanley, the geek nobody liked, getting his kicks by scaring the pee out of you."

"Stanley. God, I'd forgotten all about old Stanley," Bruce said. "Didn't I hear he ended up in Silicon Valley and was making a fortune?"

"Something like that," Jeremy said.

"You could've done that, man. You have the smarts."

"Yeah, but I hate traffic." Jeremy grinned at him. "Anyway, I didn't feel the need to leave town. I was the geek everybody liked."

The procession turned down the lane leading to Sean and Maggie's, but they had to park a distance away because the circular drive was already full of cars. The old Victorian blazed with lights.

Bruce turned to Jeremy. "Did we bring beer? We can't barge in on their party if we didn't bring anything."

"Jeff loaded us up." Jeremy climbed out of the car. Good thing Jeff Brady, owner of the Big Knobian, had given them a discount. "I have to say, this is beginning to feel like a military operation."

Bob walked back toward them. "How do you want to play this?" Bob was middle-aged and married, with a slight paunch and a bald spot. But tonight he looked like a frat boy at a panty raid. "I doubt they know we're here," he said with barely disguised glee.

Jeremy glanced at the line of cars and trucks pulling in behind him. Sean's old pickup was directly behind them, and after that about a dozen other cars had rolled in. The line extended out to the main road.

Jeremy glanced at Bob. "You don't think they saw your bubblegum machine twirling around on top of your car?"

"I turned it off before we were in sight of the house."

"Then let's ask Sean." Jeremy sauntered back to Sean's truck. "It's your house, buddy. How do you want to do this? Just go up to the front door and knock like normal people?"

"Hell, no. That's no fun. Let's sneak up on the porch and see what they're up to before we announce our presence."

"There's about thirty of us," Jeremy said. "You think thirty guys can do a decent sneak?"

Bruce came up beside Jeremy. "I can sneak with the best of them. I say let's do it that way."

"The bridegroom has spoken." Jeremy liked the way the evening was turning out. Getting drunk and watching a belly dancer hadn't appealed to him, but he'd thought that was the expected drill, so he'd arranged for it. "Sean, will you pass the word down the line that we're orchestrating a major sneak?"

"You bet." Sean looked eager to begin. "Who's the point man for this operation?"

"I am," Jeremy said. He didn't even stop to think about it. Yet he'd never taken command of much in his life, other than the Internet café and the kayak adventure last night. Or the interlude up in his apartment this afternoon. Obviously Annie was inspiring him.

A couple of minutes later, Jeremy gave a soft whistle and motioned the guys forward. He and Bruce took the lead, with Ambrose and Sean following close behind. Bob fell in with Jeff to help carry the beer.

It was a reasonably quiet procession. Once in a while a bottle in one of the cases of beer would clank, or a muffled laugh would break the stillness. But all in all, it was a most excellent sneak.

Once they reached the front porch steps, Jeremy could hear music with a Latin beat.

"Maybe they're dancing," Bruce murmured.

"Let's see." Jeremy climbed the steps carefully so they wouldn't squeak, but with the music inside the house, he didn't think anyone could hear them, anyway. Edging along the porch, he peered in the first of two living room windows. What he saw made his blood run hot.

Only one person was dancing, and that was Annie. The other women formed a circle around her as they clapped and whistled their encouragement. Annie's natural coordination made her a good dancer, but more than coordination was going on. Annie was gyrating and undulating in a combination of sexy moves that left Jeremy with his tongue hanging out. Who needed a belly dancer?

"You have one hot mama, there, my friend," Bruce said, his tone worshipful.

She's not mine. But Jeremy didn't say that. For now he'd pretend that the woman dancing so sensuously inside the circle—the woman every man in this posse wanted except maybe Bruce, Ambrose, and Sean—that woman was Jeremy's girl. Reality would hit soon enough.

The dance ended, and some bozo hanging on the porch railing lost his grip and hollered like a banshee as he fell into the flower bed. Maggie peered out the window and shrieked, and it was all over. The door swung open and chaos erupted.

A couple of minutes passed before Jeremy worked his way over to Annie. Her cheeks were pink and her skin moist from her dance, which made her even sexier. He wondered if now that the bachelor party had combined with the bachelorette party, they could both be excused for the night.

"What are you guys doing here?" She didn't look upset about it, though. She looked happy, in fact.

"I hired a belly dancer from Evansville, but she didn't show." He surveyed her outfit, a flowered dress that didn't quite reach her knees. Being near her again made him grin like an idiot. "I should've asked you to dance, instead."

Her cheeks grew even pinker. "We were playing truth or dare, and I picked dare, which turned out to be dirty dancing."

"I liked it."

She met his gaze. "Do you dance?" she asked softly.

"I . . ." He came close to admitting the truth, that he was lousy at it.

As he tried to figure out how to answer the question without lying, Ambrose showed up to save him.

"Have you seen Dorcas?" Ambrose asked.

Annie glanced around. "About fifteen minutes ago she went out back to check on Isabel. Maybe they're still out there."

"Thanks." Ambrose took off.

"Hey, Jeremy!" Bruce called from across the room. "The girls say if we're staying we have to play truth or dare. I took a poll and the guys are fine with it."

"All right." Jeremy wanted to stick around, so if they had to play silly games, so be it.

"We decided you should be the first victim," Bruce added.

"Me?" Jeremy had hoped to use the distraction of the game to slip outside with Annie. "You should go first. You're the groom."

"Exactly, which is why we picked you, my best man, to do the job for me, bro."

Jeremy sent a pleading glance in Annie's direction, but she shrugged as if to say she couldn't save him.

"So what'll it be?" Bruce hoisted the beer bottle in his beefy hand. "Truth or dare?"

Neither. But he didn't have that choice. Two days ago he could have picked truth with no problem. He'd been a man of no secrets. Now his life was riddled

with them. But choosing dare was almost as scary.
No telling what a crowd of liquored-up friends would
think of.

He took a deep breath. "Dare."

Bruce nodded. "Okay, men. Huddle." As the guys
formed a tight circle, snorts of laughter punctuated
the muted discussion.

"You should see your face," Annie said. "Want a
blindfold and a cigarette?"

Jeremy glanced at her and remembered that she'd
put herself on the line only minutes ago. He wouldn't
come off as much of a hero if he couldn't handle a
party game without passing out from fright. He
squared his shoulders and gave her what he hoped
was a nonchalant smile.

She smiled back. "That's better. Anybody who can
keep his head when kayaks are flipping over should
be able to conquer truth or dare."

"I don't mind playing the game," he said. "But I
was hoping you and I could step outside for some air."

Her smile faded. "About that. I've been thinking
that maybe we shouldn't—"

"We've decided!" Bruce took a sip of his beer while
the rest of the guys, minus Ambrose, who was still
outside, grinned at Jeremy as if they could hardly wait
to find out how he'd deal with their challenge.

"Lay it on me." But he was no longer concerned
about the game. Annie had been about to say something that he definitely didn't want to hear. Was she
going to let what happened today scare her off for the
rest of the weekend? What a depressing thought.

Bruce cleared his throat. "We dare you to dance
with Annie to the same tune she danced to a few
minutes ago. We want to see some dirty dancing from
you, bro."

Panic rose in his chest. He wasn't much of a dancer.
Correction, he was not a dancer at all. The few times
he'd been forced to dance, like at his sister's wedding,

he'd managed with a hold-the-girl-and-shuffle maneuver that had gotten him through.

Annie stepped closer to him. "You can do this."

"I don't think so."

She gazed into his eyes. "I *know* you can."

"But—"

"We're starting the music," Maggie announced. "Ready?"

Annie glanced over at her. "Bring it on!" Then she leaned closer to Jeremy. "Watch my eyes and think sex." As the music began, she began to undulate in time to it.

With her hips moving like that, he didn't know how he was supposed to watch her eyes. He stood frozen in place, mesmerized by the magic of her body.

Magic. Would that help? Ambrose hadn't said a thing about dancing, and yet . . . there had been music that night. He was almost sure of it. And some dancing.

"Go for it, bro!" Bruce yelled out. "Shake your booty!"

"Look into my eyes," Annie said as she shimmied closer. "And think sex."

Jeremy dragged his attention from Annie's gyrating breasts and hips so he could gaze into her eyes. Slowly he began to move in time to the beat. "Abracadabra," he muttered under his breath.

The result amazed him. All at once he began rotating his hips in sync with hers. When she leaned back and wiggled her shoulders, he leaned forward and wiggled his. He had no idea how he was doing that, but he wasn't going to question it. Somehow, through some process he didn't understand, he was dirty dancing.

As an added bonus, he was making points with Annie. He could tell by the way she smiled and the heat built in her eyes. He could tell by the trembling of her body as he slid his against her. His dancing was turning her on. If he'd realized how effective this could be with women, he would have taken lessons years ago.

Although most of his concentration centered on her, he was vaguely aware of all the whistles and catcalls coming his way. No one had expected him to pull this off, but by God, he was doing it. Score one for Jeremy, the guy who'd always been clueless on the dance floor.

When the music ended, he wrapped his arms around Annie as the room erupted in clapping and cheers.

She looked up at him, her eyes glazed with obvious lust. "Wow. You're something."

"So are you." He was hot and aroused. "What were you about to say before the dance started?"

She moistened her lips. "Never mind."

He had little time to savor the meaning of that before the guys surrounded them, clapping him on the back and carrying on about his studly performance. Somehow he and Annie got separated and someone shoved a cold beer in his hand. He drank the beer and accepted all the good-natured kidding, but all he really wanted was to get back to Annie.

Then, before he realized she was there, she linked her arm through his and stood on tiptoe to murmur in his ear. "Still want to get some air?"

His heart, which had begun to slow after the exertion of the dance, picked up the pace. "You bet."

"Let me get my purse. I'll meet you in the front entryway."

He leaned down and put his mouth close to her ear. "Do you think we can leave?"

"No."

"Then why bother with your purse?"

Her laugh sounded breathless. "I want to show you the prize I won for pin-the-penis-on-the-man."

Chapter 14

Dorcas walked quickly in the direction of the Whispering Forest. She'd promised Ambrose she'd keep track of Isadora, and now the wily witch had given her the slip. Dorcas should have realized Isadora was getting bored and might search out better entertainment. It didn't take much imagination to figure out where she'd gone.

Maggie and Sean's house was about a ten-minute walk from the dragon's favorite clearing. Dorcas followed a narrow trail, stumbling across tree roots and banging her head on overhanging branches. Just her luck—she was out here without her light globe, but at least the moon shining through the trees allowed her to see the biggest obstacles.

When she stubbed her toe on a rock that looked like a shadow, she cursed Isadora first and George second. If it weren't for Dee-Dee, Dorcas would demand the Grand High Wizard send Isadora straight back to San Francisco. But Dorcas and Ambrose could use some help with Dee-Dee, and much as they both hated saying so, Isadora was a witch of considerable talent. Managed correctly, Isadora could be an asset.

Her work with the smallpox plague was as famous in the wizard world as it was here in Big Knob. True, she'd been a reluctant nurse, but she'd stuck it out and saved the town from potential annihilation. Underneath her brash exterior was a sympathetic heart, which had prompted her to come back and help with Dee-Dee.

As Dorcas drew closer to the clearing, she heard Isadora's boisterous laughter float through the trees. Then George shouted, "Righteous!" followed by a chattering sound that had to be the raccoons.

"I'm all in," Isadora announced.

So they were playing poker. Dorcas had known about these nightly games for months, but she and Ambrose had never caught them at it and George was very closemouthed about the proceedings. If nothing else, she'd finally have her curiosity satisfied as to how they worked the monetary angle.

Like every dragon, George had a chest full of gold pieces in his cave under the granite spire of Big Knob. Most dragons had no reason to spend the money, but most dragons didn't strike up a friendship with poker-playing raccoons, either. Dorcas suspected the raccoons of trying to swindle George out of his fortune.

Isadora had to have brought cash with her when she flew here from San Francisco, so she'd have no trouble buying in to the game. But what about the raccoons? They had no source of income, yet they'd been playing constantly ever since Dorcas arrived in town, and probably for years prior to that.

Led onward by the sound of the game in progress, Dorcas arrived at the edge of the dirt road that was the only vehicular access into the forest from the main road. Across the way was George's favorite clearing, illuminated tonight by a battered kerosene lamp hanging from a tree branch.

George, Isadora and four raccoons were gathered around a large, flat-topped tree trunk. All the players perched on makeshift stools made from sections of another hefty tree trunk. George required three chunks roped together.

Everyone had stacks of poker chips, but the biggest raccoon had the most. His masked face and bright

eyes were almost hidden by his pile of chips. All the
supplies must have been gathered by the raccoons
over the years, swiped from campsites or unguarded
backyards. Dorcas didn't know a lot about the game,
but the basic requirements had apparently been met—
chips, cards and a playing surface.

On the ground next to George lay a mound of shiny
gold pieces. The raccoons seemed to be paying their
way with necklaces, bracelets and rings. From this distance Dorcas couldn't tell if the jewelry was valuable
or not.

If she had to guess, she'd say it was all costume
jewelry they'd found or stolen. George wouldn't realize that trading his gold pieces for a fake ruby in a
gold-plated setting wasn't a fair exchange. He'd probably rather have something colorful.

As the play continued, George turned to the big
raccoon seated on his left. "Are you serious, dude?
You're actually gonna raise my ass?"

The raccoon chattered an answer Dorcas couldn't
understand. She'd studied raccoon years ago, but this
southern Indiana dialect confused her.

Isadora sat up straighter on her tree stump. "I say
that raccoon is dealing from the bottom of the deck."

Chattering angrily, the raccoon rose up on his hind
legs and stared at Isadora with his bright eyes.

"Oh, yes, you are." Isadora lifted her chin. "I taught
your ancestors how to play, and you look just like the
one who was a big, fat cheater. I'll bet cheating runs
in the family."

Dorcas's jaw dropped. Isadora had played poker
with the raccoons back in the 1800s? No wonder the
game was so entrenched in the Whispering Forest.

The big raccoon continued to chatter his protest,
even holding up his little black hands as if to prove
his innocence.

"I don't believe you." Isadora pulled something out
of her sleeve.

Dorcas gasped. It was a small wand, and Isadora was pointing it at the raccoon.

"No!" Dorcas rushed across the road toward the clearing. "Put that away now!"

Isadora gave her a glance of disdain. "Says who?"

"Says me." George reared up to his full height and shot a flame that knocked the wand right out of Isadora's hand.

"Ouch!" Isadora shook her hand. "That hurt! What in Zeus's name do you think you're doing, shooting off your mouth like that?"

George breathed on his claws and polished them on his chest. "Just protecting the creatures of the forest," he said with studied nonchalance. "Pretty cool, huh?"

Isadora turned to Dorcas. "Are you going to let him get away with that?"

"Absolutely." Dorcas beamed at George. "That was terrific. Good for you."

George gave her a sly grin. "Think it's worth a professional case of poker chips?"

"I need to talk with you about the poker, George. I—"

"There's nothing wrong with the poker." Isadora's voice was tight with fury. "It's the cheating raccoons I'm talking about. In my day I kept them honest. Walking around hairless for a few days never hurt anybody."

"Who's going to end up hairless?" Ambrose crossed the road looking harried and out of breath. "What did I miss?"

Dorcas decided to focus on the positive. "George being a hero. He saved one of the raccoons."

"What raccoons?" Ambrose put his hands on his knees while he caught his breath.

"The four who were—" Dorcas glanced around the clearing and discovered the raccoons were gone, along with their baubles, the chips, the cards and . . .

George's pile of gold pieces. "They took everything except the kerosene lamp!"

"Of course they did." Isadora walked over and picked up her wand. "I told you they needed to be taught a lesson, but you and your friend George wouldn't let me. This wand better not be damaged or someone will be billed for it. This is not a cheap wand."

Dorcas gazed at the bare ground where the gold pieces had been. "George's missing treasure isn't exactly chicken feed, either."

"Hey, there's more where that came from." George gazed eagerly at Dorcas. "Do I get the poker chips? Huh, huh? Do I?"

Dorcas sensed Ambrose's attention focused on her. With gold pieces missing, he'd expect her to be tough. She crossed her arms. "You're supposed to be guarding that treasure, George, not gambling it away."

"I'm not gambling it away!" He drew himself up with an indignant snort. "I might be a little behind, but give me a few more nights and I'll win it back plus the jewels. Just watch. I'm gonna clean out those raccoons."

Dorcas felt a headache coming on. She wanted to believe that George was making progress, but he seemed to take one step forward and two back. As for Isadora, she was more liability than asset right now. She'd helped create this poker problem in addition to letting Dee-Dee stay in the lake, even knowing she'd be trapped there for life without a partner.

Isadora pointed her wand at a small forest plant and made it bloom. "I guess the wand's working. Now that you guys broke up the poker game, I might as well go back to that dumb party."

Dorcas turned to her. "Before we head back, let's set a time to get together and brainstorm ideas for taking care of Dee-Dee's problem."

"That stupid lake monster?" George belched loudly. "Who cares about her? Do you think my scales are turning a little more gold? I think they are. Take a look, Dorcas."

"Excuse yourself, George," Ambrose said.

" 'Scuse me. What do you think about my scales? Can you see how the gold is spreading? I'll bet that lake monster doesn't have any gold on her."

"No, she doesn't." Dorcas chose to grab whatever opportunity presented itself. "She'll always be the same color. Drab old black."

"Except in the sunlight her skin gets iridescent and it's really pretty," Isadora said. "You can see purple, and blue, and—"

"But she can't be out in the sun," Dorcas said quickly. "So nobody will ever see that. Once you turn all gold, George, you'll be beautiful." With a quick glance she tried to enlist Ambrose in the cause. "Right, dear?"

"I'm not sure *beautiful* is the word," Ambrose said. Dorcas groaned.

"I'm thinking *magnificent* is the term we should use."

Ah, she did love her husband.

"Magnificent," George said. "I like the sound of that."

"Blah, blah, blah," Isadora said. "I'm leaving before I hurl." She started across the road.

"We're right behind you." Ambrose beckoned to Dorcas. "Let's go," he said in a low voice. "She's armed and dangerous."

"Go ahead. I'll catch up in a sec." Wanting to leave George with positive thoughts, she turned back to the dragon. "I can hardly wait until you're all gold," she said. "That was wonderful what you did, sticking up for the raccoon."

George looked doubtful. "Yeah, but maybe Zorro was cheating. That's not cool."

"Zorro?"

"That's what he calls himself. Then we've got the Lone Ranger, Batman and Spiderman. You know, masked dudes. Those are all heroes, so I didn't think of anybody cheating. Maybe I should have let Isadora turn Zorro hairless."

"No, you did the right thing." Dorcas patted his arm. "And I do see the gold spreading, so that proves it. Now, I have to go."

"What about my poker chips?"

Dorcas lowered her voice in case Ambrose was still within hearing distance. "I'll look into it."

"Righteous."

As Jeremy headed out the front door holding Annie by the hand, he kept expecting someone to call them back, but nobody did. They made it down the front steps of the porch without incident. So far, so good.

"Let's go sit in the Suzuki," he said. It wasn't the coziest spot he could think of, but he wasn't prepared to go off into the woods without a blanket.

"How about my car instead?"

"Why?"

She tugged him in that direction. "It's closer."

"Good reason."

"And it has a bigger backseat."

That comment had an immediate effect on his penis. He hadn't come prepared with condoms, but they could have a boatload of fun even without those little raincoats. He felt inventive.

Taking her keys from her purse, Annie chirped the lock open. "Come on. In here." She opened the back door before he could get to it and scooted inside.

The dome light came on, so he piled in after her and closed the door so they were once again plunged into darkness. Not total darkness, though, because the lights from the house cast a faint glow into the car's interior.

What Jeremy saw when he glanced over at Annie made him gulp. She had her dress pulled over her head, revealing a virginal white lace bra and panties. And he'd thought he preferred black.

She pulled the dress all the way off and tossed it into the front seat. "Take off your jeans." Her voice was sexy-soft and breathless. "We don't have much time."

"We don't have much birth control, either." Even so, he unfastened his belt. Oral sex was a damned good alternative, especially when they'd accomplished all the foreplay a person could want out on the dance floor.

"That's where you're wrong." She grabbed her purse from the floor, pulled out a box and tossed it to him. "I told you I won a prize."

And he'd won the jackpot. He was in the backseat with a woman who craved his body *and* was packing condoms. He lost no time shucking his pants. When he encountered the obstacle of his shoes, he yanked them off without untying them. If his feet protested a little, so what?

He threw both shoes and jeans into the front seat in a jangle of keys and loose change. His shirt followed, then his briefs. He left his socks on because he doubted that she'd have the time or inclination to suck his toes.

Sucking Annie's toes had been his pleasure this afternoon, and he wouldn't mind a repeat, but this promised to be what everyone referred to as a quickie. Jeremy had never had a quickie. He couldn't remember a woman who had lusted after him so desperately that she'd settle for one.

Annie, however, had taken off her bra and was shimmying out of her panties. Jeremy thought he'd best get the condom box open. He tore it apart and ripped open one of the packets inside.

Once he had it on, Annie started to giggle. Not the type of reaction a guy looked for when he was going in for the big score.

"You're green," she said. "Very green."

Even in the dim light from the house, he could see her point. "Then let's get it out of sight."

"I love it when you talk dirty." She wiggled down onto the seat and made room for him between her thighs.

"This is extremely unromantic." But his penis was throbbing and threatening to detonate any minute, so he made like a pretzel and braced himself above her. "I haven't even kissed you yet."

"Kiss me now," she whispered. "Then do me."

He followed her instructions, finding her warm, moist mouth in the darkness. She welcomed him with her tongue, which encouraged him to find that other warm, moist opening between her legs. Then he was lost. Connecting with Annie this way fried every brain cell he possessed.

Once he was inside her, he became so involved in the experience that aliens could have landed a spaceship right next to him and he wouldn't even have noticed. All that mattered was Annie's hot, pulsing center, where he searched for salvation. Thrusting deep, he celebrated the rhythmic moans that greeted him each time he buried himself to the hilt. All the while he kept kissing her, smothering her cries so that they wouldn't be heard.

She loved this as much as he did, and he'd carry that knowledge forever. No matter what happened later tonight, or tomorrow, or the next day, he would know that right now, while he lovingly stroked her G-spot with his penis, there was nowhere she'd rather be.

During their dance she'd told him to think about sex. Now, during sex, he thought about their dance, which inspired him to use his hips in new and interesting ways. She responded by rising to meet him with such enthusiasm that he wondered whether the car had started to rock.

He didn't care. Annie had invited him into the backseat, and he would make it count. Their bodies grew slick with sweat and her fingers dug into his hips.

Their soul-blending kiss ended as they both struggled for air in the final moments. As he felt her tighten around him, heard her breathing quicken, he increased the pace. There. He sensed her orgasm hovering . . . hovering . . . *now*.

The moment she came, he surrendered to the pounding in his groin and surged forward in a shuddering, monumental climax. A red haze swirled in his brain and gradually settled again as the quivering stopped. So this was a quickie. He could grow to like it.

"Jeremy!" A guy's voice penetrated his barely conscious, sex-drenched mind. "We need you, buddy! They're gonna do some toasts!"

He dragged in a shaky breath and brushed the damp hair from Annie's face. "Ready to rejoin the party?"

Chapter 15

Even though Annie had repaired her lipstick and combed her hair, she was convinced everyone at the party knew exactly what she'd been up to out in the car with Jeremy. He looked a little mussed, too, and she resisted the urge to reach up and finger-comb his hair back into place.

They'd made a decision not to go inside holding hands or act in any way that would give the gossips even more ammunition. But judging from the smirks and knowing looks as they walked back into the living room, there would be no killing this rumor. Annie didn't mind so much for herself, but her impulsive behavior tonight could make life tough for Jeremy, and she regretted that.

Still, she couldn't make herself regret what had just happened out there in the backseat of her car. She'd never been capable of quickie sex before, and she was proud of herself. She was also feeling really, really energized.

The music still blared, but the games seemed to be on hiatus while the guests tucked into paper plates piled with goodies from the Big Knob Market's deli counter.

"Grab a plate, you two," Maggie called out to them as they walked into the living room.

Annie was starving, but three days before the wedding was no time to abandon her diet. Everything on the buffet table was loaded with calories. Not a celery stick in sight. She recognized Bradley's famous chicken salad and baked-on-the-premises rye bread. And there were desserts—a cheesecake, a Black Forest cake and little individual éclairs that made her mouth water.

"Let me get you some food," Jeremy said.

"No, that's okay. I'm not hungry."

He gazed down at her, his gray eyes warm with admiration. "Annie, if this is about losing weight, I hope you realize that you don't need to lose another—"

"No, no." She waved a dismissive hand. "It's not that."

He leaned closer and lowered his voice. "I love touching you, love holding you. It's like sinking into soft pillows."

She groaned and sucked in her stomach.

"I'm guessing from your expression that was the wrong thing to say."

"You'd be guessing right. A girl doesn't want to be thought of as pillowlike."

"I meant it as a compliment."

She couldn't help laughing. His confidence might be improving, but he still had geekish tendencies. "I know. That's what's so scary."

"Come have some food."

"No, thanks." The entire Big Knob varsity football team couldn't drag her over to the buffet table now. Pillows, indeed. "But you go ahead. There's nothing pillowy about you."

"Uh, okay, I will." He backed away from her. "I still think you should—"

"Go eat." She shooed him away and glanced around to see if Gwen was nearby. Gwen cared about Jeremy. Maybe she'd have some words of wisdom about this complicated situation.

Annie found her repairing a flower arrangement on

a table between the two front windows. "I'll bet you brought that arrangement." Annie had seen some of those same flowers in Gwen's shop the day before.

"I did. Somebody bumped into them and knocked the baby orchids off-kilter." Gwen fiddled with the arrangement some more and stepped back. "That's better."

"Can I ask you something?"

Gwen glanced at her. "Sure."

"Is it horrible for me to be involved with Jeremy when I don't plan for it to go beyond the weekend? Because when I say it like that, it sounds horrible."

Gwen adjusted her glasses. "He knows that's how you feel, right?"

"Yes. If anything, I've harped on it too many times."

"Then it's not horrible. He's an intelligent guy and he has all the facts. He could call a halt if he didn't like the odds."

Annie drew in a long, shaky breath and let it out again. "Isabel thinks I'm taking advantage of him because he used to have a crush on me. She thinks I'm using him for my own purposes. I probably shouldn't listen, but what she said hit home."

"And Jeremy could be using you for his own purposes. Maybe it's liberating for him to have great temporary sex. You can't have sex with a girl in Big Knob without strings attached. What am I saying? *Ropes* attached, like the kind they use to moor a cruise ship. You might be giving him a gift."

"I'd like to think that. He's certainly given me a gift. He says I look good twenty pounds overweight. True, he compares me to a pillow, but his heart's in the right place."

Gwen rolled her eyes. "You can teach a geek magic tricks, but you can't turn him into a silver-tongued devil overnight. He once told me my nose was nicely proportioned and my nostrils were the perfect size."

"Omigod."

"That's Jeremy. But a guy who likes you the way you are is sure good for the ego."

"Mine needed some serious plumping up, no pun intended."

"Then I say let him plump. It seems as if he's good at it."

"He is." Annie gazed at her. "Are you sure you aren't secretly in love with him? Because if I thought so, I would back away right this minute."

"I'm not secretly in love with him. He's like the brother I never had. I watched you two dancing and that was the sexiest I've ever seen him, but I still didn't get a tingle." Gwen smiled. "But you did."

"Uh-huh. Can't explain why, but he really does it for me."

"Then you should let him keep doing it, at least through Sunday. You're having a positive effect on him, too. He's like me, way too conservative. You're expanding his horizons." Gwen ticked off items on her fingers. "Sex outside by the lake, sex in the afternoon, sex in the backseat during a party—"

"That's a pretty comprehensive list. Is someone following us?" Maybe Jeremy was right and the lake monster was only a practical joke.

"Not that I know of. We just have superior intelligence gathering in this town. You lived here for eighteen years. You must remember that."

Annie lowered her voice. "Speaking of intelligence gathering, I'm going to tell you something and you have to promise to keep it to yourself."

"If Jeremy's really nine inches, I don't want to know."

"This has nothing to do with Jeremy."

"So he is nine inches?"

"No."

"Eight?"

"Focus, Gwen." For the first time Annie took note

of how flushed Gwen was. "How many cups of punch did you have, anyway?"

"A few. I've never been great with parties, but it helps to get a little looped."

"In other words, I might as well disregard all that good advice you gave me because you're smashed."

"No, actually, you should listen to the advice I just gave you, because the booze helps me tap into my inner wisdom."

Annie sighed. "And besides that, you have a great nose."

"Nice of you to notice. What's this top secret thing you want to tell me about?"

"I saw something in Deep Lake last night. Something huge."

"Are we back to the subject of Jeremy's penis?"

"No." Annie edged Gwen away from the crowd. "And keep your voice down. I'm talking about a creature sort of like the Loch Ness monster, only with a smaller head. Looks kind of like a plesiosaur, if you remember your dinosaurs."

"I'll be damned. Maybe Donald wasn't exaggerating."

"Donald Jenkins?"

Gwen nodded. "He claimed to see something big under the surface while he was out fishing last weekend, but you know how he exaggerates. Nobody believed him."

A chill shot up Annie's spine. She knew Donald, who ran the Big Knob Dairy, and he did tend to exaggerate. But now three people had seen a monster. They couldn't all be imagining things.

Gwen gazed at her with benign tolerance. "You know it has to be kids, Annie. Don't be gullible. There's no such thing as lake monsters."

"If it's kids, they're a lot more clever than we were."

"Oh, they are. I wouldn't put anything past the new

crop. Teenagers get crazy in the spring. Remember how we were?"

"You were never crazy, Gwen."

"Sadly, that's true. I've been thinking that needs to change." With a lopsided grin, Gwen tucked her arm through Annie's. "Let's go get some food."

"I'm not eating. If my mother has to let my dress out any more, she'll have to add that extra piece of material we learned about in sewing class. I think it's a gussy."

"It's a gusset, and one baby éclair won't mean you need a gusset." Gwen pulled her closer to the crystal plate holding the éclairs. "Have you ever thought about how much these are like penises? Or is it penisi?"

"Gwen, you really are toasted. Plus you're fixated on male equipment." Annie laughed. "But I can see what you mean, with the shape and the cream filling inside."

Gwen handed her one. "I dare you to take this over to Jeremy, nip the end off and suck the cream out right in front of him. I double-dog dare you."

"And I thought you were a sweet girl."

"I am sweet, and getting sick of it. Try the éclair trick. I've always wanted to but never had the nerve. A big one would be more effective, but you have to work with what you have."

"Why should I?"

"Because I know Jeremy. We're way too much alike, which is why we're so wrong for each other. He'll be embarrassed and hate it, but he'll love it, too. Trust me, he wants to break out of his ordinary routine and do impulsive things. There's a wild man inside there and you can help turn him loose."

The concept appealed to Annie. If she thought she was actually benefiting Jeremy this week, that would relieve her guilt about leaving on Sunday. "I'll try it, but Gwen, you need a hot guy so you can unleash your inner vixen. If you'll come to Chicago, I'll hook you up."

Gwen shook her head. "I think I need a Frenchman."

"I know some guys with French names." Annie could think of two in the newsroom.

"No, I mean from France."

That's when Annie remembered that going to France had always been Gwen's dream. "Can you leave the flower shop and just go?"

"Not really."

"Then how—"

"The Internet. I'll find someone and invite him here to visit."

Annie looked at her friend with new respect. Gwen had a plan and a goal. If anyone could pull that sort of thing off, it would be her. "Good luck with that. Oh, and about Jeremy, will you keep an eye on him and make sure he's okay after I leave?"

"You bet."

"Especially watch out for Isabel."

Gwen saluted. "I promise she won't get by me, coach. Now, go suck that éclair."

Jeremy had hoped Annie would decide to eat something. When she wandered over with the éclair in her hand, he concluded that his bumbling attempts to tell her she wasn't fat had worked.

"I'm glad you changed your mind." He gestured to the full plate he held in one hand. "As you can see, I went a little overboard."

"Overboard is good." Holding his gaze, she bit off the very tip of the éclair.

"I'll bet those taste great." He didn't know why he should be nervous. She was only eating an éclair.

"Mm." Then she began to lick the end of the

damned thing, and he knew why he should be nervous. "That's very cute, Annie." He was getting hard, which wasn't cute at all. The word *painful* came to mind.

After she'd licked all the chocolate off, she put the end of the small éclair in her mouth and began to suck.

He should turn around and leave. That's exactly what he should do. If he stayed here and watched her perform oral sex on that éclair, he would end up in big trouble.

The party ebbed and flowed around them, but nobody stopped to comment on what Annie was doing. He could walk away and leave her sucking her éclair by herself. But his feet wouldn't go anywhere.

"Okay, Annie, that's enough." His voice sounded as if he might be coming down with a cold. "You made your point."

She finished sucking the cream filling from the éclair, and there was a little bit of it left in the corner of her mouth. She slowly licked it away.

He didn't even realize he'd tilted his plate until the entire contents tumbled in a soggy mess onto the hardwood floor. The fork landed last with a soft clunk.

Annie glanced at the floor with a little smile of triumph. "Whoops."

That's when Jeremy knew for sure that she'd meant to make him lose his cool. Little Annie wasn't quite as sweet as she seemed, and she was way sexier than he'd imagined.

She also had a devilish streak, and she'd pay for it in ways that would bring them both some extra excitement tomorrow night. He had some planning to do before they went to the lake to look for the supposed lake monster. In the meantime, though, he had a mess to clean up.

Would the magic word work in a case like this? Now that everyone at the party had noticed the food dumped at his feet, it might be a good time to find out if the word was truly multipurpose. If so, he could use it as part of Annie's payback tomorrow night.

He glanced over at Ambrose and lifted his eyebrows. Ambrose gave a slight tilt of his head, which Jeremy took as a go-ahead sign. Concentrating all his attention on the food, he held his plate perfectly level. "Abracadabra."

The food disappeared from the floor, leaving no trace, and reappeared on his plate. The fork followed. As everyone cheered and clapped, he took a little bow, being careful not to spill the food again. No point in pushing his luck.

"Nice work," Annie said with a broad smile of approval.

"Glad you liked it."

"I have no idea how you did that," she said. "It was seamless."

"Professional secret." So secret that he didn't have a clue what had just happened. He wondered if he dared eat the food. After all, it had been on the floor. Then again, it had been put through some kind of magic transformation. He took a forkful of potato salad. "Want some?"

"Okay."

He fed her the bite of potato salad and she played it for all it was worth, closing those perfect lips around the fork and easing the salad off the fork in a long, sensuous motion. His penis twitched in response, but he was still in control. Accomplishing the magic trick had put him back in the driver's seat.

"Hey, Jeremy," Bruce said. "You've got her eating out of your hand."

"Brucey, baby, why don't you ever feed me like that?" Melody asked.

"I will," Bruce said, "once you learn to eat an éclair."

That's when Jeremy knew that everyone in the room had viewed the whole performance even though they hadn't seemed to be watching. Annie definitely had something to answer for.

He glanced at her and spoke in a low voice no one else would be able to hear. "You know those rules you set up for tomorrow night at the lake?"

"Uh-huh."

"They've been officially canceled."

As he watched the anticipation build in her eyes, he began to think he might have the combination that would convince her to stay in Big Knob. She needed excitement. He'd see what he could do about that.

Chapter 16

Dorcas slipped out of bed early the next morning. Ambrose was still asleep and probably would be for at least another hour. He'd felt frisky after the party the night before and they'd had quite a time on the fold-down sex bench in their bedroom. The bench was Ambrose's invention, a sturdy alternative to chair sex.

Sean Madigan had built it for them last winter, and now they no longer destroyed wooden chairs with their enthusiastic lovemaking. Even better, the bench folded up against the wall when not in use. That was a good thing, because otherwise Ambrose would turn it into a clothes rack and it would lose its charm in a hurry.

After a night of partying and sex, Ambrose always slept in. That suited Dorcas's plans perfectly. Eventually Dee-Dee would have to get used to dealing with men, but for now she seemed comfortable talking only to women.

Dorcas dressed in a purple warm-up suit and running shoes while Sabrina pranced around her purring in anticipation. On the way downstairs, Dorcas thought about what she wanted to say to the lake monster. She'd heard that the owner of the Big Knob Dairy had claimed to have seen Dee-Dee, but fortunately nobody believed him. Still, caution was important right now.

Sabrina streaked out the back door when Dorcas opened it, but waited at the bottom of the steps. Dorcas glanced out to the lake but couldn't see much because of the pearl-colored mist rising from the surface. The air smelled of damp pine, and the rubber soles of her shoes squeaked on the dew-soaked wood as she descended to the path that led to the lake.

All this moisture was good for her complexion. That was one thing she worried about in Sedona. She'd had to counteract the effects of the dry air with a special antiaging potion, but she hadn't bothered with it here.

The sun hadn't yet topped the hills to the east of town. When it did, the mist would disappear, but for now it softened the landscape, as if some giant hand had adjusted a lens and everything was slightly out of focus. The ethereal atmosphere suited Dorcas just fine.

Sedona almost never had mist. The seasons weren't as pronounced there, either, which wasn't a huge deal, but Dorcas had somewhat enjoyed watching a snowy winter morph into a green spring. This summer she'd try swimming in the lake, and perhaps talk Ambrose into skinny-dipping with her.

Sabrina seemed to like it here, too. This morning she bounded from one side of the path to the other, obviously hoping to flush a grasshopper or a chipmunk. Dorcas would never have been able to allow this kind of freedom in Sedona, where coyotes would make a meal of her in no time. Being a magical cat, Sabrina might be able to hold her own, but Dorcas hadn't wanted to take the chance.

She grudgingly admitted that Big Knob had its advantages, and the area around Deep Lake was beautiful, almost as beautiful, in its own way, as the red rocks of Sedona. But she wasn't becoming attached to the place, by any means. She might come back and visit once in a while after they left, though.

As she neared the lake, she heard waves lapping against the small beach. There was no wind, so the waves had to be caused by Dee-Dee swimming around. She might as well do it now while the mist hid her from prying eyes.

Dorcas put her hands to her mouth and was about to call for the lake monster to approach, when a familiar laugh drifted across the water. A moment later Dorcas made out the ghostly shape of Dee-Dee swimming toward her, with a familiar long-legged figure clinging to her neck. Isadora had gone for a ride.

"Hi-ho, Dee-Dee, awayyyy!" Isadora called out and waved at Dorcas. Then she leaned to her left, and Dee-Dee veered to that side and plunged toward the center of the lake. Waves splashed higher on the beach and sprayed both Dorcas and Sabrina.

Sabrina scampered back with a hiss of distaste. She obviously loved riding perched on Dee-Dee's head, but she always managed to avoid getting wet. She glanced up at Dorcas with a meow of protest. She didn't seem to like sharing her newfound friend.

"I'm not crazy about this, either," Dorcas said. "She could attract unwanted attention with a stunt like that." Dorcas also recognized another emotion digging at her. She was jealous.

She would have loved to take a ride, but she hadn't thought it wise. Instead she'd let Sabrina go while she stood guard on shore in case anyone happened along. Isadora hadn't worried about such things.

With another whoop of joy, Isadora reappeared through the mist, still holding tight to Dee-Dee's neck. She gave a little squeeze and Dee-Dee floated in place about ten feet off shore. "Come on, Dorcas!" Isadora called. "Ride with me."

"I think you should get off." Dorcas heard how prissy that sounded. She was not prissy, or at least she hadn't been until Isadora showed up.

"Not yet." Isadora was breathing hard. "I'd forgotten how fun this is. You should try it."

Dee-Dee, being shy, said nothing. Dorcas could imagine that Isadora made Dee-Dee even more shy than usual. The possibility of a good conversation dwindled, but there was the prospect of a ride . . .

As Dorcas debated whether she dared join Isadora, Sabrina meowed again and kneaded her paws into the sand as she stared intently at Dee-Dee. Sabrina wanted her ride. And so did Dorcas.

"All right," she said. "Once around the lake."

"Hooray!" Isadora leaned forward. "Move up a little more, Dee-Dee, and lower your head like you did for me."

"I knew that," Dee-Dee said in her surprisingly melodious voice. "I learned to do it for Sabrina."

"Who?"

"My cat." Dorcas pulled off her shoes and socks and waded into the cold water so she could sling a leg over Dee-Dee's neck. "Dee-Dee's been giving her rides for days. It was Dee-Dee's idea, in fact." After a small trial run, Sabrina had been more than ready to go every morning.

"And you never tried it?" Isadora asked. "Why the hell not?"

"I thought someone should keep watch. I've been very worried that someone would see her." The lake monster's skin felt like wet vinyl, and Dorcas had to be careful she didn't slip right off as she worked herself backward.

"Someone has. Taking those petitions around has netted me a ton of gossip. The dairy guy thinks he saw her."

"I know about that." Dorcas was glad she was able to say so. "Nobody believes him, though." Dorcas intended to keep her information about Annie and her experience with Dee-Dee private for now.

"They don't believe him yet, but that could change," Isadora said. "Okay, keep inching down. I'll move back a little to make room. We should both fit right at the base of her neck."

Dorcas edged downward until she was practically in Isadora's lap.

"That's good," Isadora said. "Right there. Be sure and hold on tight. She gets going pretty fast."

"If I can ride a broom, I can do this." Dorcas was feeling a little touchy. First Isadora invaded George's territory and now she'd taken it upon herself to ride Dee-Dee without consulting anyone about the advisability of doing that.

But having Isadora reacquaint herself with Dee-Dee was a good thing. If Isadora felt invested she was more likely to help come up with a solution. Still, Isadora had been mostly a pain in the ass. Dorcas hoped all the trouble she'd caused would be worth it.

Once Dorcas was settled, she realized that her cat was still on the beach meowing. "Don't forget Sabrina," she called out to Dee-Dee.

"I would never do that," Dee-Dee said. "Sabrina is my best friend." Her neck muscles flexed as she leaned down to rest her head on the sand. Sabrina hopped on.

Now that Dorcas had her arms and legs wrapped around Dee-Dee's slippery neck, she wondered how Sabrina managed to balance on top of the lake monster's head. "Does Sabrina dig in with her claws?" she asked.

"No," Dee-Dee said. "I make sure I keep my head level. But my neck will always move, so that's why you have to hang on tight. I balance Sabrina like a book on top of my head."

Dorcas wondered where the lake monster would get an image like that, and then she remembered the back issues of *Wizardry World* she'd given her. One of the articles had to do with proper posture as an aid for improving magical skills, and the author had recommended the old trick of learning to walk with a book balanced on one's head.

"Hang on." Dee-Dee pivoted in place until they were facing the center of the lake. "Here we go!"

Dorcas gasped at the surge of power as they shot forward. She slipped to the right, and if Isadora hadn't grabbed her by the waistband of her pants, she would have ended up in the cold lake. The prospect of that gave her added strength as she righted herself and tightened her grip.

"Ride 'em, cowgirl!" Isadora shouted.

The wind they stirred up roared in Dorcas's ears and brought tears to her eyes as the mist-shrouded shoreline passed in a blur. Glancing up, she watched in amazement as Sabrina sat poised on the flat part of Dee-Dee's head. Sabrina's ears were back and her nose thrust into the wind.

Somehow, she knew to trust her lake monster friend. That trust was obviously well-placed, because from this vantage point Dorcas could see how carefully Dee-Dee held her head so that Sabrina wouldn't fall. It helped that the cat already had excellent balance, but any abrupt movements on Dee-Dee's part would have sent Sabrina into the water.

About halfway around the lake, Dorcas finally relaxed enough to start having fun. This wasn't like riding a broom, because Dee-Dee was in control. From that standpoint, Dorcas would still take a broom ride over a lake monster ride. But this was pretty darned thrilling.

As they approached the beach, Isadora called for one more round, and Dorcas agreed. She had the hang of it now, and stopping seemed silly when they were all alone out on the water. So off they went, Dorcas's hair blowing in her face. Next time she'd use a scrunchie.

Next time? She didn't dare do this on a regular basis, no matter how much she enjoyed it. Summer was coming, and people would be camping on the edge of the lake. Fishermen—Donald Jenkins among them— would start coming out here early in the morning once it got warmer. The lake wasn't crowded now, but soon it would be.

They had to solve Dee-Dee's problem before then. Otherwise her loneliness might prompt her to take stupid chances that would endanger her and possibly the townspeople, too. Dorcas thought the answer was figuring out how to get a mate here, but she had no idea how they'd manage that.

"Isn't this terrific?" Isadora cried out as they sped around the lake and headed back toward the beach.

"Yes!" Dorcas gave way to the moment and let out a little whoop of her own.

"Attagirl!" Isadora gave her a light slap on the shoulder. "I knew you had it in you."

"I have to admit it's fun. I—" She didn't finish what she'd been about to say. One glance at the beach told her playtime was over. Ambrose stood there, arms folded, feet planted apart.

Even from this distance, she could tell he wasn't happy. She could also tell he was still wearing his favorite leopard-print silk pajamas, the ones he liked to put on after chair sex because he felt like a jungle cat. He had to be freezing.

Dee-Dee must have seen him, too, because she backpedaled, causing even bigger waves to wash up on the beach. Ambrose jumped back so he wouldn't get his feet wet.

"Who's that?" Dee-Dee asked.

"My husband, Ambrose."

"He looks mean. I don't like mean men."

"He's not mean," Dorcas said. "He's . . . upset." She'd hoped for a more auspicious meeting between Dee-Dee and Ambrose. She'd also figured he'd sleep longer.

Isadora snorted. "Shades of Ebenezer. If he'd ever caught me riding Dee-Dee, which he wouldn't have because he didn't know she existed, but just saying he had caught me, he would have looked exactly like that. That's why I'll never get married again. You can't have any fun."

Dorcas felt called upon to defend her husband. "We have plenty of fun." She thought specifically of one moment last night when they'd had major fun. They'd made that wooden bench wiggle like a carnival ride. "But sometimes he worries about me. It's only because he loves me."

"Uh-huh." Isadora sounded skeptical. "That's what they all say."

"In this case, it's true." Dorcas didn't regret the exhilarating ride, but Ambrose would correctly guess that Isadora had tempted her and she'd succumbed. That didn't look good from any angle. "Dee-Dee, take us to shore, please."

"I don't want to." She continued to tread water, which caused the lake to boil as if it had a volcano under it. "I don't like him."

Isadora laughed. "It's wise to stay clear of a man who adopts that kind of disapproving attitude, Dee-Dee. You can drop us off on the other side of the lake."

"No," Dorcas said immediately. "Don't do that."

"Why not? I have my broom over there. I can give you and Sabrina a ride back to your house."

"Because the sun's up and the mist is nearly gone. Flying by broom is risky enough at night, but it's insanity during the day. Honestly, Isadora, I don't know how you've kept your identity secret all these years."

"I'm incredibly fast."

"And unbelievably lucky," Dorcas said. And cocky, too, but she didn't say that. They had a situation, and arguing wouldn't solve it.

If only Ambrose would look a wee bit more welcoming, that would help. But she wasn't surprised by his attitude. He didn't know the lake monster, and Dorcas had been remiss in not getting them acquainted earlier. She'd been so intent on creating a female bond with Dee-Dee that she'd unwittingly fostered an atmosphere of suspicion between her husband and her new friend.

For Ambrose to come down this morning and find Sabrina *and* his wife out joyriding with Isadora must have been the final straw. She wondered why he was standing there in his pajamas. Whatever it was could be urgent.

Somehow she had to convince Dee-Dee to take them in to shore. Dorcas could be let off on the other side and make the five-mile hike, but she didn't have the time. She had an appointment with Annie this morning, and besides, Sabrina wouldn't appreciate being asked to walk that far before she'd had her breakfast. *Sabrina.* That was the answer.

"Dee-Dee, I promise you can trust Ambrose," Dorcas said.

"I don't think so," she said.

"Yes, you can. Check with Sabrina. She trusts him." Dorcas didn't know how Sabrina and Dee-Dee communicated, but she was positive they did. From the moment the two had caught sight of each other, some mysterious connection had been established.

"Okay," Dee-Dee said. "I'll ask Sabrina."

In the silence that followed, Isadora leaned closer to Dorcas. "Are they using telepathy?" she asked in an undertone.

"I assume so," Dorcas murmured. "I've never asked Dee-Dee about it. It's interesting, because Sabrina doesn't communicate that way with George."

"Oh, that's easy to explain," Isadora said. "George is too wrapped up in himself. He couldn't concentrate long enough to establish a telepathic link with your cat. He—whoops, hang on. We're moving."

And so they were, straight for shore. When Dee-Dee was close enough, she lowered her head and allowed Sabrina to leap off into the sand. Dorcas was so eager to reach Ambrose that she soaked her pants nearly to her crotch.

"Is anything wrong?" she called to him.

"You mean besides you sneaking out of bed trying to get yourself and everybody else in trouble? Besides that?"

She reminded herself that he was speaking out of love. "I didn't sneak. You were dead to the world, so I went for a walk."

"So I see." Arms still folded, tone still parental, he surveyed her soaked pants.

"Ambrose, I'd like you to meet Dee-Dee." She turned around to discover that Dee-Dee was gone. So, mysteriously, was Isadora.

"If you're looking for your partners in crime, they rode off into the sunrise," Ambrose said.

Dorcas groaned. "I hope she doesn't ride her broom in broad daylight."

"Did you tell her not to?"

"You don't tell Isadora not to do something. That will become the very first thing she does. She—"

"Bombs away!"

Dorcas looked up in time to see Isadora sailing overhead on her broom and some red object falling from the sky. Before Ambrose could jump out of the way, the water balloon hit him and splattered, dousing him.

He stood there dripping and staring after her. "I have half a mind to get my staff and—"

"No." Dorcas caught him by the arm. "Don't let

her get to you. Let's go in and dry off. Then we'll discuss this like an intelligent witch and wizard."

Ambrose scowled at her. "Isadora is trouble, Dorcas."

"I know, but we need her to help us with Dee-Dee."

"We need her help about as much as we need a leaky cauldron and a backfiring broom." Ambrose stomped up the path to the house.

"We do need her. She thinks outside the box."

"She doesn't have the faintest idea of what a box is in the first place!"

"Calm down, sweetheart." Dorcas hurried after him. "Don't get your karma in a twist. By the way, why did you come down to the lake in the first place? Did you hear us?"

"No, Annie called. She wants to come over early."

"Why?"

"Her sister, Melody, was talking to Bruce, who apparently went out to the dairy to check on those ice cream molds Donald Jenkins is making for the wedding."

"Melody was telling me about those. Vanilla ice cream wedding bells. Very sweet."

"Jenkins may make sweet wedding bells, but he told Bruce that come Sunday, after all the wedding events are over, he's going out on the lake with his gun. He plans to shoot whatever's down there and get himself on the cover of *Guns and Ammo*."

Chapter 17

There's a huge story here. The flash of intuition came to Annie the minute she pulled up in front of the Lowells' house. She'd always had an instinct for news, and she'd discovered that working in print instead of in front of the camera had sharpened that instinct. A tingle at the base of her spine signaled that she was about to uncover something significant, something that could change the course of her career and probably her life.

She needed exactly that, a launching pad that would catapult her out of the ordinary and cancel any remaining icky emotions left over from her divorce and the end of her TV job. But eager as she was to walk into the house and begin the interview, worried as she was about the man who threatened to shoot whatever lurked in the water, she took a moment to sit in her car and absorb this feeling of vast potential, which didn't come to her all that often.

The bra story would attract interest, but it was still a woman's kind of story, a lifestyle piece of the sort her editor expected from her. The creature in the lake was definitely front-page material. Annie suspected that the couple living in this house, with its pale lavender siding and turquoise trim, would have a lot to do with the story, too.

Taking a deep breath, she opened the door, stepped out of her car and walked up on the porch. The Lowells' doorbell played the opening notes from Beethoven's "Ode to Joy." She doubted anyone else in town had a doorbell that played Beethoven. Those that even bothered with doorbells at all would have only the two-note, ding-dong kind.

Ambrose came to the door along with a sleek black cat who pranced by his side. The cat nonchalantly surveyed Annie with luminous green eyes. Ambrose, however, looked harried. He had on jeans and a frayed T-shirt that had a bumblebee on the front and the words BLESSED BEES underneath. The bee wore a halo.

Ambrose finger-combed his damp hair, which had just enough gray to make him look distinguished. "Dorcas is still in the shower."

"I've made you both rush. I apologize."

"No, no. Not a problem, especially considering the news you have about Donald Jenkins. We have an urgent situation here."

"I think so, too." Annie's adrenaline spiked as she realized that unless Ambrose believed that the creature was real, he wouldn't be concerned about Jenkins's threat. She was as intrigued by Ambrose as she was by Dorcas, and wanted to know more about him. "Interesting T-shirt."

He glanced down as if he'd forgotten what he was wearing. "It's a band. We play . . . played soft rock."

"The band broke up?"

"Sort of." Ambrose gestured toward the parlor. "Please have a seat. Dorcas will be down any minute, but in the meantime, I'll make you some tea."

"Thanks." No doubt about it, the Lowells were different from your average Big Knobian. Nobody in town would think to offer tea as the first—and apparently only—choice of beverage. Most likely they'd start with coffee as a first choice and tea as a distant second option.

As Annie walked into the parlor, she thought about the band name on Ambrose's shirt. She'd seen the phrase *blessed be* somewhere before, and this looked like a takeoff on it.

Then she remembered where she'd seen it—the closing line on an e-mail she'd received at work about a Wiccan festival held outside the city. She hadn't been able to cover the festival. Now she wished she had.

She didn't know much about Wicca, but the little she did know convinced her that Dorcas and Ambrose were prime candidates. They were worldly enough to have come in contact with it and they used to live in Sedona, a place known for fostering alternative belief systems. The black cat was an obvious cliché, but clichés existed for a reason.

The cat chose to follow her instead of Ambrose. Annie had a choice of sitting on an eye-popping purple sofa or an equally dramatic red wing chair. She decided on the sofa because she couldn't resist the color. By sitting on the sofa, she had a chance to study the stained-glass window to her right.

At first she thought it was an abstract design of red, purple, green and gold. Then the picture clicked into focus for her and she realized she was looking at a couple having sex—frozen in the act, captured in colored glass. The window wasn't visible from the street. Otherwise someone in town would have mentioned it to her before now.

While she was mesmerized by the stained glass and pairing that with the potential Wiccan ties of a couple who would choose such a decorator item, the black cat jumped up beside her and climbed into her lap.

"Hello, there." Annie stroked the cat's amazingly

soft fur and the cat began to purr. She'd always liked cats, but Zach hadn't wanted to be burdened by the demands of a pet. She didn't even know whether her apartment complex in Chicago allowed them.

"I see you've met Sabrina." Dorcas hurried into the room wearing stone-washed jeans and a black knit top. Her hair was perfectly combed, but it looked slightly damp.

"She's gorgeous."

"Sabrina's my alarm system," Dorcas said.

"A cat?"

"Not in the usual sense. She can't bark like a dog, but she tells me who is trustworthy and who isn't." Dorcas smiled. "You passed with flying colors."

"That's good to know. You have an unusual room here."

"I tend to go for unusual effects. Obviously I like color." Dorcas paused to gaze at Annie. "I also like sex, but I'd rather you didn't use that as a quote for your article. Ambrose and I are cautious about who we invite here."

"Yet you allowed me, a reporter, in. Why?"

Dorcas's amber eyes were nearly as mysterious as her cat's green ones. "I'd like to get to know you better."

Same here. Yet she wasn't here to ruin the Lowells' existence in Big Knob. "The interview isn't intended to be an invasion of privacy," she said.

Dorcas settled in the red wingback chair like a queen on her throne. "I know, or I wouldn't have agreed to it. But before we talk about Ambrose and me, tell me what you think about this Donald Jenkins business."

"I'm horrified. Whatever's out there could be part of an important scientific discovery. Naturally I want to break the story, but I also want to protect whatever it is and not let some trigger-happy guy destroy it. Do you have any ideas?"

"A few. Back to your story, though. Are you planning to get photographic evidence?"

Annie nodded. "Tonight. The sooner the better, considering what Jenkins has in mind."

"Assuming you manage to get a picture of her, what will you do with it?"

"You think the creature's a female?" Annie had trouble containing her excitement. "Did you see babies?"

"No, no. Nothing like that." Dorcas closed her eyes and muttered something under her breath.

"What aren't you telling me?"

Dorcas opened her eyes. "There's a great deal I'm not telling you." She leaned back in her chair. "Sabrina trusts you, and that's a good start, but when it comes to this lake creature, I'm not only concerned about what Donald Jenkins will do."

"There's another threat?" Annie should have known that word would get out. This was Big Knob, after all. "Who is it?"

"You. Your story in the *Trib*."

Annie immediately went on the defensive. "It's not as if I work for a tabloid. I'll handle the story responsibly."

"I'm sure you'll try, but—"

"I'll do more than try. Once I have a picture, I'll contact the scientific community before I make anything public. There will be security to protect the creature."

"I want to believe that's possible, but I can't imagine how you could control people's reactions. I realize what the story can do for your career, and I don't blame you for wanting to take advantage of that, but—"

"Dorcas, if we don't do something before Donald Jenkins shows up on Sunday with his gun, the creature could end up dead."

"Jenkins has complicated this, I have to admit."

Ambrose came into the room with a tray and set it on the polished black coffee table. "We won't allow Jenkins to kill it."

"How can you stop him?" Annie glanced up. "You can't patrol the lake all the time, and even if you could, there's no law saying he can't hunt a creature nobody else believes in."

"The first step is for you to take a picture," Dorcas said. "I agree with that part."

Ambrose looked at her. "You really think that's a good idea?"

"I do, especially now with Jenkins as a threat. The best time is around dusk, by the way."

"There's a problem with that," Annie said. "Tonight I've agreed to have dinner with Jeremy's parents."

Dorcas's eyebrows rose. "Really? I thought you had no intention of getting seriously involved with Jeremy?"

"I don't. This dinner is just . . . a courtesy."

"Considering the importance of getting your picture, why go?"

As Annie thought about why she'd accepted the invitation, she realized how mercenary she'd sound if she explained about Lucy Dunstan's offer to set up the interview with Clem Loudermilk. By accepting Lucy's terms, Annie had reacted like the kind of person who would do anything to get the story, which was exactly what Dorcas was afraid of. She wasn't that kind of person . . . was she?

"I'll cancel the dinner date," she said.

"Which will put Jeremy in an awkward position, no doubt," Dorcas said.

"Yes, and I hate that." Annie thought quickly. "But all his mother really wants is a chance to talk to me and see if there's any chance I'm interested in hooking up with her son. If I invite her to lunch today and explain myself, that might solve everything."

Dorcas beamed her approval. "Good thinking. Then you'll have a chance to take your picture this evening. Once you have that, let's talk again."

"Have you tried to take a picture?" Annie asked.

Dorcas shook her head.

"Why not?"

"I'm horrible with cameras. Every one I've ever tried to use self-destructs."

Annie frowned in surprise. "That's strange. Cameras are so easy to use these days. It's really hard to break one."

"Not if you're a wi—woman like Dorcas," Ambrose said.

There it was, Annie thought, proof of her suspicions. Ambrose had been about to call his wife a witch, and Annie knew he'd meant it as a compliment. A hard-nosed reporter would push the issue and find out whether these two were Wiccan.

She could see the headline now—FOR BIG KNOBS AND BROOMSTICKS, HEAD SOUTH. She could imagine the headline, but she couldn't picture her byline under it. Writing a story like that would be a betrayal of these two, and she couldn't do it.

Ambrose cleared his throat. "Who wants tea?"

"I do." Dorcas looked over at Annie. "Get your tape recorder out. Let's get this interview started."

An hour later Annie left, and Ambrose turned to Dorcas. "She's way too observant."

"You have to expect her to be observant. She's a reporter." Dorcas thought the interview had gone rather well. Annie might suspect all sorts of things, but her story would be about a couple who decided to leave the rat race and find happiness in a small midwestern town.

"Don't you think you're playing with fire, encouraging her to go out to the lake and get a picture? What if she actually succeeds?"

"Oh, she'll succeed. I'll ask Dee-Dee to pose for her."

"Ye gods and little fishes! She'll run straight to the *Tribune* with it, which means the world will be at our door with scientists, divers, tourists, even *more* hunters, which will endanger Dee-Dee and eventually George. Big Knob will be ruined and so will we."

Dorcas patted his arm. "Have faith. None of that is going to happen. Annie has more empathy than that."

"How can you be so sure? She's pretty ambitious."

"Sabrina likes Annie. When it comes to judging a person's character, I'll put my money on that cat."

Annie's plan for satisfying Lucy's curiosity worked perfectly, which meant that late afternoon found her climbing into Jeremy's Suzuki Samurai for a trip to the lake instead of having dinner with his parents. In order to increase her chances of getting a picture of the creature, she'd asked Jeremy if they could get an earlier start. He'd seemed happy to do that, and she suspected he was envisioning more time for sex. But she'd decided that they wouldn't have any sex, let alone more of it.

"You sure handled my mother," he said as they drove away.

"She called you?"

He looked sheepish. "Uh, I called her. She wouldn't tell me much. I just wanted to know . . ."

"Your mom's terrific. We had a wonderful lunch and a good talk."

"So she said." He tapped the steering wheel nervously. "I suppose you talked about me."

"Naturally."

"Did she bring the naked baby pictures? She wouldn't admit it, but I know she brought the naked baby pictures."

"You weren't completely naked. You had on six-shooters."

He groaned. "I'm going to kill her. Better yet, I'm going to go over there tomorrow and steal the photo albums so she can never do that to me again."

"She loves you, Jeremy. She wants you to find a nice woman and settle down. There's nothing wrong with that." Annie had to admit Lucy had mounted a good campaign. By the time their lunch conversation had ended, Annie had known for certain that Jeremy was a good catch.

The pictures had demonstrated what a cute baby he'd been, too, which meant he'd create cute babies of his own. Annie wasn't interested in a husband, but if she had been, Lucy would have sucked her right in.

As it was, she felt guilty for treating this great catch like a boy toy. He deserved someone ready for a march down the aisle and a couple of visits to the maternity ward. Annie was wasting his time with a sexual dalliance that would go nowhere.

Jeremy was ready for Ms. Right, not Ms. Commitment-phobic. Without being the least bit obnoxious, his mother had made that clear. She was looking out for her son's welfare, and Annie didn't blame her a bit.

"She could be more subtle about her hopes for me," Jeremy said.

"In a town like Big Knob, there's no point in being subtle."

He sighed. "Guess not."

"Listen, Jeremy, after talking to your mom, I've concluded that it's incredibly selfish of me to continue to have sex with you when I have no intention of taking the relationship further. I don't know how you imagined tonight would go, but I—"

"I selfishly hoped we'd have sex."

She ignored a delicious zing of sensation. "No, *I'm* the selfish one, for taking up time that you could better spend with someone more worthwhile."

He shifted gears and took her hand. "I'm not going to ask if you like having sex with me, because I know you do. I'm going to assume you'd like to have some more of it tonight."

"That's not the issue. This isn't about me."

"Then let's make it about me. Do you see another woman waiting in the wings, hoping you'll turn me over to her? If you don't have sex with me tonight, I'll have no sex whatsoever, unless it's solo, which we both know isn't a tenth as good as what we can accomplish together."

Talking like this was getting her panties wet, which was the exact opposite of her intention on this trip. "If we don't have sex, then you can start forgetting about what it's like having it with me and start imagining having it with someone else."

He laughed and squeezed her hand. "That's so illogical I don't even know where to start. I can't imagine how denying ourselves tonight is going to do either of us any good whatsoever. You'll have to find some other way to convince me."

She was out of ideas and ready to pull over and get naked right here and now. She squirmed in the seat. "Maybe we should drop the subject for now."

"Too hot for you?" His glance was teasing.

"Let's talk about the creature in the lake, instead. I'm absolutely serious about getting a picture of it. That's another good reason for not having sex. I don't want to be distracted."

"I know. But we're out here much earlier, so I think we'll have time to have sex first and do our monster watching later."

Her whole body tightened at the thought of having sex the minute they landed. "Please talk about something else."

"Right. The creature. My opinion hasn't changed, Annie. I still think it's some fake that a few kids built to scare whoever came out here this spring."

"Dorcas and Ambrose don't think it's kids." She looked straight ahead and slowly began to get control over her runaway libido.

Jeremy parked the Suzuki in the small lot next to the beach and glanced at her. "And what do they think it is?"

"I don't know." She gazed out at the lake, as if she could will something to rise above the surface. "They're being a little bit secretive, but they definitely indicated that they think it's alive and something worth protecting."

Jeremy snorted. "Then they're nuttier than I thought. It's gotta be kids."

"Then those kids need to be careful. Now they have Donald Jenkins to worry about."

"How come? What's up with him?"

She quickly filled him in on Bruce's conversation with Jenkins. "So whether it's kids or some rare creature who shouldn't be harmed, we have a problem."

"No, we don't. Tomorrow I'm talking to Jenkins. That idiot is not going to start impersonating Rooster Cogburn, not if I have anything to say about it."

Annie pictured hothead Donald with his hunting rifle and mild-mannered Jeremy with his flash drive. It didn't seem like a fair contest. "How can you stop him?"

"Easy. His entire operation at the dairy is computerized, thanks to me, and I'm the only one he trusts to work on his system. He definitely won't want to piss me off."

"I see." Annie's recently tamed libido stirred to life again. Maybe the flash drive was mightier than the rifle, after all. She found Jeremy's take-charge attitude sexy.

"And now that we have the Jenkins problem settled, let's head for our private beach to drink some wine and watch for monsters."

So he had brought the wine. She should have known

he would. The old Jeremy would have been more tentative, and she could have easily talked him out of having sex tonight. The new Jeremy knew what he wanted and how to get it. She might simply have to resign herself to wasting a little more of his time.

Chapter 18

Jeremy watched Annie paddle across the lake with sure strokes. She was a natural at this. He, on the other hand, was clumsier than hell today, which probably had something to do with the erection straining at his jeans.

Watching a woman paddle a kayak wasn't supposed to be a sexual turn-on, but with Annie, there was no predicting what would get a rise out of him. Most anything, apparently.

"You're doing great!" he called out for no particular reason other than to let off a little steam and make at least a verbal connection with her.

"Thanks. The exercise feels good."

He could imagine another exercise that would feel even better, but he wouldn't throw that suggestion across the lake where anyone might hear him. He still wondered if there were kids lurking in the woods waiting for the right moment to activate their underwater toy.

They'd need the light to fade a lot more before they tried anything. Too much brightness and the gears and pulleys would show. The setting sun reflected off the water and made it impossible to see below the surface. He tried a few times, and then gave it up as hopeless.

"The other thing I've been doing for exercise," Annie said, continuing the conversation, "is pitching."

"Don't tell me you talked the bride into risking her nails to catch for you." Jeremy wouldn't mind volunteering for the job. They could both get a little hot and sweaty and take a shower together.

"No chance," Annie said with a laugh. "But the old net's still up in the backyard. Mom never got around to taking it down, and I found a canvas bag full of softballs in the basement. I'd forgotten how much I loved pitching."

"You were great at it. The best Big Knob varsity ever had."

Despite the intervening years, he could easily conjure up an image of Annie standing on the mound, her blond hair pulled into a ponytail high on her head. Annie had campaigned for regular baseball pants instead of the shorts and knee socks girl softball players often wore. She'd won that battle, and the knees of her white pants were usually smudged with dirt from sliding into base.

He used to sit, mesmerized, as she wound up and delivered a fastball underhand with such speed that he could hear it pop in the glove. Very few could hit Annie's fastball.

"You went to the games?"

He told himself not to be insulted that she hadn't noticed. "Hey, softball games were a great chance to hang out with girls, so I—" In the middle of that big, fat excuse, he stopped himself. "No, that's not right. I showed up at the games because I grabbed every chance I could to be near you."

She didn't respond right away, just kept dipping her paddle in the water. "That's very flattering," she said at last. "But knowing how long you've felt that way really gives me second thoughts about us."

So much for honesty. Time for a little bullshit. "That was then," he said. "I was just a lovesick kid with no social life. I've moved beyond that." *Now I'm a lovesick adult with no social life.*

"You have changed, Jeremy." She paddled steadily toward the crescent beach that still held the rocked-in fire circle they'd built Tuesday night. "I suppose I have, too. It's almost as if you found the self-confidence I lost."

As Jeremy struggled to frame a response to that, his anger toward Zach resurfaced. No one had the right to sabotage someone in order to build himself up. Annie had definitely lost some of her assurance, and Jeremy blamed Zach for that. The guy had plenty to answer for.

"See, that's why I feel guilty," Annie said. "You make me feel better about myself, so I keep finding reasons to be with you when the kind thing would be to leave you alone."

"That wouldn't be kind. It would be torture." He was close enough to shore that he could pick out the indentations in the sand where they'd had sex.

"Torture sounds a little extreme."

"No, it's an understatement, especially now that we've . . ." He wasn't going to finish that sentence, not when he wondered who else might be out here.

He'd thought about that when he'd prepared for tonight's picnic, and he'd come more prepared than he'd been last time.

"At least we got across the lake without falling in." With one more stroke, Annie propelled the front of her kayak onto the sand.

"Falling in had its advantages." Jeremy beached his kayak next to hers.

She glanced over at him. "If we hadn't . . ."

"But we did. And the rest, as they say, is history." The lust he felt when he looked at her made him shake. Somehow he managed to get out of his kayak and pull both hers and his up on the sand without making a fool of himself.

The maneuver meant his feet got wet and hers didn't, which was the idea. The cold water should have helped cool his jets, but all he had to do was watch her take off the kayaking skirt and he imagined her taking off the rest of her clothes, too.

"Our firewood's still here." She picked up one of the branches they hadn't burned on Tuesday night. "Should we start a fire?"

"I'm not touching that line." Oh, but he wanted to touch her. He had to stay focused on his plan, though, if he hoped to have a relatively private encounter in a few minutes.

"Funny." She dropped the branch and pulled her purse out of her kayak. "I should take a picture of the kayaks, in case the editor wants some kind of photo spread when the story breaks."

Jeremy opened the back hatch of his kayak and removed the blue blanket and a canvas bag. "I suppose you'll have a halfway decent story even if it turns out to be a prank."

"Maybe." She took her camera out and dropped her purse to the sand at her feet. "Especially if it's a good hoax. But what I really want is an actual creature. That could make my career."

"I'd be all for that, but I don't think it's going to happen." He dragged the two-person tent out of the bag and began to set it up.

"You brought a *tent*?"

"Uh-huh." And he hadn't put it together in ten years, either. He wrestled with the flexible poles, trying to remember how they went. He should have practiced in his apartment before bringing the damned thing out here.

"You didn't say you wanted to camp out."

He glanced up and found her looking at him with interest and . . . affection. Yes, definitely affection. "We're not camping out. Not all night, anyway. This is for temporary privacy." One of the poles flipped up and nearly hit him in the face.

"Oh." She looked slightly disappointed.

"Would you have done that? Would you have camped out with me tonight?" He shoved the pole back into what he hoped was the right position.

"Probably not. The closer we get to Saturday, the more Melody flips out. Mom appreciates having me there to keep the lid on things."

"I'll bet." Another pole sprang apart. If he hadn't been wearing his glasses, it would have poked him in the eye.

"Can I help with that?" Laughter rippled through the question.

"Thanks. I've got it." Ramming the pole into the closest sleeve, he surveyed the tent. It looked lopsided, but they were burning daylight. He stood and dusted off his hands.

"Aren't you going to stake it down?"

Jeremy eyed the pile of metal stakes. Then he gauged the position of the sun in the sky. Dusk would be upon them in about thirty minutes. He didn't want to be responsible for Annie missing her photo op.

It wasn't as if they planned to sleep in this tent, so he decided staking it down would be overkill. "No," he said. "We'll hold it down with our bodies, anyway."

She met his gaze. "Oh, we will, will we?" Her voice had dropped to a sexy murmur.

"Yeah." He reached for her and pulled her tight against him so she could feel his erection. "We will." When she didn't resist, his galloping pulse raced even faster.

"Taking a lot for granted, aren't you?" Winding her arms around his neck, she tilted her face up to his in an open invitation to kiss her.

He intended to accept that invitation right now. "Maybe." He took off his glasses and tossed them on top of the canvas bag that used to hold the tent. "Any objections?"

She rubbed her body against his. "I raised all my objections earlier. You shot them down."

"I knew that debate class would come in handy." The feel of her body pressed ultraclose coupled with the scent of her perfume threatened to turn him into a clothes-ripping maniac.

He kissed her with more restraint than he'd thought possible. Then he lifted his head. "We have some extra time. Come into the tent with me."

"Are you sure there's room?"

"Just barely."

She wiggled against him. "Nice."

He groaned and allowed himself one more heart-stopping kiss. She matched him tongue thrust for tongue thrust and gasp for gasp. This was going to be so good.

She drew back slightly and gulped for air. "About the tent."

"What?" His brain whirled with the prospect of making love to her again.

Her words were punctuated with her rapid breathing. "Have you ever undressed inside one?"

He had trouble thinking when she slid against him like that. "I . . . don't think so."

"Ever undressed a woman inside one?"

He knew the answer to that. "No."

"Then let me go in first." She untangled herself from their frantic embrace. "I'll call when I'm ready." She nudged off her shoes, opened the tent flap and crawled inside.

Despite the sexual overload shorting out his neurons, he could see the wisdom in her plan. He was very ready now. He was beyond ready. If he waited for her signal and crawled into the tent with all his clothes on, he might never get them off in time.

He'd be wise to engage in some pre-tent maneuvers, starting with his shirt. As he tugged it over his head, he heard Annie rustling around inside the tent. Then her blouse sailed out through the flap onto the canvas bag he'd left in front of the tent.

In another moment, her bra followed. Forgetting all about his own undressing plan, he became mesmerized by the lace cups that had recently cradled her breasts. Heat surged through him, expanding his already throbbing penis.

Her khaki shorts joined the pile of clothes, and then came the scrap of material that had to be her white lace panties. The clothes lay there in mute testament to her nakedness, like the movie scene where a woman undresses behind a folding screen and flips each garment over the top edge so it hangs there in a seductive display.

"Ready," she called out.

He snapped out of his daze. Maybe he should have worried about stripping down on a public beach. Big Knob had laws about such things. But at the moment, he didn't give a damn. He shucked the rest of his clothes, grabbed a condom from the kayak, and crawled, naked and painfully erect, into the tent.

Dorcas lowered her binoculars and turned to Ambrose. "Our Jeremy is turning into quite the wild man. He just stripped in public."

"I'm gratified to see that you stopped watching once he did that." Ambrose sounded a touch jealous.

"I wasn't expecting a show, Ambrose." But once she'd realized what Jeremy intended to do, she had taken the time to notice that he was very well endowed. Just because she was married didn't mean she was dead.

"Lucky for him we're on the job so he has the privacy to run around bare assed."

"He's not running around bare assed. He was only exposed for a few seconds. Now he's in the tent with Annie." She tucked her binoculars in their case and turned back toward the house. "And it's all about bonding."

Ambrose hurried after her. "What was that?"

"I said it's all about bonding."

"Shucks. I thought for a minute there Jeremy had gone really wild and was into the velvet ropes and fur-lined handcuffs."

"Now who's the voyeur?"

Ambrose cleared his throat. "I find various sexual practices fascinating, that's all."

She stopped to gaze at her husband. "Are *you* interested in the velvet ropes and fur-lined handcuffs?"

"No, of course not. I mean, well, maybe. Sort of. Yeah."

Ambrose never failed to surprise her. She thought the whole concept was silly, but if he wanted to try it, she'd go along. "We couldn't exactly find that sort of thing in the Knobby Nook Department Store."

"No." He gave her a sly glance. "But I could order it online."

"Is that what you've been doing down at Click-or-Treat? Searching for sex toys?"

"Absolutely not. I research all kinds of things. You'd be amazed at what I come up with surfing the Internet. Simply amazed."

"I'm sure."

"It's true! I got the idea of putting the fluorescent orange parking cones across the entrance to the lake road from reading someone's blog."

Dorcas had to give him that one. He'd rushed to put up the cones after Jeremy and Annie had parked so no one else would come down to the lake tonight. "It was an excellent plan."

Ambrose put an arm around her. "Those aren't just parking cones."

"They look just like parking cones."

"They started out that way, but I've been working on them down in the basement. They're spell enhanced."

Dorcas had another unsettling thought. "Where did you get them, by the way?"

"They're doing a little road work on I-64. Something else I learned on the Net."

"You *stole* them?"

Ambrose looked indignant. "Absolutely not."

"I know they didn't give them to you. That's state property. How did you get them?"

"The workers were quite a ways down the road doing something with a dump truck and a grader. I didn't want to bother them, so I took the five cones I needed and tucked money under the windshield wiper of the flatbed truck they were stacked on."

Dorcas sighed and shook her head. She supposed it could be worse. She just hoped Chief Bob didn't come around asking questions.

"So let me tell you what these little hummers do." Ambrose warmed to his subject. "They not only block people from coming down that road; they extend a circle of protection around the perimeter of the lake." He swept his hand toward the trees.

"Hm." Dorcas had her doubts, but if the spell worked, that would be very convenient. "Maybe we could use them Sunday morning, to keep Jenkins from coming down here with his shotgun."

"I don't see why not." Ambrose looked extremely proud of himself. "And then there's the whole business about outdoor sex to consider."

"Excuse me?"

"I've been reluctant to have outdoor sex in the woods near the house. Too many people are attracted to the lake and the surrounding forest. It was bad enough when we had to worry about Big Knobians, but now there's Isadora gallivanting around. This is turning into a very busy area."

"I'm sure Isadora has better things to do than spy on us having sex."

"I wouldn't put it past her, not for a minute. In any case, it doesn't matter, because I've created a Safe Outdoor Sex Zone."

"Okay." Dorcas always worried about Ambrose's tendency to pile one spell on top of another. Sometimes that could backfire.

"And even better, the cones are pyramid shaped, so that gives them added power."

"No, they're not. They're round, which is why they're called cones. They're not called parking pyramids, Ambrose."

"That's correct. I had to modify them, flatten them on four sides so they would become pyramids. So anyone within that circle of protection will feel the power of the pyramid during sex."

"So I'll have pointed orgasms?"

"Very funny, Dorcas. Do you want to keep mocking my invention, or do you want to take it for a test drive?"

"Are you proposing we go into the woods and have sex right now?"

He gave her a long, lazy smile. "I most certainly am, my little muskrat."

Dorcas thought quickly. Jeremy and Annie were otherwise occupied, and Dee-Dee couldn't make her scheduled appearance until after they'd emerged from the tent and could concentrate on taking pictures. That left Dorcas with some time on her hands.

She really did enjoy outdoor sex, especially on a balmy night like this was turning out to be. The moon wasn't up yet, but when it did arrive it would be full. She could feel the full-moon energy beginning to pulse.

Or maybe it was the effect of Ambrose's orange parking cones. Now that he'd done the deed and procured those cones, she was curious about whether they'd make a difference during sex. If so, then maybe his protection spell was viable, too. A test seemed like a logical idea.

"Okay," she said. "Do we need to get a blanket?"

He took her hand. "The blanket's already spread

out under the trees, along with a bottle of wine and two goblets."

"We can't let ourselves get distracted. I need to come back here in about thirty minutes and cue Dee-Dee."

Ambrose squeezed her hand. "Then you might have to settle for two climaxes instead of three."

A promise of triple orgasms meant that Ambrose had oral sex on his mind. Dorcas didn't want to short-change herself on that. "Maybe I can spare forty-five minutes."

Ambrose laughed. "I thought you might begin seeing things my way."

Chapter 19

Before Jeremy was halfway into the tent, Annie reached for him, desperate to feel that skin-on-skin connection that set her world to rights. As if he knew exactly what she needed, he kissed his way up her body while he crawled in on his hands and knees.

She moaned as he paused to suckle her breasts. The sensation of his mouth there, right *there,* telegraphed a message straight to her vagina. She intended to keep that line open. Arching her back, she cupped her breasts in both hands and lifted them for greater access.

"Mm, nice." He became even more enthusiastic, tugging on her nipples with his teeth and burying his face in her cleavage. Then he licked every square inch of her breasts, moving her hands away so he could get the underside, too.

She breathed in the scent of musty nylon and sex. The heat of their bodies turned the inside of the tent into a sauna, and her skin grew slick from sweat and the swipe of his tongue. She wanted to come, and she was close.

She gasped for breath as she felt the first tightening. With a little urging, that spasm could become a full-blown climax. All he'd done was use his mouth on her breasts, and it was almost enough. If he'd just

slide his hand between her thighs . . . She willed him
to do that.

Or she could do it for herself. But no, she wanted
Jeremy's hand to be at the controls. She wanted those
thick masculine fingers probing, thrusting, driving her
over the edge.

Grabbing his right wrist, she positioned his hand
right where she needed it to be. He knew the moves.
As he continued to suck rhythmically on her breast,
he shoved deep with his fingers.

"Yes," she murmured. "Oh, *yes.*" Spreading her
legs, she lifted her hips and pushed against the firm
pressure of his fingers until her world erupted, show-
ering her with pleasure.

With a stifled groan, Jeremy released her breast and
toppled to his side, but he kept his hand right where it
was, his fingers buried to the hilt. The tent swayed and
righted itself. Annie rolled to her side, too, so that she
wouldn't risk losing that delicious feeling of his fingers
moving gently as the contractions slowly subsided.

His voice was low and husky. "Lost my balance."

"My fault." She dragged in air as her body trembled
in the aftermath. She'd been too involved with her
orgasm to realize he needed both hands to brace
himself.

"My right arm's stronger."

She opened her eyes to find him gazing at her.
"Next time I'll remember that."

He smiled. "Or I could strengthen my left arm."

"It's okay." Keeping her thighs closed over his
wrist, she reached up and traced the line of his mouth
with the tip of her finger. "You stayed upright just
long enough."

"Do I get my hand back? Not that I'm complaining.
I like where it is, but my other arm is pinned under
me and my options are limited unless you give me
more room to maneuver."

"I want you like this for a little while."

"You can have me any way you like."

"That's good to know." She felt a certain power knowing that she held him a willing prisoner. By stretching a little, she could wrap her hand around his penis. "Look what I found."

He clenched his jaw and air hissed out from between his teeth. "Careful. That rocket's in final countdown."

"I can tell. It feels like I've wrapped my hand around the grip of a softball bat."

"And if you keep squeezing like that, you'll hit a home run in about two seconds. Maybe we should get the—"

"Not yet." She had an idea, something she'd always wanted to try and never had the nerve to do. Somehow being cocooned in this tent made her feel safe enough to go for it. She let go of his penis. "I'm going to reposition myself. Lie still."

"Don't worry. I'm going to lie very still and think about something besides sex."

"You can do that while we're in here naked?"

He gazed at her. "No, but it sounded good. God, you're beautiful."

She could listen to that kind of talk all day. Every time he told her she was beautiful, she felt like Cleopatra and Helen of Troy rolled into one. "You can have your hand back now." She released her grip on his wrist.

"Now I don't want to leave." He caressed her, building the heat once again. "I came out here with this tent for a solo camping trip the summer between my junior and senior year. I remember distinctly having a wet dream about you that night."

"Do you remember the dream?" Amazing how he could work her up so quickly again.

"Typical male fantasy."

"Let me take a guess. It involved my mouth and your penis."

"Yeah." He brushed his thumb over her clit.

"That fits right into my plan." Reluctantly easing his hand away, she sat up.

"No, it doesn't. Believe me, I appreciate the offer, but I wouldn't last five seconds if you tried that."

"You might if I offer you a distraction. A job of your own, as it were." She watched his expression and had to hold back a smile at the way his eyes widened once he understood. "Let's do it," she said. "I've always wanted to."

"I'm worried that I'll come too soon."

"Don't worry." She grinned. "Be happy."

"Lady, if I were any happier, I'd be floating in the air."

"That could make this next event problematic. I need you grounded." Sliding her legs to the back of the tent, which was, coincidentally, where Jeremy's head was, she wiggled into position, not touching him yet. "If you're so worried, you can start."

"Great idea." As if he'd done it a hundred times, he hooked one of her thighs around his neck, settled his mouth on her sweet spot, and proceeded with enthusiasm.

Immediately her orgasm loomed on the horizon. It was just that fast. "Stop!"

His mouth stilled, but he couldn't seem to resist taking little swipes with his tongue.

She began to shake. "Jeremy, you're going to make me come and I haven't even—"

"Good." He picked up where he left off, and before she could draw another breath she was crying out and writhing in the grip of a second climax. Apparently this position worked for her.

Panting, she tried to regain control of the situation. "Okay, that was great. More than great. You should win a medal for that technique. Now it's my turn."

He blew warm air over the place he'd just scalded with his wicked tongue. "I thought the idea was doing it simultaneously."

"You didn't." She grasped his penis at the base and prepared to assault him with the same dedication he'd brought to his assignment.

"You told me I could start first."

"Well, now I'm starting." She slid her lips over the tip of his penis and was gratified to hear his quick intake of breath. But he recovered quickly and began using his tongue to good advantage once again.

He was good at that. Too good. The more he applied himself, the less she could concentrate on her goal. No, damn it, she was going to give as good as she got. With firm resolve she used her tongue on the sensitive underside of his shaft and felt him shudder.

He didn't abandon his quest, though. If anything, he became more focused. So did she. As the spring of tension tightened within her, she took him deeper into her mouth, increased the suction pressure and danced over his skin with her tongue until they were both thrashing wildly in the tent. It seemed as if each wanted to bring the other to orgasm without losing it themselves.

Talk about a win-win situation. It was the last coherent thought Annie had before she lost control. Jeremy clutched her with both hands and wouldn't let her go. She held him just as firmly.

As her orgasm spun through her like a giant pinwheel, she heard the deep rumble in his chest and finally tasted the salty evidence of his surrender. Then, with countless snapping noises that indicated poles coming apart, the tent collapsed.

Dorcas lay on her back on the blanket feeling the cool breeze caress her naked body. She gave thanks to the gods that she'd married a man who knew his way around a clitoris. Not every man did, but she'd been lucky enough to hook up with an artist in that regard.

The glass of wine had no doubt helped, and the

impending full moon had helped, too. Maybe even Ambrose's fluorescent orange parking cones had helped. She had to admit that their lovemaking had been more creative, so she might have experienced the power of the pyramid, after all.

She rolled to her side and stroked her husband's bare chest. "That was fabulous."

Turning his head, he flashed her a smile. "Thanks."

In that moment, she fell in love with him all over again. Yes, sometimes he was a pain in the butt, and she really wished he'd buy a Harley and get rid of that dorky red scooter, but he made love like an angel. And he loved her beyond reason, even after more than two hundred years. Not many could say that.

She wouldn't mind lying here a little longer so she could spend time basking in the afterglow of great sex. But she had obligations. "I need to check on Jeremy and Annie and see if they're out of the tent yet." She located her scattered clothes, shook off the pine needles, and got dressed. "It should be about time for Dee-Dee's close-up."

"I'm still nervous that Annie will take her picture and e-mail it to the *Trib*. After all, she's with Jeremy, who owns the only high-speed connection in town."

"Yes, but she promised to come to me first."

"And then what? She thinks we have to make Dee-Dee's presence public to keep Jenkins from shooting her. We can't tell her about my orange cones."

Dorcas paused to gaze at him. "What a brilliant idea! Of course we can tell her. We can say that we'll use the cones on Sunday morning to make it look like the road's closed."

"That won't work for very long." Ambrose started pulling on his clothes. "Knowing Jenkins, he'll ask around about the road and eventually figure out the cones are bogus."

"But he still won't be able to get in because of your spell, right? Exactly how will that work, by the way?"

Ambrose paused in the act of buttoning his shirt. "Um, I'm not sure. The spell book was a little vague on the reaction someone could expect if they tried to push through the invisible barrier, but I'm pretty sure they'd start puking."

Dorcas wrinkled her nose. "Lovely. But I guess it would keep them from continuing on, so that's good. Anyway, I think we can buy some time with your cones, enough time for Annie to fall completely in love with Jeremy. Let's go see how they're doing."

Moments later Dorcas peered through her binoculars and started to laugh.

"What's funny?"

"Take a look." She handed them to Ambrose.

He raised the binoculars and trained them on the beach across the lake. "What the hell? It looks like two badgers fighting in a gunny sack!"

"My guess is they made love with so much enthusiasm that they made the tent collapse."

"Should we be worried? Maybe they can't get out."

"I'm sure they can get out." Dorcas smiled. "They just might not want to."

Jeremy felt like an idiot, especially because Annie was laughing so hard. "I actually do know how to set up a tent, believe it or not." He struggled to prop the tent up with one hand.

"Oh, Jeremy, I'm not laughing at you." She gasped for breath.

"There's some other imbecile in here with us?" While holding the tent up, he tried to turn around without kicking Annie. They had to find the front flap in this pile of nylon if they ever expected to get out. "When I get home I'm burning this stupid thing."

"Don't you dare. I love this tent." She dissolved into another fit of giggles. "Can you imagine how everything looks from outside?"

He groaned. "I hope there's not a soul out there to

witness this disaster. If there is, I'll never hear the end of it."

"It shouldn't matter. It's getting dark, anyway, and—omigod, the creature! I have to get out there with my camera!"

"Trust me, I'm working on it."

He didn't seem to be making much progress, though. "Let me help." She crawled forward and felt around for the front flap.

"Annie, don't help."

She glanced sideways at him. "What's wrong?"

"Nothing, except you're on your hands and knees, completely naked, with your sweet little tush in the air. If you ever want to get out of here, I suggest you lie down flat on the floor of the tent and look unavailable."

If he'd expected her to instantly drop in the interests of obtaining her picture soon, he turned out to be wrong. Instead she gave him a hot look. "We've never done it doggy style."

He swallowed. "No, we haven't." And if he hadn't been single-handedly holding up the tent, he would have remedied that right now. He had a condom, which was . . . somewhere. That would be the other problem. The condom was lost in the folds of nylon.

She moistened her lips. "Would you like to?"

He didn't have to think about it. "Yes." How incredible that she was looking at him with such lust in her eyes. He had to ignore that look, because once the lust had faded, she'd be furious with him if he went along with her seduction and she missed her photo op.

Nobility sucked. "But we're not going to," he said. "For one thing, the tent would be in the way, and—"

"I mean after we fix the tent."

He groaned. "I want credit for what it's costing me to say this, but . . . what about your picture?"

Gradually realization must have dawned, because

her expression changed from lustful to chagrinned. "You're right," she murmured. "Thank you for reminding me."

"Believe me, I didn't want to." Maybe if he'd found a way around the tent problem so he could keep making love to her, she'd have decided a picture of the creature wasn't important at all. Maybe she'd have decided that her job at the *Trib* wasn't the end-all and be-all, either. But it was too late for second-guessing himself.

"I do give you credit," she said. "Not every guy would have said something."

He was already regretting opening his mouth. "So are you going to lie down flat so I can concentrate on getting us out of this sorry excuse for a tent?"

"I am." She scooted to her tummy and propped her chin on her folded hands. "Better?"

"Marginally. I think it would be almost impossible for me to have sex with you while you're in that position." He continued his exploration of the tent seams, looking for the zipper.

"There are probably ways. I was reading a sex manual once that suggested—"

"*Annie.*"

"Right, right. Think of me as a chunk of wood next to you in this tent. A fallen log. Of course, fallen logs could have knotholes."

"I swear to God you're driving me crazy. Where is that damned flap, anyway?"

"You have no idea how good that makes me feel, knowing how I affect you."

He wished it made her feel good enough to want to stick around, but she wasn't saying that. "Glad to be of service," he said. "Okay, I think I've found it. Yes! Here's the flap."

"Now what?"

"I guess we crawl out and get dressed."

"Uh . . ." She hesitated. "If you'll shove my clothes

through the opening, I'm going to try and dress in here."

"I don't see how you can. I know it's a lousy alternative to go out there naked, but I don't know what else to do. I'll stand guard if you want. Or you could make a run for the privacy of the woods."

She shook her head. "I'll just do the best I can in here."

"But—"

"I have to try, Jeremy. If somebody saw me running around naked on this beach, that would become the topic of conversation for the weekend, thereby upstaging Melody. Again. I've finally realized how much she hates all the attention I normally get compared to her. She deserves a chance to be the star during her wedding week."

"Then I'll go first and do my best to hold the tent up from the outside."

"Or maybe you could use your magic."

Well, yes, he could, couldn't he? He'd forgotten all about this magical ability he was supposed to have. He was so used to blundering through on his own that the magic tended to slip his mind. "I'm not positive it will work in this context."

"So putting up tents isn't something you practiced, then? I guess that makes sense."

"It isn't that." *It's that I don't have the faintest idea what causes the magic, so that means I have no control over it.*

"So you have practiced this?"

"Not exactly." Because he hadn't practiced diddly-squat, at least not that he remembered. "But I'll give it a try."

Closing his eyes again, he focused on the stubborn tent poles that he hadn't been able to beat into submission. He visualized them coming together again and supporting the tent so Annie could put her clothes on without danger of suffocation.

Then he took a deep breath. "Abracadabra."

As if someone had reversed time, the tent sprang back into place with a snap of canvas and a click of tent poles.

She gazed at him in awe. "How did you do that?"

"It's a mystery." The line, borrowed from *Shakespeare in Love,* came to him without a struggle. Once again, he was the man of the hour. The success of the trick filled him with the confidence that he could handle anything, even the challenge of convincing Annie to stay in Big Knob.

Chapter 20

Twenty minutes later, Annie sat on a piece of drift-wood and scanned the quiet surface of the lake as light slowly faded from the sky. Sitting down would give her a better chance of holding the camera steady. Off to her right an owl hooted, but other than that, the night was quiet.

"If this is a creature of habit, it should show up anytime now," she said. "I'm pretty sure this was about the amount of light we had on Tuesday night."

"Maybe." Jeremy stood behind her. "I was focused on getting us both out of the water safely, so I didn't notice exactly how dark it was." Sand crunched as he shifted his weight. "Are you getting hungry?"

"A little." Strangely, she wasn't starving the way she had been earlier in the week. Either her stomach had shrunk or all the good sex had taken her mind off food. She imagined that her cropped pants fit a little looser than they had last week, but that could be wishful thinking.

A couple of times she'd thought of climbing on her mother's scale, but she'd chickened out. A few years ago her mother had bought a digital one. There was no fudging with that puppy, no fooling with the dial or making the needle wiggle.

"Want some wine?"

"Not yet." Annie didn't want to take a chance that

her senses would be blurred in any way while she was trying for this once-in-a-lifetime shot.

"What if the thing doesn't show up? If it's operated by kids, which I still think it is, they would get a huge kick out of making you sit there all night for nothing."

"It's not kids," Annie said.

"You don't know that."

"I do know that." Annie watched the water for any sign of movement. "One of the reasons I'm a good reporter is that I have an instinct for the big story. My editor doesn't believe that yet, but once I show him this picture he will."

"Are you sure your camera will do the job? There really isn't much light."

"It should be good enough for now. I'm sure the *Trib* will send a team of photographers out here eventually." Annie felt a pang of guilt when she said that. Dorcas didn't want a team of photographers descending on whatever lived in the lake.

Logically, though, the creature couldn't live there indefinitely without being discovered. Deep Lake wasn't big enough or remote enough to allow the creature its privacy. Someone would break this story, and that someone might as well be Annie.

Jeremy scuffed his shoes against the sand. "Assuming you get a picture, what then? Are you going to e-mail it to Chicago tonight?"

"Maybe." She could tell Jeremy was getting restless standing around doing nothing. "I promised Dorcas I'd bring her the picture before I sent it anywhere."

"How does she feel about making it public?"

"She's concerned about the welfare of the creature. So am I, for that matter. I think it needs some sort of official protection. And I realize the tourist angle needs to be managed properly, too."

He blew out a breath. "Look, I know how much you want this to be real, but it's not."

"Dorcas and Ambrose think it is, and they—"

"They're newcomers, Annie. They haven't lived here all their lives like we have. I've been swimming in this lake every summer since I learned to dogpaddle. So have you. So has half the population of Big Knob. Don't you think someone would have seen this thing in the water before now?"

She gazed silently out at the lake, willing something to break the surface and dispute Jeremy's excellent logic. Nothing did. She sighed. "I know what you're saying. I've thought those things, too."

"When you desperately want something to be true, your mind can play tricks on you. Take it from someone who knows."

She had an uneasy feeling he was referring to his daydreams about her. Maybe they were equally deluded. He had fantasies about her staying in Big Knob, and she had fantasies about breaking the biggest story in Indiana history, maybe even in U.S. history. What a pair they were.

"I think we should eat," Jeremy said. "This could be a long wait."

For nothing. He hadn't actually said that, but he didn't have to. Annie got the message that he thought they were on a wild-goose chase. Or, more accurately, a wild-lake-creature chase.

"You go ahead," she said. "I'll sit here a while longer. I still think it'll show up."

"Then I'll bring you a sandwich while you wait."

"No, thanks. I'll eat later. I don't want to have this thing pop out of the water when I'm holding a sandwich. I'll probably be freaking out, and I just know I'd try to take a picture with the sandwich."

"I can hold the camera while you eat."

She turned sideways and glanced over her shoulder so she could look at him when she responded. She didn't want him to take offense when she rejected his offer. "That's very gallant of you, but—"

"If I took the picture, you couldn't legitimately claim the photo credit."

"That's right." She searched his expression for irritation, and there was none. "I guess you really do understand how important this is to me."

He nodded. "That's why I don't want you to get your hopes up, because I guarantee it'll turn out to be a hoax."

Annie surveyed the lake again. "Tell you what. I'll wait until it's completely dark. If I haven't seen anything by then, I'll give it up as a lost cause."

"Deal." He sounded happy about that.

"In the meantime, please start eating."

"I don't have to do that, but I can get everything ready. Sure you don't want me to bring you a glass of wine?"

"Absolutely sure." She felt like a party pooper, but unless she made a reasonable attempt to get the picture, she'd regret it the rest of her life. "But you go ahead."

"Can't."

She swiveled around to look at him again. "Why not?"

"The whole point of this wine is to share it with someone you . . . care about."

As she looked into his eyes, her heart did a somersault. *Close call.* He'd almost said something that would ruin the next two days for both of them. She refused to think in terms of the *L* word, and he'd be wise to do the same.

"Just give me another twenty-five minutes." She kept her tone light, as if she hadn't picked up on what he'd nearly let slip. "Then we'll tackle that bottle."

"Right." He turned away quickly, as if not wanting to maintain eye contact. Then he got very busy getting the food out of the kayak.

She didn't blame him. She'd given him no hope for

a future together, and now it seemed possible that he was falling in love with her. He shouldn't allow himself to do that. She'd carefully kept a tight rein on her emotions, and there was no way she was falling for Jeremy.

Sure, she had tender feelings for him, but they weren't unmanageable. She was keeping her eye on the prize. Damn it, where was the creature? She concentrated so hard on the lake that it seemed as if the surface began to shimmer.

Blinking, she looked again. Were those ripples, or was her imagination playing tricks on her? Jeremy had said that desperately wanting something to be true could mess with your mind.

Yet the water seemed to be moving, although in the dim light she couldn't swear to it. There was no breeze, either. She held her breath, hoping the movement wasn't something she'd conjured up.

But if the water really was moving . . . her mouth went dry with unexpected fear. She'd been so eager for a creature to rise up so she could get the picture of the century, and yet she knew nothing about it. The long, snakelike neck might enable it to reach out and snatch her from the beach the way orcas went after seals.

Dorcas hadn't seemed afraid, but maybe Dorcas didn't have sense enough to be afraid. Maybe she'd only watched from the safety of her kitchen window, while Annie, determined to become a star reporter, had decided to get up close and personal with something huge and potentially dangerous.

Yes, those were definitely ripples, and bubbles, too. Big bubbles. Her heart beat furiously as the ripples increased in size, spreading out as if someone had thrown a giant stone into the lake. She opened her mouth to call Jeremy, but nothing came out. Her throat muscles refused to cooperate.

Jeremy was rustling around unloading things from

the kayak, no doubt setting up their dinner. A pop told her he'd opened the wine. Surely he would look up in a minute. Surely he would see that there was *something out there.*

She began to shake. Why hadn't she suggested watching from Dorcas's kitchen window and using a telephoto lens to get the shot? Why in God's name was she sitting here, paralyzed with fear and quivering so much she'd never be able to take a decent picture?

A triangular head broke the surface about a hundred yards from where Annie sat. She nearly passed out. Her heartbeat surged in her ears like ocean waves, and cold sweat trickled down her backbone. *Shit.*

The head was about the size of the middle section of a curved sofa her mother used to have. Despite Annie's terror, her reporter's brain noted the size and shape so she'd be able to write about it later. That was assuming there would be a later, and she wouldn't be pulled from the beach and gobbled up before Jeremy even missed her.

The creature's head came out of the water like a periscope balanced on a very long neck, and a dank scent filled the air, like the smell of a mudpack she used to get back in the days when she had regular spa appointments. As the head turned, Annie caught the flash of luminescent eyes. It saw her. She was sure of it.

Maybe the thing was considering whether to make her the evening meal. She couldn't see its mouth very well in the darkness, but no doubt the jaws were big enough to close right over little Annie. She prayed it was a vegetarian.

Apparently it was treading water, because the ripples continued spreading outward. Annie told herself to take heart from that. If the creature wanted to attack, it would have done so by now.

Her teeth chattered, and she clenched her jaw. *Time*

to take a picture, girl. But what if she raised the camera and the creature mistook it for a weapon? Come to think of it, the camera was the only weapon she had. Maybe she could blind it with the flash, or throw the camera, aiming for a spot between its eyes.

No, her best defense was to get up and run, dragging Jeremy with her. This thing had never been seen out of the water. Annie was guessing it had flippers, not legs. Running would be a great idea. But she couldn't seem to move.

The creature lowered its head and looked at her more closely. Annie held her breath, wondering if it would suddenly strike. But nothing happened. Then, in a motion that Annie couldn't believe was happening, the creature winked.

That couldn't be right. This was some sort of monster. Monsters didn't wink. Then the creature did it again.

What a surreal moment. This huge thing that was like nothing the world had ever seen before was *communicating with her*. Did it want to be friends? Or was the wink merely a technique to make her drop her guard, a distraction so the creature could pounce and devour her?

Whether it was a predator's trick or not, it worked well enough that Annie lost some of the terror that had gripped her when the creature's head had appeared. Slowly she raised the camera. When she had the head and neck framed on the digital screen, she pressed the button. The flash went off, and the creature slid immediately beneath the water.

"Annie?" Jeremy's feet crunched through the sand as he walked back toward her. "Did you just take a picture?"

She pointed to the ripples and the bubbles in the water. "There." Her voice sounded funny, sort of like a rusty hinge.

"Something came out of the water?"
She nodded.
"Was it the creature?"
"Yes. And it winked at me."

Annie had insisted on taking the picture immediately to Dorcas, so Jeremy had recorked the wine and packed up the food. They'd paddled quickly across the lake, and then Dorcas had invited them both to sit in the kitchen and eat their sandwiches while they discussed this so-called lake monster. Jeremy left the wine in the Suzuki, hoping he and Annie would drink it later.

Sitting in the Lowells' kitchen, he gazed at Sabrina perched on the kitchen window ledge. That cat saw a lot of what went on around here. If only she could talk, she might be able to clear up everything.

For Jeremy, the wink had clinched it. Somebody was playing an elaborate trick, and he was furious. Whoever it was had scared Annie to death at first and was now stringing her along and making her believe she was on the trail of a major news story. He hated that kind of joke and wanted to find the perpetrators and wring their necks.

"It's not a great picture," Annie admitted as she sipped some tea and looked at the small screen on the back of her camera. "I wish I'd had the presence of mind to take a bunch of them."

"It's a beginning," Dorcas said.

Ambrose brought over mugs of tea for himself and Dorcas. "I'm sure you were rattled by the whole experience."

"Which was the point, wasn't it?" Jeremy put down his sandwich. He was too angry to eat it. "I used to think this was the work of teenagers, but they wouldn't have a reason to be this mean to Annie. I'm wondering if it's some woman from her class who's harboring a grudge over the Miss Dairy Queen pageant. Or some guy who's pissed because she wouldn't date him."

Dorcas shook her head. "We saw the lake monster before Annie came back to town."

"Doesn't matter." Jeremy had his theory and he was sticking to it. "They were practicing, making sure the thing worked right."

Dorcas and Ambrose exchanged a glance.

"Don't worry about convincing Jeremy," Annie said. "He's not going to believe this monster is real, and that's the end of that."

"I can't believe the three of you think it is!"

"Well, we do." Annie gazed at him steadily across the table. "And we need to decide how to handle it. I'm counting on you to take care of Donald Jenkins and his plan to shoot it."

"Don't worry, I'll take care of Jenkins. Besides threatening him with loss of computer service, I'll also let him know it's a fake monster and he'll look like a fool if he starts shooting up something made of fiberglass and rubber." He sent a pointed look across the table at Annie. For an intelligent woman, she was being incredibly gullible.

Without commenting, she turned back to Dorcas and Ambrose. "The picture I took isn't enough to convince my editor, but I'll have a tough time getting a better one. The next two nights will be taken up with the rehearsal dinner and the wedding."

Dorcas blew across the top of her mug of tea. "Maybe you could stay over a few more days."

Jeremy turned to stare at Dorcas. *Damn it to hell!* It wasn't a jealous Dairy Queen candidate or a loser guy, after all! Dorcas and Ambrose had created the monster as part of some elaborate matchmaking scheme. The monster was designed to keep Annie here until she finally fell for him.

That kind of manipulation was just wrong. Sure,

he'd love for her to hang around, but not because she was being tricked into thinking she had a big story to investigate. He couldn't believe these two would be that devious, but now it all made sense. He had to do something.

"I might be able to stay until dusk on Sunday," Annie said. "But if I didn't get something definitive then, I'd have to head for Chicago. I could come back the weekend after that, though."

Unable to stand this nonsense another second, Jeremy stood. "Ambrose, could I talk to you privately in the parlor?"

"Uh, sure." Ambrose pushed back his chair.

Jeremy didn't wait for him. He strode down the hall, breathing fire. This was the most ridiculous situation he'd ever been in, and it was ending as of tonight.

Ambrose followed him into the parlor. "You seem upset."

"Close the door. I don't want Annie to hear this."

Eyebrows lifted, Ambrose quietly shut the parlor door.

"I know what you and Dorcas are doing, Ambrose. Stop it. Stop it right now."

"I don't know what you mean."

Jeremy clenched his hands, wanting to hit something or someone. But he wasn't the kind of guy who punched people out, so he kept his hands at his sides. "Oh, yes, you do. Just how far were you planning to carry this matchmaking scheme, anyway?"

Ambrose looked startled. And guilty as hell.

"The scary monster," Jeremy said. "Which one of you dreamed that up? I'm not even going to ask how you built it, but I'm thinking there's evidence down in the basement."

"There's no evidence because we didn't build it. The monster is real."

"Bullshit. How dare you toy with Annie like that? How dare you dangle the prospect of a story that could make her career as a reporter, when the whole thing's a fake?"

Ambrose cleared his throat. "Jeremy, it's not fake. I know that's hard to believe, but—"

"Oh, come on! This is me you're talking to, not Annie. Give it up, Ambrose. Stop the charade. I figured it out the minute Dorcas suggested Annie could stay on longer to get a better picture. You're using the monster to get us together, aren't you?"

Ambrose scrubbed a hand over his face. Then he gave Jeremy a resigned look. "Sort of."

"Aha! I knew it!"

"We did think the lake monster would help keep Annie around, which would further your cause. You two belong together, Jeremy. Anyone can see that. You both need more time to find it out."

Pain sliced through him. He thought they did, too, but not like this. Not if she had to be tricked into it. "I'm telling her." He started toward the door.

"No, wait." Ambrose caught his arm. "I swear we didn't create that monster."

Jeremy shook him off and opened the door. "So you bought it on eBay, instead. Who cares? You're manipulating her, and that's about to stop." He hurried down the hall. "Annie!"

"Jeremy, hold on." Ambrose followed quickly behind him. "Don't go ruining—"

"Annie." Jeremy stood in the kitchen doorway, breathing hard. "Dorcas and Ambrose are using this monster thing as a way to keep us together. Ambrose just admitted it."

Dorcas leaped up. "He *what*?"

"I'm sorry, my love." Ambrose edged past Jeremy. "He figured it out when you suggested Annie stay on a while longer. I couldn't lie to him."

Annie looked stricken. "The monster's a fake?"

"Yes!" Jeremy shouted.

"No!" Dorcas and Ambrose said together.

Annie stood and turned to Dorcas. "I trusted you."

"And you can still trust me. It's true that I was hoping the investigation would keep you in Big Knob a while longer. I'd like to see you and Jeremy get together."

Annie's body grew rigid. "So you built a lake monster? I suppose I should be flattered that you'd go to all that trouble, but instead I feel stupid that I fell for it."

"Annie, let's go home." Jeremy stepped into the kitchen. "No need to prolong this."

"Wait." Dorcas put out her hand and touched Annie on the shoulder. "Annie, please believe me. There is nothing fake about that lake monster. You saw it. Jeremy has never seen it. Trust your gut on this one."

Annie gazed at Dorcas for a long time. Then she sighed. "I probably should go home. I'm supposed to be here to help my sister get married, not carry on an affair and chase after lake monsters, real or imagined." She walked toward Jeremy.

He started to put his arm around her, but she waved him off and left the room. His heart ached in a way he'd never thought it could, as if someone had carved a hunk out of him. He glanced back at Dorcas and Ambrose. "Thanks a whole hell of a lot."

Chapter 21

Dorcas loved her husband, but at the moment she wanted to stick his head in a steaming caldron. "What in Hades did you think you were doing, telling Jeremy we were using the lake monster for matchmaking purposes?"

"But we are, Dorcas."

"He didn't have to know that!"

Ambrose sighed. "Yes, he did. The guy's smart, and he was already suspicious about Dee-Dee. He's drawn the wrong conclusions about her, but the right ones about us. He confronted me. I couldn't lie about it."

Hands on hips, Dorcas faced him. "Oh, for Hera's sake, you don't have to lie. You just avoid telling the truth. Don't you pay attention to the news? Politicians do it all the time."

"Which means I'd better not run for office."

"Now, there's a true statement. You wouldn't get elected in a million years." Dorcas blew out a breath and walked over to the window where Sabrina still sat looking out at the lake. As Dorcas stroked her cat, she tried to rein in her temper. Fighting wouldn't help anything.

"I'm sorry, Dorcas." Ambrose sounded miserable. "I'm not as quick on my feet as you are. That's why I like the Internet. I get to think about how I want to say things before I actually have to say them."

Just like that, her anger melted away. She'd known it was a bad idea the minute Jeremy had asked for a private conversation with Ambrose. She should have used a bit of magic to create a diversion. A stack of plates could have tumbled out of the cupboard or she could have opened the kitchen window and invited in the bat who had made a home under the eaves.

"It's okay." She turned back to her husband. "I probably shouldn't have told Dee-Dee to wink at Annie. I thought it would be endearing, but the wink is exactly why Jeremy thinks the lake monster's not real. It's not all your fault, Ambrose."

"Right," he said eagerly. "Like if you hadn't suggested to Annie that she might want to stay longer, Jeremy might never have come to the conclusion that . we—"

"But it's mostly your fault." Dorcas had thought Jeremy would be delighted with her suggestion that Annie should hang around. She'd thought he'd either agree or have the good sense to keep his mouth shut.

Instead he'd assigned himself the role of protecting Annie from being misled. Noble, maybe, but in the process he'd truly shot himself in the foot. When she'd left a few moments ago, Annie had sounded as if romance was the last thing in the world she wanted to think about.

"What do we do now?" Ambrose asked.

"I'm not sure." Dorcas walked over to the kitchen table, tasted her tea and made a face. "Cold."

"I'll brew more." Ambrose went to the stove and picked up the teakettle.

He really was a good man, she thought. In some ways Jeremy reminded her of a younger version of Ambrose. Ambrose had been an earnest young man, too, and he would have been willing to fight anyone who threatened her happiness.

Dorcas understood exactly why Jeremy was upset, and it only proved that he was very much in love with

Annie. Annie was probably also in love with Jeremy, although she would go to any lengths to deny it. The campaign was so close to success that Dorcas couldn't see herself throwing in the towel yet.

"Dee-Dee is still the answer," she said. "But I'm not sure Annie's willing to listen to me anymore on the subject."

"Or me." Ambrose turned on the flame under the teakettle.

"That leaves only two other people who know about Dee-Dee and could talk to Annie about the lake monster. I can't send Maggie, because she works for us and Annie could easily think we'd instructed Maggie to parrot the company line."

"Tell me you're not going to sic Isadora on her."

"You have a better suggestion?"

"Anybody would be a better suggestion than Isadora."

"We don't have anybody else." Dorcas measured a half inch with her thumb and forefinger. "We're *this* close, Ambrose. We can't give up, not when we have one more move on the chessboard."

"But do we? I don't see how you can manage a meeting between them. Isadora can't very well knock on the door and announce she's there to talk about the lake monster."

"No, the meeting has to be more coincidental, and it should be away from Annie's mother's house. That place will be chaos tomorrow. Let me think . . . I have it! I'll do a spell tonight that affects some of the flowers Gwen's planning to use for the bouquets."

"Like what?" Ambrose poured hot water into the teapot.

"I'll give the roses large, inappropriately shaped stamens."

Ambrose chuckled. "You definitely have a flair for this kind of thing."

Dorcas smiled at the praise. It was true, if she did

say so herself. "Gwen will call Annie over to figure out what to do, and I'll ask Isadora to drop by on some pretext."

"You won't need a pretext. Just tell her about the stamens and she'll be there in a New York minute."

"I know, but she needs an excuse for going there in the first place." Dorcas tapped a finger against her chin. "Maybe she'll decide to get a bouquet of flowers to give the Danburys because they've been so hospitable."

"Hospitable? Last I heard, Madeline was threatening to short-sheet her bed."

"Then Isadora will be buying a bouquet to win Madeline over."

"Fat chance of that ever happening. She'd as soon flip Madeline off as give her flowers. Besides, why would Isadora agree to help? Except for viewing your magically enhanced stamens, there's nothing in it for her."

Dorcas was well aware of that. It was the biggest flaw in her new plan. "I'll think of something," she said.

Annie didn't feel like talking on the way over to her mother's house. She didn't know who to believe, Jeremy with his indisputable logic or the mysterious Dorcas, who had been secretly matchmaking even though Annie had told her she wasn't in the market. Believing Jeremy made the most sense, because he had nothing to gain and something to lose by insisting the monster was a hoax.

Still, she couldn't picture Dorcas and Ambrose going to so much trouble to hook her up with Jeremy. If the monster already existed, they might not be above using it to their advantage, though. That much she could imagine.

That left her mulling over her encounters with the monster. The first time she'd been too scared to notice much, but the second time had been more controlled. She'd evaluated the size of the head and neck. She'd cataloged what the creature smelled like. The monster was extremely lifelike.

A professional model builder for a movie studio could have created something that realistic, but Annie had a tough time accepting that Dorcas and Ambrose were that talented. She supposed they could have hired someone to create it, but why? Surely not for the single purpose of fostering a romance between her and Jeremy.

"I've thought about this some more," Jeremy said as he pulled up in front of her mother's house. "It's a stretch to think Dorcas and Ambrose concocted this scheme just to keep you in Big Knob."

"I know." She turned to him, relieved that he'd come to the same conclusion. "No matter how someone did it, they'd have to spend lots of hours and quite a bit of money."

"Exactly." He met her gaze.

"So you think the lake monster's real?" If he did, then he might help her document it. The timing would be tricky with all the wedding events, but maybe they could figure out something. She wanted him on her side.

"No, I don't think it's real."

Her hopes plummeted.

"I hate that look of disappointment in your eyes, Annie. I wish I could agree that it's a real monster and you're sitting on an amazing story, but I can't."

"I wish you could, too." It would mean more than he knew to have him with her on this. "So what's your theory?" She was almost afraid to ask.

"I think Dorcas and Ambrose are after money."

"Money? That's the last motive I'd connect with them."

"People aren't always what they seem. Think about it. They create this monster and make sure you see it.

You're a reporter for a major newspaper. You break the story, and suddenly everyone heads for Deep Lake. Who owns the house closest to the lake? Who could set up a gift shop and a restaurant right next to the main attraction?"

Annie shook her head, rejecting the whole scenario. "That doesn't fit. Not with their personalities, and certainly not with their religion."

"What religion? I didn't see anything religious in their house."

"I'm almost sure they're Wiccan."

Jeremy frowned. "I'm not clear on what that is."

"I'm not totally up on it, either, and you have to promise not to spread this Wicca thing around town."

"I don't know why I should feel an obligation to protect them. They've been manipulating you, and I—"

"Maybe." She touched his arm, the first contact she'd made since they'd climbed in his Suzuki. "And I appreciate how you came to my defense. I do."

Jeremy looked down at her hand. "Why do I feel as if this is the kiss-off speech?"

Reluctantly she removed her hand. "I don't think we're on the same page anymore."

"You think this monster is for real? It's not! It's a huge scam, and that might be your big story, how an enterprising couple moved into a small town and figured out a way to turn their lakeside property into a gold mine."

"Sorry, I don't buy it."

"Because you think they belong to some religious group you don't completely understand? That's crazy, Annie. You don't have enough information to make that kind of judgment."

She could hear his frustration, and she didn't blame him. He was a logical guy, and logic was on his side. "Dorcas told me to trust my gut, and that's what I'm going to do. I think the monster is real. I'm still not sure how I want to deal with that, but I'm going forward on that assumption."

Jeremy turned away and stared out the window. "And I think you're playing right into their hands. I hate to see you do that."

"I'm sure you do." She swallowed. This was more painful than she'd anticipated. She'd counted on having him as an ally, but that wasn't realistic. She'd enjoyed having him as a lover, but that wasn't fair. "Jeremy, it's been . . . I've had a great . . ."

"Please." He opened his door. "Save the speeches." Then he came around and opened her door, because he was, no matter what the circumstances, a gentleman.

She managed to get out of the car without touching him. The night had cooled, and there was a hint of rain in the air. "We still have to pretend to be on good terms for the next two days."

"I can do that. It's not like I hate you, Annie."

"I don't hate you, either." A nearby streetlamp gave just enough light for her to see how terribly sad he looked. She resisted the urge to throw her arms around him and say that she agreed with him about the monster and the larcenous plans of Dorcas and Ambrose.

But she didn't agree, and besides, she and Jeremy had no future, anyway. Maybe emotionally parting ways now would make things easier in the long run. She hoped so, because this moment was excruciating. They'd come to mean a great deal to each other in the past few days. Even though she'd known it couldn't last, she'd avoided thinking about what it would be like to end everything between them.

"You'll talk to Donald Jenkins?" She didn't like asking, but Jeremy had the most leverage.

"I said I would."

"Right. I didn't mean to question your word."

He rubbed the back of his neck and gazed up at

the cloudy sky. "And I didn't mean to bite your head off for bringing it up. In the beginning, I told you I'd take what I could get. But I suppose it's human nature to be greedy."

"Jeremy, if I had any intention of getting involved with someone, you would be the—"

"Don't say it." His look was forbidding. "You'll only give me hope that someday things will change."

She nodded. "That would be cruel, to leave you hanging with a maybe."

"Yeah." His voice was husky.

"Good night, then."

"Good night, Annie."

Clutching her purse to her chest, she ran up the walk. So she was crying. So what? A few tears never killed anyone.

As Jeremy unloaded the kayaks and the picnic supplies, he came across the corked bottle of wine. He didn't want it, but it was good wine. Someone should get use out of it, and delivering the bottle gave him an excuse to see Sean.

He thought Sean should hear his reservations about Dorcas and Ambrose. After all, Maggie worked for them, and Sean wouldn't want her dealing with a couple of shysters. He wondered if Sean had heard anything about this so-called lake monster. Time to find out.

First he let Megabyte out to do her business, and then he called Sean. With a couple like Sean and Maggie, a person was wise to call before dropping in. Just because Jeremy's sex life was in the dumper didn't mean he had to interrupt Sean's.

But Sean answered and told him to come on over and bring his dog, too. Sean had just finished the baby's room and wanted to show it off. Jeremy hoped he'd be able to work up some enthusiasm for the renovation project.

Maybe Megabyte would be enthusiastic enough for both of them. His dog was pathetically happy to be going anywhere with him. Ever since Annie had hit town, Jeremy hadn't paid much attention to the Irish wolfhound. Fortunately Meg was an easygoing dog, but Jeremy felt guilty all the same.

Driving up to Sean's house, Jeremy thought again about what a transformation Sean and Maggie had made to the old Victorian. They'd taken a run-down wreck and made it into a home. With lights glowing from the tall windows and fresh paint on the gingerbread trim, it looked like a picture in a magazine.

Jeremy's apartment above Click-or-Treat was fine while he was baching it, but he couldn't expect a wife to live there with him. He certainly couldn't expect Annie to do that. But of course that didn't matter, because Annie wasn't even a slight possibility.

Seeing Sean and Maggie's house made him finally admit that he'd had unrealistic dreams when it came to Annie. No matter what she'd said or he'd told himself, he'd begun weaving fantasies about marrying her. He'd even started thinking about what houses were available for sale in town. Talk about delusional.

Grabbing the bottle of wine, he climbed out of the Suzuki and let Megabyte out before mounting the steps to the front porch. Sean must have heard him coming, because he opened the door before Jeremy could use the brass knocker.

Sean took one look at the bottle of wine, the cork sticking partway out of the neck, and rolled his eyes. "This can't be good. That wine was supposed to be for you and Annie."

"Yeah, well." Jeremy shrugged and handed it over. "You can put it to better use, I'm sure."

"That's a damned shame." Sean stood back so Jeremy and Megabyte could come in. "What happened?"

Jeremy glanced around. "Is Maggie here?"

"As a matter of fact, she's not. She and Denise Woolrich are on their way back from Evansville. There was some shoe sale going on over there, and Maggie was going to look for cribs, too."

Jeremy raised his eyebrows. "You two will look a little silly if the process takes another year or so."

Sean looked down at the floor, and when he glanced up again, there was a cat-who-ate-the-canary look on his face.

"Maggie's pregnant?"

Sean seemed to be smiling all over. "That's what the home kit says. Of course we want her to get the official word from Doc Pritchard. She has an appointment tomorrow."

Jeremy clapped him on the back. "That's great, just great. Congratulations."

Sean held up the bottle of wine. "She won't be able to have this, and I wouldn't feel right drinking it in front of her when she loves it so much. You might want to find someone else to give it to."

"We can figure that out later. Right now Megabyte and I want to see the baby's room."

"Right this way." Sean led Jeremy and Meg through the living room with its cozy overstuffed furniture and up the massive staircase to the second floor. A light was on in the small room next to the master bedroom. "Maggie did most of the actual decorating. I just finished putting in a window seat, and she'll need to get a cushion for it, but otherwise the room's done."

Jeremy followed Sean into the tiny room, and Megabyte came too. The three of them nearly filled the space, but a kid's room didn't need to be big. Jeremy's chest tightened as he realized how far he was from this point. He hadn't known he wanted kids, but seeing this room made it obvious he did.

The walls were pale lavender, and one of them was covered with a fantasy mural of what looked like elves and fairies dancing in the clearing of a mist-shrouded forest. Wildflowers bloomed everywhere and a couple of unicorns could be seen through the trees.

Jeremy studied it. "This is pretty. Who did it?"

"Maggie. She insisted on painting that wall with all sorts of magic stuff. I didn't know she could draw, but she's great at it. I think there's even a cute little dragon in there somewhere. Whatever turns her on is fine with me."

Jeremy gazed at him. "Has she said anything to you about something living in Deep Lake?"

"You mean that creature Donald Jenkins keeps yapping about? Not really. I'm sure she thinks like everyone else, that it's Jenkins's way of getting attention."

"Have you ever asked her if she's seen anything in the lake?"

Sean studied him. "You were just there, weren't you? Did you see something?"

"No, but Annie claims she did. And Dorcas and Ambrose both think there's something there."

"Really." Sean rubbed his jaw. "When did they say this?"

"Apparently Dorcas admitted as much to Annie on Wednesday night during the bachelorette party. Then tonight, Annie snapped a picture of it, and we took it over to Dorcas and Ambrose so they could—"

"Whoa, whoa. You're saying there's an actual picture of this thing? Who has it now?"

"Annie, and it's a lousy picture. But that's not the point, Sean. The point is that I'm convinced Dorcas and Ambrose either built the creature or had someone do it for them. Somehow they operate it from their house, and they're trying to get Annie to write it up for the *Trib*."

Sean looked at him as if he'd lost his mind. "That makes no sense, buddy. Why in hell would they do something so ridiculous?"

"To create a Loch Ness monster type of tourist attraction and clean up. They're situated in the perfect spot to have the restaurant, the gift shop, the—"

"No, that's not like them. They would hate that kind of commotion. I don't know where you got that idea, but I can't believe they would come up with a scheme like that."

"Or you don't want to believe it because Maggie works for them."

"Yes, she sure does, and she loves those two people. She wants them to be the godmother and godfather to our baby."

"You might want to rethink that."

Sean shook his head. "Not if I want to stay married, I don't."

"Hey, I know it could cause problems with your situation, but something's going on down there."

"Apparently, if Annie took a picture. Look, I don't know if there's really some creature in the lake or it's kids playing a prank, but I can guarantee that Dorcas and Ambrose are not trying to build themselves a Loch Ness monster tourist business."

Jeremy sighed. "Okay, but when the shit hits the fan, don't say I didn't warn you."

"If the Lowells are scam artists, I'm Bugs Bunny."

Jeremy gazed at him. "What's up, doc?"

Chapter 22

After a quick cup of coffee, Annie drove over to Beaucoup Bouquets. Skipping breakfast wasn't a hardship. When Zach had bailed on their marriage, she'd eaten every carb in sight, but ending her affair with Jeremy had left her with no appetite at all. Lousy feeling, but a great weight-loss program.

She had to handle this flower situation quickly because she was due at the Loudermilks' house at ten. She couldn't imagine what was going on with the wedding bouquets, but Gwen had sounded frantic. She'd stammered something about odd-shaped growths on the roses, and yet they'd looked fine earlier in the week. They were in a greenhouse, so that ruled out weather issues and bugs.

Annie's mom had asked her to handle this crisis because Melody was embroiled in a fight with Bruce over the rehearsal dinner. The Millers, aka Bruce's parents, didn't want to pay for wine to be brought over to the Hob Knob from the Big Knobian Tavern, and Melody was insisting on serving wine. Bruce had offered to pay for it, but Melody wouldn't let him because she thought the wine issue was a sign that his parents didn't really support this marriage.

In other words, typical day-before-the-wedding drama. Annie remembered having a huge fight with

Zach over whether she'd wear his mother's pearls with her wedding dress. His mother had been reluctant, but Zach had pushed the issue. Annie had worn them against her better judgment, and of course the string had broken halfway through the ceremony, scattering pearls everywhere. She should have taken it as a sign.

By some miracle she hadn't run into any of Zach's relatives so far this visit. Then again, she hadn't spent much time in the shops on the square, which is where most people met. She hadn't yet eaten a meal at the Hob Knob or browsed through the Big Knob Bookstore. Tomorrow morning the female members of the wedding party would gather at the Bob and Weave for the hair and nail appointment, and Annie would get all the town gossip then.

Chances were excellent that she and Jeremy were one of the hot topics of conversation. She dreaded the questions that were bound to come her way, but she'd stirred up the gossip, so she couldn't complain about it. Less than three days to go. She planned to stay until dusk on Sunday and hope to hell she got a decent picture of the lake monster. Then she'd blow this popcorn stand.

She parked her car in front of the flower shop, which was located on the corner of Fourth and First. As she got out, she glanced across First and noticed Maggie Madigan headed into Doc Pritchard's office. If she remembered correctly, everyone expected Maggie to get pregnant any day now. Maybe she had and was going for her first checkup.

Annie felt an unexpected pang of regret. The idea of having kids had been pushed way to the back of her mind. Zach hadn't wanted a pet, let alone a kid, and Annie had been content to focus on her TV career.

Now that she'd ruled out marriage for the time being, kids were really a long way off. Most likely

Melody would present their mother with the first grandchild. That should make Melody happy, to finally get the jump on Annie in something.

A bell rang over the door when Annie opened it, and Gwen hurried in from the side door that led to the greenhouse.

Gwen looked frazzled. "I've never seen anything like this," she said. "Every single white rose is affected."

"Affected how?"

"You'll have to come and see." Gwen pushed open the door into the greenhouse and led the way down the aisle, which was lined with every kind of flower imaginable.

Besides being a riot of color, the greenhouse was warm and moist. No wonder Gwen's complexion always looked so good. She spent her days in a sauna. Annie breathed in the mixture of sweet floral scent and damp potting soil. She could understand the appeal of this job.

"Look at this." Gwen stopped in front of the white roses that Melody had chosen for her bouquet.

Annie glanced at the roses and gasped. "What part is that called? I learned it in biology, but I—"

"Those are the stamens, the male part of the flower."

"They certainly are . . . male." Annie couldn't believe what she was seeing. Three-inch, penis-shaped stamens poked boldly out of every rose. "Is it a mutation?"

"I have no idea. I came out here this morning to water and there they were, flashing me. If we were going with, say, orchids, it might not be so obvious, but usually you don't even see the stamens on roses until the buds are fully opened. These are still semi-closed and—"

"Erect."

Gwen nodded. "Yeeesss."

"How about going the Lorena Bobbitt route?"

"Tried that." Gwen held up a wilted rose. "This happens. I'm glad you're here instead of Melody. She'd flip."

"Yes, she would." Annie felt a giggle coming on, and she swallowed it. "I guess you'll have to substitute a different color."

"She was very specific about white."

Annie glanced at her. "Yes, I know, but you can't have her walking down the aisle with those things"— she paused to clear her throat—"waving in the breeze."

"Probably not." Gwen stared at Annie and her face grew pink. Then she clapped her hand over her mouth as a snort of laughter escaped.

That was all it took. Annie lost it, too, and they both cackled like fiends, alternately holding their stomachs and pointing at the offending flowers.

"I would give *anything* to see that," Annie said. "Can you imagine? Everyone stands up and turns around as the bridesmaids come in, and then they look at the bouquets and see . . ." She dissolved into laughter again.

"The Full Monty!" Gwen wiped the tears streaming down her face. Then she held up her hand. "Shh. I think I just heard the shop bell."

"Hello!" called a woman from the shop. "Anybody here?"

"I'll be right out," Gwen called back. She took a tissue out of her apron pocket and blew her nose. "I haven't laughed so hard in ages. But I still have a small problem, here."

"A three-inch problem."

"Stop it." Gwen grinned, and then she hiccuped. "I have a customer to deal with. I'll be right back."

"I'll wait here. And think of solutions." Once Gwen left, Annie reached out to touch one of the stamens, and damned if it didn't seem to enlarge. She touched another one, and the same thing happened. What in hell was going on?

She heard Gwen in the shop explaining to the customer that she had no white roses available. How weird that someone would come in this morning and ask for them. Annie thought she recognized the voice, but she couldn't remember from where.

"Let me at least look at them," the woman said, and Isabel walked through the greenhouse door. Today she wore a long purple skirt slit up to midthigh and a low-necked white peasant blouse. "Oh, hello, Annie. I didn't realize you were here."

Gwen followed close behind Isabel. "Annie's helping me figure out what to do about the white ones, which we'd planned to use for the wedding bouquets tomorrow." She avoided looking at Annie. "I could fix you a nice arrangement of yellow, or perhaps pink."

"I prefer white. I—oh, *my*." Isabel's eyes widened. "How in the world did you accomplish that?"

"I didn't," Gwen said. "It happened overnight."

"Indeed." Isabel moved closer. "I like it."

Annie and Gwen exchanged a glance and looked quickly away again.

Isabel reached out toward one of the roses and Annie caught her wrist. "You might not want to do that."

"Why not?"

"It makes them get bigger."

Gwen gasped. "Bigger?"

"Watch." Annie let go of Isabel and touched one of the stamens. It quivered and enlarged.

Behind her glasses, Gwen's eyes looked enormous. "Oh . . . my . . . God."

"This is my kind of flower!" Isabel stroked a stamen and laughed. "Give me two dozen."

"I'd rather not sell them," Gwen said.

"Not sell them? Are you insane? Figure out how you did this and you could make a fortune."

"That's just it. I don't know what happened, and there could be some kind of plant weirdness going on."

Isabel shook her head. "You need to loosen up, girl. I sense some sexual repression going on."

"This has nothing to do with sex." Gwen sent a pleading glance in Annie's direction. "Whatever it is, I need to keep it contained in this greenhouse."

"She's right," Annie said. "If she lets these go out the door, she could have the Department of Agriculture breathing down her neck. She's a small business owner. She doesn't need that kind of grief."

"Oh, all right." Isabel glanced around the greenhouse. "Let me have some of those yellow ones, then. Just a dozen in whatever cheap vase you can find."

"All right. You might be more comfortable waiting in the shop."

"I'm sure I would. And Annie will come keep me company, won't you, Annie?"

"Uh, sure." Annie was willing to make conversation if it kept Gwen's customer happy.

Leaving Gwen to gather what she needed for the arrangement, Annie and Isabel walked back into the shop. Isabel took a seat on one of the stools beside the counter where Gwen kept all the catalogs. Annie decided to stand.

"You're a reporter, aren't you?" Isabel said.

"That's right."

"Then I assume you might be interested in something I saw out at the lake a couple of nights ago."

Annie's heart rate picked up. "Like what?"

"A large amphibious sort of creature, bigger than an elephant, with a long neck and a triangular head."

Annie longed to have Jeremy here, but then again, he probably wouldn't believe Isabel, either. "Yes, I would be interested." She did her best to not show how much.

"You've seen it, too, haven't you?"

Annie decided there was no point in pretending ignorance. "Yes. Twice."

"What do you plan to do about it?"

"Ideally I'd like to get the story without ruining the town or jeopardizing the safety of the creature."

Isabel nodded. "That's a tall order, chicky. You want fame for yourself but you want to keep things low-key for Big Knob and the Nessy. I don't know if that's possible. Something's got to give."

Annie thought so, too. She'd spent part of her sleepless night trying to work out a solution. But until she had a picture that confirmed the existence of this thing, no solution was necessary.

Knowing that Isabel had seen the creature brought up a new possibility, though. "Is that why you made the trip from San Francisco? Did you come here to see whatever is living in the lake?"

"In a way."

Annie looked more closely at her. Maybe it was the long skirt and the peasant blouse, but suddenly she knew who Isabel looked like. "You probably haven't noticed, but you look a lot like the bronze statue we have on the square."

"Funny, isn't it?" Isabel met her gaze. "And it's not a square. It's a pentagon."

"Everyone knows that, but you can't hold a Fourth of July picnic on the town pentagon."

"I suppose not."

Then Annie realized something else. The symbol for Wicca was a five-pointed star with a circle around it. Big Knob was laid out that way, but there was no circle. Or was there? She remembered the walking path that linked each point of the star.

Nothing fit together yet, but she had a feeling it would if she could only put some time into research. Unfortunately, she had another story to file for the *Trib* and wedding activities that would suck every spare minute. But she was here now with Isabel, and she might as well take advantage of the moment.

"What do you know about Wicca?" she asked.

"A few things." Isabel turned to a catalog and began flipping pages.

"I've figured out that Ambrose and Dorcas are Wiccan."

"Bully for you." Isabel kept her attention on the catalog.

"I'm betting you are, too."

"Maybe."

Excitement churned in Annie's stomach. She was on to something. "Somehow the lake monster ties into all this, but I haven't figured out how."

Isabel looked up. "You're the reporter. You figure it out." Then she slid off the stool and walked out of the shop.

Moments later Gwen hurried in, a vase of yellow roses in her hand. "Where'd she go?"

"She left." Annie took the vase from Gwen. "Let me buy these. My mother needs a lift."

"Annie, you don't have to do this. It won't be the first time somebody stiffed me."

"I want the flowers, okay? And as for the problem with the white roses, I say use your palest pink and she won't even notice the difference. If she does, tell her it's the light."

Gwen nodded. "That's what I'll do, assuming the white roses still look the same tomorrow as they do today."

"Why wouldn't they?"

"I don't know, but they got that way overnight. Maybe they'll go back to normal overnight, too." She glanced at the front door Isabel had recently gone through. "What do you make of her?"

"Honestly? I think she's a witch."

"Hey, she's not that bad. She's actually kind of funny."

"I'm not saying she's not a nice person. I'm saying she's Wiccan."

"Wiccan?" Gwen scrunched up her face. "Is there really such a thing?"

"Oh, yeah." Annie was becoming more convinced with every hour that went by.

"I can't believe Wiccans would be in Big Knob."

Annie decided not to mention her theory about the five-pointed star with the walking path around it. "Well, they are," she said. "And I'm beginning to think they've been here a while."

Jeremy thought he was functioning pretty well on no sleep. He'd managed to keep everything running smoothly at Click-or-Treat plus run interference on several wedding issues. He'd stepped in and offered to pay for the wine that was becoming such a bone of contention for the rehearsal dinner. That allowed Bruce to tell Melody that it was taken care of and Bruce wasn't paying for it.

Then he'd straightened out a misunderstanding with the Evansville DJ who'd been hired for the reception. The DJ had somehow come to the conclusion that he should play all Hawaiian tunes during the reception. Jeremy had recommended Top 40, some eighties classics and a few fifties numbers. The DJ could throw in an occasional Hawaiian tune if he felt the need.

Big Knobians would respond to "The Hawaiian Wedding Song" and "Blue Hawaii," but that was about it. Hawaii was like a foreign country to them, and they would want the tunes they heard on the radio, tunes they knew how to dance to.

Jeremy was damned proud of himself for functioning so well, considering he'd tossed and turned all night. But then he'd faced his biggest challenge of the day. Annie came in to write her story about Clem Loudermilk and his famous bras.

She gave him a tentative smile as she walked in the door. He smiled back as if his heart wasn't in shreds and his ego hadn't been reduced to the size of a termite. He might be left with nothing else, but by God, he'd hold on to his pride.

"How'd the interview with Clem go?" He was proud of his casual tone, which struck exactly the right note, as if they were old friends, not lovers who'd just broken up.

"Very well. I have a picture of his first working model of the bra."

"Is that the one he strapped on a life-sized statue of Venus de Milo?"

"That's it." She shifted her purse to her other shoulder. "Have you seen it?"

"No, not many people have. Sean built them a sunroom earlier this year, so he told me about it. He says there's this marble reproduction of Venus in the corner of the living room, and she's wearing a bra."

"Yep. That statue wearing the bra is the focal point of the living room. The statue's in this dark nook and he's trained a couple of black lights on it so the bra seems to glow."

"Yeah, Sean mentioned that." Jeremy became aware that this wasn't the greatest topic in the world. Thinking about bras made him think about Annie's underwear, something he'd never have the pleasure of removing again.

"I guess if you make several million dollars on something, you want a way to display it."

"I suppose so." Money wasn't a good subject, either. It made him remember Dorcas and Ambrose, who were no doubt imagining how they'd spend all the tourist dollars they were about to earn.

She gazed at him as if she could read his mind, and maybe she could. He'd never been good at being inscrutable. Everything he thought showed on his face.

"I need to get busy," she said. "After this I'm making the place cards for the reception, and I have to get them done before the rehearsal this afternoon."

"How's Melody?"

"A pain in the butt. How's Bruce?"

"Bruce is getting nervous, like most guys do the day before they get married." But Jeremy knew that if he had the chance to marry Annie, he wouldn't be nervous. He would be too busy dealing with extreme happiness to be nervous.

"It'll be good to get this over with."

"Yeah." He said that because it was expected of him, but he didn't really think so. Once the wedding was over, he'd have no more reason to hang around with Annie. Much as it hurt to do that, he'd rather hurt than not see her at all.

"I'll take the terminal over there, the one beside your dog."

"That's fine. Want some coffee?" He'd been living on the stuff, so she might be in the same condition.

"That would be great." She walked over, stepped around Meg and sat down.

He decided to bring her a cookie, too. She looked thinner, probably the result of the way she'd starved herself this week. What a dumb thing to do, when she'd looked so gorgeous the day she'd arrived.

He set the mug of steaming coffee and the napkin with the cookie on it by her right hand. "On the house, by the way."

She glanced up from the screen, and there were smudges of weariness under her blue eyes. "You don't have to do that, Jeremy."

His heart squeezed at the softness in her expression. She was heading for disaster with this lake monster business, and he had no idea how to stop it. At this point he had no proof of anything.

"I like doing things for you," he said.

Her gaze softened. "I know. You're a good guy."

"Annie, I—"

"I wish you'd stop being such a good guy. I wish you'd act like an SOB." She swallowed and looked away. "And I really need to write this story." She swiped at her eyes and turned back to the screen. "Thanks for the coffee."

"Anytime." He walked away, feeling helpless. There had to be something he could do to protect her from getting hurt. There just had to be.

Chapter 23

The rehearsal wasn't quite as painful as Annie had been afraid it would be, partly because there were so many people around. All the practice was focused on the processional because Melody couldn't seem to get the pace right as she walked down the aisle with her mother. They ran through the recessional once, which was the only time Annie had to walk arm in arm with Jeremy.

During those necessary moments of body contact, she'd concentrated on the lake monster and Jeremy's belief that Dorcas and Ambrose were greedy opportunists. That helped to keep the sizzle factor at bay when she touched him. Other than that, she did her best not to look at him at all. The slightest glance in his direction made her want to jump his bones.

How she could have become obsessed with him in such a short time was beyond her. Even Zach hadn't affected her that way, and everyone had agreed he was hot. Zach had thought he was, too, which might have been part of the problem. Jeremy didn't think he was hot, which made him all the sexier.

Wine was served at the Hob Knob during the rehearsal dinner, but Annie didn't have much. The wine had to be poured into water glasses because the Hob Knob didn't have any stemware, so consequently nobody could gauge how much wine they'd had and most of the wedding party got very happy except Annie and Jeremy. Annie pretended to sip with each toast, and she smiled until her cheeks hurt.

At last this particular ordeal was over, and she drove her tipsy mother and sister back home. About an hour later, as she crawled into her childhood twin bed in her old room upstairs, she heard a ping against the windowpane. Another ping followed, and another.

She walked over to the window and looked out to find Jeremy standing below, tossing pebbles at her window. The tail of his dress shirt hung out and his hair looked as if he'd been driving around town with all the windows down in his car.

She shouldn't have been glad to see him, but she was. Her whole body was glad, responding with a flush of pleasure that tingled. Grabbing a terry bathrobe from a hook on the back of her bedroom door, she put it on over her nightgown and hurried downstairs.

By the time she opened the door and stepped barefoot out on the cool painted surface of the front porch, he was on the steps, and he'd already taken off his glasses, as if he fully intended to kiss her. Her lips warmed at the thought.

"Tell me to go away." His voice sounded rough, almost angry. He crossed the short distance between them and stood inches away from her. "I have zero control over my need to see you, but you're probably in better shape. So tell me to leave, and I will."

"I don't want you to go away."

With a groan he swept her up in his arms and covered her mouth with his.

He tasted of desperation, and she kissed him back so hard she would probably have bruised lips in the morning. She didn't care, didn't let up. Grinding her pelvis against his, she signaled she was ready, so ready.

Before long he'd untied her bathrobe and had both hands up under the hem of her nightgown. She climbed him like a firehouse pole, and he helped by cupping her behind and lifting her up against his erection.

Panting, he drew back from the kiss. "We can't do this here."

She ignored the fact that they shouldn't do this at all. Wanting him had eliminated all her good sense. She dragged in a breath. "There's a hammock out back."

"Someone might hear us."

"We'll be quiet."

"We can try." Hoisting her more firmly into his arms, he managed to get down the steps without dropping her.

"I can walk."

"No. You're barefoot." He staggered around the side of the house.

"You'll throw your back out."

"Ask me if I give a damn." He made it over to the large canvas hammock, which hung between two oak trees in a shadowy part of the yard. Somehow he'd managed to avoid the softball net where she'd practiced her pitching every morning.

He paused beside the hammock and struggled for breath.

"You can put me down."

"Not yet."

"Second thoughts?" She thought she might die if he had second thoughts. She wanted him inside her. Five minutes ago wouldn't have been too soon.

"No." He was still breathing hard. "Just figuring the logistics. It's dark back here and I've never done it in a hammock."

"Dark is good."

"I know, but I don't want us to dump. Not after the tent thing."

She cupped his face in both hands and kissed everywhere she could reach. She was dizzy from wanting him. "Put me on top. I'll take it from there."

"Good plan." He turned his back to the hammock.

Still holding her firmly, he sat on the edge of the canvas. The ropes groaned under their weight. "This is probably a terrible idea, but I'm too far gone to care. Hang on and I'll get us horizontal."

"Just for good measure, say your magic word."

"God, why not. Abracadabra." Then he flipped back into the hammock, taking her with him. It swung wildly and the ropes made a whining sound as they sawed back and forth, but Annie and Jeremy stayed in.

Even before the hammock stopped swinging, she'd moved to one side so she could unzip his pants. "Condom." She knew he wouldn't have made the drive without one. Not Jeremy.

"Here." He fumbled in his pocket, pulled one out and ripped open the packet.

By then she'd freed his glorious penis, so she grabbed the condom and rolled it on.

He blew out a breath. "Sweet Lord, please hurry."

"I'm hurrying." Either necessity or magic must have given her dexterity, because she handled the job in record time. Then slowly, so as not to start the hammock swinging again, she eased one leg over him.

"What can I do to help?" He sounded as if he might be talking past a clenched jaw.

"Nothing. Just lie there." Rising above him, she untangled her nightgown from around her legs with one hand while bracing her other hand on his shoulder. It was a tricky maneuver, but well worth the effort once she was in a position to slide down over the object of her desire. And slide down she did, with a moan of delight.

He gasped and his muscles clenched. "I will not come," he muttered. "I will not come."

"Yes, you will." Both hands braced on his shoulders, she eased upward and slid down again.

He groaned and grasped her hips. "I mean not yet. Hold still."

"I can't." She moved restlessly in his grip, surprised by how strong he was. He held her so that she couldn't ride him, but she could rock gently back and forth, which was good, so very good. She moaned as her body tightened deliciously.

His fingers pressed harder. "Stop." His chest heaved. "I want this to last more than two minutes."

She gazed down at him but couldn't see his expression in the dim light. With great effort, she held herself rigid. Even then, her blood sang through her veins, urging her to reach for her climax. She'd never felt so sexually hungry in her life.

"You make me crazy," she murmured.

"Good." He moved one hand around until his thumb brushed her clit. "Let's see if I can make you even more crazy."

She closed her eyes as he began to fondle her. "You can." She moistened her dry lips. "I'm no challenge at all."

"Oh, you're a challenge. Just not this kind." He wiggled his thumb faster.

She drew in a breath as her orgasm hovered. "Are you saying I'm easy?"

"Easy to love."

If she hadn't been about to come, she might have warned him not to use that word. But she didn't have the breath to talk right now, and when her orgasm hit, she had to focus on not yelling like a banshee. Ah, that was *good*. Writhing in his grip, she leaned forward and gulped for air.

He made a sound low in his throat, which she took to mean that he was closer to a climax than he wanted to be. She forced herself to stop moving.

"Thanks," he muttered, his voice like footsteps on gravel.

"I think I should be thanking you." She leaned down a little more so she could touch her lips to his. "How're you doing?"

His breath was warm and sweet against her mouth. "I'm right on the edge."

"You might as well give in." She ran her tongue over his lower lip.

"I wish we were in a bed."

"Want to come up to my room?"

"No." He sucked in air. "That's all we'd need, to have your mother catch us together in your bedroom."

"How did you know which one was mine, by the way?"

"Zach told me once. He tried to figure out how to climb up, but there aren't any trees close enough."

"I wouldn't have let him in."

Jeremy ran his hands up her bare back. "But you'd invite me up?"

"Uh-huh." She nuzzled his neck under his shirt collar. "I was a virgin then, but I'm not anymore."

"Virgins are highly overrated." He moved his hands under her nightgown so he could cup her breasts.

She sighed as he massaged her breasts. He had such a deft touch. "Wanna come up and share my twin bed?"

"Sure, but I'm not going to."

"Why not?"

"Because."

"Because why?"

He drew his hands out from under her nightgown and cupped her face. "Because I can't afford to get that close to you." He kissed her gently. "I'm too close already."

She understood. He wasn't talking about how their bodies were intimately joined right now. He was talking about a deeper connection, one that he was fighting for all he was worth.

"Then let me make you come," she said.

"Yeah." His voice had grown husky again. "I'd like that."

Clutching his shoulders, she rose up so that she had

better leverage. "Don't yell," she said softly. Then she rode him hard and fast. As she could have predicted, her second orgasm came sailing in when he was obviously on the brink himself. Gulping back her cries once again, she surrendered to the inevitable, knowing he would climax without any more prompting from her.

When he did, he bucked beneath her and tossed his head from side to side, but he muffled his response behind tightly closed lips. He didn't want to wake the neighborhood, and neither did she. This was their own private moment. No one needed to know about it but the two of them.

Much later, he carried her back to the porch and set her gently on her feet. Then he brushed the hair back from her face. "I'm glad you didn't send me away."

"So am I. I hated the way we'd left things between us."

"Now we can remember this, instead."

She knew what he was saying. Tomorrow night the wedding festivities would go on until all hours, and as maid of honor and best man, they were obligated to stay until the bitter end. There would be no time for stolen moments like this. Their affair was officially over.

Sure, he could visit her in Chicago, but why? Even if she eventually decided to remarry, it wouldn't be to a guy who wanted to stay in Big Knob for the rest of his life. More contact would only make them miserable.

Grief brought a lump to her throat and she couldn't speak. Giving him a feather-light kiss of good-bye, she hurried inside before she spoiled the tender moment with sobs of regret.

Inside the magic circle drawn around the cauldron bubbling in their basement, Ambrose danced his jerky little cha-cha to Frankie Avalon's "Venus." As usual, Sabrina performed her kitty cha-cha right behind him while Dorcas looked on and tried not to laugh at the goofy pair. Ambrose had talked her into a scrying session to invoke the goddess of love and ask for her help in getting Annie and Jeremy together.

The session was definitely needed. Dorcas had taken heart when the steam rising from the cauldron had revealed Annie and Jeremy getting it on in a hammock. But after that they'd parted so sadly that Ambrose had decided to dance his cha-cha some more and stir up another batch of love vibes.

That meant replaying the Frankie Avalon tune, something that Dorcas could do without, but Ambrose believed in the power of Frankie. He was convinced that Frankie's last name, Avalon, was no coincidence and that he was somehow linked to that magical island of fairies and King Arthur legends. Half the battle was believing in your magical methods, so Dorcas sprinkled her favorite herbs in the cauldron and Ambrose danced to Frankie.

"They're splitting up," Dorcas said. "Who are we following?"

"Jeremy." Ambrose made a rolling motion with his hands as part of his cha-cha. Then he flung his left hand in the air and, after that, his right. "Let's see where he goes when he leaves Annie's house."

Dorcas concentrated on the image of Jeremy's Suzuki driving down dark roads. She knew this route. "He's coming here. No, wait, he's turning down the lake road. Maybe he wants to wallow in memories. Lovesick guys do stuff like that."

"Uh-oh." Ambrose stopped dancing so abruptly that Sabrina bumped into him. She meowed in protest and swatted his leg with her paw. "The cones are still there," Ambrose said.

"He's getting out and moving them."

"This is not good, Dorcas. The spell's in place."

"Can you do something? Unspell those cones?"

"Not that fast. I'd need my staff, and there's a special incantation I got out of the *Book of Shadows*. I'd have to look that up, and . . ." He stared at the misty picture. "This is not good."

"Oh, dear." Dorcas put a hand to her mouth. "Poor Jeremy. His rehearsal dinner just came up."

"What a shame. But at least we know the spell works." Ambrose brightened. "That's a plus. I really wasn't sure it would. I did a fine job on that spell, by golly."

"While you're busy patting yourself on the back, maybe you can tell me how you propose to instill a longing for romance in a man who's whoopsing his cookies?"

"It does present a problem."

"Once he leaves, I insist you go down there and remove the spell. The lake is a romantic rendezvous spot for those two, and they might even find themselves coming back after the wedding tomorrow night to work out a solution. Throwing up hardly ever furthers the cause of true love."

"I suppose not." Ambrose picked one of Sabrina's hairs off his trousers. "Uh, maybe you should contact Annie and warn her not to come to the lake tomorrow night, just in case."

"Why would I do that?" She peered at her husband as a dreadful possibility occurred to her. "You can remove the spell, can't you?"

"I, um, think so."

"Ambrose Lowell! You're never supposed to cast a spell you aren't certain you can remove. What about when summer comes and everyone drives down to the lake? We'll have Big Knobians barfing all over the place."

"I can remove it. I think."

"You'd better hope you can. Which reminds me, you will remember to turn on the exit sign on Highway 64, right? We'll have out-of-towners galore coming in for the wedding. The belly dancer was a minor glitch, but if it's off again tomorrow, the wedding could be ruined."

"The sign will be on." Ambrose gave her an injured glance. "And I promise the spell will be removed. I'll stay up all night if I have to. I was only trying to help."

She couldn't stay mad at him when he gave her that sad puppy-dog look. "You won't have to stay up all night. I'll work with you on it."

"Don't feel obligated."

"Oh, but I do." She stood on tiptoe and kissed him. "Now, let's close the circle and get on with the spell. If we're lucky, we'll have time for some chair sex before we go to bed."

Chapter 24

Early Saturday morning Annie got a call from Gwen. "The white roses are back to normal," she said. "I can't figure it out. One day they're X-rated and the next they're back to G."

"Weird. But I guess it's a good thing." Annie was relieved that at least something was going right. Melody had started her day with the announcement that she hated her wedding dress and couldn't imagine why everyone had encouraged her to choose an off-the-shoulder style. Both Annie and her mother were ready to let bridezilla get married in shorts and a tank top.

"That Isabel woman came back in late yesterday," Gwen said. "I keep thinking I know her from somewhere."

"That's because she looks like the statue of Isadora Mather," Annie said. "I would say she's a descendant, except that I don't think Isadora had any kids."

"They say everyone has a double somewhere, so it's probably a coincidence. Anyway, I understand why you're afraid she'll come after Jeremy once you've left town. The woman's fixated on sex."

"I know." When Annie thought about Jeremy having sex with anyone else, especially Isabel, she felt sick. "That's why I want you to keep an eye on her."

"That won't be hard. She seems to have taken me on as a project. She thinks I'm repressed."

"Compared to Isabel, everyone is repressed." After the past few days, though, Annie couldn't very well claim to be repressed. As a prime example, Jeremy had showed up at her doorstep last night and shortly thereafter she was shtupping him in the hammock. "What does Isabel plan to do about your supposed condition?"

"She wasn't sure yet, but she promised there were several options that would give me, as she phrased it, a sexual wake-up call."

"Wow. You'll have to keep me informed. Just don't let her give Jeremy any wake-up calls."

"I'm on it, boss. Anyway, I just wanted you to know the flowers are fine. I'll have the pews and the altar decorated by two. I like to leave plenty of time before the ceremony, in case there are any last-minute changes to be made."

"We'll be over there by three," Annie said. "Or we will unless Melody decides my mom has to make her a whole new dress. If that happens, we may not make it in time for the ceremony at five."

"I thought you had the dress issues."

"Miraculously, my dress looks halfway decent on me now. Even the peach color isn't too bad."

"It must be that glow a woman gets from amazing sex. Isabel says I desperately need some of that sexual afterglow, and since it seems to have worked for you, she may be right."

Annie decided not to mention that her glow might already be fading because she no longer had a ticket on the sex train. Last night had been an unexpected bonus, but she and Jeremy had come to the end of the line. The finality of that hadn't hit her yet, but she knew it would, probably about the time she saw him this afternoon looking yummy in his tux.

"I wouldn't count on Isabel to find you a guy," Annie said to Gwen. "I like your Internet plan to locate a Frenchman much better."

"Yep, me, too. Well, gotta go. I have white roses to arrange. I just wanted you to know the good news about the great penis caper."

"Thanks." Annie was smiling as she hung up, but as she thought of what lay ahead, her smile faded. In a matter of hours she and Jeremy would have to go through the charade of pretending to be casual lovers when they were no longer lovers at all.

And as for the casual part, it had never been that. She was through kidding herself. She was in love with him. But that didn't mean she had to give in to that emotion, abandon her dreams and come back to Big Knob to be with Jeremy. She was tougher now. She could walk away.

After hurling in the bushes next to the lake road the night before, Jeremy had figured he'd have to battle a stomach flu all day today. But once he'd left the lake area, he'd been fine. Well, *fine* being a relative term. Knowing he would lose Annie soon meant he might never be fine again.

Going to the lake had been dumb, anyway. He'd had some idea that he could sort things out if he went back to the place where he and Annie had first made love. But he'd forgotten his kayak, which was a good thing, considering that his stomach had been so messed up.

Fortunately, he was cured of the stomach problem now, so he'd been able to fulfill his duties as best man throughout the day, which mostly involved keeping Bruce sober. Jeremy and the two groomsmen, Jeremy's buddy Sean Madigan and Jeff Brady, hung out at the bar playing pool. The guys let Bruce win a lot and monitored his beer intake.

It wasn't the most fascinating day Jeremy had ever spent, but joking around with his friends had helped take his mind off Annie. Sort of. He'd still caught himself wondering what she was doing and whether she was thinking about him. He was glad he'd gone to her house last night and discovered she'd been as hot for him as he'd been for her.

Apparently she wouldn't let that keep her from going through with her plans, though. If he'd hoped she'd call him first thing this morning and say she wanted to spend the rest of her days in Big Knob, it hadn't happened. Barring that impossible fantasy, he would have liked her to call and say she'd come to her senses about the lake monster and was now doing an exposé on Dorcas and Ambrose.

But she hadn't called with either news flash, which had left Jeremy free to concentrate on the grumpy groom. Nothing the guys dreamed up—pool, darts, *South Park* reruns—had improved Bruce's sour mood. He'd spent the whole day complaining that this was the biggest mistake of his life. He was still babbling about it as he stood beside Jeremy at the altar of the Big Knob Interdenominational Church.

"What kind of idiot gets married *before* he moves to Hawaii?" Bruce muttered under cover of the pre-ceremony organ music. "The minute I got that promotion, I shoulda broken off the engagement."

"Hey, you love Melody. You guys will have a great time in Honolulu."

"This was my chance to party, man. I blew it. I coulda had me a ukulele baby who knew how to hula and wore those sexy grass skirts and itty-bitty bikini tops."

"Get Melody hula lessons and a grass skirt. You can have it all—a Hawaiian fantasy and safe sex."

"Wouldn't work. Melody has two left feet. Annie, now, would be great at the hula. That woman has moves."

Jeremy didn't want to think of Annie dancing the hula. That image could leave him standing at the altar with an erection denting the front of his tux pants.

The organist switched to the processional. "This is it, buddy," Jeremy said. "You're up to bat."

Bruce groaned. "You got the ring?"

"Yep."

"Shit. Wish you'd forgot it."

"Shut up and smile."

Bruce's dark-haired niece Emily, age four, trotted down the aisle strewing rose petals from a white basket. She flung them with enthusiasm, taking great wads and throwing them everywhere, including on the guests sitting in the pews.

Bruce chuckled. "Wouldn't mind having a munchkin like that someday."

"See?" Jeremy relaxed a little as the first bridesmaid, Bruce's sister Georgia, walked slowly toward them in a pale blue dress. "You actually do want to get married."

"I guess."

That was the most positive thing Bruce had said all day. Jeremy decided he might not have to put Bruce in a headlock to get him through the ceremony. "Think of all the good stuff you can look forward to."

"Yeah. Melody makes great spaghetti. Lasagna, too."

Jeremy hoped Bruce and Melody weren't basing their attraction mainly on Italian food. But then again, it wasn't his problem. No, his problem had just walked in.

Annie stood inside the door of the vestibule poised to follow Melody's best friend, Carol, down the aisle. Jeremy's mouth went dry.

She'd complained about the peach dress, but it must be a girl thing, because Jeremy had never seen a more beautiful woman in his life than Annie as she started toward him. The dress's scooped neckline revealed cleavage that made him remember every single time he'd touched her there, kissed her there, taken her nipples in his . . . No, he couldn't think about that or he'd be in big trouble.

Maybe he could admire her hair, instead. The women

had been over at the Bob and Weave for most of the morning, and these tricky arrangements must be the result. Annie's hair had been caught up in some swirly deal on top of her head and decorated with rosebuds, but a few strands curled softly around her face and neck in the sexiest look Jeremy had ever seen. He wanted to kiss her so much he started to shake.

"There she is," Bruce murmured.

"Yes." *There she is, the woman I love. But she doesn't love me, at least not enough to hang around this tiny town.*

"She's beautiful," Bruce said.

Jeremy glanced sideways, not sure he liked the idea of Bruce describing Annie in that worshipful tone. But then he realized Bruce wasn't looking at Annie. His gaze was focused on Melody, who stood at the back of the church, arm in arm with her mother.

Jeremy gave Melody a passing glance. "Yeah, she's okay." Then he returned his attention to Annie, who had taken her position on the opposite side of the altar.

"Okay?" Bruce sounded angry. "What do you mean by *okay*?"

"She looks very nice." Belatedly Jeremy figured out that Bruce's devotion to Melody had finally kicked in.

"She's way more than nice. She's *hot,* man."

At this point, Jeremy wasn't sure whether it was wise to agree with Bruce or not. If he also proclaimed Melody hot, Bruce might punch him for being disrespectful of his bride-to-be, but if he said nothing, Bruce might punch him for lacking the proper admiration for his beloved.

Finally he settled on, "She's perfect for you, buddy."

That seemed to work for Bruce, because he grinned. "Damn straight. I deserve a hot woman like Melody."

Jeremy wondered if he deserved a hot woman like Annie. From all the evidence, apparently not.

The ceremony passed in a blur, and before Jeremy was quite ready for it, he had to walk Annie, a vision of peaches and cream, back down the aisle. He offered his arm and she slipped her warm hand though. He could feel the burn all the way through his jacket.

The scent of the roses in her hair and in her bouquet filled his head with dreams of making love to her on a bed of rose petals. He made sure he kept his gaze far away from her cleavage. There was only so much a guy could take.

He ached for what he couldn't have and had to swallow the lump in his throat before he could speak. "You look great," he said as they walked past the applauding guests.

"You, too."

"Ah, it's just a monkey suit."

"You look good in a monkey suit."

The gentleness of her tone gave him courage. He turned his head but kept his attention firmly on her face. Anything below her neck was off-limits. "Thank you for last night."

Color bloomed in her cheeks, but she didn't look at him. Instead she smiled at the wedding guests. "It was a crazy thing to do, wasn't it?"

"Yeah, and I loved every minute."

"How are you doing?" she asked softly.

"Miserable. How about you?"

"I've been better."

They'd barely made it to the end of the aisle before Bruce's sister Georgia swooped down upon them. "Pictures, pictures!" she said. "Everyone has to hurry over to the square for pictures!"

In the hubbub that followed, Jeremy was separated from Annie for the short walk to the square. The picture taking was chaotic, too, and Jeremy wondered if that brief trip down the aisle would be his only private moment with her.

Eventually the pictures were all taken and the wed-

ding party moved to the far side of the square, where
white canopies had been set up along with round
linen-draped tables surrounded by white folding
chairs. The trees were strung with twinkling white
lights and the DJ from Evansville had set up his sound
system in the gazebo. A temporary dance floor was
laid out nearby.

As dinner was served, Jeremy figured now he'd have
a chance to spend some time with Annie. After all,
they were sitting at the same head table. But each
time he made an attempt to talk to her, she found a
reason not to be drawn into conversation with him.

After the third coincidental interruption, he faced
the truth—she was deliberately avoiding him. Moments after that concept registered in his love-
besotted brain, he began to drink.

After the meal and the cutting of the cake, the dancing began. Annie had been avoiding Jeremy ever since
she first caught a glimpse of him in the black tux with
the dove gray vest and tie. She'd wanted him so much
at that moment that she'd had trouble catching her
breath.

Sometime during the evening his tie had come un-
done and now it dangled on either side of his shirt
collar. He'd unfastened a couple of shirt buttons, and
he couldn't have looked more appealing if he'd tried.
She was deathly afraid of what she might do if she
had to be in close contact with him. Embarrass herself
in front of the whole town, most likely.

Half the population of Big Knob was here, from
babies to octogenarians. If she kissed Jeremy the way
she wanted to kiss him, with open mouths and plenty
of tongue involved, she'd shock everyone, plus she'd
steal attention from Melody, which she'd promised
herself not to do. But wow, did she want to kiss
Jeremy.

Because of that, she was reluctant to dance with

him for fear temptation would overcome her. But refusing to do that would have brought even more attention to the situation. When the DJ called for them to come out, she told herself to be strong and joined him on the floor. She'd stay for one dance, and one dance only.

"Hey, schweet thang," he murmured, gathering her close. "Wanna see some magic?" Then he pinched her butt.

She gasped. "Jeremy, you're drunk!" She struggled to hold him upright as he staggered around the dance floor.

"Mm-hm."

"How much have you had, anyway?"

"Dunno. Lost count."

At least she didn't have to worry about a hot French kiss in the middle of the dance floor. Jeremy wouldn't be able to manage it without falling down.

"You need coffee." She steered him in the direction of the table where Madeline was serving coffee and wedding cake.

"Nope. Need you. With nothin' on. Nekkid. Hot."

His drunken mumblings shouldn't have had the slightest effect on her, but between the tux and his rumpled, sexy appearance, she was an easy mark. Even totally smashed, he had the power to turn her on.

She pretended to be unmoved. "As blitzed as you are, you wouldn't know what to do with me."

"Would so. I know *zackly* what to do with you." He leaned down and put his mouth close to her ear. "Screw you blind."

"Stop it." He'd never talked to her like that, probably hadn't talked to any woman like that before. She ought to be highly incensed. She wasn't. She liked the concept of Jeremy screwing her blind. But that wouldn't be happening for a number of reasons, including how large doses of alcohol affected a man's sexual abilities.

She noticed that Sean and Maggie were out on the floor. "Sean, could I get a little help, please?"

Sean glanced over. "What's the—oh, I see the problem."

"No problem, buddy." Jeremy's grin was lopsided. "I be dancin' with schweet Annie-fanny. She's sooooo hot."

"And you're soooo wasted." Sean put an arm around Jeremy's shoulders. "How about if Annie and I buy you a cup of coffee?"

Jeremy shook his head. "Don' wanna sober up. Feel good."

Guilt washed over Annie in a huge wave. She was to blame for Jeremy soaking up the booze. *Nice going, babe.* She'd known from the beginning that Jeremy could fall hard, but had she worried about it? Not much, at least not as much as she should have.

Sean helped her lower Jeremy into a folding chair near the coffee and cake table. "I'll get the coffee," Sean said. "You stay with him."

"Don't worry. I will." Annie pulled up a second chair and sat knees to knees with Jeremy. She took his hand and rubbed it, as if she could rub out all the damage she'd done. "I'm so sorry. I should never have allowed us to become involved with each other. Now I've hurt you."

"No r'grets." Jeremy's glasses were askew and he clumsily straightened them. "We're good."

"No, *you're* good." She felt awful. "Too good for the likes of me."

"Don' say that, Annie. Don' put yourself down. You're amazin'."

"So are you." Her throat was thick with sadness and she had to clear it before she could go on.

"Talked to Jenkins."

She nodded. "I knew you would. You're a conscientious guy."

"How 'bout hot? Am I hot?"

"And hot. Very hot. To top it all off, you're even a magician."

He frowned and stared at the ground. "Nope."

"Yes, you are. You're a terrific magician. I don't know how you do those tricks."

He shoved his glasses back up to the bridge of his nose. "Me, neither."

"Oh, come on. Of course you do. Maybe not now, when your brain is fried, but when you're sober, you know."

Sean walked toward them. "Here's the coffee. Want me to stick around for a while?"

"No, that's okay." Annie took the steaming mug. She'd let it cool a bit before giving it to Jeremy. "I have things under control. Thanks, Sean."

"I'll be back to check on you two in a little while. Take care of the big guy, Annie."

"I'll do my best." She was afraid her best wasn't all that great, but she vowed to stay with Jeremy until he could navigate without bumping into things.

"I mean it, Annie," Jeremy said.

She glanced at him. "Mean what?"

"I don' unnerstan' the magic. It jus' happens."

"But I thought Ambrose taught you how to do it."

"Ambrose." Jeremy scowled. "Slime bucket."

Annie decided there was no point in arguing with anything Jeremy said at the moment. He wouldn't remember it later, anyway. She blew on the coffee and tested it. In the chill of the night air it had cooled quickly. "Here, drink this."

Jeremy took the mug, but instead of drinking the coffee he gazed into the murky brew as if deep in thought.

She couldn't imagine how deep his thoughts could

be when his brain was pickled. She put a hand on his knee. "Jeremy? You need to drink that, sweetie."

He glanced up, and for a moment his intelligence shone through his drunken stupor. "Didn' think of that. Should've."

"What?"

"Ambrose. Magic. Monsters."

"I don't understand."

"Thas okay." He gave her a loopy smile. "You're so pretty. Let's go to the lake. Look for monsters."

"You're in no condition to do that."

"Oh. Can I have cream?"

"Uh, sure. I should have asked." Funny that they'd shared so much and yet she didn't know how he liked his coffee. "Stay there. I'll be right back." She stood and hurried over to Madeline. "I need cream for Jeremy's coffee, please."

Madeline reached behind her and came up with a plastic bucket full of creamers. "I have to keep them back here. Otherwise the kids will grab them and drink them straight from the packet."

"Thanks." Annie took several and walked back to where she'd left Jeremy. But he was gone.

Chapter 25

While Annie was getting Jeremy the cream he didn't need, he stood. He was a little shaky, but this was important. He slipped quietly through the crowd. When he'd almost made it, Donald Jenkins stopped him. Jenkins had a bottle of beer in his hand, and he took a swig. "You sure there's no monster in that lake, Dunstan?"

Jeremy wasn't sure, not anymore. If Ambrose could make magic, then there could be a monster. "I gotta go."

"Go where?" Jenkins's eyes narrowed. "I've been thinking about what you told me, that it was a fake, but I have the feeling there's something more to it."

"Nope. Nothin' more. 'Scuse me. Gotta take a leak." Then Jeremy turned and made his way as quickly as his foggy brain would allow toward Click-or-Treat. Yeah, he was somewhat trashed, but not so much that he couldn't do what he had to. He had a magic word, and he intended to use it.

Getting the kayak out of the storage shed and onto the roof of his Suzuki turned out to be tougher than he'd thought. He dropped it a couple of times but finally got it tied down. Good thing he usually left his keys under the seat of his car. He wasn't up to climbing the stairs to his apartment to get them.

Driving to the lake wasn't much of a challenge.

With everyone at the wedding, there was no traffic, and he'd made the trip so many times he could get there blindfolded. This trip felt a bit like that until he remembered to turn on the headlights.

The dented orange cones weren't across the road down to the lake anymore, thank God. He didn't feel like getting out to move them. He didn't bother to park straight, either. Nobody else would be parking there, anyway.

He was eager to get this done, eager to try and prove that there was a monster in the lake, after all. Annie would be so happy. He didn't know if having a monster there would make a difference so far as hanging out with him was concerned, but logically she'd be in Big Knob a lot more while she worked on the story for the *Trib*.

She was hot for him. That was a plus, he reminded himself as he pulled the kayak off the top of the car. He bonked himself on the head, but it didn't hurt too bad. That was the good thing about being toasted. Stuff didn't hurt.

He remembered his life jacket at the last minute. He had to take off his tux jacket to get it on. Once he'd managed to shove his arms through the armholes of the life jacket, buckling it was way too much trouble, so he didn't.

Finally he launched the kayak and climbed in. No need to bother with the kayak skirt, either. Too much work for what would be a quick trip.

Paddling wasn't all that easy, either. He kept slapping the water, splashing himself and laughing. He'd never splashed Annie with the paddle. If she went kayaking with him in the summer, they could have fun doing that. Nothing like a splash fight on a hot day.

When he was somewhere in the middle of the lake, he stopped paddling. This was it. The big test. He filled his lungs with air and shouted, *"Abracadabra,"* as loud as he could.

Nothing happened. He shouted it again. Still nothing. Shit. This had to work. It always had before. He stood up in the kayak. *"Abracadabra!"* he called across the water.

Standing in the kayak wasn't the brightest idea he'd had, especially because he wasn't very steady to begin with. The kayak started wobbling, and he tried to sit down again before it was too late. No good. The kayak flipped and he hit the cold water, losing his glasses as he went under.

He got his head above water, but the life jacket got tangled up and was more trouble than it was worth, so he got rid of it. But then he realized his arms were sort of tired. So he'd just hang on to the kayak, except he couldn't find it. Treading water, he felt the weight of the tux like an anchor dragging him down.

He should take it off, but it wasn't his. It was rented, and there would be hell to pay if he didn't return it in good condition. The stupid thing was dry clean only. What was up with that? All clothes should be washable. He wondered how he'd explain the water stains on the tux.

God, he was tired. Too many beers and too little food. Not enough sleep. A wave slapped him in the face and he swallowed water. Damn. He really was drunk. And he didn't think he could swim to shore, either. He wasn't quite sure which direction it was, anyway. Things were not looking good.

Annie combed the crowd looking for Jeremy, but no one had seen him. She couldn't believe he would take off. He was the best man at Bruce's wedding, and what could be more important than celebrating his good friend's special day?

She knew the answer. She was more important. Sorting out their differences would loom huge in Jeremy's mind, especially when he'd had enough to drink that he wasn't thinking straight.

But he'd been babbling about Ambrose and magic. And monsters. She had a bad feeling he might have gone to the lake in an effort to prove or disprove the presence of a lake monster. But he was too drunk to be anywhere near water.

She could check out her theory fairly quickly. Without telling anyone, she quietly left the celebration on the square and walked over to Click-or-Treat. Her peach-colored heels, dyed to match the hideous color of the dress, weren't the greatest for making good progress, but she walked as fast as she could.

No lights shone from the upstairs windows. She went around back to see if his Suzuki was still parked there. Gone. He was at the lake. She just knew it. But she could be wrong, and there was no reason to interrupt the wedding celebration . . . yet.

She'd left her car over by the church, and the keys were under the seat, a habit everyone had in this crime-free town. Rather than walk back along the square where she might be seen, she cut across the back alley behind the stores on Fifth in order to get to the church.

It was dark back there, and she stumbled over rocks and weeds. The peach heels would be ruined, but she didn't give a damn. She'd never wear them or the dress again, anyway.

She got into her car with a sense of urgency, started the motor and drove to the lake road. As she turned down it, her car's headlights picked out two vehicles. One was Jeremy's Suzuki, parked at a crazy angle in the lot. The other was Donald Jenkins's truck, with the boat trailer backed up to the water.

Rolling down her window, she heard the soft putt-putt of Jenkins's motorboat. Both men were on the lake looking for a monster. Jeremy wanted to find it for her, but Jenkins wanted to kill it.

Annie reached for her purse to pull out her cell phone and remembered that she'd left her purse with everyone else's at the church. No one had wanted to carry purses to the reception. She was stuck out here by the lake in a peach matron-of-honor dress, high heels, and no cell phone. Ducky.

She climbed out of the car, leaving it running with the headlights on. As she did, the scent of a spa mudpack drifted toward her. Her heart began to hammer. *It's out there.* She peered out over the lake but could see nothing.

The headlights of her car reached only to the edge of the water, and beyond that she couldn't see worth shit. If anything, the headlights made the lake seem darker, so she went back and shut off the motor and the lights. The moon wasn't up yet and no lights shone from the Lowells' house because they were still at the reception.

The sound of Jenkins's motorboat grew fainter, so he must be cruising on the far side of the lake. But the waves were lapping here, which meant something was out there swimming, something big. Where was Jeremy? She thought of calling out to him, but if the monster was close by, she didn't want to startle it into doing something that would endanger him.

Where was the damn moon? Then, as if she'd beckoned it, the moon topped the trees and washed the surface of the lake with light. What the moonlight revealed nearly made her pass out.

The lake monster swam toward the shore with something in its mouth. As it drew closer, she could make out what it was. With growing horror, Annie recognized a limp form wearing tux pants, shirt and vest. Jeremy. She screamed, an involuntary sound that carried across the lake like an emergency siren.

Jenkins's boat revved up and roared across the lake. The monster swam faster in Annie's direction.

"Don't hurt him!" Annie cried out. "Please don't hurt him!" Yet for all she knew, he was already dead.

If he was, she might as well be dead, too. Dear God, he couldn't be dead. Not Jeremy.

"I've got it handled!" Donald Jenkins cut the motor and his boat bobbed several yards away from the swimming creature. "I'm gonna shoot that son of a bitch!"

That was fine with Annie if the monster had killed Jeremy. Science be damned if that thing had destroyed the gentle soul of Jeremy Dunstan, the man she loved. But Annie didn't choose to stand by and trust Jenkins to take care of things.

Keeping her eye on the monster, she leaned down and picked up a rock the size of her fist. She'd always had excellent aim thanks to her softball practice, and a well-thrown rock could do damage. Look at David and Goliath.

She forced herself not to think about Jeremy's apparently lifeless body dangling from the jaws of this prehistoric aberration. She clung to the hope that he was still alive. She had to believe that killing the creature, or at least stunning it, would allow her to rescue him.

In order to zero in on her target, she was forced to look into the monster's luminous eyes, and as she did, she paused in confusion. There was no menace in that gaze. There was only . . . caring. Was that possible? Could this reptilian thing be rescuing Jeremy instead of devouring him?

She had a split second to decide. Jenkins had taken aim and was ready to fire. She could throw the rock at the monster's head or she could throw it at Jenkins's arm and ruin his shot. If she chose to save the creature and she'd guessed wrong, she could be putting Jeremy in even more danger, assuming he was still alive.

Taking a deep breath, she wound up and let the rock fly. Jenkins cried out, and his gun splashed harmlessly into the lake. Gunless, he fired off a barrage of swear words and threats of lawsuits.

Annie ignored him as the lake monster swam toward her, its eyes focused in her direction. About ten yards out, it paused to tread water.

"I'm trusting you," Annie said. "Don't let me down." She held her breath as the monster came nearer, and nearer still.

When it was almost at the shoreline, it lowered its head and deposited Jeremy gently on the sand. Annie rushed forward and fell to her knees. He was breathing! She lifted his head into her lap as hot tears of gratitude ran down her face.

Tearing her gaze from Jeremy, she glanced up to thank his rescuer. She was just in time to see the lake monster bob its head once before sinking back into the lake.

Jeremy stirred and opened his eyes. "Annie? What happened?"

"Nothing much." She stroked his cheek and choked back a sob. "Just another crazy day in Big Knob, Indiana."

When Dorcas couldn't find either Jeremy or Annie, she convinced Ambrose that they needed to head home and check the lake road. Leaving the festivities, they walked back to the church, where they'd left the red scooter.

"The spell should be gone." Ambrose climbed on and started the motor.

"I'm sure it is." Dorcas gathered the skirts of her purple velvet dress so she could ride on the back of the scooter. "I just feel the need to make sure nothing's amiss down there."

"There's always the chance our lovebirds are down at the lake canoodling," Ambrose said as they took off.

"I doubt it." Dorcas thought she and Ambrose

would look much more daring in formal wear on a
Harley instead of this little putt-putt. "Jeremy was
knocking back the drinks, which is not what you want
in a man when canoodling is involved."

"Well, we'll know soon enough."

"If we had a real motorcycle, we'd know almost
immediately. Does this thing go above forty-five?"

"Yes, but I don't like to push it, my love. I want it
to last me a while."

Dorcas rolled her eyes. Just what she needed, a
scooter that would hang around for the next twenty-
five years.

Before they even made the turn down the lake road,
she could hear some man yelling obscenities. "Goose
it, Ambrose. We've got trouble."

To his credit, Ambrose tromped on the gas and they
shot forward so fast that Dorcas's head snapped back.
They pulled into the parking lot and Dorcas jumped
off before the scooter came to a stop. In the moonlight
she saw Annie kneeling on the sand holding Jeremy's
head in her lap. It didn't look like a love scene, especially with Donald Jenkins speeding toward the beach,
swearing loud enough to be heard over the noise of
his boat.

Dorcas picked up her skirts and ran toward Annie
and Jeremy. "Is he okay?"

Annie looked up and the moonlight gleamed on her
tear-streaked face. "I think so."

"I'm okay." Jeremy's voice was weak, but at least
he was talking.

"Damned bitch ruined my shot!" Jenkins ran his
boat up on the sand, cut the motor and jumped out.
"I'll sue your ass, girly-girl! My arm hurts like hell.
Might be broke."

Ambrose stepped in front of Jenkins before he
could reach Annie. "You might want to calm down,
Mr. Jenkins."

"Outta my way, Lowell." Jenkins shoved Ambrose

aside. "That woman threw a goddamned rock at me. I had a perfect shot, and she ruined it. Now my gun's at the bottom of the lake, and that's a damned good gun. Missy here has a lot to answer for."

Dorcas exchanged a glance with Ambrose. He nodded and laid a hand on Jenkins's shoulder. "Why don't you come with me?"

"Yeah, like I want to do that, pretty boy." Jenkins tried to pull away.

"I think you will." Ambrose applied more pressure.

"Hey, let go of me!" Jenkins struggled, trying to get away. "What you got, some effing black belt or something? Let go!"

"We're going up to the house." Ambrose propelled him in that direction. "I'll bet you could use a drink."

"I don't want a drink. I want . . . Well, hello, mama." He glanced up the road. "I wouldn't mind having some of that."

Dorcas glanced over her shoulder, quite sure Isadora had appeared. Not surprising, with all the psychic energy swirling around this spot. Whatever had happened, Dee-Dee had been involved. Dorcas could feel it.

"Looks like there's a party going on down here," Isadora said. "Can I join in?"

"Sure thing," Jenkins said. "This night just got a whole lot more interesting."

"I was about to buy Mr. Jenkins a drink," Ambrose said.

"I see." Isadora glanced at Dorcas. "Everything cool with Annie and Jeremy?"

"Looks like it," Dorcas said.

"Then I'll go with these gentlemen up to the house. I mix a mean drink, Ambrose. You might want me to do the honors." With that she linked her arm through Donald's and they walked toward the house.

Annie glanced at Dorcas. "We need to get Jeremy

up to the house, too. Do you have your cell phone?
I think we should get Doc Pritchard over here."

Jeremy coughed. "I'm fine. Just help me to a car."

"Not yet." Dorcas dropped to her knees next to
Annie. "Can you move your arms and legs?"

Jeremy made some feeble movements. "Yeah. What
was Jenkins blathering about? Did he see the lake
monster?"

"He just thought he did." Annie combed the damp
hair away from Jeremy's forehead.

"You threw a rock at him? Why'd you do that?"

Annie shot a quick look at Dorcas. "Somebody was
going to get hurt, and I was afraid it might be you."

Jeremy frowned as if trying to put it all together.
"I guess I swam in. I remember falling overboard,
but then . . ."

"You were probably on automatic pilot," Dorcas
said.

"Guess so. That's probably what Jenkins saw, me
swimming in."

Dorcas knew that in a few minutes, it wouldn't matter what Jenkins saw, because Isadora and Ambrose
would slip a memory potion into his drink of choice.
He'd probably always wonder what happened to his
gun, but Dorcas thought Jenkins without a gun was a
good thing.

She gazed down at Jeremy. "Annie and I are going
to help you stand up. If you can manage that, we'll
see about getting you up to the house." Murmuring a
healing incantation under her breath, she helped Jeremy sit up.

"Dorcas, did you say something?" Annie stood and
grasped Jeremy under one arm.

"Just a little prayer," Dorcas said. "A prayer of
thanksgiving that Jeremy didn't drown. Okay, on the
count of three, we'll lift him."

"This is silly," Jeremy said. "I can stand up just fine."

"We'll see about that. You've had quite a shock to your system." She was dying to find out what Annie knew, but that would have to wait. "Here we go, now. One, two, *three*."

She and Annie got Jeremy upright, but he was wobbly. Without both of them supporting him, he never would have made it up to the house. When they staggered awkwardly into the kitchen, Isadora, Jenkins and Ambrose were singing drinking songs.

"Dunstan needs a drink!" Jenkins said.

"No." Annie helped Dorcas lower Jeremy into a chair. "One thing he definitely doesn't need is a drink."

"Hell, everybody needs a drink!" Jenkins lifted his glass. "Isabel and Ambrose make one damned fine martini, let me tell you."

"I'm sure they do." Dorcas sent them each a look of gratitude for a job well done. "But some of us could use a cup of hot tea. I'll make it." She walked over to the sink and ran water into the teapot.

Annie came over and stood beside her as Jenkins started singing again. Annie leaned over and spoke in a whisper. "The lake monster saved Jeremy."

Dorcas nodded. "I thought as much." She glanced at Annie. "And by the way, her name is Dee-Dee."

Chapter 26

An hour later, Annie sat alone at the Lowells' kitchen table, sipping tea and waiting for them to come back from taking Jenkins down to his truck. Isabel had gone for a walk by the lake, and Jeremy, wearing some old clothes belonging to Ambrose, was asleep on the purple sofa in the parlor. Sabrina was curled up at his feet.

Every time Annie had gone in to check on him, Sabrina had been purring to beat the band. Dorcas had said the vibrations would help Jeremy regain his strength so he'd be right as rain tomorrow.

Annie wondered what right as rain would be for Jeremy. If Ambrose had given him the ability to do magic, what other alterations had the Lowells done to Jeremy's personality in the name of matchmaking? She intended to ask them once things quieted down.

After Jenkins had passed out, Dorcas and Ambrose had hauled him outside and used a wheelbarrow to get him down to his truck. They planned to let him sleep it off in the cab. They'd assured Annie that when he woke up, he'd simply think he'd had too many beers and had decided to go out for a moonlit boat ride. All memory of the lake monster would be gone.

Annie no longer questioned anything they said or did. Whatever their powers, they were way beyond anything she'd ever experienced. Her view of reality had undergone a major shift in the past two hours. And she *really* wanted to know what sort of transformation they'd created in Jeremy.

What he'd said about his magic made sense now. Ambrose had somehow transferred those powers temporarily to Jeremy so he could impress her. They might have put some sort of confidence spell on him, too. The Jeremy she'd fallen for might not even exist.

The kitchen door opened and Isabel came in. "Had yourself quite a night, didn't you?" She took a mug out of the cupboard as if she owned the place and helped herself to some tea from the pot sitting on the table. She didn't sit down.

"Quite a night." Annie studied Isabel and decided the resemblance to Isadora Mather was probably not a coincidence, especially because Isabel seemed to have a relationship with Dorcas and Ambrose, so she was probably Wiccan, too.

Isabel leaned against the counter and drank her tea. "I'm quite proud of my girl, Dee-Dee. She just told me her version of what happened. She was so scared that Jenkins would shoot her, but she couldn't let Jeremy drown, so she took a chance. That's guts."

Openmouthed, Annie stared at Isabel. "You *talked* to the lake monster?"

"Sure. She leads a boring life, so normally she's not the greatest conversationalist, but tonight's story was riveting. Without Dee-Dee, our boy in there would be sleeping with the fishes. She heard him thrashing around and sure enough, he was drowning, so she picked him up and brought him to shore, ignoring her personal safety."

"Okay, Isabel, who the hell are you?"

Isabel gazed at her over the rim of her mug. "I'm not sure you need to know that. You being a reporter and all. It's bad enough that you know about Dee-Dee. I suppose the reward for her gallantry will be

that she becomes part of a freak show for the
tourists."

Annie cringed. She didn't want to be responsible
for that, but Dee-Dee's days of seclusion would be
over sooner or later. "If I don't break this story, I'm
just delaying the inevitable. Someone else will get a
glimpse of her and might handle it way worse than
I will."

"Ah, but what if no one else ever sees her?"

"I don't see how you can guarantee that. She's been
popping up pretty regularly this past week."

Isabel nodded. "That's true, but there were extenu-
ating circumstances. For one thing, there was the
whole matchmaking gig with you and Jeremy, and for
another, she's lonesome as hell, which makes her more
prone to put in an appearance."

"Lonesome?"

"Yeah. She needs a boyfriend." Isabel drained her
mug and crossed to the window. "Don't we all. I—oh,
here comes Dorcas with an empty wheelbarrow. I tried
to talk her into dumping Jenkins in the lake, but she
wouldn't go for it. Knowing Dee-Dee, she would have
saved him, anyway, even though he tried to kill her.
That lake monster has the softest heart in the world."

Dorcas came through the kitchen door looking
weary. "That's settled. Ambrose is bringing your car
up and putting it in our driveway, Annie, so whenever
you feel ready to go home, it's right there."

"Thank you." She wondered if that was a subtle
hint for her to leave. She wasn't going anywhere until
she had some answers.

"But before you go," Dorcas said, "we need to talk
about Dee-Dee."

"Don't bother." Isabel waved a hand in Annie's
direction. "She's convinced that it's only a matter of
time before Dee-Dee's discovered, anyway, so it might
as well be her getting the glory."

Annie bristled. "That's a crummy way of saying it."

"But accurate." Isabel's glance challenged her. "Aren't you after the glory?"

Annie couldn't deny it. "I also want to protect Dee-Dee as much as possible."

Dorcas pulled out a chair and sat down. "That's just it. If we can come up with a way to transport a male lake monster to Deep Lake without arousing suspicion, then I'm convinced Dee-Dee will be content to stay out of sight, at least for another hundred years or so. We won't have to worry about protecting her, at least not for a while."

Annie's brain was on overload. She could barely comprehend that she was sitting on a story about a lake monster who was older than any living creature on Earth, a Loch Nessian animal who could talk, reason and feel compassion. On top of that, Dee-Dee was lonely and wanted a boyfriend to make her feel complete, which meant there were other creatures out there like her. Any journalist who published that news would be famous forever.

Isabel pointed at Annie. "Look at her face. She's writing the lead to that story in her head right now. You're not going to keep her from reporting on this unless you give her a memory potion, and my guess is that she won't drink anything other than tea in this house ever again."

Dorcas shrugged. "Then I guess Annie will do what she has to do." She turned to Isabel. "Our main concern right now is finding a way to airlift a male lake monster the size of a Goodyear blimp without traumatizing the entire population of Big Knob."

Isabel blew out a breath. "I have an idea, but I'm not comfortable talking about it in front of the press."

"Oh, for heaven's sake," Annie said. "I'm not *the press*."

"You're not?" Isabel lifted her eyebrows. "If you're not the press, then who are you?"

Annie met her gaze and realized she had no answer. Breaking news was what she did, what she was good at, her pathway to the career she'd chosen. But was that who she was? She'd like to think there was more to her, but if so, she was having a tough time putting her finger on it.

And if she didn't know for sure who she was, Jeremy was an even bigger question mark. "Putting my identity crisis aside for the moment, I'd like to ask you a question, Dorcas."

"All right." Dorcas looked as if she'd been expecting it.

"I take it Ambrose gave Jeremy some magic powers."

Dorcas nodded. "He couldn't have taught him enough technique in the short time we had, so he placed a magical spell on him."

"For how long?"

"It's expired now."

Annie wondered how Jeremy would feel about that. She'd written a story proclaiming him the Internet Café Magician, and now he wouldn't be able to perform those tricks. "Was there anything else? He seemed more confident than I remembered."

"We gave him a potion to boost his confidence," Dorcas said. "He only had a few days to win you over, so we wanted him to have his best shot, but it wouldn't have worked if he hadn't—"

"So everything was a lie." Annie felt sick to her stomach. If she could have chosen, she would rather have the lake monster be fake and Jeremy's personality real.

"Not a lie," Dorcas said gently. "An enhancement. You see—"

"I don't really know anything about him," Annie

said. "How can I make decisions based on some magical *enhancement*?"

"You know more than you think you do," Dorcas said.

Isabel yawned. "Frankly, I'm bored with the whole subject."

Annie heard Ambrose come through the front door. That was her cue. She pushed back her chair and stood. "You know what? It's been a long day. A long week, come to think of it. I need to go home and get some sleep."

"If you insist." Dorcas looked relieved.

"I do. If you think Jeremy's recovered enough, I can take him back to his place, too."

"I'm sure he's fine. That's a good idea."

Dorcas probably hoped Annie would spend the night with Jeremy. Annie hated to disappoint her, but she no longer knew who Jeremy was, really. She wasn't so sure who she was, either, and she needed to figure that out, pronto. Sex would only cloud the issue.

Dorcas stood with Ambrose at the front door and watched Annie help Jeremy into her car. "I hope she comes to the right decision," she said.

"About Dee-Dee or Jeremy?"

"Both. I have to admit I'm worried. She's thinking with her head instead of her heart, and that's bad."

"All the more reason to get a boyfriend for Dee-Dee so she'll be tough to find if Annie chooses to go public with this and the news crews show up."

"You're right. Isadora says she has an idea."

"I do," Isadora called from the kitchen. "Get your butts back here so we can discuss it. I have a hot poker game waiting for me in the Whispering Forest. By the way, thanks for the stake, Dorcas."

Ambrose turned to his wife. "Is that what you bribed her with?"

"I had to come up with something."

Ambrose lowered his voice. "You know perfectly well that Isadora is not a good influence on George. She could undo weeks of progress with one late-night poker game. Plus every time they play, the raccoons steal another chunk of George's treasure, which won't sit well with the council. At this rate we'll never get back to Sedona."

Dorcas smiled at him. "About that. Have you noticed that the boredom factor has all but disappeared around here?"

"Guys, I'm waiting," Isadora called out again.

Ambrose nodded. "I can't say I'm bored. And your point is?"

"No point. Just mentioning." She gave him a light pinch on his tight derriere as they walked back into the kitchen. Their sex life had improved since moving to Big Knob, too. She wondered if that had anything to do with the large granite phallic symbol northeast of town. Probably.

Jeremy tried to convince Annie to stay with him in his apartment, but she refused, saying they were both exhausted and they'd talk in the morning. She made sure Megabyte went out to pee, and then she announced that she'd come back at first light and take him to the lake so he could retrieve his car. He was in no shape to seduce her into changing her mind, so he let her go back to her mother's house.

Sure enough, the sky was barely growing light when someone pounded on the back door of Click-or-Treat. Rousing herself, Megabyte started down the stairs. Jeremy threw on jeans and a Click-or-Treat logo T-shirt, gargled some mouthwash, put on his glasses, and followed Meg down. On the way he ran a hand over his jaw and winced. He must look like a homeless person.

Annie, however, looked terrific. She stood at his back door wearing a long-sleeved knit top the color of lime sherbet and a pair of snug jeans. She would probably complain that they were too tight, but he thought they were perfect.

Annie gave Meg a head rub as the dog walked past on her way to the yard. Turned out Meg got a friendlier greeting than Jeremy did.

Annie didn't offer to kiss him, didn't touch him at all, in fact. "Let's go get your car." She said it gently, which was sort of comforting, but otherwise she was all business.

"I need to feed Meg first."

"That's fine."

"Want to come in?"

She shook her head. "I'll wait out here."

He didn't like the distance she was putting between them, didn't like it one bit. Last night she'd seemed to care a lot. She'd even been crying. Today—not so much.

He took Meg back upstairs, poured out her ration of kibble and waited the ten seconds it usually took her to gulp it down. When he came back downstairs, she followed him.

He opened the door and gestured to his dog. "Can she come?"

"Sure, why not?"

He felt better having Meg along, riding in the back-seat and sticking her head between the front bucket seats. Meg loved him unconditionally, whether he knew magic or got drunk or almost drowned himself. Annie probably didn't love him at all, conditional or un. If she did, she wouldn't be acting so standoffish today.

Having her drive him was a new experience that gave him a chance to study her, and he could tell from the set of her jaw that she was tense. But even tense, she was gorgeous.

He loved looking at her hair, which was a million

shades of blond, especially when it caught the light. He wasn't sure if she had on makeup or not because she was good with that kind of thing. She could be wearing it and he wouldn't know it.

Whether she was wearing makeup or not, she'd spent time on her appearance before coming to pick him up. Normally that would be a good sign, but judging from her expression, she wasn't feeling soft and cuddly. "You said we'd talk today," he said. "Maybe we should do that."

She let out a breath. "Maybe we should. I found out a few things from Dorcas last night while you were asleep on the Lowells' sofa."

"And?"

"I don't know if you realized it, but they gave you some herbs and stuff that . . . well, they're sort of a mood enhancer. They wanted you to feel more confident in approaching me."

Jeremy didn't want to hear that. He'd suspected as much, but he hadn't asked for fear he'd discover the truth—he'd been operating under some sort of mind-altering substance. All that personal power he'd felt had been fake.

Still, he had a morbid fascination with the topic. "Did you ask about the magic?"

"I did. They helped make all that happen, too."

"I don't see how. They weren't always around when I tried magic tricks." Vaguely he remembered struggling to conjure up the lake monster last night with his magic word, but most of the evening was very unclear.

"I'm not sure how they did it. They have some very developed abilities." Annie approached the turn to the lake road and made a left.

"And you all still think there's a lake monster out there?"

"Probably." She drove slowly down the narrow road to the lake. "I hope you're convinced by now that the

Lowells didn't make it up so they could cash in on the tourist business. They do some unorthodox things, but not because they want to get rich."

Jeremy had to admit that scenario didn't fit very well anymore. "Yeah, I'm convinced." As they neared the parking lot, he saw the crazy way his Suzuki was parked and groaned. "I must have been really sloshed last night."

"You were, which is mostly my fault."

"That's not true."

"Yes, it is." She pulled her rental up next to Jeremy's car and gazed out through the front windshield toward the lake. "Except now I know that Dorcas and Ambrose deliberately tried to make me fall for you, so I don't feel *quite* as guilty."

"You shouldn't feel guilty at all. I was the one with ulterior motives." Jeremy was not encouraged about how this was going. He unfastened his seat belt, but she didn't. She didn't shut off the motor, either. Bad sign.

She turned her head to look at him. That was the first time he realized she had tears in her eyes.

"Oh, Annie, don't." He started to reach for her.

She waved him away and sniffed. "I'm too vulnerable right now."

He felt pretty damned vulnerable, too, but he didn't say that. His rep had already taken too many hits. "I don't want you to be sad."

"Can't be helped." She wiped at her eyes and took a shaky breath. "I'll be driving back to Chicago this morning."

He'd expected that, too, but expecting it and hearing it were two different things. He couldn't have prepared himself for the pain he'd feel. "Are you coming back anytime soon?"

"I . . . I don't know. I got in over my head with you, Jeremy. But it wasn't really you, was it?"

He gazed at her. "I'm not sure I know the answer to that."

"And if you don't, I sure don't. With Zach I fell in love with an image, and I'm not about to do that again. I need distance. Time to think."

He had no choice but to accept that. No doubt about it, he wasn't as advertised. The Lowells' plan had backfired and he was left wondering if Annie would have been interested in him without the magic. It was a little late to find out.

When he started to speak, he had to clear the misery out of his throat first. "Have you decided what you're going to do about the lake monster?" He'd wanted to find it for her, but he'd failed at that, too.

She glanced away. "I'm still thinking about that."

"If you want to come back and try to get a better picture, then I'd be glad to—"

"We'll see." She glanced at him and swallowed. "For now, we'd better just say good-bye."

Agony ripped through him. Even Megabyte must have sensed it, because she whined and nudged his arm with her wet nose. She was probably telling him to get the hell out of the car before he started doing something unmanly, like begging.

Somehow he met Annie's gaze and nodded. Reaching blindly behind him for the door handle, he opened it and climbed out of the car. It took him forever to find the mechanism to let the front seat down so Megabyte could come out. No question that he'd lost his Mr. Smooth persona.

"Jeremy, this week has been . . ."

Heaven and hell. "For me, too. Good-bye, Annie."

" 'Bye," she said softly. Then she put the car in gear, made a quick U-turn and barreled out of the parking lot with the tires spitting gravel as she left.

Jeremy watched her until she was out of sight. All week long he'd wondered if this time with Annie was too good to be true. Now he knew the answer. It was.

As he stood beside his car trying to get himself together so he could drive home, he heard a droning sound off in the distance. Glancing up, he saw a blimp several miles away. Must be a golf tournament in Indianapolis today.

With a sigh, he walked around to the passenger side and opened it for Meg. "Come on, girl. Looks like it's just you and me again."

Chapter 27

Annie rolled her car windows down and let the breeze dry her tears as they fell. With the window open, she had no trouble recognizing the steady drone of a blimp's engines overhead. She saw and heard blimps all the time in Chicago, where they were used for various outdoor sporting events. This one must be on its way to somewhere else, because there would be no reason for a blimp to hover over Big Knob.

A creature as big as the Goodyear blimp.

Dorcas's words came back to her. No, that was too crazy. But it wasn't any crazier than some of the other things that had happened this week. Annie pulled off the road and leaned out the window to get a look at the blimp. Sure enough, it was headed in the direction of the lake.

Up ahead was a wooded side road. She drove to it, pulled in and managed to turn the car around without getting stuck. So far, so good. Now she had to wait for Jeremy to drive by and hope he was so distracted that he didn't notice her car back in the trees.

Soon his Suzuki whizzed by, Megabyte's massive head sticking out the passenger window. With Megabyte riding shotgun, Jeremy wouldn't be able to see into the woods on the right side of the road, anyway. She was in luck.

Once she was positive he wouldn't see her, she

headed back for the lake, but parked on the side of the road before she'd reached the turnoff. If she was right, she didn't want to announce her presence.

Taking her camera from her purse, she left the car and cut through the trees toward the lake road. The blimp drew nearer. Her chest tightened in anticipation and a tingly feeling traveled down her spine. Once again, she was poised on the brink of something amazing.

She crept through the trees, making sure she didn't rustle leaves or step on dried branches. The sound of the blimp's motor would probably block out any noise she made, but she still didn't want to take a chance on being spotted. At last she had a clear view of the lake.

The blimp approached, barely skimming the trees, its Goodyear label making it look completely authentic. But Annie didn't think Goodyear owned this particular model.

"Almost there, Norton," Dorcas called out to the blindfolded lake monster as she and Ambrose flew underneath the two-and-a-half-ton beast. She was giving her broom a true test, but so far it had kept up nicely with Isadora's sporty model.

Besides disguising Norton as the Goodyear blimp, the magical trio had disguised themselves and their brooms as the undercarriage. Ambrose was in charge of making the noise of the motor, which meant he couldn't talk, but so far he'd done a fine job. He sounded exactly like a blimp.

Dorcas couldn't believe they were going to pull off this caper, especially because no one had slept at all, but things were looking good. Once Isadora had described her idea last night, she'd left Dorcas and Ambrose to scry a soul mate for Dee-Dee. They'd come up with Norton from North Lake, only twenty-six miles away as the witch flies.

Dorcas and Ambrose had traveled there immediately and done some fast talking. Fortunately, Norton was as lonely as Dee-Dee. In spite of an intense fear of flying, he'd been willing to grab this chance to meet what Dorcas and Ambrose had convinced him was his true love.

They'd summoned Isadora by cell phone, and she'd reluctantly left the poker game to help them create the spell and fly Norton to his lady love.

"By the way," Isadora said, "you might want to know that George is pissed about this lake monster matchmaking deal."

Ambrose's motor sound stopped. "Dear Zeus, why did you say anything?"

"Motor, Ambrose, motor," Dorcas reminded him, although she felt like swearing, too. "I wish you'd let us tell him, Isadora."

"I couldn't help it. When you called on my cell, I was holding the nuts hand and had to throw it in. Naturally George demanded to know what was going on, so I had to tell him. Like I said, he was pissed."

Dorcas groaned. "What exactly did he say?"

"That this proves you like Dee-Dee better, and now there's gonna be *three* magical creatures when there should only be one, and, oh, yeah, why didn't you fly Dee-Dee to Norton's lake, instead. I had no answer for that one."

Dorcas wasn't about to admit she'd become attached to Dee-Dee and wouldn't have wanted to see her go. "Logistics," she said. "North Lake is more secluded. We could take off from there. A blimp taking off from Deep Lake would have aroused too much attention."

"Whatever," Isadora said. "One other thing George mentioned was that he might like a soul mate, but obviously you didn't care whether he ever got one."

"And he's never getting one if he doesn't earn his golden scales." Dorcas saw this as a definite setback for George, but she couldn't worry about it now. She reached up and patted Norton on the tummy. "How are you doing, Norton?"

"I'm really scared."

"We're almost ready to land. You've done great."

"Not scared about flying. I got over that after a while. I'm scared I won't be the lake monster Dee-Dee needs."

Isadora laughed. "Are you kidding? She'd take—"

"You in a heartbeat," Dorcas said, cutting off whatever lame-brained thing Isadora had been about to say. "She's going to love you, Norton."

"I hope so."

"We all hope so," Isadora said. "Because—"

"Hey, gang, we're here," Dorcas said. "Ambrose, start throwing your voice and make that motor seem as if it's receding in the distance."

Ambrose nodded.

Dorcas cocked her head and listened. Her husband was good at this. If she didn't know better, she'd swear there really was a blimp leaving the area. "That's great. Everybody ready?"

"I don't know," Norton said. "Maybe—"

"You're ready." Dorcas patted him on the tummy again. "Here we go, everybody. It's showtime."

Annie stood transfixed as the blimp began sinking toward the lake. The sound of the motor was no longer attached to the blimp. The sound alone moved off over the trees as if the blimp was flying away. It wasn't, though. It was right here . . . and then it wasn't a blimp anymore.

Annie forgot to breathe as she got her first look at the full body of a lake monster. It was bigger than she'd imagined, larger than the eighteen-wheeler she'd compared it to earlier. It had flippers instead of legs, and a whiplike tail. The head was triangular, like Dee-Dee's, but the brow was more pronounced.

At first she couldn't figure out how such a huge creature was floating gently down to the surface of the lake. But then she saw Isadora on a broom underneath the monster's belly, and on the far side, barely visible, were Dorcas and Ambrose on a second broom.

She raised her camera. Then she lowered it again. She couldn't see as well through the camera, and she couldn't bear to miss anything. A little to the right of where the monster would land, Dee-Dee lifted her head, gazing upward in obvious anticipation.

Annie's heart squeezed. She remembered how carefully Dee-Dee had carried Jeremy last night and how gently she'd laid him on the sand. Without her, he could be dead. And now this sweet-natured being was getting her reward, the lake monster of her dreams.

When the creature was almost at water level, the two brooms zipped out from under its belly and shot into the air. The lake monster landed with the mother of all cannonballs, sending waves onto the beach that might have been surf worthy.

Then the creature popped up again and bobbed in the waves for a moment, looking around. Dee-Dee was bobbing not far away. They looked at each other and slowly began swimming through the heavy waves. At last they were close enough to reach out and touch noses.

Annie felt wetness on her cheeks and realized tears were streaming down her face. She might not have found true love, but Dee-Dee had.

Movement in the sky caught her attention. As she looked up, she laughed in delight. The three who had orchestrated this were obviously celebrating, with Dorcas and Ambrose on one broom and Isadora on the other. They sailed over the heads of the creatures, doing barrel rolls and high-fiving each other every time they passed.

Once again she raised her camera . . . and lowered

it. She would not be taking pictures this morning. She would never tell anyone what she'd seen. Dee-Dee deserved that much.

Glancing again at the lake monsters, she noticed they had started to submerge. Slowly they sank under the surface, until only a trail of bubbles showed where they had been.

Still smiling, Annie turned and walked back through the forest. So much for fame and fortune.

Twenty-four days, six hours and . . . Annie paused to glance at her watch . . . fifteen minutes since she'd last seen Jeremy. Not that she was keeping track or anything.

She succeeded better at not thinking about him when she was at the *Trib,* but she couldn't hang out there every day of the week. That would make her look pathetic. So sometimes she had to come home to her boring apartment, like now, and while away a couple of hours surfing the Net.

She usually started by checking out Ambrose's MySpace page. Ambrose had joined the Knob Lobbers softball team and played left field. Through his page she kept up on the team, which was currently at two and two. Jeremy, who played third, had four hits for the season. Not that she'd searched for that stat, either.

Oh, hell, she might as well face the fact that she missed him desperately. She'd been reading the *Big Knob Gazette* online and thinking they could use a features writer with some talent. After being certain she wanted the big stories, she'd covered a high-profile murder case and had hated every minute of it. She didn't know if she could be satisfied writing human interest pieces for the *Big Knob Gazette,* but the prospect of having Jeremy around 24/7 would give her another kind of satisfaction, a kind she craved.

But it wasn't only about the sex. Granted, it was

partly about the sex, but mostly she missed the guy himself. He was funny, smart, considerate and very brave. So what if he wasn't the smoothest dude on the planet? So what if he couldn't make a rabbit appear from a hat? Whenever she'd been with him, she'd felt happy.

And yet . . . she kept coming back to the enhancements Dorcas and Ambrose had given him. How much had they had to do with his attractiveness? She'd thought about taking a weekend off and going back to Big Knob to find out, but she'd always chickened out. She'd rather miss Jeremy and hang on to her fantasy than risk discovering he was not the man she thought he was.

As she scrolled through the Knob Lobbers' stats on the official Knob Lobbers Web page, a Web page probably designed by Jeremy, she heard the click of an e-mail coming to her in-box. Probably Kendra from work asking if she wanted to go out for drinks and a little manhunting. Annie did not. No guy she'd meet in a bar could possibly compare to Jeremy, or at least the image she had of Jeremy.

But she clicked on her mail icon, anyway. No point in leaving Kendra hanging. When she saw the e-mail address, her breath caught: jdunstan@ClickorTreat.com.

She'd thought about e-mailing him a million times. She'd held off, having no idea what to say. She was even more worried about what he'd have to say. What if, after all they'd shared, his e-mails turned out to be boring? She couldn't bear the disillusionment.

But here he was, e-mailing her. She wasn't physically capable of ignoring it. The curiosity gene was dominant in her, which was why she'd felt so at home with journalism, essentially a career of voyeurism.

Heart pounding, she opened the e-mail.

Hi—How R U? J

She groaned. Talk about an unimaginative e-mail. Well, she could be unimaginative, too. *Hi—I'm fine. A*

The response came back immediately. *U busy?*

Why would he ask if she was busy? She hoped that didn't mean he was about to call her. She couldn't think of anything more awkward than a telephone conversation. The longer this inane communication lasted, the more she decided that she'd been harboring false hopes that she and Jeremy had a future.

Always, she typed. *Going out the door in two minutes.* That should forestall the phone call, if he'd had that in mind.

I see. Better let U go.

She hit REPLY and simply typed *Bye.* Then she turned off her computer and discovered she was trembling. The exchange had been stupid and ordinary, but the words had still come from Jeremy. She didn't seem to be as over him as she would have wished.

She got up and began to pace her living room. Could it be she *liked* boring, if it could come packaged with hot sex? Or could it be that she'd fallen in love with the guy and he could type a message that included the weather report and she wouldn't care, because he had sent it. After all, she'd been cherishing each and every Knob Lobbers stat because Jeremy had compiled and posted them.

God, she was a mess. And furthermore . . . She stopped pacing as she heard something right outside her front door. A dog whined. Then it scratched on the door. *What the hell?*

She lived on the third floor of an apartment building. Stray dogs couldn't just wander up here. She crossed to the door and unlocked it. Maybe her neighbor's toy poodle had slipped out and—she gasped. Megabyte sat there brushing the hall floor with her humongous tail. She held a rolled newspaper in her mouth.

Adrenaline rushed through Annie and she glanced up and down the hallway. "Jeremy?"

He stepped around the corner and smiled at her. "Hey, Annie."

"Hey, Jeremy." She couldn't stop smiling herself. She supposed to anyone else he'd look like a regular, glasses-wearing guy dressed in jeans and a white polo shirt. But they didn't know him the way she did. Or at least the way she thought she did.

Suddenly her old reservations returned. "I thought you were still in Big Knob, since you were e-mailing me."

Jeremy held up a BlackBerry. "The marvels of modern technology." He glanced at her ratty shorts and T-shirt. "But I don't want to hold you up. You said you were leaving."

"Oh." A flush warmed her cheeks. "I . . . ah . . ."

"Wanted to brush me off?" He strolled toward her, still smiling. "I can understand that. You don't know me very well, but that's going to change."

She looked into his eyes and saw the kind of determination and confidence that had always turned her on. But she didn't know what to believe anymore. "Did Dorcas and Ambrose give you any—"

"Special herbs? No. And I can't do magic, either. You're going to have to love me for other reasons." He paused about two feet away.

"L-love you?" The minute she said that, she knew it was already a done deal.

"That's right. But if you have places to go and things to do, I can come back another time so we can work on it."

She began to tingle all over, exactly the way she did when she was on the trail of a good story. This could turn into an outstanding story, and she wanted to work on it *now*. "That's okay. I can skip it." She backed into her apartment. "Why don't you come in?"

"Then I guess we will, won't we, Megabyte?" He motioned the dog through the door and followed after her. "By the way, Annie, that newspaper is for you. It's a special edition of the *Big Knob Gazette*."

"Why, uh, thanks." She reached for the newspaper, but Megabyte didn't want to give it up.

"Meg, give Annie the newspaper."

As Annie tried again, Meg held on more firmly and wagged her tail.

"I think she wants to play tug-of-war," Annie said.

Jeremy sighed. "I *knew* I should have practiced this with her a few more times. Meg, this isn't a game. Give me the newspaper."

Meg lumbered out of the way, and her wagging tail knocked the magazines and a bowl of fruit off Annie's coffee table. Miraculously the bowl didn't break when it hit the carpet, but peaches and nectarines rolled everywhere.

"God, I'm sorry." Jeremy surveyed the situation and glared at Megabyte. "This seemed like a good idea at the time."

"Maybe you should just tell me what's in the newspaper. Is it a wedding edition so the family can have a keepsake?"

"No." Jeremy approached his dog. "You're not helping, Meg. Now, give it here." Grabbing the paper, he pulled it forcefully from her mouth, and it partly shredded. Jeremy groaned.

"Here, let me see it." Annie took the paper and unfolded it. "A little Scotch tape and—" Speechless, she stared at the front page of the paper and the headline emblazoned there. WILL YOU MARRY ME? There was a big rip in the word MARRY and dog slobber all over the page, but there was no mistaking Jeremy's intent.

The paper rattled in her hand as she began to shake. Then she looked up to find Jeremy gazing at her, all his hopes shining in those caring gray eyes.

"I can see this is a shock," he said. "But I'm prepared to move here. I've already talked to Denise

Woolrich about selling Click-or-Treat, and I can open the same sort of Internet café in Chicago. Meg's a big dog, but she doesn't need much space. We can do the apartment thing here as well as we could in Big Knob."

"No." Annie shook her head.

"You won't marry me?"

"I won't have you giving up everything you love to move to Chicago."

"Annie, everything I love, every*one* I love, isn't in Big Knob. And if moving here means I have a chance with you, even if you're not ready to marry me yet, then I'll do it. I'll do whatever it takes. I love you."

Annie clutched the paper to her chest. "I won't let you make that sacrifice."

"But I want to."

"But you don't have to." She gazed at him, and joy bubbled inside her as she finally realized what she wanted. "I'm coming home."

"You are? Why?"

"Because I love you, and I also love Big Knob, and I've never been happier than I was that week I spent writing crazy stories about the locals and making sweet love with you."

"Oh, Annie."

How she cherished his goofy smile and the light in his gentle eyes. She was going to love being married to Jeremy Dunstan.

She laid the paper on the coffee table, and Megabyte immediately snatched it. "I'm afraid that won't make much of a souvenir," she said.

"I have a spare."

She laughed as she walked toward him. "I'm not surprised."

He drew her into his arms. "But you were surprised when I showed up, right?"

"I have to admit, that surprised me."

"Good. I don't want to be predictable." He cupped

her face in one hand. "And if you're not ready for the marriage thing, then I can wait."

"You can?"

"You bet. Waiting I can manage. Being without you is something I can't seem to manage at all."

"I see." She reached up and took off his glasses. "Well, you'd better kiss me, Jeremy, because I can't wait another second, and the answer is *yes*."

Epilogue

Hours later, after Annie and Jeremy had properly celebrated their engaged status in Annie's bedroom, Jeremy went in search of his jeans.

"Don't feel obligated to get dressed," Annie said as she admired her husband-to-be from the rear. "We can order from the Chinese place down the street whenever you're hungry."

"I'm not getting dressed, although I'll have to eventually so I can walk Meg." He picked up his jeans from the floor and fished something out of the back pocket. "Dorcas asked me to give you this. She said I should only give it to you if you agreed to marry me, but when you said you would, I went sort of crazy."

"And I loved it." Her clothes were old and she hadn't minded at all that he'd torn them off of her.

"Anyway, I forgot the letter until now." He handed it to her.

She switched on a light next to the bed so she could see better in the late-afternoon gloom. After being stuck in Jeremy's pocket all day it was wrinkled, but the purple envelope looked very much like Dorcas. The lavender sheet of stationery inside contained loopy handwriting that also fit Dorcas.

Annie held the paper toward the light and read silently.

Dear Annie,

If you're reading this, then you've wisely chosen to marry Jeremy. You two are soul mates, and I'm so pleased that you've found each other. You may think we've been too interfering, but we were only trying to help.

In that vein, I have another offer. Jeremy says he's willing to live there, but if you would consider moving back to Big Knob, I can get you a job reporting for Wizardry World, *the newspaper serving the entire magical community. In addition to reporting on the dragon and the lake monsters living here, you'll be able to cover stories involving magical creatures and events all over the world.*

Jeremy, of course, can't know about this, and we can take measures that will assure that he won't find out. This writing will disappear the moment you've read it.

Blessed be,
Dorcas

Annie pretended that she hadn't finished reading so she'd have a chance to compose herself before she met Jeremy's gaze. That wouldn't be easy, because she wanted to jump up and down on the bed. Big Knob also had a *dragon*? And that was only the beginning! She would be transported all over the world to write amazing stories. And she'd worried about being bored!

"You look pretty happy about that letter," Jeremy said.

"I am." Finally she dared to glance up. "Dorcas says we are truly soul mates. I guess she should know, since that's her field."

"I didn't need Dorcas to tell me that." Jeremy sat down next to her on the bed. "What else did she say?"

"Mostly that. The soul mate thing. Wishing us well and all that."

"Gonna let me read it?"

"Well, I would, but you know Dorcas and her flair for drama." Annie turned the paper around so he could see it. "She wrote the letter in disappearing ink."

Jeremy shook his head. "I have to say, that woman's a little weird."

"Yes, but in a good way." A *very* good way. Thanks to Dorcas, Annie would have a writing career the likes of which she never could have imagined. "So you knew we were soul mates? When did you decide that?"

"When I was fourteen." He stretched out on the bed beside her and gathered her close.

"Too bad I didn't know it, too." She nestled against him and was gratified to discover he was aroused again. "We could have saved a lot of time."

"True." He nuzzled a spot behind her ear. "So the way I have it figured, we have to make love twice as often because of all that time we lost."

"Works for me." Annie brushed her mouth over his collarbone as she anticipated another most excellent session between the sheets with her honest-to-goodness soul mate. And next week she'd get to meet a dragon.

Read on for an excerpt from

CASUAL HEX

Coming from Onyx in February 2009

Tied game, bottom of the ninth, bases loaded with the Mariners' designated hitter at the plate. Seated directly behind home plate between two of the hottest babes in Seattle, Prince Leo sipped his ice-cold brewski and smiled. October, and his favorite team was still in the hunt. Life didn't get any better than that.

Then his cell phone rang. Worse yet, it was his mother. He could ignore it, let it go to voice mail, claim the ring had been drowned out by the roar of the crowd. But Queen Beryl wouldn't buy it. Fairy princes, of which he was one, had incredible hearing.

Because of that ability, he'd overheard this morning's conversation at the palace between his mother and one of her oldest friends, a witch from San Francisco named Isadora Mather. Very odd, that conversation. Unless his mother had been joking, she was having second thoughts about handing over the kingdom to her one and only son. Yeah, she was probably joking.

Still, the discussion had made him briefly consider giving up his primo seats and the company of the Dempsey twins this afternoon so that he could stick around and get the 411 on what he'd thought was a done deal—his becoming king of Atwood in the near future. In the end he'd hadn't been able to make himself miss the game.

Besides, he had every confidence that he'd end up on the throne. He'd reached the required age, so it was mainly a matter of finding a good coronation date. He'd tried on his late daddy's crown, a little dusty after sitting around all these years, and it fit just fine. Soon he'd be the big boss in the forested kingdom of Atwood, a misty island at the far reaches of Puget Sound.

True, his mother had the power to deny him that job, but she wouldn't disinherit her own flesh and blood, even if she was irritated with him these days. So what if he liked to party? Was that a crime? And maybe he hadn't put much effort into those charitable projects she was so big on, but there would be plenty of time to get serious once he was king.

She'd probably known he was listening and had wanted to give him a little scare when she'd told Isadora that she might pass the crown to a commoner. He didn't believe for a minute that she'd do such a thing, but just to hedge his bets, he answered the phone.

"Hey," he said. "Let me call you back after the game."

"I'm afraid not." His mother had adopted her imperial tone. "This is of utmost importance."

Leo sighed. "What's up?" He couldn't imagine anything of more importance than a game-winning grand slam, which would put the Mariners in the playoffs and cause the very stacked Dempsey twins to leap out of their seats and jump up and down, which would promote major jiggle. He watched the pitch come in.

"The time has come for you to prove yourself worthy of the crown," his mother said.

Swing and a miss. Damn. "I don't remember hearing anything about that before." He had to watch what he said. The Dempsey twins thought he was just another sexy guy with excellent moves. When dealing with nonmagical women, he kept his fairy status a secret.

Letting it be known would only cause problems. For one thing, people assumed all magical fairies were tiny. Tiny was an option, one he didn't use much. At full size, if he suddenly announced he was a fairy, it would be misinterpreted, to say the least.

"You're hearing about it now," his mother said. "I have an assignment you must complete first."

"This is sounding like *Mission: Impossible*." Leo winced as the batter missed another fastball.

"You'd better hope it's not impossible." His mother was obviously in a mood. "You're perilously close to losing your birthright."

Leo rolled his eyes. Oh, the drama. Meanwhile, the Red Sox catcher called a time-out and loped to the mound to confer with the pitcher. If Leo hoped to finish this phone call before the next pitch, he'd better play along. "All right. What's the assignment?"

"I'm sending you to Big Knob, Indiana, where—"

"Big Knob?" Leo felt the twins' attention on him and realized he'd said that a little too loudly. He gave them both a lazy smile, as if he'd been referring to himself. "Oh, yeah. Big Knob." He hoped to hell his mother wasn't expecting him to deal with George, the juvenile-delinquent dragon living in the woods near that podunk town.

"Your assignment involves a young woman by the name of Gwen Dubois. She owns the local florist shop, Beaucoup Bouquets."

Now, that was more like it. A woman. Maybe even a Frenchwoman. "Is this a rescue situation?" He could get into that, especially if she happened to be gorgeous. He didn't want to have to fight any dragons, but from all reports, George didn't like to fight. Leo turned his attention to the game as the catcher hunkered down behind the plate.

"It's sort of a rescue," Queen Beryl said. "She lacks self-confidence with the opposite sex."

Just his luck she'd be ugly. "And why isn't she self-confident?"

"She doesn't consider herself particularly attractive."

Bingo. "Mom, I don't think—"

"I want you to give her the kind of attention that will change her self-image and make her feel sexy."

Leo preferred his women to be sexy from the get-go. "I'm not really into stuff like that."

"Which is exactly why I'm assigning you this task, Leo. You're to ignore your obsession with external beauty and consider someone else's feelings for a change. You must prove yourself capable of a selfless act."

That hurt. "I can be selfless."

"I've seen very little evidence of it. Oh, and when you go, stay out of the Whispering Forest and away from that dragon, George."

Earlier Leo had hoped not to be assigned to George, but he hated being told what to do. "Why?"

"The dragon is Dorcas and Ambrose Lowell's project."

"Mmm." Leo had heard of the witch and wizard who'd been banned to Big Knob because they'd screwed up some spell or other. Leo was curious about that, too, but not enough to make a trip to some piddly small town. "There must be some other assignment you can give me."

"I'm afraid not. Do you want the crown, or don't you?"

He wanted it, and apparently he'd have to jump through hoops to get it. He sighed. "Yeah, okay. I'll do it." The pitcher went into his windup. "When do I have to go?"

"Next week."

With a crack of the bat, the hitter sent the ball

over the center-field fence. Leo jumped to his feet and cheered while the Dempsey twins leaped around and bumped into him with their generous assets. Sweet. "Sorry, Mom!" he yelled into the phone. "Next week is out."

"Why?"

"We're in the playoffs! We might end up in the World Series! Maybe I could go in late November."

"Won't work. You'll need plenty of time, and Gwen's closing the shop in mid-December to spend the holidays in Arizona with her parents."

If it hadn't been for his acute hearing, Leo wouldn't have picked up on that last sentence. Pandemonium ruled at Safeco Field, and the Dempsey twins became orgasmic in their joy. He looked forward to capitalizing on that in his hotel suite tonight.

"January, then!" he shouted into the phone. "Gotta go, Mom! 'Bye!" He snapped the phone shut and shoved aside all thoughts of his assignment. Party time!

Now Available
From Vicki Lewis Thompson

OVER HEXED

Dorcas and Ambrose, former matchmaking sex therapists for witches and warlocks, are now working for mere mortals—although the handsome Sean Madigan is kind of an Adonis. That is, until Dorcas and Ambrose strip him of his sex appeal and introduce him to his destiny, Maggie Grady. This time winning a girl's heart won't be so easy for Sean. It means rediscovering the charms buried beneath the surface. But what a surface!

"A snappy, funny, romantic novel."
—*New York Times* bestselling author Carly Phillips

Available wherever books are sold
or at penguin.com

Don't Talk Back
to Your Vampire
by Michele Bardsley

*Sometimes it's hard to take your own advice—
or pulse.*

Ever since a master vampire became possessed and bit a
bunch of parents, the town of Broken Heart, OK, has
catered to those of us who don't rise until sunset—even if
that means PTA meetings at midnight.

As for me, Eva LeRoy, town librarian and single
mother to a teenage daughter, I'm pretty much used to
being "vampified." You can't beat the great side effects:
no crow's-feet or cellulite! But books still make my
undead heart beat—and, strangely enough, so does Lorcán
the Loner. My mama always told me everyone deserves a
second chance. Still, it's one thing to deal with the usual
undead hassles: rival vamps, rambunctious kids adjusting
to night school, and my daughter's new boyfriend, who's a
vampire hunter, for heaven's sake. It's quite another to fall
for the vampire who killed you....

"The paranormal romance of the year."
—MaryJanice Davidson

"Hot, hilarious, one helluva ride."
—L.A. Banks

Penguin Group (USA) Online

What will you be reading tomorrow?

Tom Clancy, Patricia Cornwell, W.E.B. Griffin,
Nora Roberts, William Gibson, Robin Cook,
Brian Jacques, Catherine Coulter, Stephen King,
Dean Koontz, Ken Follett, Clive Cussler,
Eric Jerome Dickey, John Sandford,
Terry McMillan, Sue Monk Kidd, Amy Tan,
John Berendt…

You'll find them all at
penguin.com

*Read excerpts and newsletters,
find tour schedules and reading group guides,
and enter contests.*

Subscribe to Penguin Group (USA) newsletters
and get an exclusive inside look
at exciting new titles and the authors you love
long before everyone else does.

PENGUIN GROUP (USA)
us.penguingroup.com